P9-BXV-857

A Well-Behaved Woman

ALSO BY THERESE ANNE FOWLER

Z: A Novel of Zelda Fitzgerald

A Well-Behaved Woman

A Novel of the Vanderbilts

THERESE ANNE FOWLER

ST. MARTIN'S PRESS
New York

This is a work of fiction. All of the characters, organizations, and events portrayed in this novel are either products of the author's imagination or are used fictitiously.

 Printed in the United States of America. For information, address St. Martin's Press, 175 Fifth Avenue, New York, N.Y. 10010.

www.stmartins.com

Designed by Ellen Cipriano

LIBRARY OF CONGRESS CATALOGING-IN-PUBLICATION DATA

Names: Fowler, Therese, author.
Title: A well-behaved woman : a novel of the Vanderbilts / Therese Anne Fowler.
Description: First edition. | New York : St. Martin's Press, 2018.
Identifiers: LCCN 2018019687| ISBN 9781250095473 (hardcover) | ISBN 9781250202758 (international) | ISBN 9781250202765 (signed) | ISBN 9781250095497 (ebook)
Subjects: LCSH: Belmont, Alva, 1853–1933—Fiction. | Vanderbilt family—Fiction. | Socialites—Fiction | United States—Social life and customs—1865–1918—Fiction. | GSAFD: Biographical fiction.
Classification: LCC PS3606.O857 W45 2018 | DDC 813/.6—dc23
LC record available at https://lccn.loc.gov/2018019687

First Edition: October 2018

10 9 8 7 6 5 4 3 2 1

To John, for all the reasons

A woman's lot is made for her
by the love she accepts.

—GEORGE ELIOT

Pearls

Her eye of light is the diamond bright,
Her innocence the pearl;
And those are ever the bridal gems
That are worn by the American girl.

—FROM *THE YOUNG LADIES' OFFERING*
(AUTHOR UNKNOWN)

I

WHEN THEY ASKED her about the Vanderbilts and Belmonts, about their celebrations and depredations, the mansions and balls, the lawsuits, the betrayals, the rifts—when they asked why she did the extreme things she'd done, Alva said it all began quite simply: Once there was a desperate young woman whose mother was dead and whose father was dying almost as quickly as his money was running out. It was 1874. Summertime. She was twenty-one years old, ripened unpicked fruit rotting on the branch.

"Stay together now, girls," Mrs. Harmon called as eight young ladies, cautiously clad in plain day dresses and untrimmed hats, left the safety of two carriages and gathered like ducklings in front of the tenement. The buildings were crowded and close here, the narrow street's bricks caked with horse dung, pungent in the afternoon heat. Soiled, torn mattresses and broken furniture and rusting cans littered the alleys. Coal smoke hung in the stagnant air. Limp laundry drooped on lines strung from one windowsill to the next along and across the entire block from Broome Street to Grand. The buildings themselves seemed to sag.

"Stay together?" Alva's sister Armide said. "Where does she imagine we'd go?"

"To the devil, surely," one of the other girls replied. "Like everyone here."

The speaker was Miss Lydia Roosevelt of the Oyster Bay Roosevelts, a cousin or niece (Alva couldn't remember which) of one of the charity group's founders. She would tell every Roosevelt ancestral detail if asked. Alva wouldn't ask.

Among the "everyone" here were numerous haggard, bundle-laden girls and women moving to and from doorways; a few old men propped on stoops or reclined against walls; and the dirtiest assortment of children Alva had ever seen—barefooted, most of them—playing in the street.

Miss Roosevelt's act-alike friend Miss Hadley Berg said, "To be fair, what else can you expect? These people are born inferior."

"You don't really believe that," Alva said.

"I don't believe what?" Miss Berg asked, adjusting her hat to keep her face in shadow. "That they're inferior?" She pointed to a little boy with greasy hair and scabbed knees who picked his teeth while he watched them. "That their poverty is natural?"

"Yes," Armide said. "Certainly circumstances play a role."

Alva glanced at her. The two of them knew this well. If their circumstances didn't improve dramatically and soon, they and their two younger sisters might be the ones living in a single room with no running water, doing their business in a dim alley or open courtyard where everyone could see. Already they were rationing food, restricting their entertainments, managing with two servants when they'd once had nine—and disguising these truths as best they could.

The group waited while Mrs. Harmon directed the coachmen to unload their baskets, each of which held twenty muslin bags tied with twine. Every bag contained a small sewing kit of two needles, thread, pins, and a thimble; a bar of soap; a short book of simple, uplifting poems; a lollipop; and four pennies. They'd spent the morning assembling the kits and now were to hand them out to some of Manhattan's poorest children—foundlings, runaways, immigrants, orphans, street urchins, what have you. Mrs. Harmon said that once able to sew, a highly skilled person could earn as much as ten dollars a week. Even the younger ones could earn twenty cents in a day, which might make all the difference.

Miss Roosevelt said, "You can clean up the white ones and send them to school, but it's not as though the boys will become gentlemen. They can't. It's not how God made them."

Miss Berg added, "If this sort could resist going for the bottle when difficulties come—"

"That's just it," said Miss Roosevelt. "The Irish are practically born drunk, and their men—why, drink is a part of everything they do. Even the women are susceptible. We had to fire a maid for it last week. My mother caught her roaring drunk and stuffing silverware into her pockets!"

"The Germans are nearly as bad," said Miss Berg.

Armide said, "We *did* have a terrible German governess . . ."

"Did? Who tends your sisters now?" asked Miss Roosevelt.

"Armide does," Alva said. "She's very capable, and with our mother gone, the girls prefer her."

"Four motherless, unmarried girls." Miss Roosevelt shook her head. "*So* unfortunate."

"But it's the Jews who are the worst," Miss Berg continued. "Not with drink; I think liquor is against their beliefs. They're . . . sneaky and underhanded. *Conniving*, that's the word."

Alva said, "But white Christian Americans are perfect, I suppose."

Miss Roosevelt rolled her eyes. "We're simply stating facts, Miss Smith. Perhaps if you were better educated, you'd recognize how stupid you sound."

Armide stepped between them. "I think Mrs. Harmon is ready."

"All right then, girls," said Mrs. Harmon as she joined them. "I remind you that good Christians are generous in deed *and word*." She directed them each to take a basket and choose a partner, then said, "Every one of us can improve ourselves, no matter the circumstances of our births. Given sufficient tools and training, we can all be clean, responsible persons."

"Yes, Mrs. Harmon," they chirped.

Clean and responsible. That might be the most Alva and her sisters could hope to be unless at least one of them married well—a difficult achievement when there were no offers. Having first come to New York from the now-disgraced South and then returned here after spending the war years in Paris, the Smith girls were no longer quite good enough for Knickerbockers, those well-to-do gentlemen whose families were deep-rooted Manhattanites. Nor were they important enough to attract the social-climbing nouveaux riches now coming to New York in droves. They'd had to aim for the narrow in-between.

Yet even that had proven profitless. Here was the trouble: they were four perfectly nice young ladies among a throng of others of equal merit, and there were so many fewer gentlemen to try for since the war. Given all of this, Alva had reluctantly agreed to participate in a marriage plot for one of those in-between fellows, to be concluded a few weeks' hence.

Mrs. Harmon entered the building and the young ladies filed in behind her, so that they were all standing inside the oppressive, odorous hallway. The air here was much warmer than outside. Mrs. Harmon pressed her handkerchief to her neck and forehead in turn. Miss Roosevelt pressed hers to her nose.

Mrs. Harmon said, "If we act efficiently, we won't need to be here long." She assigned Miss Roosevelt and Miss Berg to the first floor, and then worked her way down in rank, up in floors. "You Smith girls, you'll have the fourth," she said, then gave a nod toward the building's dark interior. "All right? I'll be outside if you need me."

"I'm very sorry for your luck," Miss Roosevelt said.

Miss Berg said, "Yes, too bad. I hear they house the lepers and idiots up top."

"Even lepers and idiots deserve our charity," Armide replied, giving Alva a look of warning to leave it alone.

Alva marched up the stairs. She would not give them the satisfaction of believing she was offended. First floor, fourth floor—what difference was there, really? Circumstances. Nothing inherent.

Armide was close behind Alva. The scent of urine was stronger now, trapped in the stairwell along with the hot air. Trying to breathe through only her mouth as she went, Alva hooked the basket in her elbow and used both hands to keep her skirts off the greasy treads. Below, the others were already knocking on doors. *Good afternoon, madam . . .*

Their instructions: two girls to a floor, a stop at each dwelling, where they were to *knock politely; announce yourselves; inquire about children in the home. If invited inside, stay in the doorway and avoid touching anything. Lice and fleas jump!* They were to offer one kit for every child over the age of six but under the age of fourteen. At fourteen you were on your own. At fourteen, you might already have a means to avoid being removed from your home and shipped out from Grand Central Depot to lord knew where, sent to work on farms or ranches or plantations or in mines. Alva had heard that some Southern families were taking children to replace the slaves they'd lost in the Emancipation. Some girls who were sent west, to the territories, were being put to service as wives. She imagined it: orphaned *and* exiled *and* married off to an old pockmarked tobacco-spitting homesteader, rising before dawn to milk the goat or cow, a runny-nosed baby on one hip and another on the way . . . Alva was glad that Julia, her youngest sister, was fifteen.

She and Armide reached the dim fourth-floor landing and paused to get their breath. There was a strange metallic scent here, pungent and sharp. Alva started to remark on it, then spotted a young woman lying inert beside the second door. Blood, so dark that it looked black, had pooled around her sodden skirts. Armide gasped, turned, and ran down the stairs, calling for Mrs. Harmon to find help.

Trembling, Alva knelt at the girl's shoulder and took her hand. It was cool and pliant. She watched the girl's chest; it didn't move. She put her ear to the girl's breast. Silence.

Alva sat back. Her hands were shaking, her whole body trembling so much that she put her arms around herself and clamped them to her ribs.

Dead. After being frightened and in pain.

At a party Alva had been to a few years earlier, two women of middle age, well fed and well turned out with pearls and furs, remarked on a tour they'd taken of the Five Points slums not long before:

Wasn't it fascinating?

Yes, horrific! Imagine that being your life—a short one, probably.

People are simply dying to get out of there!

Then laughter at their cleverness. Alva had smiled, too, as yet unaware of how narrow the gap between privilege and poverty. *Dying* to get out, ha!

Now she sat at a dead girl's side. Had the girl been lying here terrified by what was happening to her, or relieved by what was possibly her best prospect of escape?

The sound of someone running up the stairs—

"Katie?" said a girl whose resemblance to this one was unmistakable. "Oh, no, no, no—" Alva moved aside as she kneeled down and grabbed the dead girl's shoulders, attempted to lift her. "Katie, come on," she said. The dead girl's head lolled backward. The other girl's eyes were panicked. "They said someone went for a doctor, but it could be hours. Where's she bleeding from? What can we do?"

"It's too late," Alva said. "I'm so sorry. She wasn't breathing when I— We were too late."

"This can't be!" the girl cried. "What happened to her? She was perfect when I left this morning."

"I am so terribly sorry."

In Alva's purse was perhaps fifty cents. Her hands shook as she held it out to the girl. "There's not a lot here, but—"

The girl slapped it away. "Money's no fix!"

"It can help—"

"*You people.* Get out of here," she said. Her face was red and streaked with tears. "Go!"

"I'm sorry," Alva said again, and left the girl there to wait for help that would not help, her words sounding in Alva's mind. Money was no fix for that girl, true—*But please, God,* she thought, *let it be for me.*

II

THE OTHER MARRIAGEABLE girls were too lovely, all of them, those rose-milk complexions and hourglass waists and silks that gleamed like water in sunlight. The Greenbrier resort's dining room was filled with such girls, there in the company of clever mothers whispering instruction on the most flattering angle for teacup and wrist, and *sit straighter, smile brightly, glance coyly—lashes down.* The young men, who were outnumbered three to one, wore crisp white collars and linen coats and watched and smiled and nodded like eager buyers at a Thoroughbred market.

Miss Consuelo Yznaga, Alva's closest friend since their childhood summers in Newport, Rhode Island, had originated the plot now under way. She'd insisted Greenbrier was *the* place to secure a husband—for Alva. Consuelo, with her money, alliances, and beauty, was in no rush for herself. She had no need to be. Her father had so far managed to keep his wealth.

The Yznaga money came from Cuban sugarcane. Each summer before the war, the family decamped Cuba for temperate Newport, often renting a cottage on the same road as the cottage the Smiths took to escape Manhattan's muggy heat. Mr. Yznaga liked to say, "A man must be a faithful steward of the land that built his fortune," a veiled criticism of Alva's father, who was better suited to selling the family plantation's cotton than to growing it. The international markets were in New York, and so Murray Smith had settled his wife and girls there. Alva and Consuelo, unconcerned with any tension between their fathers, had attached themselves to each other with the unreserved love that carefree childhood encourages, their similarities far more important than their differences.

During the war years, they met in Paris for a few weeks each spring. When apart, they corresponded by post. Then Consuelo's father, seeing new business opportunities, bought a house in Manhattan soon after Alva's family returned there, reuniting the friends. Alva knew Consuelo's heart as well as she knew her own. Nothing could divide them. Even as troubles had come for the Smiths, Consuelo remained the steadfast friend she had always been.

And now she had decided on William K. Vanderbilt for Alva, having first gotten acquainted with him while in Geneva the year before—W.K., they called him, a young man whose wealthy family, now in its third Manhattan generation, was having little success gaining entry into best society. As Consuelo had presented the matter to him, Alva's family's spotless ancestry combined with the Vanderbilts' money and influence would tip the social scale, and the Vanderbilts and Smiths could rise together.

This was an optimistic prediction.

Still, by Consuelo's measure, W.K. was receptive to her campaign and receptive to Alva. By Alva's, he was a cheerful puppy; in the few times they'd met, he had given her little more than a happy sniff before gamboling away. Oh, he seemed to like her well enough. But he seemed to also like playing pranks with his friends and racing four-in-hand in Central Park and doing card tricks and crewing in yacht races and talking jovially to attractive young ladies, of whom she was merely one among many. *Alva Smith? She's a clean, responsible girl,* he'd tell his friends, and then attach himself to someone with better adjectives.

"Oh, look." Consuelo pointed to a trio of men entering the broad, high-ceilinged room. "I told you he would be here." She beckoned a waiter to their table and handed the man her card, on which she had already jotted a note.

She said, "The one in the blue coat over there, Mr. Vanderbilt—say we'd like him and his friends to join us."

The waiter left and Alva sighed heavily.

"Are you anxious?" Consuelo said. "Don't be. He'll come."

"And then what?"

"Then you hold your teacup like *so*—"

"Honestly, Consuelo."

"And stop frowning! 'A pale, smooth, pleasing visage is required of every young woman who hopes to attract a husband of quality and taste'—I read that in a manners guide. Not to mention frequent frowning ages you *six years.* It's been scientifically proven." Consuelo paused, and frowned. "Oh dear, what's this?"

Alva turned to see another waiter arrive at the gentlemen's table while their own waiter was still making his way across the vast room. The first waiter handed something to W.K. and indicated a nearby table of ladies from whom the something had evidently come. As the men stood, W.K., with his dark blond hair and dimpled smile, wasted no time, barely pausing to take Consuelo's card from the just-arrived waiter and pocketing it as he went.

"Well," Alva said, facing Consuelo again, "so much for your plotting."

Consuelo said, "So much for your faith! I concede that Theresa Fair *is* beautiful. Imagine having hair that red! But Mrs. Fair is so overweening that she's certain to scare off any but the most desperate man."

"Beautiful and young," Alva said. "She can't be more than fourteen."

"Greek society bring their girls out at ten—that's the legal age in New York as well. At least you're not competing against a ten-year-old." Consuelo reached for her cup. "Do not distress yourself. W.K. doesn't need to weight his pockets with Fair silver. His grandfather is quite rich."

"His *grand*father."

"Who's already ancient and won't live forever." Consuelo watched the group. "I wonder how much he's actually worth?"

"W.K.?"

"His grandfather, Commodore Vanderbilt. I read that his steam yacht is as big as a warship and cost *a half million* dollars *twenty years* ago. And W.K.'s father is situated nicely, too. What they need is your untarnished ancestry to offset the gossip about war profiteering and political bribery and all that business about the son."

"What? Which son?"

"His uncle, C. J. Vanderbilt. Papa calls him a dissolute gambler who never pays his debts. Also, he has fits. Convulsions."

"You never mentioned this before!"

"Haven't I?"

"If I had known—"

"You'd have ruled him out? You can't afford that."

Alva turned to look again. "Miss Fair's dress . . ." She shook her head.

"It is a masterpiece of figure—flattery, true. But as I said, her insufferable mother—"

"Won't live with them."

"Wouldn't," Consuelo corrected, pointing at Alva with her spoon. "If. But that *if* is not a real possibility because Miss Fair is common. Whereas you are a prize."

"Only in comparison."

Before the war, before New York society closed ranks to most everyone whose money wasn't local and old, the Smiths had been as good as any of the Knickerbockers—better, Alva's mother Phoebe Smith had asserted: they were more cultured and much broader of mind, as she had been taking her daughters to Europe from the time each could hold herself up at a ship's rail. What's more, their ancestry, deep and impressive in America's South, was even deeper and more impressive in Europe: they were descended from royalty in France and Scotland both. "My girls are *born* to wear crowns," she had told everyone who would listen.

Consuelo was saying, "It's always in comparison. Don't look a gift horse in the mouth."

"'Bad teeth are a bad bargain at any price,' that's what Lulu says."

"What does an old slave know? Anyway, look at him. He has lovely teeth."

"Yes, well, it would be lovely if he would stop displaying them to Miss Fair."

Alva fiddled with her neckline. The dress was old and no longer fit as well as it had. It was one of the last she'd ordered in Paris before her father moved them back to New York. She hadn't understood, then, that his cotton-trade business was dying as quietly but surely as her mother was.

With his Old South manners, his enduring belief that a handshake was still sufficient assurance of a man's intent, he sank under the ceaseless waves of unscrupulous, undercutting cotton dealers, the lot of them climbing atop one another in an attempt to keep their noses above water. Worse, he'd invested badly, betting on the Confederacy and Southern banks. The wealth that had arisen from a grand cotton plantation, money that had lifted her forebears into prominence and come to her father in turn, was now all but gone.

Consuelo said, "Leave your dress be. And stop *frowning*."

"I'm sorry, but this is demeaning, you must see that." Alva picked at her thumbnail, resisting the urge to chew it. "I wish we'd gone to London when the empire fell. Jennie Jerome met Lord Churchill there. And Minnie's going to have a title, too," she said, referring to another of their friends. "I always thought I would marry a gentleman with a title and lands and people. With *history*. My mother fed me on that dream."

"They all do."

"It's a worthy aim," Alva said. "She wasn't wrong about that."

"Yes, your mother had a fine aim but a terrible approach. Why did no one ever intervene? That's what I wonder."

Throughout her youth, Alva had thought her mother to be a calculating but charming and effective navigator of society. She was disabused of this belief on an evening in a Tuileries Palace drawing room when, seated behind Empress Eugénie (and thrilled by the proximity), she overheard the empress say, "I believe Mrs. Murray Smith is the most ridiculous figure at court. Always going on about her royal descent—which was centuries back, if it's true at all. But hearing her tell it, one would think her people still rule."

Alva wanted to die on the spot. The empress was speaking of her mother. The empress thought her mother ridiculous. The *empress*.

Her companion replied, "A pompous creature, I agree. It's quite entertaining! Every one of her perfect daughters is fated to be a queen. Or an empress. Beware!" She laughed.

Empress Eugénie said, "I am not entertained. I feel sorry for her poor girls; no one good will consider them seriously."

Alva hadn't dared draw attention by leaving her seat. There she sat, horrified, burning.

Her mother was a laughingstock.

No one good would ever consider them seriously.

Now her mother was in her grave and Alva was here in West Virginia perspiring through her corset and vying—not very well—for a common gentleman's attentions.

Now she was stuck with New York, with its long streets of dingy, uninspired row houses and shopfronts fringing rickety tenements and swampy squalor. There was no grace in Manhattan—few grand homes, no soaring cathedrals or charming garden parks like the ones Louis-Napoléon had carved into the Parisian arrondissements. They had ugly brick and brownstone and boards and soot and one-legged vagrants and dead horses rotting in the streets.

Now she was a charity case.

For a time the two young ladies drank their tea in silence. Alva could see her friend's mind working like Austen's Emma's. Consuelo had introduced her to W.K. earlier in the year, when she took Alva to dine at another friend's home. Consuelo had arranged Alva's invitation to his sister's debutante ball. Consuelo sought him out whenever she could, making sure to bring Alva to his mind in some way or other, extolling her qualities, overemphasizing her outstanding ancestry and her father's Union Club membership, promoting an alliance as a cure to his family's society frustrations. No Knickerbocker mother would marry her daughter to a Vanderbilt. Alva Smith was the next best thing.

Consuelo tapped her spoon against her palm. She said, "I don't see why he . . . Not that I'm truly worried, you understand. It would be so convenient if there were a terrible rumor about Miss Fair afloat. Something scandalous—like, she's been seen leaving a stable hand's quarters."

"Except that she hasn't. Has she?"

"Who can say for certain?"

Alva said, "That coal man from Pittsburgh who was seated beside me last night at dinner—"

"Alva."

"He's sweet, and nice enough to look at. Perhaps it's not so bad that he's first-generation—"

"*Alva.*"

"He's probably worth more than W.K."

"Only at the moment. Stop it."

Alva lowered her voice. "He has money. I need money. He might be the best I can do."

"He is a parvenu. You are a *Desha.* Your grandfather was a congressman. Your uncle was a governor. You will *not* let yourself go to some upstart with coal dust under his fingernails."

"My mother was a Desha; I am a Smith. Daddy is an invalid who can't pay his bills, and if I don't marry into money soon, we'll be letting rooms and taking in wash."

She could see it plainly: her father lying prostrate, too weak to do more than sip broth; odd-smelling strangers stomping in and out of their house at all hours; she and her sisters slaving at the stove and the hearths and the sink, swatting away flies in summer heat, lining their shoes with rags in the winter, their lives every bit as miserable as those she'd seen that day at the tenement, their futures as insecure as the dead girl's sister's must be now. No decent man would have any of the Smith girls, and they'd all get some kind of pox or grippe and die ignominiously, four spinsters whose mother had once declared they would be duchesses or marchionesses, or ladies of the peerage at the very least. Probably they would die in winter, in the snow. An Italian immigrant would find them and, in his grief, write an opera about their beautiful, tragic deaths, for which he would become renowned, tour the world, earn a fortune, and marry a destitute but titled European maiden who would change her name to Armide.

Alva said, "We're being hounded by the grocer. We haven't paid the laundress or Lulu since . . . I don't even recall."

"Yes, all right, but I know you: money alone isn't enough."

Alva turned for another look at W.K., secondborn son of the firstborn son of the man who was running almost every railway in the east, who had built Grand Central Depot, who often had President Grant's ear. He and two friends were seated with Theresa Fair, Mrs. Fair, and the two other married women in their party. Mrs. Fair was speaking animatedly, her head bobbing like a hen's.

He was pleasing to the eye. Almost beautiful, in fact. He did have good teeth. And he was amiable. Everyone said so. Lively and fun-loving, the nicest fellow, as good-natured as God made. Certainly he had better credentials than the Pittsburgh coal man. Watching him, Alva let herself imagine a life of comfort in which she was never anxious, never cold, never fearful that no one would want her. A life in which she wore every season's best fashions and headed a polished mahogany dinner table with him at the opposite end, their friends and acquaintances lining the sides, enjoying French wines and stuffed squab and delicate little puff pastries *au crème* . . .

So his grandfather the Commodore was said to be boorish, eccentric, coarse in language and manner. So his uncle was too fond of cards. So W.K. had no title or lands, nothing exalted in his history, no claim to glory—even by extension—in any war in any country at any time. The fact was that Alva had no chance to be Lady Anyone. If she pursued the Pittsburgh man, she might gain security, but socially she'd be Mrs. Nobody. As a Vanderbilt she could at least be a very comfortable Mrs. Someone.

When Alva turned back to the table, Consuelo was assessing her through narrowed eyes. "Which dress did you bring for tonight's dance?"

"The gray faille—I know what you're thinking, but Lulu altered the bodice. It isn't current, but it's closer."

"You really should have taken my mother's offer to dress you this year, instead of capitulating to your father's pride."

"Pride is all he's got left."

Laughter erupted from the Fair table. Look how W.K. grinned at Miss Fair! Look how she blushed! Now it was Miss Fair Alva saw at the polished mahogany table with W.K., Miss Fair in *her* seat, drinking *her* wine, eating *her* squab, licking the cream from *her* pastries off her delicate little silver-ringed fingers. It was Miss Fair sitting across from the husband Alva might have had, while Alva was up to her elbows in scalding water and lye scrubbing some customer's—probably the Vanderbilts'—sheets.

Consuelo reached for Alva's hand and declared, "You'll wear my new rose muslin."

"And that, of course, will solve everything. No," Alva said, "thank you, but I look awful in pink."

The Fair party rose and sauntered to the French doors, Miss Fair's hand on W.K.'s sleeve, and then outside they went.

"That's the end of it, then," Alva said. Whatever Consuelo had been led to believe, Mr. Vanderbilt clearly had other plans.

"You cannot give up so easily. Where is my spirited friend who used to race all the boys and steal backstage at the opera and—"

"That friend has limits," Alva said, rising. "I will not chase a man who is supposed to be pursuing me. Let Miss Fair have him. Or *you*—you rate him so highly, after all."

Consuelo didn't reply, and it was just as well, as that reply would almost certainly be one Alva did not wish to hear: that she, Consuelo, had higher aims for herself than a Vanderbilt, along with the means to hit her mark. That for all the tough talk, Alva had no currency to back her words. That Consuelo was doing her best for Alva and Alva ought to be grateful.

Gratitude. How perilously close to resentment it could be.

After tea, while the other ladies napped, Alva stood at her room's window, too uneasy to rest. Consuelo was correct: marrying for money alone was not ideal. Alva hoped for status, too—though not for the reasons her mother had sought it, self-importance and admiration. Status gave a woman more control over her existence, more protection from being battered about by others' whims or life's caprices.

No one gave a whit about the coal man from Pittsburgh (who might not choose her, anyway). The Vanderbilts, though, were already influential in politics and policy. Alva read the papers. The Vanderbilts' bread was already half buttered. She should temper her pride and pursue W.K.; it would only be to her advantage. And if she somehow did manage to get them into best society, she could have not only butter but raspberry jam, too. Any time she liked. That would be delicious.

She rang for the bellboy and bade him fetch Lulu. "Tell her we're going into town."

They went to a dry goods shop, where Alva bought four yards of black tarlatan. Then she directed the coachman to a hillside covered in wildflowers. Using sewing scissors and swatting at bees, she and Lulu cut armfuls of goldenrod and brought it back to Alva's room. Two hours later, the room resembled a sloppy seamstress's workshop, with fabric scraps, bits of thread, scissors and needles and pins scattered over the table, unspooled ribbon and leftover tarlatan draped over a chair. Discarded leaves and stems littered the floor.

It was the fashion, then, to tuck little blooms into one's hair or to tack a few flowers onto a bodice or the cap of a sleeve. Alva had gone further. She and Lulu had draped the tarlatan around the gown's skirt like bunting, then spread the gown across the bed and painstakingly tacked onto its skirt garland-like lines of tiny goldenrod bouquets.

"How . . . striking!" Consuelo said as she swept in wearing the rose muslin. "The flowers—"

"She had me out there in the hills like some field slave," Lulu said.

"For almost no time at all."

"I work in the *house*."

"You wouldn't have let me go by myself!"

"Mr. Smith, he'd have my hide if I did."

"It was a gorgeous hillside, full of fragrant flowers—"

"Full of bees," Lulu complained. "And you out there without your hat . . ."

Consuelo took Alva by the hands and assessed her from hair to hem. "It's inspired," she said. "Do I take it you're back in the fight?"

"I don't want to end up in a tenement."

"Do *not* permit such a thought. Setting one's mind on positive subjects leads to positive results." She released Alva, saying, "Now, when W.K. finds you—and he will, if he knows what's good for him—make the absolute most of it. A man needs to feel he's won a prize all his friends will envy. Woo him, Alva. Flatter him. Do you understand? *Be* the prize."

Alva realized her miscalculation as soon as she reached the ballroom. She had forgotten its walls were painted the deepest rose; the ceilings were paler pink; the very light in the room was rosy. She could not have made a more disharmonious choice.

Every other girl in the resort seemed to have anticipated the décor. They wore gowns in ivory, cream, buff, silver, pearl, gray, sage, pale blues and greens, every shade of pink. A daring young lady was dressed in deep garnet, the dress and her chestnut hair set off with strings of seed pearls. Perfection! Whereas Alva stood there near the doorway in her black-and-gold . . . confection.

She was certainly drawing the attention of the others:

"Miss Smith! How . . . unusual."

"Well! I haven't seen that particular style in ages."

"I do hope your partners aren't sensitive to goldenrod."

"Rather an *autumnal* theme, isn't it?"

"Mourning summer's end?"

Teeth clenched, Alva turned—and ran directly into Theresa Fair's mother.

"My dear Miss Smith!" said the saccharine Mrs. Fair, so elegant in dove gray with silver-set diamonds at her ears and neck. And waist. And wrists. And fingers. "Look at you! Those flowers! And . . . are you wearing hoops?"

Alva was not wearing hoops—but she'd added an extra crinoline to support the skirt and was paying for it in streams of perspiration that trailed over her bottom and down her thighs into her stockings.

Mrs. Fair said, "Why, you're practically a Southern belle."

"Well," Alva said, "I *am* from Mobile, Alabama. My father comes from Virginia. My people were in the South a hundred years before the Revolution."

Whereas the Fairs were Irish immigrants, now in Alva's circle only because Mr. Fair had, some years earlier, gone west to prospect and, with two compatriots, stumbled upon one of the biggest silver lodes ever found. Before his strike, Mrs. Fair had run a boardinghouse.

Mrs. Fair said, "That's a fine trick to pull here, with so many Southern gentlemen afoot."

"Why would *I* need to play tricks?" Alva said. Then she turned back toward the ballroom and glided inside as if she had every confidence in the world.

Her unusual attire was succeeding, in part: She danced for an hour or more, handed off from one Southern gentleman to another, most of them showing subtle signs of the genteel poverty one could get away with more easily in the South. Their proud bearing seemed to say, Yes, they had to wear cotton gloves instead of kid, and yes, their boots had polished scuffs. They had been devastated by Northern troops, so many men dead, their fields destroyed, their homes burned or ruined by hard use and neglect. Their slaves were gone, their houses in disrepair, their land still unworked nine years after the Confederate defeat. But their impressive family names were intact. Had they known that Alva had nothing beyond her own name to offer, she would have passed that hour standing in discord with the rosy wall while W.K. danced with nearly every other girl present.

After taking her through a waltz, the Pittsburgh man kept hold of her arm, telling her, "I have meetings with some important men in New York soon. Coal is the future of this country's power. I mean political power. Not everyone realizes that. There are men working right this minute on coal-fired generating systems that will, when extended as power grids throughout a city—I mean physical power . . . well, electrical power, which is a kind of physical power—allow for the extension of electricity into both the individual, meaning private, and commercial establishment . . ."

As Alva searched the room for Consuelo, hoping for rescue, behind her came a voice saying, "Please excuse me for interrupting—" Alva turned, and there was W.K. He said, "Might I have a few minutes of your time, Miss Smith?"

"Of course!" she gushed—too eagerly? Had she just dampened whatever interest he was exhibiting, which might not be interest at all, might be nothing more than a desire to ask her about goldenrod?

Her companion, though obviously put out, made no argument. He bowed and left them, while Alva said, "I'm pleased to have a chance to—"

To what? What would Miss Fair say? "To—to merit some of your time. It's a genuine pleasure," she added. "Truly."

He gestured for her to precede him through doors that led to a wide stone terrace and extensive sculpted gardens. The Allegheny peaks were violet against the mauve sky. A mockingbird recited its chickadee-cardinal-wren-titmouse litany at the top of its voice. Were it not for the scene she was supposed to be staging, she might have been able to properly admire and enjoy her surroundings. She might have been able to admire and enjoy W.K. Instead, she fought to control her nervousness and, as ladies did, waited for the gentleman to speak first.

They left the terrace and entered the gardens and he said nothing. Strolling the paths—nothing, still. Nothing for so long that she couldn't stand it anymore and said, "You seemed to be enjoying yourself, dancing."

Dancing with everyone else, that is.

"Did I? Yes, well. Unlike my elder brother, I'm not willing to spend all my youth at a desk calculating profit margins on shipping rates. *You* were quite good in there. Quite popular, too."

Then why didn't you ask me to dance?

(No one good will ever consider them seriously.)

"Thank you," she said. "I learned the dances in Paris—at *court*," she emphasized, in accord with the plot. "Armide, my older sister, had her debut in the Tuileries Palace at one of Emperor Napoléon's balls, and I attended several when I was old enough. My mother was quite intimate with Empress Eugénie and her celebrated friend, the *salonnière* Countess de Pourtalès."

(An overstatement.)

(*Be* the prize.)

At those balls, her mother had been displaying her to the highborn gentlemen as though she were a coming attraction, something to look forward to, to plan on, perhaps. Maman would tell the men that she danced well and was fluent in English, French, and German. Not a beauty, perhaps, not yet. But pretty enough and already so poised, *n'est-ce pas*? And her ancestry . . .

W.K. invited Alva to sit beside him on a bench, where she attempted prize-like conversation.

Her: *Do you enjoy that new game, lawn tennis? I'd wager you're awfully good at it.* (Bat eyelashes. Smile.)

Him: *I do play, and fairly well, it seems. A bit hot for it now, though. Yachting, that's the thing.*

Her: *Have you spent much time in London? Paris? Parlez-vous français?* (He did. Geneva. School.)

Him: *I'm keen on horses—breeding them, racing them; they're the most magnificent animals, don't you agree?* (She—silently—did not.)

Even with the pleasant banter, he didn't appear to be enjoying himself. He rubbed his eyes. He sneezed, withdrew a handkerchief, wiped his nose. Alva's stomach was knotted and painful. They went on this way, a rowboat idling in an eddy seemingly forever. Her smile felt pasted on her face. Finally she blurted—

"I'm loath to tell you this. But I've recently heard a rumor. About Miss Fair. The sort of thing *I* would want to know if I were befriending a lady."

His eyebrows were lifted in curiosity, so she continued. "It seems she may have become . . . quite close . . . to a young man who works for her family."

"Oh?"

"A stable hand, actually." His eyebrows went higher. Alva said, "So I heard. I can't say that it's true, but . . ."

"I did have some reservations about Miss Fair," he said, then sneezed again. "This only confirms them."

"I dislike spreading rumors, but in this case . . ."

"Miss Smith," he said, laying his gloves on the bench. He picked them up again. Laid them down. Patted them.

"Miss Smith," he repeated, "Corneil—my older brother—has three children. Margaret, my oldest sister, has four. My younger sister Emily has one and—if I may—is currently in anticipation of another."

"That's a lot of nieces and nephews," Alva said. "Holidays must be lively affairs."

"They are."

"And I'm certain *you* make them all the brighter." This, in her best prize-like tone.

He picked up his gloves and clutched them.

He sneezed.

"I think it's the"—he gestured as he pressed the handkerchief to his nose yet again—"the flowers on your dress."

"Oh, I'm so sorry," she said, and began to pluck off the offenders and toss them aside.

"Please." He waved off her apology while shifting farther from her on the bench. "What I have been intending to say is that I understand your father is having some difficulties right now."

She stopped plucking. He wanted to speak about her *father*?

"Well," she said, "yes, that's true, but it's only temporary. He's been ill, you see. Once he recovers—"

"Certainly. But if you have no objections, it would please me to be in a position where I could aid him in the meantime. I thought I might speak to him when I return to New York."

So the Vanderbilts were now also in the lending business and W.K. was fishing for clients? Perhaps she had misjudged his merits. Perhaps she should go this minute and find the Pittsburgh coal man.

"That's kind of you," she continued, gathering her plucked skirts and rising, "but I suspect he would prefer to—"

"As his son-in-law, I mean," he said, standing.

"As his son-in-law."

"I—yes. That is, if you're amenable to that plan. I've been meaning to see you alone for days. This was my aim in coming here. I realize my proposition might seem surprising—"

"To say the least! You didn't even ask for a dance."

"I do apologize. I . . . well, it's . . . Miss Smith, seriousness doesn't come easily to me. I had to work up my nerve to speak with you. Because as my family has rightly advised me, it's time that I . . . Well, I've considered this carefully, and as I'm certain you know, we—all of us—are given a small array of choices that suit our situations, and you seem to me a good choice, and from what I can tell, it seems that you feel similarly. About me."

She stood there stupidly, blinking. Then she began to laugh.

"Miss Smith?"

Was it really as simple as this?

He said, "I'm afraid I don't see the joke."

A few strokes of flattery and a few gushing remarks, once the scene had been set?

Recovering her composure, she said, "You're certain?"

"I am."

"I'd thought that perhaps Miss Fair . . ."

He shook his head. "She wouldn't suit. But you—you do find the prospect appealing?"

"Yes. Yes! Wonderful, in fact. It's what I had hoped for."

He grinned that happy-puppy grin. "Good. Then we shall continue our acquaintance in New York. I think you'll find I'm an agreeable fellow—and if not, you'll call it off."

"I find you completely agreeable already. Please, Mr. Vanderbilt, do see my father, as soon as you can."

"Call me William, won't you?"

"If you'll call me Alva."

"Alva," he said. "Alva. Good. It's all arranged."

The next morning, Alva met Theresa Fair in the corridor.

"Clever Miss Smith," said Miss Fair in a voice even more childlike than she. "You made like you were after the Southern gentlemen last night, but obviously it was a ruse. I saw you in the gardens. You're in love with him, aren't you?"

"In love—?"

"With Mr. Vanderbilt. Don't pretend otherwise."

Love him? Alva thought. *I hardly know him.*

She said, "I suppose it's obvious, then. I may as well admit it. He proposed marriage to me, and I accepted. I'm sorry if this means disappointed hopes for you. There will be many excellent opportunities in your future. I wish you well."

Love was a frivolous emotion, certainly no basis for a marriage—every young lady knew this. *You must always put sense over feeling*, Madame Denis, Alva's favorite teacher, had said. *Sense will feed you, clothe you, provide your homes and your horses and your bibelots. Feelings are like squalls at sea—mere nuisances if one is lucky, but many girls have lost their way in such storms, some of them never to return.*

Alva did not need to love William Vanderbilt; she needed only to marry him.

III

"I'VE BEEN TELLING Father and Grandfather all about you," William said as he and Alva, en route to dine at the Commodore's house, strolled in nearby Washington Square Park. "They can't wait to see for themselves what a fine match I've made. I believe Grandfather even trimmed his sideburns for the occasion."

"The pleasure will be all mine, I'm certain." Already she was enjoying herself; who would not be flattered by such enthusiasm? It was endearing, really.

He said, "I would temper your expectations. The papers refer to him as 'the old tyrant' for a reason."

"And is he a tyrant?"

"Oh, not at all. He is—shall we say?—less accomplished in the social graces than the gentlemen you're accustomed to."

"If you fear I might judge you by his behavior, rest easy; my practice is to give every person a fair trial on his own merits."

"Good! This is my practice as well. Society's gotten so caught up with convoluted rules and standards—"

"Hasn't it, though? It can be maddening."

William said, "It pleases me that you're so understanding—and intelligent! I told them, 'She's not one of those insipid girls who can't think for herself.' That dress with the flowers—granted, those particular flowers didn't agree with me—but I told them how you were the only girl there with an original approach."

"And you were the one gentleman there whose opinion I valued."

This compliment was not exactly a lie. Had she delivered it convincingly? Artful doublespeak did not come as naturally to her as it seemed to do for others she'd seen—the ladies in the French court, for example. They had made a sport of it, a sport that had amused her when she'd been merely an observer.

At their destination, they were shown into the Commodore's drawing room, a high-ceilinged, well-appointed but not ostentatious space where the two men stood up to greet them. Mr. Vanderbilt, William's father, was a stout, balding man with dark, bushy muttonchop whiskers and friendly brown eyes that were almost Asiatic in shape. The Commodore was much the same in countenance, but with white hair and piercing blue eyes. He was taller than his son, and lean—strapping, one might call him, despite his having turned eighty years old earlier that year. His sideburns were indeed neat.

He came to Alva and took her hand. "Welcome, Miss Smith! The boy here has been talking of you without end."

"I do hope the descriptions were favorable; if not, you must confess it so that I can run away right now."

Mr. Vanderbilt took her hand in turn, saying, "Fear not. He used only the most glowing terms."

"Glowing? Oh—well, now I'm worried I shall never live up to your expectations."

"What, you can't actually glow?" said the Commodore. He looked at William's father. "Billy, the lass can't glow!"

"How very unfortunate," said Mr. Vanderbilt. He shook his head in mock disappointment.

"That's it, then. Out with ye!" The Commodore gestured toward the door.

Encouraged by this favorable reception, Alva said, "If you must know the truth, I truly can glow—but to display my talent might mean outshining you all, and I don't wish to be immodest."

"Aha! A bright girl," the Commodore declared, nudging William. "Shine away! Already our boy here is showing good effects from it." The Commodore pinched William's cheek.

Alva smiled demurely. (*Glance coyly—lashes down.*) It was not *so* difficult to be the prize, not when it meant exercising one's mind in the process. She hoped William possessed the same wit she was seeing demonstrated by these men—though she had yet to see signs of it.

They dined on beef rib roast, candied carrots, creamed spinach, pickled beets. Alva savored every delicate bite she brought to her lips, no forkful actually full—one did not wish to appear *over*eager. What a pleasure it was, though, more so even than the repartee. If William did not prove to be clever, she would regardless eat very well, just as she'd envisioned that day at the Greenbrier. She'd done right in allowing Consuelo to lobby for her, for this.

As they ate, the Commodore, who'd begun life as a Staten Island farmer's son, did much of the talking, regaling them with dramatic stories of his steamboat days in the wilds of Nicaragua, and New Jersey. Mr. Vanderbilt, far more modest in attitude, told about the Vanderbilt family history and how he'd gotten his own start farming the family land before his father brought him in to manage the railroads.

The Commodore said, "He tells it too simply—when he was a young man, I knew he was stupid. *Blatherskite*, I called him. Always going on in his plodding way. *He plods, he ought to plow!* I thought. So I gave him leave to run the farm—didn't see him being any good to me here. He showed me, though, believe it. Smart like a fox. That farm never saw so much income! So I put him in charge of the whole works—all the roads, operations, accounting—the whole works, I tell ye, and we're more profitable than ever."

"Not that business profit should concern Miss Smith," said Mr. Vanderbilt with equanimity. "Likely she prefers more feminine subjects." He then asked after Alva's father, inquired politely about each of her sisters, and bade her talk about her years in Paris.

Time to play huckster once again:

She told them that she had attended a good school, "though I much preferred the city over confinement within the school's walls. My mother was active in society and at court. We attended the opera, the ballet, so many plays and concerts. *Je parle très bien le français,* as you would expect. It was a fine upbringing. So much emphasis on art and beauty. I confess I used to wish I could be Empress Eugénie's daughter. But not anymore," she added. "My fate could not be happier."

At the conclusion of the most satisfying dinner Alva had eaten in a year or longer, the Commodore raised his glass of what was a marvelous Garrafeira port and said, "William, my boy, I speak for your father and myself when I say you've done well by the family. Miss Smith here is a fine, well-behaved woman, there's no doubt in it—no, none at all. Marry her, with our blessings."

She was comporting herself perfectly and reaping the benefits. Yet all the while, Theresa Fair's accusation—that Alva loved William—sat on her shoulder speaking into her ear the way her mother's pet mockingbird used to do. Love. *Liebe. L'amour. Amore.* Love, for a man. She'd read of it, had seen it seem to happen to other girls, but could no more imagine how it felt than she knew how it felt to fly.

She believed that what Madame Denis had cautioned was true, but was there *any* benefit to this type of love, any advantage? Fact: emotions were unstable, unreliable, time consuming. Emotions were forever getting the heroines of stories into trouble. Only when Elizabeth Bennet stopped fretting over Mr. Darcy and he over her did the wisdom of their pairing prevail. Only when passionate Mr. Rochester had been tamed by grave injury was he worthy of sensible Jane Eyre's affection and commitment.

Besides, one could not conjure love.

William had selected her, would marry her, and they would in time become something like his parents. Alva would manage his household. She would bear his children. She would be at the very least a prominent second-tier society matron. She would never have to live in a tenement, or die in one. That ought to be enough.

"Mother is home from her summer travels and would like you to come to tea," William said, standing by the window in Alva's cramped drawing room on a late September afternoon. He'd stopped in to see her before leaving for Long Island, where he and some companions were going to hunt quail. Alva's youngest sister, Julia, sat nearby ostensibly writing a letter to a friend.

The sisters, having seen only a little of him, were intensely curious about this Vanderbilt fellow who would be their savior. They'd given up waiting for Armide to receive an offer; now twenty-seven, she was far too old to be anyone's first wife. Jenny, nineteen, was prettiest, but Jenny was painfully shy and suffered from melancholy. Fifteen-year-old Julia was flighty and spoiled and in no way ready for marriage, even should an offer come her way. They'd pinned Alva with their hopes the way a naturalist pinned a frog to a pan.

Alva observed William. He was slender and of a good height, with gray-blue eyes and ruddy cheeks. His hair was golden in the sunlight. He was in fact a golden boy. She was the one who'd gotten the prize.

He continued, "She says Thursday would be best, if you're free. Three of my sisters will be there, and Corneil's wife, Alice. George, too. He's about to be twelve, but Mother indulges him. Everyone's eager to finally meet you, as you might imagine."

"And I them. I'll send a note right now." She went to the desk and told Julia to go.

"Why should I?" said Julia, not budging.

"Because I asked you to."

"You didn't ask, you commanded."

"Will you please leave us?" Alva said sweetly.

Julia turned to William. "Must I?"

"Go," Alva said. "You see? This is why I commanded."

William smiled as Julia went off pouting. "All right now," he said, resuming the conversation while she penned her note. "Let's see. You might bring some orange daylilies. Are they in season? Or violets. Mother likes those, too. I should tell you, you're not the sort she'd choose for me. She's retiring and gravitates toward similarly quiet friends. But she'll like you just the same. Better, I should think."

"I know I'll adore her. All of them."

He paced the short distance between desk and doorway. "Oh—she loves opera. She and my father take Florence, Lila, and George to every performance. You might mention some you've seen."

"Opera," Alva said. "Good. I—"

"Actually, *don't* mention opera."

"Oh?"

"It's a sore point. The academy refuses to sell my father a box. 'War profiteering,' they say, though they took his contributions readily enough and in every way profited from the war themselves." He turned to her. "I apologize. I shouldn't get in such a temper."

"No, the snub is unmerited, I agree."

"It frustrates Father no end, and distresses Mother, of course."

"So I won't bring up the opera."

"Unless, that is, you believe you might have some influence there?"

She had none. "Perhaps I do," she said. "I'll give it some thought."

"It isn't only the opera. Florence was terribly disappointed to be left off the list for Miss Astor's debutante dinner dance."

Alva chose not to say that she, too, was left off.

"And it's been quite tiresome to be denied membership in the Union Club. I'm grateful to your father for mounting a campaign on behalf of my brothers, Father, and me."

"He's eager to help," she said, though he'd done nothing more than sign the letters she had written to the membership committee and to key friends who had a regular presence there and were current with dues. Daddy had not a single political bone in his body; Maman had been the one for that.

Alva finished the note, folded it, and handed it to William. "Give this to your mother and leave all the rest to me."

He took the note, then pulled her up from the chair. "You see, this is what I like so much about you. Other ladies would fret and wave their handkerchiefs. 'Oh, what can *I* possibly do?' You are a lady of action. Thank you," he said. "You'll make me the family hero." Then to her dismay, he kissed her.

This was not the first time she'd been kissed. On her grandfather's plantation when she was ten, the overseer's son had found her alone in the orchard and dared her to let him do it—a chaste, childlike kiss. Later she had kissed the young Parisian pianist whose mother was their music teacher. Maman caught them and slapped her and sent her to her room for three days. She fired the teacher and told everyone that the son preyed on young girls. Had Alva been his prey? If so, why had Maman slapped *her*? The entire matter had left her embarrassed and confused. William's kiss was having the same effect.

He let her go, saying, "Forgive me. I took advantage."

A noise in the hall suggested Julia hadn't gone far. Alva stepped away from him. "I hope there's good weather for your travels."

"I rather hope there isn't," he said, moving to get his hat from the table. "A man likes a rugged sea!"

"Be safe," she said, surprised by the tenderness she felt. Or perhaps fear was what tightened her throat: if William came to a bad end, everything would be ruined.

❧

The morning was warm, so Alva and Consuelo, in Union Square to browse Tiffany's, found a bench in the shade of the oaks. Pairs of ladies done up in summer muslins with parasols to match strolled past them, petticoats rustling over the bricks as they went.

Quick study though Alva was, it was taking some time to learn the Vanderbilt family members' names and keep them straight in her mind. Part of the trouble was that in addition to there being so many people, there were so many repetitions of names.

"William and his father and one of his nephews are all Williams," she said to Consuelo, who was helping her review in advance of her tea date the next day. "So many Williams in the world—William Shakespeare, William Blake, William Wordsworth . . ."

"General William T. Sherman, too, let's not forget."

Alva said, "Certainly Atlanta recalls him well."

She continued, "The Commodore's name is Cornelius, as is the younger of his two sons, as is his oldest grandson—William's brother."

Consuelo said, "You know, I liked the brooch with the emerald in the center and the enameled leaves. You should get W.K. to buy you the opal you admired, the one flanked with diamonds. Or that black velvet choker with the gemstone swirls." She made a swirl motion with her hand.

"And both Cornelius the son and Cornelius the grandson are called Corneil," Alva went on, ignoring her. Jewelry was the least of her concerns right now. "And although the son is technically the second Cornelius, he's Cornelius *Jeremiah*—C.J., and it's the grandson, William's older brother, who's 'the second.' "

"C.J. is the one who's no good, remember. If his name comes up, you pretend ignorance."

"I'll do that. His *brother* Corneil, however, is a shining example of all that's right in the world."

"Yes. And saying so—as often and as publicly as possible—will get you into his wife Alice's good graces; she'll be the Vanderbilt matriarch one day, you know."

Alva looked up from her notes. "That should be an *earned* position, don't you think?"

"You only say that because W.K. isn't first in line. You'll have to have Corneil poisoned or something if you want to advance."

"We don't have a feudal system here. I could be matriarch."

"As easily as that?" Consuelo laughed. "You think Alice will simply stand aside and allow it?"

"Don't bother me about details. I'm very, very busy."

Alva glanced again at her notes. Alice and Corneil's oldest son, four years old, was William Henry II; they called him Bill. Their younger boy, a year old, was Cornelius III and was called Neily. Alice and Corneil had named their firstborn (Neily's big sister) Alice. Alva said, "Does this family have no imagination whatsoever?"

"Just learn your lines."

Tucking the paper into a pocket, Alva said, "Suppose Mrs. Vanderbilt doesn't like me. William says I'm not the kind of girl she'd choose for him."

"She would never say so to your face."

"How very helpful you are! I'm worried, though. I really don't have any influence beyond what I've already done."

"Perhaps not. But you can still spend the money."

"Do you suppose I can elope? Next week would be perfect. The landlord will be around soon for the rent."

"Oh, yes, elopement would be excellent for your standing in society. Do that."

"If I were a man, I could have resolved my family's problems ages ago."

Consuelo kissed Alva's cheek. "If you were a man, I would marry you."

"No, you'd hold out for a nobleman."

"You're right. But I'd still love you best."

In the Vanderbilts' drawing room the next day, Alva had hardly settled into a chair when Mrs. Vanderbilt, whose entire mien conveyed kindness, said, "My son and I had a conversation. If you feel you could agree to a short engagement, it seems to me a December wedding would be ideal."

Three of William's sisters and their sister-in-law Alice observed Alva as if she were that pinned frog. She'd hoped to also meet George, but it seemed he had better things to do than sit in an overwarm room inspecting his brother's intended. What was there to see, after all? A dark-haired girl of medium stature with prominent nostrils in a squarish face. Not unpleasant to look at; her brown eyes were intelligent, her eyebrows expressive, her skin pale and clear. Nothing to warrant an interruption in what George was doing, however—reading, probably; William had said (with some puzzlement) that he rarely saw George without a book in hand.

"It's soon, I know," continued Mrs. Vanderbilt, "but we're very eager to have you. And your reputation is so good, I can't imagine anyone finding cause to speculate."

Alva loved her immediately.

"December?" said Lila. "Oh, I agree. Imagine, you might even have snow!"

Fourteen years old and as pretty as a rosebud, Lila was being brought up in quite a different environment than her older siblings had been. Mr. Vanderbilt had outlined the history for Alva. The American Vanderbilt family went back to 1650, Staten Island, when a forebear named Aertson from the Dutch town of De Bilt came as an indentured servant. William and his seven siblings were born on the Staten Island farm the Commodore had given their father to run before bringing him into the railway business. It had been years now since they'd migrated to the city. Lila and George, the youngest, were city children.

The Commodore had been raised on that farm. His father was both farmer and ferryman, and the Commodore became a ferryman, too. Next steamships, then railroads. But he didn't build his home in Manhattan until 1846, making him a Johnny-come-lately here—another reason the family was not among the "best" New York Dutch—the Beekmans and Stuyvesants and Schermerhorns and Joneses. And then there was the problem of unmentionable Uncle C.J.

"Snow? I should hope not," said Alice, who was settling little Alice, a delicate six-year-old with a winning smile, into a chair beside Alva. "Imagine our wet hems and shoes."

Lila said, "*I* think it would be romantic."

"Yes," lisped little Alice. She wore a dress in the same soft yellow as her aunt Lila's. "And I shall serve everyone tea."

Alva patted her head. "Will you do that? It would be such a help."

"She'll take you at your word," Alice warned. "Best not to give her false hope."

Alva told the child, "Perhaps you can serve tea to the most special guests on the day before. You'll be far too busy on the day of the wedding."

"What shall I be busy with?"

"Why, carrying flowers, of course."

They discussed the details. The reception breakfast would be here in his parents' home, a four-story corner house with its own stables in the rear. Florence thought Alva should be married in white, as Queen Victoria had done, and adopt, too, Her Majesty's decision to serve a sublime white cake. "To symbolize the bride's purity," Alice said, gazing at Alva with round, apparently guileless eyes. "And of course the ceremony must be held at St. Bart's."

"Oh, but we attend Calvary. I wouldn't think of offending Reverend and Mrs. Washburn."

"But you will attend St. Bart's after your marriage," Alice said. It wasn't a question.

Alva smiled politely. This was not the time for debate. She said, "Of course, if that's my husband's desire."

William had told her nothing about Alice beyond her being his oldest brother's wife of seven years now. Alva had not expected her to be so . . . lovely. Her heart-shaped face was perfectly appointed: delicate yet full lips, clear blue eyes, enviable lashes and well-behaved eyebrows slightly darker than the burnished blond hair on her head. From the slimness of her figure, one would not imagine she'd borne three children in the space of four years, the youngest being barely a year old. Alva's waist had not been so narrow since she was twelve years of age, if then.

"Miss Smith," little Alice said, "when you marry Uncle William, I should like cousins I can visit at your home."

Her mother tapped her arm. "Don't be rude, Alice."

The child looked abashed. "Oh. If you please, I mean."

Alva said, "First let's think about the flower girl's dress, shall we?"

"And yours!" Lila said. "You've got to outdo my sister Margaret's. She thinks too much of herself."

"Margaret's the eldest," Florence explained. "You must use Mrs. Buchanan—she does the Astor girls' dresses when they're not buying in Paris, and the Stuyvesants', too."

Mrs. Vanderbilt shook her head. "You girls make it out to be a competition."

"Forgive me, Mother," Florence told her, "but it's been a long time since you were married, and a lot of things have changed." To Alva she said, "Mother has Roosevelt relations, which she needs to make more of, for our sake."

"Tell me."

Emily said, "Her father's mother was Cornelia Roosevelt. *Her* father, Isaac Roosevelt, was among our state's first senators after the Revolution and was a Federalist ally with Alexander Hamilton. They called him the Patriot."

"Senator Roosevelt," Alva said, thinking of snooty Lydia Roosevelt and her superior airs. "That's quite impressive."

Emily said, "You wouldn't know it from the way we're received—or not received, as has been the case too often."

"Is it possible that society is ignorant on the matter?"

"It seems so," Florence said. "Mother feels it's impolite to boast."

"Society's objection lies with our grandfather, the Commodore," Emily explained. "The newspapers call him—and I quote—'the robber baron of our modern feudalism.' "

Florence added, "They say he's a 'railway despot.' Alice has helped to make some progress, though."

Alice shrugged modestly, and Emily went on, "Her father, Mr. Gwynne, though he's from St. Louis, is regarded very well by his law colleagues, which has made it easier for some of their wives and daughters to accept us. But Alice is so busy now with the children and church," she added breezily. Too breezily. "We're counting on you, Miss Smith, to further the cause."

Mrs. Vanderbilt again shook her head. "I don't pretend to understand all of this 'best society' nonsense. Who's allowed in, who's kept out. It's as though someone made a new rulebook after the war and only certain women possess a copy."

Florence said, "It's not so difficult, Mother. The things that matter foremost are family history and reputation."

"That's right," Emily said. "Four generations of gentlemen in a family line, that's become the standard. Like Miss Smith's got—your family was here in the early 1700s, isn't that correct?"

"We were," Alva said. "Though not in Manhattan."

"Even so," said Emily.

Mrs. Vanderbilt shook her head. "Getting one's daughters into the right circles and properly married is almost like sport! It didn't used to be this way."

"Take heart," said Florence. "Now we have Miss Smith to lead our charge."

Except that Miss Smith had no weapons, no troops. Miss Smith might well be fraudulent goods sold to an unsuspecting sap. Miss Smith, if she were wise, would change the subject.

"Mrs. Vanderbilt," she said, "I wonder if you would be able to suggest an agent to help William and me find a suitable house. What I have in mind—"

"Tell her, Mother!" Lila interrupted.

"Tell me what?"

"She has a surprise for you."

Little Alice jumped up. "She has a surprise!"

Mrs. Vanderbilt smiled at her granddaughter. "I can't very well keep it secret any longer, can I? My husband is acquiring a house on Forty-fourth Street as a wedding gift for you and William. We thought we would help you two get started."

"A house *and* servants," Emily said. She laid her hand on her rounded middle. "You'll need help before too long."

"One hopes," said Mrs. Vanderbilt. "Now, for servants, I use an agency—"

"Good heavens," Alva said, going over to kiss her. "This is incredibly generous. I can't begin to thank you enough."

Mrs. Vanderbilt blushed. "Please. Do sit. It's a small gesture—and really, it's for me as much as the two of you. I feel better when I know everyone has what they need."

Regaining her chair, Alva said, "You mentioned an agency, for the servants? That will make things simpler. I've got Mary, whom I'll bring with me—"

"Mary?" said Mrs. Vanderbilt.

"Our housekeeper's daughter. She's only fifteen, but she's been helping with our hair and clothes practically since she was born."

Alice looked confused. "A child worked for you?"

"Well, her mother, Lulu, was a slave who stayed on, and it was only natural—"

"You don't mean to have a Negro girl as your lady's maid," Alice said.

"I do mean to. It's an ideal position, and she's well suited for it."

"The best families use only white servants," Alice said.

Alva was losing patience with Alice. "I like her and I trust her and she's going to have to go out to work before long anyway, so I mean to keep her with me."

"Can she even read?" Alice said.

"Lulu sent her to school, yes." Alva forced herself to keep her tone even.

Mrs. Vanderbilt said, "I do hope she's not too dark."

"She's actually very light," Alva said, "not that it should—"

"Who's her father?" Alice asked.

"I don't see how that's any concern."

Mrs. Vanderbilt interjected, "Never mind. It's good of you to want to improve her circumstances."

"Thank you," Alva said, forcing a smile for Alice, who returned an insincere smile of her own.

"When you're free," said Mrs. Vanderbilt, unmindful of the exchange, "I'll take you to see Mrs. Coleman at the agency and we'll see about setting you up. What a treat all of this is!" She drew her granddaughter onto her lap. "I do love to play house."

IV

"NINE MORE WEEKS," Armide said, closing their father's ledger. It had a balance of seventy-five dollars, against their monthly expenditures of ninety-five, barest minimum. Already they were subsisting mainly on potatoes, cheese, eggs, and bread.

She continued, "If I put some people off, we should be able to get by. I've paid the laundress and the grocer, and I'll make excuses to the rest."

Consuelo mimicked, "'Goodness, we simply *forgot* to pay, what with all the chaos of the upcoming wedding to Mr. *Vanderbilt.*'"

"That ought to do it," Alva said. "You should practice, Armide."

They were in the parlor, where Consuelo was teaching Alva a card game she'd learned in London and picking silly tunes on her banjo. Upstairs, Murray Smith rested and read, which was how he spent most of his days now. Anything more strenuous risked bringing on another heart episode.

"And speaking of your wedding," Armide said.

"Let's not," Alva told her. "We're having such a nice time."

Now that she'd secured her future and her family's, practical truths were encroaching: she would have to leave home, which meant living apart from her sisters for the first time ever. The thought was strange, frightening—they'd been four lifeboats lashed together in a rough sea, and now her line was going to be cut.

And Lulu, who had overseen Alva since birth, would no longer be there to tell her all the things she was doing wrong.

And she would have a husband who would make "demands" of her, and while she wasn't clear on the particulars of such demands, she knew close physical contact was involved and she dreaded it. She was *supposed* to dread it, at any rate, according to the *Lady's Book* and according to her mother and according to God, and therefore she had persuaded herself that she did.

Marriage also meant children, which meant pregnancy and childbirth, which meant untold agonies along with risk of death—and given the number of orphans in literature and life, that risk, as Mr. Shakespeare might say, was grave.

Consuelo put her banjo aside. "No, let's do. Have you settled on a design for your gown?"

"Has anyone told you how poorly you take direction?"

"All the time," Consuelo said. "So, the gown?"

"Mrs. Buchanan hasn't had time for me yet. She's doing a ball gown for Mrs. William Astor. She'll see me a week from Tuesday, I'm told."

"Oh, well, of course," Consuelo said. "One cannot delay *Mrs. Astor's* order, because *Mrs. Astor* commands the moon and stars and the rain, too, I am fairly certain. As well as Mr. McAllister, of course. Her Lord Protector."

Ward McAllister, a fellow Southerner who hailed from Savannah, had been a fixture of their Newport summers, a happy drone flitting among the families, pollinating everyone with his enthusiasm and advice. He did this here as well, under doyenne Caroline Astor's watchful gaze.

"I rather like him," Alva said.

Consuelo nodded. "All the ladies like him."

"Mrs. Astor doesn't command *Mr.* Astor," Alva said. "Or perhaps she does."

"Does Mr. Astor actually exist?"

"The papers speak of him often enough." However, he owned a steam yacht and appeared to prefer life at sea over unending social commitments.

Armide said, "Shall we mind our own business now?"

"If we must," said Alva.

"Important as the wedding gown is," Armide said, "what needs to be discussed is what happens on the wedding night."

Consuelo poked Alva. "When the gown is down, one could say."

Armide said, "I wish I knew more. What I do know, however, should keep you from entering the situation completely ignorant of what awaits you." She paused. "You *are* ignorant?"

"I prefer *uninitiated*," Alva said.

"It has to be just so with you, doesn't it?"

"Not always. *Ignorant* is pejorative, that's all."

Consuelo said, "You should credit Alva, not criticize her; precision is the hallmark of success."

Alva said, "Success is the hallmark of success."

"Indeed it is," Consuelo said. "Correct again."

"Precisely."

Armide said, "You should take this seriously."

"Who isn't serious?" asked Alva. "I epitomize the word."

Armide tried again. "The purpose of marriage is, as you know, procreation—"

"The purpose of *my* marriage is salvation."

Consuelo said, "Fairly certain you're bargaining for both."

"Procreation ensures salvation, it's true."

"Like money in the bank."

"Girls, please," Armide said. "At least pretend to be serious."

They folded their hands in their laps and sat up straighter. "Proceed," Alva told her.

"As I understand it, men, well, they have particular needs that have to do with . . ." Armide paused. "Think of the pegged planks that made the walls of Grandpa's slave quarters, remember? The wife is the plank and the husband is the peg. That is, he, um, he *has* a peg. All men do, where we have our—"

The other two burst out laughing. "A peg!" said Consuelo.

"I'm merely illustrating—"

"But it's made of flesh, obviously," Alva said. "Is it . . . is it like a finger? With bones inside it, I mean. Or one bone, perhaps?"

Armide frowned. "I don't know. I suppose it must be."

Alva imagined something like a tiny elephant's trunk. She'd seen an elephant once, at P. T. Barnum's Hippodrome. Did elephant's trunks have bones? She said, "Can a man move it at will?"

"Alva, really." Armide's face was crimson.

"Don't you wonder?" she said. "How long is it? Does it get tucked down against a man's leg when he isn't . . . um . . . engaged in . . . construction?"

Consuelo erupted in laughter again while Armide said, "Never mind. *He'll* know how it works and how to proceed. What I do know—and this is important: you mustn't act as though you like whatever he does to you. I used *plank* as a metaphor deliberately. Keep your arms still. Don't . . . don't writhe."

"Don't writhe!" Consuelo said.

Alva frowned at her sister. "Honestly, Armide. I'm not an *animal.*"

But she *was* an animal. How else to explain what she'd done when she was younger? Meandering through her school's parklike grounds in Neuilly-sur-Seine, lying facedown on a fallen log for the sensation she got when pressing herself against it. Secretly riding her pony unsaddled with her legs astride its back. Washing herself in the bath, deliberately rubbing that place she knew better than to touch except in strict necessity. Maman had been adamant about the way a girl would ruin herself if she indulged such filthy impulses. Alva didn't want to be ruined. But she couldn't help herself; the sensation was glorious, and as no one seemed to see any difference in her, she had kept doing it. Until the day her mother came into the bathroom and caught her at it. She'd yanked Alva from the tub, and, not even allowing her a bath sheet, made her place her hands on the washstand while she raised a hairbrush—

Are you some kind of animal? (Smack!)

I will not have a daughter of mine behave in such filthy ways. (Smack!)

Lustfulness is a sin. (Smack!)

Do that again and no decent man will ever marry you. Do you understand?

Alva understood.

Armide was saying, "It's only that when men get with women in this way, they can succumb to their baser instincts. They want to . . . to rut. It's your job to prevent that."

"Rut?"

They all looked at each other helplessly. Then Armide shrugged. "That's what I heard Madame Whitaker say." Madame Whitaker had been a neighbor of theirs in Paris. Armide attended her Wednesday evenings at home, when many fashionable ladies and men, too, gathered to drink Cognacs and Madeiras and to gossip about whoever wasn't immediately within earshot.

Armide said, "Let's suppose it means behave basely."

"And *basely* in this context would be . . . ?"

"I don't know. I don't know! It doesn't matter. I'm only telling you this part because you're sometimes unladylike, asserting yourself the way you do, and—"

"What nonsense!" Consuelo said. "These are modern times—"

Armide put her hand over Consuelo's mouth. "Alva, if you give your husband *any* signal that makes him imagine you are less than virtuous—"

"I won't," said Alva. "I'll be a plank."

"Because she'll be scared stiff!" Consuelo laughed.

Armide said, "Who wouldn't be?"

A few days later, a somber William came by to say that his niece, little Alice, had unexpectedly succumbed to a fever. The family was stunned; the doctor had said her ailment was nothing serious. She had declined so quickly that there wasn't even time to send for the clergyman. Even as Alva sat there, stricken, listening to him, heartbroken for the child's parents and anxious about her own situation because the wedding would have to be put off, another very different (and guilty) feeling overcame her: relief.

The gown need not come down—not for a little while longer, anyway.

V

ALVA'S RELIEF LASTED precisely as long as the mild weather and their meager store of summer produce did. Come January, getting by on two meals a day so that Jenny and Julia, still growing, could have more to eat, Alva no longer cared what might occur on her wedding night or any night afterward. Her stomach gnawed at her all the time. Her collarbones and cheekbones grew prominent enough that at church one Sunday, Mrs. Washburn took her aside and said, "Miss Smith, you're so thin and pale! I must ask: are you tubercular?"

"Goodness, no, I'm quite well," Alva assured her. "It's bridal nerves, that's all."

"Still, you've got to eat!"

Yes, she needed to eat—and did, in vivid dreams of steaming hot meat pies and thick stews and pastries straight out of the baker's oven, only to cruelly wake again to a breakfast of a single egg or cup of porridge, weak coffee, and Julia grousing, "Why did that child have to die?"

Alva scolded her. "Have you no sympathy for anyone beyond yourself?"

"She's already dead; my sympathy can do nothing for her. I'm hungry. The house is always cold. Daddy's room gets all the coal—"

"Would you have your invalid father freeze to death?"

"We're cursed," Julia said. "We used to live so nicely, and now I have to sleep in a room where I can see my breath and have to share a bed with Jenny."

Alva said, "I should think her a benefit in wintertime."

"Her nose whistles when she breathes. What happened to us? Why did everything have to go so wrong? When will Daddy be well again? He's not going to die, is he? I won't be able to stand it if he dies, too. It isn't fair."

Alva could not endure three more months of this. She might ask William to advance them a portion of her settlement; undoubtedly he'd be glad to assist them this way. Was it not bad enough, though, to be undertaking the marriage solely for his money, without begging for his aid even before she'd bound herself to him? Nor did she wish to beg from Mr. Yznaga or any of her distant uncles. Leaving aside the embarrassment it would cause her father, she did not wish to always be turning to some man or other for solutions to her troubles. As helpless as so many of her sex preferred to be, she was determined to be the opposite. All these ladies of privilege, pale feathers drifting on the breeze. No. She would aid herself.

To save coal, her father had taken to staying in bed with hot water bottles, pillows, and quilts tucked around him. Alva found him lying on his left side (the doctor having said it was best for his blood circulation) with his mouth hanging open, exposing the dark gaps where his molars once had been. Even in sleep, his breath was shallow and labored. As she set his tray on the bureau, she heard him rouse.

"Is that you, my dear?"

"It's Alva," she said, turning to face him. "I've brought your lunch."

He propped himself on one elbow. "You can tell your father I agree. I'll do it."

"What are you saying, Daddy?" The stramonium bottle on his bedside table lay on its side, empty. The Fowler's solution was empty as well. She put the bottles in her pocket. "Did you have another episode? Are you in pain?"

"I'll give up the law and work for him in Mobile. It's what you want. Though God knows I'm no salesman."

She kneeled down next to the bed. "Daddy, it's Alva. Your daughter." She reached for his wrist to measure his pulse.

He pulled his arm away. "You shouldn't be in here, Phoebe. Go on, before someone comes along and sees you."

"Stop it, Daddy, I'm *Alva*. Maman's gone. It's 1874—"

"Go on, won't you," he hissed. "If my mother finds you here, you're ruined. Please. *Go*."

"All right." She fought back tears as she stood. He was puffy and his color was terrible, save for the hectic pink of his cheeks—which in its way was awful, too. He might not have four months left in him. He might not have four days. "I'm leaving." She went to the bureau and took a box from the bottom drawer, then hurried out of the room.

The narrow blue velvet box, which Maman had called her treasure chest, was decorated with gold thread filigree. It held eight items, all of which had been promised to the girls, two apiece, as their inheritance. Their mother liked to take out each item and unwrap it tenderly, laying it on her dressing table while the girls gathered around her. A short string of pearls. Three gemmed brooches. A diamond-and-ruby ring, emerald earbobs, a gold bracelet encrusted with opals, and a stickpin with an enameled peacock design. Its eye was a small but vivid diamond, and its tail feathers had arrays of colored gems. Each girl had her favorite, though Julia was forever changing her mind. It didn't matter; they didn't believe the jewelry would ever come to them, because to get it they had to lose their mother, and such a loss simply wasn't possible. When later they were forced to face that loss, Armide put the box away. "Maman said to keep it for our weddings—one piece each, and then the second at the birth of our first child."

And so they would. First, however, Alva would pawn it and get as much money as she could bargain for. Then once she and William were married, she would repay the pawnshop from her own household account, reclaim the jewelry, and tell her sisters she had packed the box away with her belongings when preparing to move to her new home. An inspired plan, if she did say so herself.

Dressing to go out, she pushed the box into the balding fur muff she'd been using for as long as she could remember. As she passed the parlor on her way to the front door, Armide said, "Where are you off to? It's terribly raw out there. Icy rain—"

"I have to go to the druggist's," Alva said, turning back to the parlor doorway, the box hidden inside her muff. "Daddy has gone through his medicines. And then I am off to Mrs. Buchanan's, finally."

Armide pulled her shawl close around her neck and set her book aside. "Oh, the wedding gown—I had forgotten that's today! I'll get my wrap—"

"No, you have to stay. Daddy's not well, and Lulu's out with the girls."

"I hate to think of you going there on your own. What of Consuelo? Might she go with you?"

"She's still in Cuba with her mother. You're sweet to worry, but I don't mind. Truly."

"You should be chaperoned—"

"It's just town."

"Now is not the time to be risking your reputation."

Alva said, "You worry too much. Everything will be perfect. Keep a listen for Daddy. He's . . . well, he mistook me for Maman. You might bring him a coffee, help him clear his head."

Armide's alarmed expression was the response Alva was aiming for. Her sister would shift her concern to their father and Alva could carry on without interference.

Outside, the rain clouds were beginning to lift. The wind carried scents of wet wool and acrid smoke. Glimpses of sun amid rolling clouds did little to offset the wind's bite. Alva wondered if William might like to spend winters somewhere warmer, perhaps Marseille. The food in Marseille was itself worth the trouble of getting there. Bouillabaisse . . . lapin à la provençale . . . pieds et paquets . . .

After seeing the druggist, Alva caught the horsecar for downtown. Working-class girls coming from the shantytowns eyed her from beneath untidy hats and hair, contempt plain in their expressions. She turned her gaze away.

The streets were thick with carts and carriages, the cobblestones wet from the rain. Shopkeepers were extending their awnings. Chairs and tables were set out in front of cafés in weak approximations of a Parisian street. What she wouldn't give to be in Paris, with the Seine in the sunlight, accordion music and *le français* filling her ears, an adoring husband, chaussons aux pommes and café au lait, a charming wrought-iron balcony on her pied-à-terre from which she would watch the beautiful rigs with their beautiful passengers . . .

At Chambers Street the trolley lurched, the team balking as a cart overturned ahead of them. The cart pulled its horses with it, mud and manure flying, the intersection blocked, men yelling, people rushing to get a better look. A child wailed. The girls near Alva stood up and made for the exit. "Best stay put," one said as she passed. She sounded Russian. "Don't want to get yourself dirty."

"Da," said her companion. "Too precious for this street."

Too precious? My, how outward appearances could deceive. Yet Alva said nothing; she had no rebuttal: her fiancé's father had a monthly dinner date with the president.

She waited for them to go, then got up and followed them off into the crowd.

Pushing through, she struggled to make her way to the far opposite curb. The fallen horses were screeching in pain or panic. People rushed past and around, bumping and shoving and calling out. Alva's hat went askew and she reached up to protect it, finally seeing the curb ahead as she did.

What a relief to find the sidewalk, to be out of the mud and chaos and wind! As she stood in front of a tobacconist's, she used both hands to secure the hat while she scanned the storefronts for a pawnshop—

Both hands.

"No!" she yelled, startling a pair of men nearby.

She must have dropped the muff in the commotion of getting through the crowd.

Back into the melee she went, pushing and bumping, her gaze on the street . . . nothing.

The car! It was still idled. She hurried over, climbed inside, her heart pounding while she searched the seats and floor.

"It has to be here!"

"Lady?" said the driver, stepping back inside.

"A muff: did you see it? Or a box, a blue velvet box."

"I found a half a sandwich . . ."

Back into the street again, searching, praying—but of course it was no use.

On the sidewalk once more, she wiped angry tears and choked back the rest. *I will figure it out later. I will figure it out.* Right now she had other important business to transact. It would not do to appear in Mrs. Buchanan's shop all teary and bedraggled.

She reached into her coat pocket for her purse to get fare for the ride up to the shop on Fourteenth. The purse, too, was gone.

As Alva walked, she attempted to fix her mind on a plan for Mrs. Buchanan, and not on her stupidity, not on the loss. Stupid pride. Oh, yes, she was solving problems brilliantly on her own! Well done, Alva Smith.

Stop it, she told herself. *It couldn't be helped. You can figure it out later.*

In order to maintain bargaining authority with Mrs. Buchanan, she must give no sign of her agitation. She must encourage the dressmaker to create a vision of a modern bride heretofore not seen outside of royal weddings, outdoing Margaret Vanderbilt Shepard as instructed. She would insist on the best price, and then her father would settle the account later from the sum he'd receive after the wedding. If her stomach growled, she would pretend that it had not.

Entering the shop, Alva heard, "Mrs. Vanderbilt-to-be, I presume! A pleasure!" Mrs. Buchanan, who was younger and more handsome than Alva had expected, rushed over and grasped her fingertips. The woman looked to be in her thirties. Keen gray eyes, light brown hair, nose rounded at the end like a berry. She reminded Alva of a squirrel.

The dressmaker said, "I read of your engagement to 'young Prince Vanderbilt'—they called him that, and by the sketch I'll say he looks the part! Come, give me your coat! Now sit and tell me precisely what it is that will make your wedding day the most glorious ever."

That it should happen, Alva thought, seating herself on a jacquard chaise and unbuttoning her gloves. Mrs. Buchanan sat at the opposite end.

"Supposing you mean my gown—" Alva said, unpinning her hat and setting it aside. Her mother had taught her this process—the undressing before being asked to undress. It conveyed sophistication, Maman had said.

Experience. A perception that one was not to be trifled with in regard to materials or price. That way, by the time one was down to chemise and corset for measurement, one felt in control rather than exposed.

"A heart neckline," Mrs. Buchanan said, and gestured to a dour woman who'd been hovering nearby. "Take this down. Pale green satin—"

"White," said Alva. "It makes a statement."

"Ah, another anglophile. I had so hoped Victoria would go out of fashion, but the woman simply keeps on!"

"With wide flounces," Alva added.

"A riot of flounces! And a neckline to flatter the décolletage. Stand up, dear."

Alva stood. "I don't know that further emphasis of my . . ."—she looked down—"is necessary."

"Fashion dictates," said Mrs. Buchanan. "We must comply."

"My husband—"

"Will admire you tremendously, as will his gentleman friends—a perfect outcome!"

"It *must* be modest," Alva said. She pointed to her neckline. "Perhaps you can put lace here?"

"Oh, certainly. A chemisette of the very best lace, the finest of the fine. Woven by angels! And I'll find you silk so supple that you won't believe it isn't poured from a bottle. Japanese baleen in the bodice, of course, and . . . hmm." She put her hands on Alva's hips and moved her one way, then another. "Seed pearl beads? Opals?"

"Opals would be marvelous." And expensive. But with the marriage settlement, her father could afford it. She said, "Prince Albert was quite fond of opals."

"Make a note," Mrs. Buchanan told the dour woman.

They discussed sleeves and seams and embroidery and buttons. After they'd gone through the process of taking Alva's measurements (Mrs. Buchanan scolding her for being too thin), the dressmaker said, "We'll have a sketch for you to review on Monday next."

"Wonderful. I do appreciate your making time for me this way. I'm sorry I had to delay our appointment."

"A terrible situation that could not be helped! The thing to do in all such cases is to look for the silver lining. Yes. That's my way. There's always something to be— Wait: a silver lining *in the gown*! The primary underskirt. Yes, oh my, an excellent idea. Make a note!"

"I suppose you know best," Alva said without conviction.

"I do know best! Wonderful! What a wise girl you are," Mrs. Buchanan said. "We'll meet on Monday, at . . ."

"Eleven A.M.," said the dour woman.

"At eleven A.M. Yes? Upon your approval, we'll take a deposit of fifty percent and get the work under way."

"A deposit?"

"Oh, don't be affronted. It's not personal. But you see, not everyone in this city is trustworthy—to say the least! We can't simply sell off a gown if the client changes her mind or—and this has happened!—suddenly can't afford to pay. Men play the markets like it's only a game. Some win. Some lose spectacularly! So we now require a deposit from everyone, even Mrs. William Astor. It's strange times, strange times indeed. We must adapt!"

"Certainly," Alva said, as if this requirement changed nothing. "My father will want to know the price—"

"It's too soon to say."

This was unexpected. How could she negotiate if there was no price? "A range, then."

The dressmaker looked at the ceiling, as if the figures were stamped there on the tin. "Eight hundred to twelve hundred—a wide range, I know, but I won't be able to say better until I've selected the beads."

"As much as that?" Alva said. "That seems . . . rather high." Her mother had never paid more than one hundred dollars for the most elaborate of gowns, even from the best Parisian dressmakers.

Mrs. Buchanan nodded. "Yes, I know—it's terrible how postwar inflation is taking its toll. But I wouldn't dream of offering the future Mrs. Vanderbilt anything but my very, very best."

Alva suspected the inflation had more to do with the name Vanderbilt than with the economic effects of a war that had ended a decade earlier. Regardless, she was sunk. A deposit of four hundred or six hundred dollars—or even fifty—was impossible.

"Of course," she said. "Wonderful. *So* very exciting."

Seeing her to the door, Mrs. Buchanan again grasped her fingertips. "Until Monday!"

"Yes," Alva said, stepping outside. "I look forward to it."

Now she could go home, put her feet in a basin of hot water, and think of how to get herself out of the mess she had made. Such a clever young lady. Oh, yes. A lady of action indeed.

Miss Lydia Roosevelt, just out of her expensively plain landau, approached.

"Miss Smith," she said, plump and privileged in her lustrous blue wool coat with its delicate fox-fur collar. "How pleasant to see you. Did you have business with Mrs. Buchanan? Do you not adore her?"

"Yes, completely," Alva said. "She's planning my wedding gown. You know I'm marrying a cousin of yours."

"A cousin?" Miss Roosevelt looked confused. "I'd heard your betrothal was to William Vanderbilt."

"As I said."

"I'm afraid you've got something wrong, dear. The Vanderbilts, much as they may wish it, are no relations of ours."

"Oh, but you're mistaken. My fiancé's mother is a Roosevelt granddaughter."

"Was her name Roosevelt?"

"No, it was Kissam. But her grandfather was Senator Isaac Roosevelt."

Miss Roosevelt said, "That's *how* many generations back? I'm afraid you're grasping at straws, dear. The only fact that matters to anyone is that Commodore Vanderbilt is a crass, boorish criminal."

"Really, Miss Roosevelt. Such slander diminishes you."

"It's said." Miss Roosevelt adjusted her fur collar to deflect the wind. "Besides, he spit tobacco on my father's shoe."

"Intentionally?"

"Does it matter?"

"You're all being quite unfair to the Vanderbilts. Mrs. Astor—Caroline

Schermerhorn, before she married her husband—lifted the Astor family's similar reputation."

Miss Roosevelt said, "She was a *Schermerhorn.* Not a Kissam/Roosevelt twice removed." She started to move toward Mrs. Buchanan's door, then stopped and said, "You know, I'm sorry for you, Miss Smith."

"Sorry for me?" Alva said.

"Oh—obviously the rumor hasn't yet reached you."

Walk away, Alva told herself. *Don't give her the satisfaction. Say "good day" and leave.* She saw herself doing it, saw Miss Roosevelt's disappointment—

She said, "Tell me the rumor, and I will put it to rest."

Leaning closer, Miss Roosevelt put her hand on Alva's arm. "You know Mr. Gordon Bennett, whose father owns the *Herald Tribune*? He was entertaining some friends last week on a short cruise to see the whales, and your Mr. Vanderbilt was, I hear, quite taken with another of the guests, a girl whose father made a fortune in silver mining. Fair, I believe. A Miss Fair, yes."

"You're mistaken. My fiancé is in mourning," Alva said. "He hasn't been at sea with Mr. Bennett."

"Perhaps not, *if* he's observing custom." Miss Roosevelt shrugged. "Little matter. Even supposing he does marry you, it's not as if you can buy your way into best society. But at least you'll have the gown—no doubt an improvement on the one I heard you wore at Greenbrier."

If only Alva were ten years old again, so that she could knock Miss Roosevelt to the ground and pummel her the way she had done to the boys who made fun of her for climbing trees and building little castles from sticks and rocks. Why was someone always interfering, judging her and her family, making her feel wrong and inferior when the things she was trying to do were neither?

Alva stood taller and said, "Good day, Miss Roosevelt."

"Good day, Miss Smith."

As she walked away, her mind turned immediately to the rumor. *Had* William been sailing with Gordon Bennett? And Theresa Fair: Had she really been aboard as well? Would William have paid the girl so much attention (she was younger than Julia, for heaven's sake!) that others would say he'd been "quite taken" with her?

It was possible. How well did she know him, after all?

If it hadn't happened, why would anyone say it had?

If it had, why had it? Was it that he was merely a flirt? Or was he so inconstant that he'd decided he needn't hitch his wagon to an old horse like Alva, not when Theresa Fair was younger and prettier and had no want of his money. When she so clearly adored him, might even love him.

Alva had given a good performance of those sentiments. But perhaps not good enough.

I should love him, she thought.

In time, perhaps she would.

She would not, however, get prettier. Or younger.

The blisters that had formed on both of her feet during her walk to Mrs. Buchanan's had now swelled and split open, searing her left heel and little toe and her right first and third toes, and a spot toward the outside of that foot . . .

William, entertaining Theresa Fair on Gordon Bennett's yacht. Why would he do this?

She could survive him breaking the engagement, if it came to that—though she would be a pariah where all other gentlemen were concerned; none would take up with another's castoffs.

Still, it would not be the end of the world. She would have to forget the entire plan that's all, and learn to make do.

Forget the buttered bread with raspberry jam.

Forget the life of the empowered, well-off lady,

the stuffed squab,

the paid bills,

the goose-down beds,

the full stomach,

the warm house.

Forget the protection afforded by being married well.

Forget supporting Armide and Jenny and Julia. And Daddy. And Lulu and Mary. Who had all come to count on her, whose comfort and well-being and safety depended upon her marrying William or someone like him.

I have to try harder.

Alva stopped to let a fish cart pass in front of her. She was so weary, and so hungry, and her troubles seemed to be multiplying by the minute.

Money's no fix! the tenement girl had said.

It is, though, she thought. *It can be. For me, it can be. It will be. It has to be.*

Alva made herself concentrate on facts. Miss Roosevelt might be wrong about everything. And even if she wasn't, there might yet be a way for Alva to turn back the rising tide. She would have to seek an expert's assistance—a man, unfortunately. As needs must, and pride be damned. For now.

❧

Mr. Ward McAllister was expected back soon, his housekeeper told Alva. "You're welcome to remain here in the vestibule if you like."

Alva sank onto a bench. "Thank you, I will."

The McAllister townhouse was a tasteful residence not far off Fifth Avenue on Sixteenth Street, where Mr. McAllister lived with his wife, Sarah, a quiet woman whose most remarkable feature had been the money she was to inherit from her steamship-tycoon father. Mr. McAllister was known to stroll Fifth Avenue regularly, observing his neighbors and, of course, being observed. And while it was true that the most fortunate of New York's residents (including Caroline Astor and the notorious abortionist Madame Restell) lived at the corners of Fifth Avenue on increasingly higher-numbered streets, plenty of good people continued to reside in New York's lower blocks, the McAllisters among them.

What were the gentlemen wearing this season? Chestnut gloves or gray? Top hats a little shorter this year, or no? Beaver for those hats, or wool? Brooks Brothers or Wetzel for the best tailcoats? Enameled shirt studs or simple gold? These would be some of his concerns—he wanted always to dress currently. But it was societal fashion, not sartorial, that was his strength, the reason he was sought after by ladies of all ages and stations.

Mr. McAllister was even better informed of the goings-on of the city's best citizens. Indeed, this was his stock-in-trade. At one time he'd been an attorney; the law, though, was less interesting than his friends' lives. Take, for example, the question of whom Miss Carrie Astor might marry when the time arrived. She was not yet sixteen, hadn't officially debuted, but already there were a few young (and some not so young) men making love to her at picnics and parties and balls. Her mother, Mr. McAllister's close friend Caroline, was reportedly concerned that the youngest Miss Astor would fall for one of these Lotharios. She might disregard her parents' direction the way her sister Emily had done in marrying that ridiculous widower James Van Alen last year. Would Carrie remain obedient? If she did not, which unsuitable suitor was she most likely to choose? Mr. McAllister claimed he could occupy himself for entire days with the permutations of such matters, and often did.

Gossips said he'd been in line for a million-dollar inheritance only to see his expectation thwarted when his aunt, whose support and influence had been his entrée into New York society when he was a young man, divided her estate between the Georgia Historical Society and the Presbyterian Church. So he had joined his father and brother in their California law practice. He liked to say that the three of them did quite nicely there, helping to secure claims and settle disputes when gold was all but jumping out of the hills. But the rush couldn't last forever, and although ambitious, he hadn't the form of Commodore Vanderbilt or Wall Street traders Mr. Drew or Mr. Gould, or the increasingly impressive Scotsman Mr. Carnegie, say, men who went at their obstacles like bulls, heads down and horns out. Therefore he'd had to marry well, and had been lucky in that, at least. His wife's father had left her a fortune sufficient for him to retire from the law and apply himself to all those things he did best.

Alva heard a carriage come to a stop. A few moments later, the front door's latch gave way.

"Why, Miss Smith!" said Mr. McAllister, entering. "To what do I owe this pleasure?"

She stood and offered her hand. "Thank goodness you're here."

"Indeed I am," he said, giving her a curious smile. "And here you are as well."

With ceremony he removed his hat, gloves, overcoat, and muffler, and gave the garments over to the housekeeper. "Come in, won't you? Give Mrs. Shaffer your things."

Little in his appearance had changed in the years Alva had known him. He was a bit rounder, perhaps, and a bit balder, but his mustache and goatee were still present and well trimmed, if grayer than she'd noticed before. A man of average height, he managed to come across as shorter. Despite the care he took with his appearance and his attempt to be distinguished, there was something of the banty rooster about him.

Alva gave the housekeeper her coat and unpinned her hat once again, saying, "I'd hoped to find you at home. I'm in need of your expert advice."

"And a warm drink, I'll wager. Tea or coffee—or would you enjoy chocolate? My man gets the most exquisite cocoa. Imported from Denmark, don't you know."

"Yes, thank you—the chocolate."

Mr. McAllister led her into the drawing room. "If I may, how is your father's health?"

"He's following his doctor's directions," she said, taking a seat in an armchair. She spoke then about those directions, and about her concerns for her father (though she downplayed his current state), and of how, once she and William were wed, her father and sisters would move to a more comfortable house. "That is," she said, coming to her point, "if I actually succeed in being married."

"What? Has there been a rift?"

"I was aware of none, but a rumor to that effect has reached me. Mr. McAllister, may I ask your counsel?"

"By all means!"

"The Vanderbilts are a fine family. They give their time and money to good causes. They're active in their church. They have friendships with most everyone of merit—including President Grant. Yet your friend Mrs. Astor, for example, has never once received any of them, not even my fiancé's

mother, a woman of exceptional taste and irreproachable habits—*and* a descendant of Isaac Roosevelt, whose contributions to New York are manifest, as I'm certain you know."

"What a speech!"

"Forgive me. It's just that I *must* remedy this situation." She lowered her voice and added, "because in this remedy lies my own success."

"You desire a place in best society, too—"

"No. That is, yes, of course I do. More to the point, it's that my value—as a bride, I mean—lies in being able to improve the Vanderbilts' social standing. I am doing all I can, but—"

"But perhaps it's not enough to validate his choice, is that it?"

"This is my fear, yes."

"And you worry he'll withdraw his offer of marriage."

She nodded. "The Vanderbilts deserve to be known for the excellent people they are. They *deserve* to be in best society. You can't disagree."

"No, in fact I quite agree. Why, I used to see the Commodore often, and was fast friends with his son, C.J.—that is, before the good man lost his way, poor fellow."

Alva was heartened by this. She said, "Then will you help me design a solution of some kind? Just now I've only my gratitude to offer in return—"

"Who would wish for more?" he said. "I am pleased and honored that you sought me out. I am precisely the man for the job, don't you know."

"I was certain you would be. Perhaps first you could advise me on this pressing matter: for my wedding gown, I've been to see Mrs. Buchanan—"

"One of my dear friends!"

"Yes? Well, supposing you and I find a way to maintain my engagement—"

"We shall," Mr. McAllister asserted. "You may place your faith in me."

"I have to pay a deposit for the gown in advance, and I am unable to pay it. The gown will be marvelous—a showpiece, truly, and worth every bit of the thousand dollars it's likely to cost. How might I persuade her to defer all payment until my father receives the settlement?"

"Miss Smith, I think I see what you're about, but my word, a thousand-dollar gown is *not* what you need. Oh my, no. You need a simple gown—*litotes*, my dear. Sublime understatement is what you want, if you hope to be received by Mrs. Astor and her set."

The maid brought a plate of teacakes and biscuits and the chocolate pot, and served them while he continued, "Your father's financial difficulties are understandable. These things happen to even the best of us. Why, many of my Southern compatriots have found themselves in similar straits. A terrible thing, the war. Terrible. You should not be blamed for such misfortunes! And although I don't seek to deny my dear friend Mrs. Buchanan the opportunity to have your business, I wonder if you might, for this, look to a gown you own already, one that can be altered, say, in some divinely original manner. Your mother's wedding gown—is that in your possession?"

"I believe so. But it's blue."

"All the better! We've had thirty years of white! How predictable, how dull! Now, Mrs. Buchanan is too expensive for this endeavor—and to be frank, too fond of her nouveau riche clients' tastes, though she'd never dare foist those tastes on Mrs. Astor. No indeed. And as the social circles don't overlap, Mrs. Buchanan manages to have the best of all of them. This is how it's done, don't you know."

"Actually, I—"

"Take your mother's gown to Miss Donovan, a young but exceptionally talented seamstress on Prince Street. Tell her what I said—sublime understatement. She'll know what to do. As for Mrs. Buchanan, tell her that you've had a fit of sentimentality in regard to your late mother and simply must wear her dress for your wedding, as you're the first of the Smith girls to wed. And in the same breath, tell her that you adore her work and that you'll visit her again when you're home from your honeymoon, when, as your dear friend Mr. McAllister advised, you will order your entire wardrobe for the following winter."

Alva was unconvinced. "You're certain this is the better approach?"

"You did ask my counsel."

"Of course. Forgive me."

Mr. McAllister inclined his head, then continued, "It is essential that when you converse with these ladies, you include my name. It is, we might say, the wave of a wand in cases such as these." He waved the metaphorical wand. "Magic is ever a trick, and yet the beholder believes."

Alva would like to believe. She said, "You are a wonder. I'm much obliged."

"And as to demonstrating your value," he told her, "I have just the solution: if you and your fiancé agree the timing is all right—considering mourning, I mean—you shall be among my most especial guests for the Patriarch Ball in February, where I shall personally present you to Mrs. Astor."

"Do you mean it?"

"Most seriously."

"It was my impression that neither my fiancé nor I qualified—"

"My dear, you must trust that I know what I'm about. As you said yourself, I am expert in these matters."

"Of course. I didn't mean to suggest otherwise. This invitation—well, it was too much to hope for," she said. "But it is precisely what I need. I'm certain my fiancé's family will approve."

"I suspect they will. Tell him right away; he'll want time to spruce up his formal wardrobe. And for this event, too, I advise that your gown be understated." Mr. McAllister paused. "Mrs. Astor enjoys seeing ladies in rose colors, don't you know, so you'll only improve your case by wearing one such gown. Here again Miss Donovan can be your guide. Be sure to say I advised you so, and that she should feel comfortable deferring her fee until April."

"Mr. McAllister, I am grateful beyond words," Alva said, trying to keep her emotions in check. After all, by connecting him securely to the Vanderbilts, he would profit as much as she. It was a business arrangement. Gentlemen made such arrangements all the time and certainly none felt weepy when a deal was made. How amusing it would be, though, if the Wall Street sidewalks were filled with men walking about, dabbing their eyes and clasping their hands as they looked heavenward.

He said, "Nothing pleases me more than to aid my good friends. "Here." He held out the plate of treats. "Perhaps now with your mind at ease, you'll regain your appetite. You've grown far too thin."

She took a biscuit. "My appetite is as good as ever—in fact I'm hungry all the time. I am this thin only because our meals are budgeted. We've no more money and I—" Her voice thickened and she paused to regain her composure.

It was no use. Angry tears came as she told him, "It has been an awful day. I was robbed."

"Robbed? My word!" He handed her his handkerchief. "Were you injured?"

"Only my pride—though my family is injured by the loss. I was wrong to go out alone."

"You mustn't be critical of yourself. One can see you are well intended! I'll direct my grocer to send over some goods, and you'll order more on my account—no, do not attempt to object. Consider it a wedding gift in advance. And you'll need cab fare," he said, drawing his wallet from his jacket and giving her two dollars.

Recovering herself, she said, "You are a godsend. I'll repay you, for all of it, as soon as I can."

"Don't think of it. Friends aid friends." He clapped his hands. "Now, your goal is unlikely to be accomplished solely by attending this ball—you do understand. Wars are campaigns, not solitary battles. Your attendance at the Patriarch's is not an assault," he said. "It's a quiet initial incursion."

"I understand."

"Very good. Feel free to call on me for any need. You'll want some advice, perhaps, in arranging your household. Have you chosen a place already? I can recommend an excellent property agent."

"My fiancé's father has found us a house on Forty-fourth Street near Fifth Avenue."

"Above the Forties! Ah, very good. A fine location for young people who are unbothered by the time it takes to travel such a distance. It's becoming more fashionable, to be sure. I will commend my friend on his choice. Off with you, now," he said, rising. Alva stood, too. "Your fiancé will be pleased to get your news—so pleased, I'll wager, that he may attempt to elope!"

"You're quite the optimist," Alva said.

"The world is wonderful, *wonderful*, I tell you, if one only views it in the right manner."

After buying two chocolate-dipped langues de chat from a baker's cart, Alva got a cab and, en route to the Vanderbilts' house, sat back with a sigh of relief as much for her feet as for her stomach as for her *life*.

What a tale she had for Consuelo! Except, might it be better to let everyone believe that the invitation to the Patriarch Ball had arisen only due to Mr. McAllister's high esteem? Though she trusted her friend completely, this plan would be most effective if no word got out (even if merely by an accidental slip) that Alva had been instrumental in arranging it.

Wave a wand, cast a spell.

At 459 Fifth Avenue, Alva went to the door and rang the bell. "Alva Smith to see Mr. Vanderbilt. William, that is. W.K."

She attempted to disguise her limp as the butler led her into the parlor. He gestured to a sofa—"Please wait here"—and she dropped into it with relief the moment he turned away.

"What a surprise," William said when he joined her. She noted he did not say *pleasant*.

Feigning confidence, she told him, "I have news that demanded to be given in person."

"Good news, I hope."

She nodded. "While I was out this afternoon, I happened to see Mr. McAllister. He would like to invite us to the Patriarch Ball."

"He told you this?"

"He did. Knowing that we're to be married, he's taken special interest in bringing us into society this way. He's known my family since I was a child," she went on, improvising. "It means a great deal to him to do this for me. For the two of us, that is." She made herself smile as she'd done on the night he proposed they marry. Her prize-like smile. A smile that contained all she had to offer that Theresa Fair did not and could not offer, ever.

"Well, that's capital," he said, smiling now, too. "Won't my sisters be delighted with this news! Did you know this was in the offing?"

Alva attempted a coy expression. "Perhaps."

"Will you stay for tea? Mother and Lila are out, but Florence will want to get every detail, and it won't be nearly as satisfying for her if she has to hear it all from me." He rang for a maid. "Cook's got some excellent lobster salad she puts on buttered toast. Mother says you ought to eat more."

"I do want to oblige your mother. I will be glad to stay."

❧

In bed that night, after attempting to sleep, Alva relit the lamp and turned to face Armide. "Wake up. I need to confess something."

Armide kept her eyes closed and stayed burrowed under the quilts. "Alva, go to sleep."

"It was only because of our situation," Alva said. "I was going to fix everything."

"What are you on about?"

"I lost all the jewelry."

Armide opened her eyes and sat up. "You mean—"

"From the 'treasure chest,' yes, and no use scolding me because I already feel terrible and there's nothing to be done. I was on my way to a pawnshop. But there was a scene—an accident, and crowds of people, and the box was stolen from me." She said, "Do *not* tell the girls. I'll replace everything later, when I have my own budget."

"But it won't be the same. Those were heirlooms!"

"Well . . . I'll buy better things, with better history."

"But not *our* history."

"This is all I can do! I'm sorry."

Armide drew a heavy breath. "I know."

Alva put out the lamp and they lay in silence for a while, but she knew her sister was still awake. She said, "I wish I liked him better."

"What are you talking about?"

"William. He has fine looks, and he's perfectly pleasant, but . . . well, he's not especially interesting. I always imagined my husband would be stimulating and sophisticated and clever, concerned with more than sport."

Armide turned over to face Alva. "You don't *have to* marry him. We can find ways to earn our living, meager as it may be. Or Daddy might be persuaded to move out of town, and we could till a big garden for our food, and—"

"What? No!" Alva said, thinking of tales she'd read of failed crops and marauding vagrants and the inevitability of flea-ridden beds. "I am certain my affections will improve, with time. He has excellent teeth."

Snow had fallen steadily for two days, resulting in a foot of accumulation and a need to trade out coaches for sleighs. Now, on the night of the Patriarch Ball, the snowfall had ended and the clouds had cleared, revealing the starlit sky. Manhattan's freshly whitened streets delighted Alva. The city was so much more festive in the snow! Sleigh bells rang out from equipages both nearby and in the distance as William's coachman handed her into the sleigh. William, bundled in a beaver fur overcoat, got in and sat beside her while the coachman climbed into the front, took up the reins, and urged the horses on their way.

Mr. McAllister had advised Alva to arrive late so that he would be available to lead them to Mrs. Astor straightaway. "It won't do for word of your presence to reach her before you do. And remember: all we desire is that she grant you recognition. A small incursion, that's our goal."

A small incursion, on a snow-bright evening with a handsome gentleman at her side. A handsome gentleman who evidently still wanted to marry her, who did not want to marry a red-haired silver heiress and may not have ever even considered such a thing or sailed with Gordon Bennett or doubted that Alva Smith was the girl for him. Whether he had or not, Miss Lydia Roosevelt had inadvertently done them a great favor by making Alva think so.

"Excited?" William asked.

She nodded. "Pleased as well. This is such a vote of confidence for our future."

"It is! You should have seen Lila, fussing about my tie, forcing different shirt studs on me—"

"She wants to make everything perfect. Our success will benefit her and Florence and my sisters as well. They'll be very much in demand, I'm certain."

"In no small part due to you, dear. I'm looking forward to seeing our names in tomorrow's society page report. I think Father may have it framed!"

The Patriarch Ball had been formed under Mr. McAllister's direction a few years earlier. He had gathered some of New York's top gentlemen and they'd crafted a list of twenty-five men (themselves included) whose families had been responsible for establishing Manhattan's society well before the British occupation of 1776 and who, through means the men chose not to examine too closely, had by now acquired a net worth of one million dollars or more. They then named this group the Patriarch Society. They tasked each member to invite to the ball, held near the end of winter, twelve other suitable guests—that is, persons with roots at minimum two generations deep, preferably three.

Special tickets were printed, upon which the name of the invitee would be written by the patriarch (more often, his wife or her secretary). A theme was designated. Formal dress was required. There would be no entry without the special ticket—which, as Mr. McAllister had foreseen, immediately became the most sought-after object in town. The surest way to create desire is to first establish denial.

For his final creative act, Mr. McAllister had recruited Caroline Astor to be the feminine face of the organization, its ceremonial head and symbol of preeminence. There could be no better choice; the Astors went back to when there were more Indians than white men on Manhattan Island. Besides which, he liked her better than anyone else in society, calling her privately "my Mystic Rose." Or so the story went.

The influx of so many arrivistes—the instant millionaires of the gold and silver strikes out west, of stock speculation, of land sales, of war profiteering—had amounted to a steady wave of uncouth, sometimes unwashed nouveaux riches flooding New York, eager, insistent, loud, expecting entrée into the social scene. Most of these people didn't know a soupspoon from a tablespoon. They understood calling etiquette not at all.

They had no sense of propriety. Reports said that some were showing up at the Academy of Music on the fashionable nights demanding the best seats, and when denied they attempted to buy boxes from the boxholders directly.

Alva suspected that Mr. McAllister found this both entertaining and useful, as it had created a need for the clear establishment of order—which created endless opportunities for him to guide desperate mothers in getting their daughters into better circles, if not the best one, a process in which wallets were opened and thousands spent, from which he benefited in myriad ways.

At tonight's ball, Mr. Astor would as usual be absent. He sailed his yacht every winter to the hospitable climes of Jacksonville, Florida, staying until he was required for church appearance at Easter. Thus Mr. McAllister was obliged to be Caroline Astor's escort, as he often was. Once she'd made her rounds, however, she would be content to sit on a velvet settee on a dais with a carefully selected coterie of sycophantic admirers at hand. There she reportedly would watch the younger set perform the figures. She would be at turns generous and critical in her commentary. She would listen to "news" and proffer opinions that would be widely cited in the homes of all the best families in the weeks ahead as the ladies went about making their calls.

If Alva could gain Mrs. Astor's favor this evening (such a thing was not *impossible*, after all), she would be able to rest easy for as long as she remained in that favor. For years, possibly. Perhaps forever. Really, why shouldn't Mrs. Astor judge them worthy additions to society's top echelon?

Mr. McAllister had not wished to set Alva's expectations too high; this was understandable. However, there were no two less offensive individuals of quality in all of New York than William and herself, and Mrs. Astor, if she was as wise and discriminating as her reputation would have one believe, would happily welcome them into the fold.

By eleven o'clock, when William and Alva arrived, three hundred guests were crowded into Delmonico's dining-room-cum-ballroom, its perimeter lined with chairs, its floor milk-polished to a perfect sheen. A chamber orchestra performed from a narrow gallery above. Attendees mingled, too, in an adjacent salon, where Chef Ranhofer would lay a delectable supper in buffet style.

Alva spotted Mr. McAllister in conversation nearby. As with the other gentlemen, he wore a starched white shirt and collar and white silk tie inside a cutaway black tailcoat, along with a black top hat. Unlike the others', his waistcoat was pale yellow—an unexpected choice for such a conservative event. She suspected he would like to be able to powder his shining brow and cheeks and chin and nose the way the ladies did, and the Frenchmen of the old days. The French court would have been a far better fit for him—though he was making do nicely in Caroline Astor's ersatz monarchy.

He hurried over to greet the couple. "Good evening to you both!" Standing back to behold Alva, he said, "What a perfectly understated gown! Garnet is a bit darker than I advised, but I must say, it suits you very well. The tone-on-tone trimming is quite subtle—did I not tell you Miss Donovan would do right? And that neckline—very tasteful!" Her train, too, was modest, with no balayeuse. Rather, she looped it over her wrist in the traditional manner. Mr. McAllister said, "Miss Smith, you've done me proud—and you, sir," he said to William, who anyone would say was *le plus beau*, "you give a fine presentation, my young friend. Fine indeed."

William bowed. "Thank you—and for the invitation as well."

"Of course! I thought, who is more deserving than the gentleman who managed to catch New York's most eligible young lady? And here you are, impressing me further."

Alva wanted to kiss him.

"You're quite dapper yourself," she said.

"I went to Matthew Rock for this suit and paid *fifty dollars*, a travesty of a price. In London I would pay half that—though I would of course have to go to London to accomplish this, and there's simply been no time, of late, for travel! In addition to directing the programs for the Martha Washington Reception and Old Guard Ball and the ball of the Société Français L'Amitié, I was thick in the planning for tonight. It's the capstone event for the winter season, don't you know. I couldn't very well leave it to someone whose interest isn't vested. But how I do go on! Come, let me present you to Mrs. Astor. I expect a good result: wine has been flowing all evening—an Italian Piedmont varietal from before unification—'52, I believe it is, a particularly favorable year for the Nebbiolo grape, according to the chef."

Mr. McAllister led the couple to where Caroline Astor was seated on the dais conversing with Mrs. Cooper and Mrs. Dresser. As evidenced by Mrs. Astor's high color and slightly unfocused smile, she was indeed enjoying the wine.

"Allow me to present Miss Alva Smith and Mr. William K. Vanderbilt, who are to be wed in the spring."

William bowed and Alva extended her hand—and Caroline Astor, without looking at either of them, turned to Mrs. Cooper and said, "And tell me, my dear, how did you find the *coffee* in Calcutta? Was it astonishing or terrible? I have heard accounts on both sides of the matter."

Alva felt her color rising to match her gown. She hadn't expected an embrace, but this? This was not called for! How incredibly insulting—how hurtful, and what reason could the woman have for such behavior? She, Alva, was a perfectly nice, perfectly turned out young lady of good reputation who had received a legitimate invitation to this ball. Her fiancé was her counterpart in every aspect.

As she was about to say as much, Mr. McAllister deftly took her by the elbow and turned her away, giving William a look that said to follow.

In Alva's ear he said, "She's being boorish, but you mustn't react. I told you, this is an incursion. Rise, Miss Smith, float, stay above it all, show everyone else here how dignified you are. Demonstrate your refined manners."

Alva raised her chin, collected herself, smiled at her fiancé, and said in a clear loud sympathetic tone, easily heard by everyone around them, "How unfortunate that Mrs. Astor's hearing and sight are failing so."

Mr. McAllister did not wait for responses from others before moving Alva toward the buffet, saying to her as they walked, "Heavens. That was quite unexpected, my dear! I must say, anyone who claims to be bored by society is simply not paying sufficient attention. The fates of empires have turned on dramas such as this!"

Alva felt sick. Her pride had again gotten the better of her. She had set out so hopefully this evening, imagining they might win over Mrs. Astor. She should have taken Mr. McAllister's caution to heart.

Yet, when she glanced at William she saw undisguised admiration. Others around them wore similar expressions.

William told her, "Wait until the Commodore and Father hear about this! Please, allow me to get you some champagne."

VI

ON A MID-APRIL afternoon, Alva set out to meet Mrs. Vanderbilt at the Forty-fourth Street house, which she had not been allowed to see the inside of until today. Rather, she had been directed to keep her attention on the wedding preparations and leave the house to her future mother-in-law.

Alva had seen nothing, too, of William since the end of winter season. He and a group of his friends had sailed with Gordon Bennett to St. Augustine. He'd been writing her short dispatches on two-penny postal cards and sending them from port towns along the way. *Glorious day at sea! Thinking of you.* And, *I mean to get myself one of these and name her Alva!* And *Mother writes of a surprise for you. She is so good with daughters.* And the last she'd gotten: *Home next week. Do you miss me? Not long to wait now.*

She'd sent her replies care of the St. Augustine post office. Likely he'd gotten several at once. *Enjoy the waves!* And *Signs of spring this week: warm breezes, budding trees!*

Insipid missives, but what else could she write?

—What's your favorite color?

—I once held my breath for so long that Maman smacked me to make me breathe.

—Do you know what to do on our wedding night? Do you know how to do it?

Because no, she did not miss him. If she was impatient for his return, that impatience was to have the wedding (and wedding night) done, the marriage secured, all of the associated changes made. After five years of managing one crisis after the next—their exile from Paris, her mother's illness and death, her father's illness, their loss of fortune, the constant strain of trying for a worthwhile husband—Alva wanted simply to feel settled and safe.

"Hello!" Mrs. Vanderbilt called, waving from the doorway of the four-story townhouse. The building, done in brownstone, was narrow and plain, unexceptional in every aspect, but relatively new and pleasing enough outside. (Beggars should not attempt to also be choosers.) The street was pleasing, too, abutting Fifth Avenue on one end, Sixth on the other. A sidewalk was laid with brick, and the street was graded well, with few ruts. Young maple trees sported their early leaves, lime green in the sun.

"Hello there!" Alva hurried up the steps. "I was just taking it in. What a charming place!"

"Isn't it? I do hope the two of you will be content here. I want all of my children to be content. It's a lot to ask for, isn't it? With so much upheaval, so many changes happening so quickly nowadays." She kissed Alva. "Never mind me. Come in!"

In the parlor, six servants awaited them shoulder to shoulder in a line, all at attention. As Mrs. Vanderbilt introduced each individual, that person glanced at Alva, nodded, and either bowed or curtsied. First, the butler and the housekeeper, who had been promoted from other Vanderbilt homes. Then the cook, a footman, and a housemaid. At the end was Lulu's daughter Mary, who smiled nervously. In this lineup, she seemed darker than Alva had thought. Perhaps it was the contrast; the housemaid, an Irish girl named Bridget, was as pale and pink as fresh snow at dawn.

"It is very good to meet you," Alva said. "Except Mary, that is—I've known Mary her entire life. Her mother keeps house for us—for my father, that is. But *you* should be pleased to know her."

These six people would comprise Alva's everyday existence. Their welfare would be her responsibility, and hers would be theirs. Harmony was necessary. Authority, wielded properly, created harmony. And so, feeling awkward and young and very much the impostor, she continued, "I'm hopeful that you will treat one another with respect and kindness, so that this home is a pleasant place for everyone in it. Each of you is essential to me. To us—that is, Mr. Vanderbilt and myself—and to the smooth operation of the household."

Her face felt hot; she had gone on too long. So she adopted a severe tone and added, "Most importantly, I will not tolerate . . . hippopotamuses; anyone found in possession of a hippopotamus will be summarily executed, without a trial."

They smiled, thank God, and Alva asked Mrs. Vanderbilt to show her the house.

After leading her through the well-appointed first-floor rooms, Mrs. Vanderbilt moved toward the stairs. "I'm eager for you to see your bedroom. Lila and I put particular thought into getting it just so."

The room, at the far left of the landing, had windows facing the street. From here, one could see the entire five-acre Croton Reservoir. Nearer, at the Forty-fourth Street corner of Fifth, was the site of what had been the Colored Orphan Asylum, attacked and burned by rioters protesting the '63 draft. Alva had been astonished at the brutalities inflicted upon those children. Children! Attacked because they had the same skin color as the people white men had enslaved and a president then declared should not be enslaved, and Southern slave owners didn't like being told what they shouldn't do and started a war that then required poor white Northern men to be drafted to fight. Angry white men who took out their anger on defenseless Negro children. Men who called themselves Christians. She did not blame them for not wishing to fight a war they had no stake in, but their actions were inexcusable. She was glad to have a view that would remind her of what angry men were capable of doing, a reminder not to take her good fortune and the safety it brought for granted.

The bedroom windows were done up in fuchsia-and-white-striped chintz, as were the lower walls, as was the dressing table, as was the bed and its canopy. Alva *hated* it.

"It's lovely!" she said.

Mrs. Vanderbilt gave a relieved smile. "I'm *so* glad you think so. You should be comfortable here."

"Without question. How thoughtful of you to go to so much trouble on my behalf. I don't deserve a bit of it, but I am more grateful than I can say."

This was the truth, at least.

❧

Dressed in her mother's expertly amended wedding gown, Alva went to her father's room to say good-bye.

He sat up and looked her over. "Phoebe . . ."

"No, it's Alva, Daddy. Your daughter."

He blinked, confused, and squinted at her. "I . . ." He rubbed his face, blinked again, sat back against his pillows. He continued to stare, and in another moment or two, recognition came. "Ah, yes. Alva." He paused. "Is it your wedding day?"

"It is, yes. Good." She squeezed his hand. "I'm leaving in a minute for the church."

"Can you forgive me for missing it?"

"Daddy, shhh. I know you would come if you could."

"It's a shame your mother isn't here for this," he said. "You look like her, in that dress."

Miss Donovan had reduced the skirt, removing two tiers of furbelow and shaping it to accommodate a bustle, then added a white train made from delicate, almost sheer silk. She'd created cap sleeves and trimmed the neckline with the same white silk as the train. There was not a bow or ribbon or bit of lace, but it was, as promised, sublime. In it, Alva could almost feel herself the fairy-tale bride she once imagined she would be.

She whispered, "I do, I know," and kissed him.

Armide was waiting in the hallway downstairs with Lulu, who handed Alva a flower bouquet. "No goldenrod," she said.

Alva smiled. "Lulu, I'm going to miss having you to boss me."

"Now you'll boss yourself. I remember that day you climbed up on that fountain at the Tuileries Garden and put your arms out wide. I guess you were about ten years old. You said, 'I'm going to be empress!' and then you turned in a circle and fell backward right into the pool. Another child woulda cried, but you, huh-uh, you just stood right up in your sopping dress and your hair all hangin' over your face and said, '*Une serviette,* Lulu, *s'il vous plait.*' "

Alva laughed. "I don't remember this at all. You're making it up."

"Not a bit of it. Go on now, the Vanderbilts' coachman is out there and he doesn't have all day."

"Of course," Alva said, nodding. She drew a deep breath and then let it out, saying, "So long. Mary and I will send you postcards from Saratoga Springs!"

When the sisters arrived at the church, Consuelo was waiting in the nave with her father, who was standing in for Mr. Smith. She took Alva's hand while Armide went to join Jenny, Julia, and the other bridesmaids inside.

"You look radiant!" Consuelo said. "Could it be that you're actually in love?"

Alva let the question be rhetorical. Her radiance was a false advertisement. She felt none of the fluttery warmth Elizabeth Bennet came to have for her Mr. Darcy, no sense that this union was the alignment of kindred spirits in angelic harmony. If anything, she was having second thoughts about the wisdom of marriage—to anyone. Inside the chapel was an amiable but uninteresting gentleman who in a few minutes would, by the terms of God's divine law and the laws of the country, own her. Whatever he believed was correct in regard to her keeping, he could enact. *Jane Eyre*'s Mr. Rochester believed his wife to be mad and put her away in his attic while he then pursued other women. If, some hours from now, when night had fallen and they were alone, William decided to rut (whatever it was), what could she do about it? Nothing. If he grew displeased with her in any way, he could lock her up or send her away. He could beat her.

He will not beat me, she thought. William Kissam Vanderbilt was a good man.

She ought to love him. In her place, at this liminal moment, Theresa Fair would be swooning in her regard for him. Well, probably her own swoon was delayed, that's all. Being more grown-up and experienced than Miss Fair, she was less susceptible to all those things that set a young girl aflutter. The swoon would come later, when she'd had time to take the full measure of William and he of her. Then they would be gloriously content with each other.

The organist began to play. "Here we go," Consuelo said as the doors opened before them. She proceeded up the aisle.

The pews held hundreds of splendid beings, all of them turned out in their best springtime attire. White ribbon bows and floral sprays were displayed at every row. The bridesmaids were beautiful, the groomsmen impeccably turned out, William the very picture of enthusiasm. After the service, they would receive scores of guests at her in-laws' home. A team of six would take William and herself in a beribboned coach from the church to the house, and then to Grand Central, where they would board a private Vanderbilt train carriage to Saratoga Springs. A happy start to a happy life.

Mr. Yznaga put his arm through hers. "Shall we?"

Suppose her rapid pulse and nervous breathing indicated not only eagerness but love, too, and she hadn't yet learned to recognize it. And William—what was he feeling right now? Suppose she went through the doors and up the aisle to find that while she had been occupied with the business of winning over his family and surviving the delay and securing his confidence and planning the wedding, William had fallen desperately in love with her? The real test of this was not the vows they were about to swear before God and all, but rather what would come at day's end in the Saratoga Springs hotel.

When Alva and William were alone together—that is, left completely to their own devices, neither of them seemed to know what to do.

They had arrived at the Grand Union Hotel and gone inside. William signed the register, and they were shown to a suite of rooms. They removed their hats. Alva pulled off her gloves and clutched them. William's hounds lay down near his feet. Mary and Maxwell, William's valet, stood silently nearby.

"I suppose this is a good time," he said, looking at her.

She waited. He seemed to be waiting, too.

"For . . . ?"

William turned toward Maxwell. "The case," he said.

"Oh. Yes." Maxwell hurried out of the drawing room and into the bedroom William would use, then was back a moment later with a substantial wooden case the size of a shirt box.

William took the box. He held it out to Alva, saying, "A small gesture to mark the occasion. I hope you like it."

She took the box. Cradling it in one arm, she opened the lid. Inside on a bed of midnight-blue velvet lay a coiled rope of glossy pearls. "My word," she breathed.

William said, "You'll especially enjoy their provenance: their first owner was Catherine the Great. More recently, they belonged to Empress Eugénie; I gather she had to give them up with her change of circumstance."

"The empress—why, I believe I saw her wearing them! How in the world did you—?"

"The Commodore. I'd initially thought gemstones, but he recalled you speaking of your girlhood in France and put me on the hunt for something related to that. My grandfather is a man who sees details and opportunities. I merely acted on his advice. Though to give myself some credit: it did take some doing to find and procure what I very much hope is an ideal gift for you."

Alva took a pearl between finger and thumb and rolled it. This stone and all of these marvelous stones had rested against the skin of two women Alva admired more than perhaps anyone else who had ever lived.

She glanced up at her husband (*her husband!*) with newfound pleasure and respect. "I'm speechless."

"But pleased, yes?"

She nodded. "Thank you so much. Really . . . I can't . . ."

"It is my pleasure. You might wear them tomorrow evening."

"Yes, I will, absolutely."

He rubbed his sideburn with his thumb and said, "Well. You'll want to retire, I would imagine," and she said, "Yes, it was a very long day," and Mary followed her to the adjacent bedroom to help her undress. William's man followed him and the dogs to his room.

Her bedroom, lighted by a happy fire in a tiled hearth, was a French dream. Bluebells on a white background covered the walls between panels of polished walnut. A high four-poster bed sat in the center, on a plush blue carpet. White satin draperies glowed in the firelight. Suppose she simply locked herself away here, just put on her pearls and lay down and closed her eyes without a care, ignored the question of whether she would have to display her body for William's gaze, and what he might expect from her, and whether she would like the sensations, and how wrong it would be if she did . . .

"It's a long day," Mary said. "Let's get you undressed."

"Oh. Of course." Alva extended her arms so that Mary could undo her buttons. To distract herself, she asked, "How did you pass the time?"

"Well, I liked watching out the window. It was my first time in such a fast train—the Sixth Avenue el never goes faster than a person can walk, does it? These fancy trains are something! I can't figure how the locomotive can be as strong as it is, to pull all those heavy cars."

She took Alva's bodice, saying, "I did a little bit of reading, too. It's a kind of magic, being able to read, don't you think so? Mama said the best thing about Emancipation is that I could be taught right out in the open to write and read."

Alva said, "When I was a girl, I hardly gave a thought to you all being *slaves*. 'The servants,' that's what my parents always said." Alva stepped out of her skirt. "*Owning* human beings. I realize that my parents grew up in a very different place and time, but I don't really understand it. Did you feel owned?"

Mary shook her head. "I was just a baby."

"What are you reading now?"

"Right now it's the story of a young Castilian lady who's meant to marry her cousin, but he comes home and confesses he's already gone and married another. *A Terrible Secret,* it's called."

"I'll say that's terrible."

Mary paused, the peignoir in hand. "But she's a pain in the behind, so I don't know as I blame him."

"And the one he did marry?"

"Sweet and docile as a calf."

"Well," said Alva as Mary put the nightgown over her head, "the author understands men, all right."

Dressed now in the thin peignoir, Alva was glad of the room's warmth. She sat at the vanity and Mary handed her a tiny bottle of perfume, which she uncapped, then touched the cap to her wrists and the spots beneath her ears. How many times had she seen her mother do this very thing? How exotic the toilet of the married woman of society had seemed to her little-girl self. Her mother had taken every step of the ritual as seriously as a devout churchgoer at Mass.

"Hair?" Mary said, indicating Alva's still-upswept hairdo.

"I . . . I don't know. Should we plait it like usual, or . . . ?"

"In that novel I was telling you about? The jilted lady, she's got 'raven tresses' she lets fall over her shoulders. He—the cousin—can't keep his eyes off her."

Before Alva could form a reply, Mary said, "What if you put on those pearls?"

"All right," Alva said with a grin. This was an easy choice. "But only for a minute." She took the strand from its box and said, "Heavens!" The string was several feet long and heavier than she'd expected. She gathered it up and held it pooled in her hands, then gestured to Mary for her help.

"To think . . ." Alva said when the strand was draped in four rows that lay against her breastbone. She pressed her palm to the pearls. "I am not at all worthy of these—but, Mary—to *own* them . . ." She shook her head. "Catherine was Russia's greatest ruler—quite progressive, so intelligent. Empress Eugénie must have prized these."

Mary said, "And now here you are."

"I'll bet she misses them . . . and everything from that life." Alva looked at Mary. "But I'm not sorry to have them. Mary, think of it: Catherine the Great wore these a hundred years ago." She shook her head in wonder. "All right. Let's put them up before I cry."

When the pearls were again on their blue velvet bed, Mary said, "Your hair—will you have it down?"

"I'll think about it. But you go on, I'll see you tomorrow."

"Mama said remind you to use the pot before you get into bed, and again right after." At Alva's puzzled expression Mary said, "After he's done."

"Oh. Yes, of course. I'd forgotten about that. With so much else going on." She couldn't admit to Mary that the girl knew more about all of this than she did.

Mary paused near the door. "You know, I've never seen a room so perfect as this one. Mama said when slave girls got their wedding nights, it was in a plain room with a sheet hanging up for privacy from the others. As for the husbands . . . I don't mean to say our men are terrible because they aren't, most of them, but *yours*, he's so clean and so . . . nice. So generous. That's a gentleman right there. Some men I know about, they're rough and they don't smell very good and they want girls to let them put it in their mouth before they—"

"Put what in whose mouth?" Alva said.

"Oh. Never mind, I was going on about nothing. Blessings on you," Mary said, and hurried out of the room, closing the door behind her.

Suddenly understanding what Mary meant, Alva said, "Oh. My word." Were such things done? Would she be expected to do that? What other bizarre acts might she have to face?

She turned toward the glass and studied the nervous young lady staring back at her. "You look like you want to run."

What if she did run? She was married now. Her father had been paid. Suppose she put on a travel suit and snuck out of the hotel, got herself a train ticket to someplace west. Buffalo, say. Niagara Falls. Have her own honeymoon. Put all her expenses on a Vanderbilt account. She could go on to Chicago, to St. Paul. The middle of the country was supposed to be a beautiful place, if still rather wild. She would avoid the wilderness, leave the Indians to their business, stick to the cities. Were there any cities after St. Paul? San Francisco, of course—a long way in between, though, with mountains in the divide. Mountains that were said to rival the Alps, though that was probably a gross exaggeration. People coming from the West were so often prone to hyperbole.

Entertaining as these musings were, she knew they were born of fear, and fear was an emotion she must not indulge. Whatever was coming, she must face it straight on. She was a married woman now. No more childish worrying over things that most every woman in history had experienced, for goodness' sake, and they didn't all go around fussing about it.

She let down her hair, used the pot as Mary had instructed, climbed onto the bed, and settled herself against the pillows.

Hands in lap, or no?

Legs crossed? Uncrossed?

Was being uncovered too immodest? She pulled the sheet over her lap, then felt silly, as if she were awaiting her bedtime story. She got out of bed, pulled the covers back up, sat again on top.

All this mystery and uncertainty! Was she supposed to sit up or lie down? Should she put out the lamp? Stoke the fire or leave it?

You're the plank, he's the peg . . .

That long-ago day in the bathtub, before her mother came in, Alva had trailed the cloth along her thighs, one and then the other, watched the water sluice down to her center, that place of mysterious purpose. Then and now she thought of paintings she'd seen abroad in museums and at court. Languid nude females attended by cherubs, by nymphs, by hand-servants, by courtiers, entwined with swans sometimes, creamy breasts and bellies and thighs unabashedly displayed for the artist's gaze . . .

What are you, an animal?

Those were celebrated works of art coveted by collectors, displayed in galleries and museums in the world's great cities. Why was sensuality all right for art but not for life? Suppose Maman had it all wrong?

A noise outside the door made her jump. Any moment now, the knob would turn—

Silence.

She waited, hot-faced, for her husband to come in.

He would note her flushed skin and accuse her, reject her, send her back to her father or lock her away under a doctor's care.

He would note her flushed skin and be flattered. He'd gaze at her adoringly. He'd kiss her until she was senseless.

Nothing. The knob didn't turn.

. . .

The rooms were quiet.

. . .

A log cracked and shifted, and the firelight dimmed.

. . .

No sounds from outside her room.

. . .

Her heart slowed, and almost without realizing it, she fell asleep.

Alva woke chilled. The fire had burned down and the room was nearly dark. Her husband knelt on the bed beside her, his face near hers. He was wearing what appeared to be a nightshirt. His breath smelled of bourbon.

"We ought to do this," he said, not looking at her face. He reached down and took hold of the peignoir, pulled it up to her hips. "I'm sorry. I'll try to be quick."

He avoided her eyes as he positioned himself, fumbled for a moment while she lay there mortified, then pressed, pushed, forced himself inside her while she fought to lie silent and rigid despite the pain. Muffling her yelps with her fist, she stared past his ear at a bedpost and willed herself not to cry.

"I'm sorry," he said again, not stopping. It went on and on. "I'm . . . trying . . ." he said, and now she couldn't hold back her tears. They slid down to her ears and hair, down the edges of her jaw. She thought of them trickling, cooling, leaving trails while he kept going, the pain now a steady burn. How long this went on she didn't know. Then his rhythm changed, became erratic, and in another moment he stilled, groaned, shuddered, and then, after a moment more, un-mounted her.

"There now," he said and patted her hip. Righting his nightshirt as he climbed off the bed, he continued, "When we have a child, he should learn French *first*, don't you agree?" Before she could form any sort of answer, he said, "I'll leave you to rest now. We had a long day. Good night."

She lay there, stupefied. The part of her body that no one ever named, the place she knew was capable of exquisite pleasure—it was meant for *this*?

"Ha!" Laughter rose out of her, she couldn't help it, and she was crying, too, and thinking, *This* is what we're fashioned for, this bizarre, painful, embarrassing task? God designed it all so? He really didn't care much for Eve, did he?

Waking in the pretty blue-and-white room, Alva didn't know where she was. Then it all came back to her, and her throat tightened.

I will not cry.

Though the sun shone in slivers from between the draperies, the room was cold, and there was no wrapper in sight. What was she supposed to do next? Where was Mary?

I want to go home.

What William had done to her last night he would do again, any time he pleased.

(*There now.*)

And the only reason she would stand for it (lie down for it) was money.

Which meant she was a kind of prostitute. Didn't it?

No, it did not. She said it aloud: "No, it does not. I didn't do it *only* for money. And I am a great deal more to him than an object for amusement. I will run his house. I will bear his children. I will be the most gracious hostess anyone's ever seen. He adores me—does his behavior not prove it?"

She rose, stoked the fire, and washed at the basin. Mary came in to help with her toilet. Alva said nothing, couldn't meet her eyes, not even when, while brushing out Alva's hair, Mary said, "Mama says your hair is quite the asset, you know."

Mary twisted and tucked and pinned it, then took a beaded silver comb Consuelo had given Alva and slid it into place above her left ear.

"All put together," Mary said. The reflection in the glass agreed. "Now, which dress for today?"

"The yellow one," Alva said. "No, the green. No . . ." She covered her face with her hands. "I don't know."

"The green," Mary said. "It's a happy color."

"Yes. All right." Alva lowered her hands and attempted a smile. "A happy color. That's just the thing I need."

William was cheerful at breakfast, which the couple took together in the dining room downstairs. Alva attempted to respond in kind, though her gaze refused to rest on him and he seemed shy as well. While she indulged herself with eggs Benedict and sausages and toast and jam, they spoke of carriages and whether she might like a new one of her own. He told her which horses were favored for the day's races. He said he would like to buy her a new hat. Would she like a new hat? Some dresses, too? He'd noticed she had been making do. A new parasol, perhaps? She stared in silence, attempting to reconcile this scene with the previous night's events.

Evidently, as demonstrated last night and here this morning as well, he was the truest of gentlemen, a man who did not burden his wife with strange requests, a man of impeccable manners. And she had been a plank. They were, thank heavens, precisely as they were supposed to be.

Alva said, "Yes, that'd be lovely, thank you."

Having apparently gained some confidence in the action, William repeated his wedding-night performance each successive night for twelve nights running. Only when Alva indicated to Mary that her monthly had come was there a break. On that night, Mary stationed herself outside Alva's door. Alva listened from her bed as William arrived and Mary told him, "The missus is indisposed. For the week," she added, and not another word was mentioned.

Alva's relief was profound—and yet she wondered if in feeling it, she was deficient. He had only been doing what he was supposed to do. She was supposed to want the same thing he wanted, that being to produce a child as soon as possible. In order to get with child, one had to be with one's husband in this way. So she should want to. But she didn't.

You mustn't act as though you like whatever he does to you.

Ha! As if there were any chance of that.

This was all so confusing.

She must be going about it wrong, somehow.

On arriving home after nearly four weeks upstate, weeks that had been spent at the racetrack and the polo field and the theater, weeks of dining out with numerous new acquaintances, evenings spent disguising with cheerful conversation her grim anticipation of what would occur at night's end, Alva shut herself in her new striped bedroom and stayed burrowed under the quilt for the entire day, glad to see no one but Mary.

On her second day home, she went in her new carriage, wearing a new hat, to pick up her sisters at their new residence, a bright, spacious house in which her sisters each had a bedroom and the larder was well stocked. Nothing for it but to get on with married life—the married life she'd been so desperate to have, the one that was providing her with all those comforts and advantages she'd longed for. If they came with a price that she was not as eager to face—well, such was the nature of marriage, and she would be wise to remember that.

"Is Daddy awake?" she asked her sisters, who were in the middle of luncheon. Tall windows that looked onto the street filled the small dining room with light. The table was set with new china, ivory-colored plates encircled with delicate periwinkle blooms and leaves, perfect for the season.

Jenny shook her head. "But he seems more comfortable. The doctor has him taking morphine."

"That's good, then," Alva said, though it was not at all good in the sense one usually intended the word to mean, and the four of them knew this.

"Come with me," Alva went on, "and I'll see him later. Let's have some fun. We'll go to Mrs. Buchanan's."

Julia said, "Mrs.—?"

"The dressmaker. My treat."

Armide said, "What need have we for new dresses? Stay, and tell us all about your honeymoon. Did you enjoy the races?"

"Speak for yourself," said Julia. "I need new everything."

Alva said. "Jenny?"

"It's better than Christmas," Jenny said. She and Julia went to get their wraps.

As they were about to leave, Lulu came downstairs. "Our own Mrs. Vanderbilt! And don't you look it?"

Alva said, "Oh, this is only the start of it. We are off to fit ourselves out as fine ladies of good society."

"That daughter of mine like to have forgotten I'm still here," said Lulu. "One postcard is all. I sure do hope she's not as lazy being your maid as she is being a daughter."

"What? Lazy? Not at all; she's doing very well," Alva said. "She's indispensable, in fact. We've been busy, is all. You'll see her on Sunday. How is Daddy?"

Lulu glanced upstairs. "He's got no appetite and only wants to sleep. You might spend a minute."

"I will, after we get back. We're on a mission."

When they arrived at the shop, Alva told the dour woman, "We don't have an appointment, but we do have a Vanderbilt to pay the bill."

"Mrs. Buchanan will be happy to see you."

Alva was home five days when, in her new carriage and a different new hat, she again traveled the few blocks to her father's new residence, arriving in time to sit at his bedside and watch him die.

A blessing, they all said. No more suffering, they all agreed.

New York, July 1, '75

Dear Consuelo,

This Viscount Mandeville—Lord Kimbolton—George Montagu—eventual Duke of Manchester fellow who has won your hand—does he know what a gem he's getting by choosing you? I admit to some envy . . . Remember how in Paris we girls played "Duchess," making up the names and confusing all the titles?

One day I will be addressing you as "Your Grace"—try not to let it go to your head, and I will try not to think about how much I'm going to miss you, as I'm certain you'll be in England perpetually, New York all but forgotten.

You needn't apologize for tardiness in replying to my last note; why shouldn't you think more of enjoying yourself than of your old married friends? I wish I, too, were there in Saratoga Springs, dancing every night until dawn. It will be some time before I'm able to attend dances at all. I loved my father, but I do not love the rules of mourning. Why must it last so long? The dresses I ordered in May will now sit boxed until next spring. And suppose I find myself with child and can't wear them then, either? It's wasteful, and who does it benefit, save the dressmakers? Daddy would not object to my wearing green or blue or yellow instead of black. I wouldn't miss him any less were I to wear scarlet.

Thank you for including the note from our dear Lady Churchill. It sounds as though she's besotted with her new son, if not with her Lord and keeper—or perhaps I am misinterpreting what she says about Churchill's absence and the reasons for it?

My days are occupied with paying calls and the tasks of running a household—it's such a comfort to finally have a predictable routine. Evenings, we entertain a great deal. The young-heirs set reveres William, with his knowledge of racing trotters and his coach-and-four skill; he says Oliver Belmont, whose father partnered with Lady Churchill's father in the Jerome Park Racetrack, has become virtually his shadow. I heard a rumor that the Belmonts are Jews—but, as old Mr. Belmont married Commodore Perry's daughter, I really can't credit it; the Perrys are as solidly Christian as they come.

William and I leave for his grandfather's Staten Island house tomorrow morning—he's lent it to us and Corneil and Alice for the rest of the summer, being himself too unwell to use it. What a pleasure it will be to get out of the city!

Do write soon—and tell me you'll be married here in New York where all your friends can revel in your reflected glory.

Utmost affection—

Alva

VII

THE GEORGE MONTAGU–Consuelo Yznaga wedding did in fact take place in New York that next spring, and was written up in the press with great enthusiasm, though for the most part the reporters gave their energies to lauding the future duke and said little about the lady he had taken as his wife.

"But whatever they do or don't write," Consuelo told Alva, paying one last call before leaving for England, "I am in fact Lady Mandeville."

"Future Duchess of Manchester. You've gotten everything you wanted."

"Yes, indeed. We're having a *marvelous* time," said Consuelo, grinning slyly while she put a cigarette into a silver holder and then lit it.

Consuelo hadn't smoked before her association with Mandeville. Was she trying on sophistication, Alva wondered, practicing it before she was presented to the English court? American women didn't smoke in public, but perhaps Englishwomen did. If Alva's father had sent the family from Paris to London, she would know with authority what Englishwomen did. She might have become one herself. She might this moment be the one who was a future duchess.

Not that she prized Mandeville himself. He was a glib greyhound, an insincere dandy with an edge to him, a coarseness she found off-putting—though if she were to acknowledge the truth, she found him exciting, too. As if he might encourage a lady to do something against her will. As if the lady might like it if he did.

Alva tried not to think about this.

"I'm very happy for you," she told her friend.

"And yet you sound the opposite."

"Well, I'd like to be having a marvelous time. That is to say, my material needs are well met, and I'm embraced by William's family—"

"You're bored."

"Not at all," Alva said. "Even with my activities limited by mourning, I hardly have a free moment in my day! But . . . it isn't a matter of how I go about my *days* . . ."

"Quit being cryptic and just say what the trouble is."

"The marital act. It's awful," Alva blurted. "Painful. Humiliating. Am I meant to endure it forever?"

Consuelo blinked in surprise, then said, "Certainly not. You could keep him out, if it's truly as bad as all that."

"What, post a servant outside my door every night?"

"That's not necessary. You simply tell him."

"*Tell* him?" Alva said, unable to imagine it.

"The same way you'd say, 'We're dining with my sister tonight,' or any such thing."

"But then I might never conceive," Alva said. "You and Mandeville—do *you* enjoy it?"

The mantel clock chimed the hour. "The time!" Consuelo said. "My carriage will be waiting." She rose and Alva stood, too. "Do I enjoy it?" she continued as they went to the entry hall. "I did say I was having a marvelous time, did I not? Your situation will improve if you tell William what you like and what you don't. I've never known you to be reluctant to speak your mind."

"No, of course," Alva said, embarrassed to admit that reluctance. She'd read *Woodhull & Claflin's Weekly,* with its exhortations for feminine independence (not to mention free love). She ought to be as modern and advanced as her friend.

She said, "I've been accommodating him, is all—"

"A proper lady."

"A plank," Alva pretended to joke.

"What terrible advice that was!" said Consuelo, laughing. "It's little wonder so many men see whores." She reached for Alva and embraced her. "I do hate to have to leave you now. But I'll write you endlessly—so often that you'll get sick of hearing from me and start burning my letters on arrival."

"And I'll write you not at all, to punish you for abandoning me."

Consuelo hugged her once more, tightly. "Au revoir," she said. She had tears in her eyes.

"Au revoir," said Alva, and watched her go.

Alva thought about their conversation throughout the afternoon and evening, about Consuelo's easy use of the word *whore*, which she'd never before heard from her friend's lips. Evidently, Mandeville's coarseness had contaminated Consuelo, infected her. Her advice on this matter could not be trusted. Alva should not desire the Mandeville version of "marvelous." She did not wish to be disrespected—for surely Mandeville did not respect his wife or any woman. She was sorry she'd raised the subject.

That night, William came to her bed. As he worked himself against her, she made herself think of Provence in summer, the lavender, the sunflowers . . . A few more thrusts, then his small groan and shudder.

—It was terribly undignified, even for him, she realized with sudden sympathy.

He un-mounted her, said good night, and left the room.

Three weeks later, when her monthly failed to arrive, Alva summoned the doctor to tell her whether the one thing she most wished for and most feared had occurred. Seated across from her in the parlor, the doctor inquired as to the state of her appetite (vigorous), her moods (variable), and how long it had been (he asked delicately) since she'd last experienced "her unwell period of time." He then examined her eyes, her neck, and the skin of her hands, and said, "It's highly probable that you are in fact in the delicate condition. You can expect to experience nausea, often upon waking each day, but it will pass." He took a small notebook from his coat and jotted something. "I'll be by to see you again in a few weeks," he said, "though you should of course send for me sooner, if need be. I anticipate a birthdate in late February, perhaps early March. Is your husband about?"

"I believe he's at his office in Grand Central," she said. "Or he might be at his club."

"The Union?" asked the doctor, and when Alva affirmed this, he said, "I'll inquire at both places if need be, and inform him of your status."

"Do you think I'm incapable of giving him the news?"

"Incapable? Not at all. The matter is one of authority. I am a physician."

"I'm the one who will gestate the child."

"Mrs. Vanderbilt," he said, patting her arm, "I'm saving you time, not to mention the distress of being doubted by your husband, who would only send for me to confirm your statement, possibly while I am in the middle of my supper. This way he's certain to come home later with excellent wine and a bouquet. Leave it to me."

The doctor was correct: William arrived at day's end with both of those items, as well as a porcelain music box on which was painted a delicate spray of roses and greenery. "Look inside," he said so eagerly that he was practically wagging his tail.

She lifted the lid. On a bed of black velvet lay an elaborate filigree diamond pendant, the stone nearly as large as her fingernail.

"A gem dealer of my acquaintance lost to me in cards, so I got a discount. Even so, I had to borrow from Father to pay for it," he said, taking it from the box. He reached to hook the chain behind her neck. "Though I doubt he'll ask for the money back. He's quite partial to you."

"My word, William," Alva said. She lifted the pendant from her breastbone. It was heavy and cold and ridiculous and she loved it.

"This is only the beginning," he said. "Think how decorated you'll be when our home is overrun with children."

Procreation ensures salvation. And apparently decoration.

She said, "I'll treasure this. Thank you."

"A lady ought to have something for her troubles."

VIII

ALVA, IN A sweeping red gown, her neck weighted with her pearls, waltzes with Louis-Napoléon by the fountain at Luxembourg Garden while Empress Eugénie applauds from atop a tall marble pedestal. The sound Eugénie's hands make grows louder, like thumping, pounding, and her cheers become rapid barks—

William's bedroom door opened and the dogs spilled down the stairs, still baying their alarm as he hurried after them. Alva fumbled for matches to light the lamp.

His voice carried from the hallway, louder than the barking: "What in God's name—"

"The Commodore, sir," a man yelled. "He's dying."

"Who sent you?" her husband said, quieting the dogs.

"Your father, sir."

"And he's convinced this time, is he?"

"It seems so," the man replied.

Finally. The poor Commodore had been suffering for months, while reporters from the *Times* and *World* and *Tribune* and *Sun* and the lesser papers, too, milled in front of his house, waiting for him to die. Since spring they'd been there, hoping to be first with the report, sometimes jumping the gun and exciting the stock market with false headlines. In July, they'd missed out on centennial celebrations because the Commodore was supposedly a mere step from the crypt. No one had anticipated that he would enact dying with the same tenacity with which he'd lived. Why, only a few weeks earlier he'd gone to the window of his second-floor bedroom, pushed up the sash, and shouted "All you dirty vultures be damned! I ain't gone yet!"

William knocked on Alva's door, then opened it. In his nightshirt, with his bare feet and tousled hair, he resembled George. But bookish, quiet, thoughtful George was in temperament the opposite of William. Nor was George like stern, humorless Corneil or steadfast Frederick. "We hardly know what to make of him," William had said.

Alva replied, "He's exactly himself. How is that troubling?"

"There are only a few ways to be a man in society, and George is none of them."

The hounds bounded into Alva's bedroom. William whistled them to his side. "I gather you heard. Grandfather's very ill. I've got to go."

"I'll join you."

"You needn't trouble yourself—especially in your condition."

"I wish to," she lied. Watching yet another person die was the last thing she wished to do. "Alice will be there with your brother."

He nodded. "No doubt."

"Then I have to be there as well." She pushed the covers aside and got up to stir the fire.

"You've become so—"

"Round?" She placed a hand on her stomach as she straightened.

He averted his eyes and turned toward the door. "I'll send your girl in. Let's be quick."

Mary was there moments later, looking sleepy but moving briskly. She took over building up the fire, then helped Alva dress. Chemise. Drawers. Stockings. Petticoat. (No corset—perhaps the best feature of her condition.) Bodice. Crinoline. Skirt. So much effort! "What do you suppose would happen if I went in my nightclothes?"

Mary smiled. "I suppose Mrs. V. would tell you to let your maid go."

"I'd *almost* sacrifice you for that pleasure," Alva said.

Mary twisted Alva's hair into a quick chignon. "It's a temporary condition. And a blessing, don't forget."

Alva had not forgotten. In fact she had savored these months. They'd been the happiest of her marriage—in large part because William no longer visited her bed. She told Mary, "A blessing, yes. Though I'm beginning to wonder if I will ever see my toes again. Would you listen to me? An excellent man is dying while I stand here complaining like a spoiled child. Thank you for your help. Go back to bed."

A soft snowfall was coating the lintels and steps of the quiet brownstones on Washington Place as the driver coaxed the horses through a crowd of grateful reporters and curious citizens, then stopped at the curb of No. 10. Alva was grateful, too; the Commodore had made a terrible invalid. Such a man ought not wither like a blighted poplar; he should be felled all at once, mercifully, like a mighty hickory in a hurricane. He was stubborn, though—of course he was; an easier, amiable, pliant man would never have accomplished what he had done in his eighty-three years.

The sum of those accomplishments—the literal sum—was the preoccupation of stockbrokers, stockholders, newspaper editors, and envious citizens not only in New York City but across the country. How much was the old codger worth, they asked, and who would get the money? His last will and testament had been kept secret, its content unknown even to Alva's father-in-law. The Vanderbilt men were nervous. The Commodore was just stubborn enough, just crazy enough, just unpredictable enough to do something outrageous, like leave all the money to his team of six. He loved those horses in a way he loved hardly anything or anyone else. And why wouldn't he love them? They pleased him. They were gorgeous and obedient. They never asked for anything, and they never let him down. Alva would not be surprised if he left his two sons only enough money to sustain them while compelling them to work as hard as he had done if they wanted to achieve as much.

"Mr. Vanderbilt!" a reporter called as William alighted from the carriage. "What have you heard about the will? How much has he got?"

William handed Alva out to the sidewalk without replying.

"Mrs. V! How much do you hope to inherit?"

William said, "They really are vultures."

"Hyenas," Alva said. "They don't even wait for their prey to die."

The Commodore's bedchamber was a large room with high ceilings, carved crown moldings, lush velvet curtains, a substantial hearth in which a fire now roared, and few furnishings: a four-poster, an armoire, a pair of upholstered side chairs, and, as of two weeks earlier, a polished oak harmonium upon which his second wife, Frank, played hymns at his request. However, the present occasion demanded the addition of numerous settees and chairs, and so the room was now arranged as if the bed were a stage, with the furniture around it placed in successive rows for an audience currently gathered to witness what they all hoped would be a simple one-act drama of short duration.

The star of this drama lay in the bed's center beneath a fine wool sheet and blanket and a brocaded blue silk coverlet, sometimes mumbling, sometimes dozing, sometimes groaning. By his vehement direction, the four saltcellars placed beneath his bed as advised by his friend Mrs. Tufts, a Spiritualist who'd touted them as "health conductors," remained in place. Yet he had also sent for his longtime friend, the Reverend Dr. Deems, who now stood in a corner consulting with Dr. Linsly and Alva's father-in-law. Evidently the Commodore was even now hedging his bets.

Along with Frank and her mother, the Commodore's siblings and children and the various spouses constituted the first row around the bed. Behind them were the grandchildren with their spouses, as well as some of the great-grandchildren—so many people in all that there was not room for everyone to sit; several of the younger men stood in the back. The audience members were overwarm and overtired and, as was unavoidable under the circumstances, overfragrant.

"Might we open a window?" Alva said.

One of the old aunties in the row ahead of her turned around. "And risk vapors giving me consumption?"

"Or grippe!" said another. She gave Alva a severe look. "What *can* you be thinking? Isn't your time near upon you?"

Indeed, she had perhaps six or eight weeks remaining, all the more reason she would like to be made comfortable so that the restless babe would not revolt and upstage the Commodore's final act by arriving on the spot. Or worse.

Until recently, Alva had known little about childbirth. A woman somehow conceived through the coupling act, she knew that—but precisely how the baby was expelled was a mystery. Gathering her nerve, she'd asked Mrs. Vanderbilt to explain. After all, the woman had been through the whole process eight times. They'd been in Mrs. Vanderbilt's parlor. Neither of them looked the other in the eye. Mrs. Vanderbilt said, "I do wish your mother were here," before going on to say: "When the baby's time comes, you will expel it through—well, it's very much the way you have your monthly." Red-faced, she went on, "God has made us so that we can . . . temporarily accommodate the passage." Alva, envisioning this, could say only, "Oh." Mrs. Vanderbilt said, "The doctor will attend you. Trust in God," and left it at that.

Now the first old auntie sniffed. "I hadn't thought you would be so selfish. My brother spoke affectionately of you—but then, he's known to be swayed by feminine wiles."

"With due respect—" Alva began.

"Mind, Jane, speak thee well of a dying man lest your harshness be returned to you on your own deathbed."

Alva tugged at her collar. "I do not possess *wiles*. Further, modern science has proven that ventilation is beneficial to our health. Fresh air—"

"Modern science: pah! Those saltcellars haven't'a cured him!" said the one.

The other said to Alva, "You are about to be a mother. Time to stop thinking so much of yourself."

"You'll excuse me," Alva said, standing.

These ladies were ancient, and the Commodore's daughters hardly seemed younger. An ungenerous assessment, Alva would admit, but she had never been one to wallpaper a water stain. They truly looked aged to her. Tired. Worn down by the waiting. Worn down by their lives. Remnants of an era that had passed.

Fanning herself, Alva observed the array of Vanderbilt ladies. Anywhere else in the world, a man such as the Commodore, a man who had conquered his foes and prescribed the policies of the land, would have made himself its king. His daughters and granddaughters would be princesses and would act in accordance with their place. They would not allow an overbearing doyenne like Mrs. Astor to behave as if she were the queen. Alva had made some small progress to that end. What she wanted, though, was for her sisters-in-law, her sisters, and herself to be recognized in best society for the upstanding people they were. It was only fair, especially when someone like Lydia Roosevelt enjoyed that status.

What she really wanted just now was for someone to please God open a window.

They watched the Commodore as he lay there, weak, helpless, his face sallow, his skin papery, the whites of his eyes now yellow as buttercream. His breath rattled. His chest heaved. His clouded blue eyes stared upward at the ceiling, or perhaps beyond.

"Play that song again, that song I like," the Commodore said in a hoarse whisper.

It was now a few minutes past ten in the morning. The Reverend Dr. Deems was at the bedside in conversation with William's uncle C.J., who was very pale but had flushed areas on his neck and face. Alva wondered if he might be about to have one of his seizures. Or was he simply distressed over being so near the man who for years had refused to see or speak to him?

"The song," the Commodore repeated.

"What was that, sir?" Dr. Deems asked.

The Commodore whispered, "I think I'm nearly gone."

Deems motioned for the family to give him their attention. Then he kneeled at the Commodore's bedside and bowed his head.

"Now God himself and our Father, and our Lord Jesus Christ, direct our way unto you . . ."

"The song!" insisted the Commodore.

Frank, who'd seated herself on the edge of the bed, jumped up and went to the organ. In tears, she began to play and sing "Come, Ye Sinners, Poor and Needy."

The Commodore raised his hand from where it had been lying, veiny and bloodless-looking against the coverlet, and waggled his fingers to encourage the family to sing along. They obliged—especially Corneil and Alice, who, Alva had learned, met while teaching Sunday school at St. Bartholomew's. How loudly their voices rose in harmony above the others in the crowded room! Did they imagine that excessive volume demonstrated superior godliness?

And the Commodore, too, attempted to sing, but the sounds that emerged from his cracked lips were the noises of a weak cat being strangled. Alva put her hand to her mouth. Beside her, Lila covered her face. George got up and left the room.

This theater of death was certainly no place for young children. Yet Alice had brought her two boys and her newest child, a girl, right into the bedchamber this morning, their presence meant to signal the parents' unquestionable devotion to the Commodore—in case he would be moved to make a last-moment alteration in the will? Or was it to *prevent* a last-minute alteration that might get made out of spite? Was Alice so political?

Alice and Corneil's boys stood in front of their parents' knees with wide eyes and somber expressions as they, too, sang—but not littlest Gertrude, who was in her father's arms. Gertrude's head, with its soft, dark curls, was drooping against his shoulder and her thumb was in her mouth.

The last notes of the hymn faded into the quiet rustling of skirts and the delicate sniffles of some of the ladies as they also dabbed their eyes.

"Billy!" the Commodore barked, making everyone jump.

"I'm here, Father. Don't excite yourself. Everything will be well."

The Commodore relaxed again. Long moments passed. Alice and Corneil's oldest boy, six-year-old Bill, turned to his mother and said, "Is he dead?" Alice bent over and whispered something in his ear; he faced the bed and stood up straighter.

Dr. Linsly leaned close to the Commodore and listened. He studied the Commodore's face, then stood upright again. "The sight's gone. Mr. Vanderbilt has passed."

Frank gave a single wet sob—but no: the Commodore's hand rose again. He moved it slowly, so slowly, toward his face. And then, with his fingers extended, he dragged his hand over his face in order to close his eyes. That done, he rested his hand against his chest.

He exhaled heavily. More long moments passed. The assembled family looked at one another and at Dr. Linsly, who shrugged. They waited. The Commodore sighed. A noise issued from beneath the covers. He sighed again. Then silence.

Dr. Linsly took his watch from his pocket. He leaned over the Commodore's face once more. He pressed his fingers to the Commodore's neck. He put his ear against his chest. When he rose, he checked his watch again, then said, "I believe this time I am correct."

Now Frank began crying in earnest. Not to be outdone, several of the Commodore's sisters and daughters joined her. The men coughed and shifted and stretched.

Three-year-old Neily tugged at his father's coat hem. "What happened?"

"Great-grandfather has gone to be with God and Jesus in heaven."

Neily frowned. "No he hasn't. I can still see him."

"Hush now."

William came over to Alva and said, "I'm going out to the stables for a bit."

"Find George," she told him. "He'll want to know it's over."

Neily was protesting to his father, "He hasn't gone anywhere, he's right there."

Alice said, "His spirit has gone."

"I didn't see it go."

"One can't. It's invisible."

"Then how do you know it went?"

Alice's lips tightened as she glanced at her husband. Then she said, "The Bible tells us. We have it as God's word."

"Was that noise I heard his spirit getting out?"

Corneil said briskly, "Let's go have a muffin, shall we?"

At the mention of muffins, Alva's stomach rumbled. At her stomach's rumbling, the baby gave a kick in its direction, then rolled mightily.

Though William (unsurprisingly) wanted a boy, Alva hoped for a girl as sweet as little Gertrude, whom it had been her pleasure to hold and rock and sing to in her first months, to play pat-a-cake with more recently. The child made a pleasing distraction during Alva's otherwise interminable visits with Alice, who found fault in everything. Alice proclaimed that her bath soaps were too fragrant, her cook's piecrusts too dense, her landau too springy, her lady friends too concerned with hairstyles and hats and not concerned enough with God. Her house was too small to properly entertain the St. Bart's clergymen, whose work she supported wholeheartedly and who deserved to be honored by many more people than she could seat. Perhaps a bequest in the Commodore's will would allow her to change this. Alva felt certain Alice was wondering exactly that.

Neily brightened at the prospect of muffins, but he was still not satisfied with his parents' responses to his question. He said, "How does a spirit get past the ceiling?"

Bill said, "It can move through anything, like a ghost."

"Mrs. Keillor baked *apple* muffins, with cinnamon," Alice said. "Can you smell them?"

Gertrude perked up and pronounced, "Cimmanin!"

"I'd like two, please," Neily said, having received from his brother the answer that actually made sense to him.

"Then come along, we'll go down to the kitchen and see Mrs. Keillor."

With Frank and the older women still snuffling and dabbing, Alva gave a last glance at the inert Commodore, so strangely still, so remarkably quiet, so *absent*, and followed the family out through the sitting room crowded now with old men, and to the hall, where a grand pastoral painting of grazing horses was displayed with prominence. Here the scent of cinnamon wafted up through the stairwell and made her mouth water.

When they reached the parlor downstairs, Alice said, "You should sit, Alva. I'll have the maid serve you."

"Thank you, I will." She pointed to Gertrude, still in Corneil's arms. "Corneil, leave her with me, we'll have a little visit and you can join William. He's gone out back to the stables."

With Gertrude settled beside her on the tufted blue sofa and no one else in the room, Alva put one arm around the child. With her free hand, she rubbed her belly, trying to soothe her own little one.

"Are you hungry?" she asked her niece, whose second birthday was only a few days off.

Gertrude nodded. Her thumb was in her mouth again.

"So am I."

Gertrude patted Alva's hand with her own free one and then pointed at a painting across from them.

"Do you like that one?" Alva said. Gertrude nodded. Alva told her, "That's your great-grandmamma Sophia. She'd be glad to know you regard her well."

Gertrude then pointed at an object on the mantel. Alva said, "The shepherdess? Yes, it's a very pretty statuette. Your great-grandfather grew up on a farm, and Sophia did, too—and your papa was born on one. Do you know what a sheep is?"

Gertrude took her thumb from her mouth and said, "Baa." She grinned.

"You are a bright one," Alva said. "Tell me, what do you imagine will become of us now?"

⁂

At the conclusion of the Commodore's funeral service in the Church of the Strangers, Ward McAllister found Alva seated alone in a side gallery pew, where she'd gone to get off her feet for a few minutes while departing guests lingered in conversation with the family.

The balconies were draped in black bunting. Urns and sprays of lilies made bright spots against so much heavy wood and black fabric. Still, elegant as the flowers were, their scent was oppressive.

Alva wished she could go home and have a nap.

"That was an excellent service," said Mr. McAllister. "Frigid day! But what a turnout, just the same. I'd wager there were more than a thousand in attendance here, would you say so?"

"Easily," she said.

Mr. McAllister seated himself beside her. "I'll suppose you've seen the newspapers. Every detail of the will and its reading, there for the public to salivate over. They seem to have spies everywhere!"

"They must," Alva replied. She adjusted her pearls, which lay heavy against her swelling breasts. Her body hardly seemed her own anymore. "The family is displeased with the publicity. It's quite invasive."

"But I'll suppose they are not displeased with the will itself—save for my dear old friend Cornelius Jeremiah, I daresay."

In the will, which had been read to the men a day earlier, were numerous (and for the most part, modest) bequests made to Frank and the sisters and daughters and assorted others. The grandsons were treated more generously—far more than anyone anticipated: an estimated five million dollars in stock to Corneil and two million each to William, Frederick, and George. Two million dollars to William. Two *million*! Alva had not allowed herself to imagine such a figure—hadn't even thought it possible.

To Uncle C.J., however, the Commodore left a mere two hundred thousand to be held in trust, so that the money could not be spent all at once. The remainder of the estate—an unreal ninety million dollars—went solely to Alva's father-in-law, who upon hearing the news had reportedly bowed his head and wept.

Mr. McAllister said, "As regards your father-in-law's share, there's not that much money in the U.S. Treasury." He said it with wonder, as if speaking of a visit of angels to Earth.

"Astonishing, isn't it? Though I'm certain some of society believe so much money is gauche."

"Some of our friends are yet mired in the cloistered past. Times are changing, though. I remember very well the gold rush days of only twenty or so years ago, when the notion of even *one* million dollars had been so startling that the newspapers put the word *millionaire* in quotation marks. And here the Commodore amassed a hundred such sums—which is, I should note, several times the estimated fortune of my dear friend Caroline's husband, who is among the richest men in the country's history. Gauche? Oh, that I could be so afflicted with such poor taste!"

Alva said, "The real trouble, though, is that Uncle C.J. feels he's been mistreated and is bringing suit against my father-in-law for a greater portion of the estate. It isn't in the papers yet, but of course it will be as soon as they can set the story and run the presses again."

"Ah. And wasn't he mistreated?"

"Yes, of course he was."

"But your husband's inheritance shouldn't be at risk. So what is it that worries you?"

"The papers. The spies. How far will they go in attempting to report the 'news'? How badly will the family's reputation be damaged? You have friends in all the important places; might you discourage them from printing gossip about us?"

His expression was pained. "Would that I had that much influence! I'm afraid that when it comes to potential income, the press is rather like a runaway locomotive, to use a most apt turn of phrase. The family should, of course, be vigilant for anything libelous. Beyond that, you can only hope the two Mr. Vanderbilts will resolve the matter quickly."

"You used to litigate lawsuits, and you know both of these men. Tell me, do you think they will—resolve it quickly, I mean?"

He gave a short, rueful laugh, and Alva said, "Yes, that's what I'm afraid of."

"Keep your head high, my dear, that's all you can do—and make certain to put some of that money to obvious good use."

Alva decided to attend a meeting of the Society for the Betterment of Working Children, which Armide had joined not long before. The group met once each month at the home of its president. Miss Annalisa Beekman was a young Knickerbocker lady whose pale eyes and pale hair and pale skin made her vulnerable to disappearance if she stood too near draperies or wallpaper of similar tones. Alva joined her and some ten other young ladies in the Beekman drawing room, which looked out onto Tenth Street. Among those ten: Lydia Roosevelt, who upon seeing Alva assessed her figure and said, "Well, Mrs. Vanderbilt, who would have expected you here?"

"This is a cause I support heartily. When my sister told me of the meeting, I didn't wish to miss it."

"How good of you. Do accept my condolences on the loss of your husband's grandfather. Who knew he was *so* well off? It does, of course, enable you to be charitable—which is only to our benefit."

"Rather, to the benefit of the children, you mean," Alva said.

"Of course."

"Of course. And you will recall that I have been engaged with charitable efforts for years."

Miss Beekman said, "Ladies, shall we come to order?"

"Do forgive me for being late," called Armide as she hurried into the room. Behind her was a young lady Alva didn't recognize. Armide ushered the lady in with her.

"Allow me to introduce Miss Mabel Crane. She's newly arrived from San Francisco, California, and is eager to involve herself with good endeavors."

The others gave polite smiles. Miss Beekman said, "California, you say? My, that's far from here."

"It was a really long journey," said Miss Crane. She was a handsome girl, and well dressed. There was, however, no question that she was different. Her skin tone was more golden, her cheeks freckled, her hairstyle less formal than anyone else's here. She was dressed as well as any of them, though, suggesting to Alva that she came from money but that the money was new.

"And will you be in our city for a while?" asked Miss Roosevelt.

"Oh, yes, I live here. My father got a house on Park Avenue near Fortieth—which I guess is a good part of town?"

"Many new residents are buying there," Miss Roosevelt said. "Most of *us* live here in this area of town, where New York's first families settled."

Alva said, "Thank you, Miss Roosevelt. We all needed that history lesson."

Armide and Miss Crane found seats, and Miss Beekman, appearing flustered, said, "I was about to bring us to order, so I'll proceed."

"Yes, do," said Alva. "I know we are all eager to get to the business of this event."

Miss Beekman laid out the agenda for the meeting, the first item being the secretary's report on what they'd done at the previous month's meeting, followed by another report of the activities they had accomplished on behalf of the society in the intervening weeks as well as in recent months. Alva listened with diminishing attentiveness; her back was aching, and the baby kept kicking her beneath her left ribs, and these reports were interminably boring.

"Forgive the interruption," she said, shifting in her chair. "I want to be certain I understand the nature of this group. By what I've just heard, it appears that you raise money by hosting subscription teas and luncheons and dinner dances, and then the society writes a check to one children's aid agency or another."

"Yes," said Miss Beekman. "That's correct."

"How many of the workplaces have you seen in person? That is to say, do you visit the factories? And what about the hospitals or the homes where the maimed children convalesce? This is not to malign any particular agency—but how do you know how the money is being spent?"

Miss Roosevelt said, "Have you forgotten our visit to that horrible tenement? I told these ladies all about it. None of us is interested in going to those places."

"She said it was quite horrible," Miss Beekman reiterated. "Seeing a dead girl—"

"Miss Roosevelt did not see the girl, she—"

"We prefer not to risk exposure," Miss Roosevelt pressed on. "We send money."

Alva smiled. "Well, this is of course commendable. But it risks ineffectiveness," she said, addressing the group. "I believe we should see for ourselves what the real needs are, and then direct the money specifically and confirm its uses. Certainly you read the newspapers; too often the money ends up in the pockets of crooks. I'd like to propose an outing for midmorning tomorrow. We'll visit the hospitals and inquire as to what materials these children most need."

"That is a fine idea," Miss Crane said. "We should have specifics, and give money directly."

Miss Roosevelt sat forward in her chair. "Miss Beekman, it is apparent to me that there is a tremendous chasm between our approach and that of our prospective new members. Rather than see an eruption of conflict, which might delay our charitable efforts unduly, I move to invite those prospective new members to form their own society, separate from this one."

Alva said, "You're denying my membership?"

"Yours and Miss Crane's, and any others who prefer your approach. All in favor?"

The secretary said, "You need someone to second your motion."

"I second it," said one of the other ladies.

"All in favor?" Lydia said, looking straight at Alva while she raised her hand.

Alva stood up, her own hand raised. "I could not approve more heartily."

The next morning found Alva, Armide, Miss Crane, and Alva's younger sisters at Charity Hospital on Blackwell's Island, their first stop on a tour of welfare facilities throughout New York City. Avoiding the wards housing prisoners or anyone with contagions, they met children missing limbs and eyes, children who cried about being unable to work again, children who stared blankly at dingy walls and did not respond to conversation. They questioned nurses and doctors about how best to help and made lists of needed supplies.

In Alva's parlor that evening, Jenny made tallies while Alva poured wine for everyone. She handed around the glasses. All of them were weary and overwhelmed by what they'd seen.

Julia said, "I didn't wish to go this morning, but I suppose I'm glad I did. We almost ended up like those people. I mean, not injured, but so poor! If Alva hadn't married William . . ."

Miss Crane said, "Before my daddy found himself a little bit of gold and started building hotels, we lived in a two-room shack that didn't even have water. I had a job digging rocks out of wherever the city was putting sidewalks in."

Jenny drank her wine all in one go, then handed back the glass to Alva for refill. "I'll go slower this time, don't worry."

Armide said, "One can see why Miss Roosevelt and the others prefer their approach."

"Yes, it is easy to see," Alva replied. "In the morning, I'll make a list of the factories we should visit next week."

IX

IN THE IMPROVING economy, William's two million grew to three in short order. With so much money looking for purpose, William, who until the Commodore's death had lived on what he called a salary but which was more accurately an allowance, made some charitable gestures that were highlighted in the papers alongside his brother's—but mainly, he bought things. Alva observed him with fascination as he ordered new crystal glassware from a glassworks he knew of in Geneva, went to Matthew Rock and bought a dozen new suits, three topcoats, two capes, every style of hat, butter-soft gloves in kid and peccary, numerous shirts, shirt studs and cuff links in every style and finish. He met with a furrier and returned home with beaver lap robes, chinchilla bed coverlets, a fox coat for himself, a mink wrap and muff for Alva, and an exquisite white blanket in rabbit for the baby to come. Remembering that he'd slept on some exquisitely smooth bedding in some French inn or other, he asked Alva to track down its origin and acquire several sets for his bed and hers, too. While she inquired among friends and wrote letters to hoteliers, he spent most of February away with his friend Oliver Belmont visiting horse farms in the South, having promised to be home for the birth of their child. And if he bought horses, he would need land, too, for a hunting estate and maybe a track. He might like a yacht as well. He was a very busy man.

One night when Alva lay in her pink-striped bedroom, hands on her domed belly, unable to sleep, she got up and went to her desk to calculate how far three million dollars (and then some) could go:

- Her sisters' allowance, at three hundred dollars a month: ten thousand months. Eight hundred thirty-three years. Not that all the money could go to them. Not that they would live for hundreds of years.

- Mary's salary, which she'd raised to thirteen dollars a week: more than two hundred and thirty thousand weeks (though of course she'd deserve a raise before then).

- One million five hundred thousand pairs of two-dollar-a-pair shoes: a new pair every day for four thousand, one hundred, and nine years. Not that Alva cared much about shoes, with her swollen feet and lack of desire to walk—or even, for that matter, to stand.

- Any dress she desired, any object, any carriage, any horse or bird or dog or giraffe—or hippopotamus (though of course she'd forbidden those).

She could fund a new, clean, safe barracks for young unmarried women in the city. Do more for children. Look into ways to improve the everyday lives of those who had no prospects of ever being rescued from their poverty by millionaire husbands. This was the thought that truly animated her.

This baby inside her, this future child, would live his or her whole life in comfort. No material need would ever go unmet. The child would never be hungry. This was the thought that soothed her.

In bed again, Alva considered what the inheritance could mean for them socially. Lydia Roosevelt had said Alva could not buy her way into best society. Well, if Lydia Roosevelt and her sort were representative of that society, Alva did not care to be a part of it whether she could buy her way in or not. Except that not to be in it was to see her family excluded unfairly from certain opportunities and events for no reason save the desire of people such as Lydia Roosevelt and Caroline Astor to feel themselves superior.

Alva quite liked the idea of disabusing them of that sensation, and that alone was reason to find a way in.

She was not thinking about society on March 2 as she labored in her pink-striped bedroom, in fits of loudly expressed agony, to deliver her child while William waited downstairs at first, and then, she was told, escaped to his club to await word in peace. She was imagining death—hers or the baby's or both.

"Is it supposed to be so painful?" she moaned to the doctor, or rather *at* the doctor. The severe-looking man in shirtsleeves and a heavy white apron annoyed her. She didn't like the hair in his ears. She didn't like his patrician nose. His eyes were beady. He wore a large gold signet ring on his right middle finger. "I'm not certain I can do this."

"Mrs. Vanderbilt, women have been giving birth for centuries. I assure you, you'll be all right."

"Women have been *dying* in childbirth for centuries," she said as another wave of pain began to overtake her. "What use is that hundred million dollars if it can't help this?"

The doctor said, "I believe it's time for the chloroform."

"No! I told you, I won't have it."

"Queen Victoria was anesthetized in her deliveries. Don't you think yourself deserving, too?"

Deserving or not, Alva couldn't abide the idea of being unconscious and manhandled. The very thought of lying prostrate and limp while this man, this stranger, had his eyes and hands on her most intimate parts . . . This was not to mention the gleaming steel forceps he'd placed on the bedside table. They could have only one purpose. She would not have her child extracted from her with that torturous-looking device. And suppose she went under and never came back up?

"Here now," the doctor said, laying a mask over her mouth and nose. She pulled it aside. He directed his nurse to hold her wrists and laid the mask in place again, saying, "You wouldn't want me to report this uncooperativeness to your husband. Be still for a moment, and when you come to, all the difficulty will be done."

Lying prostrate as she was, with her arms pulled up above her head, her effort to free herself was pathetic and short-lived. As the doctor raised a dropper before her eyes to squeeze chloroform onto the mask, she held her breath.

He applied the drug, saying, "This is childish. You must breathe, or you'll endanger the infant."

She continued her effort, counting silently and slowly, as she had learned to do as a child. She had once gotten to 137.

"You'll have to breathe before long," the doctor said, but his expression was anxious. Perhaps he was imagining what he'd hear from her husband if, due to his own stubbornness, something went wrong.

The clock on the mantel ticked, loud in the silent room.

The nurse said, "Doctor, perhaps since she doesn't wish it . . ."

The clock ticked on. Finally he pulled the mask away, saying, "All right, suffer if that's your wish."

Alva did suffer when the next wave came, and again and again and again, but a short while later she brought into the Vanderbilt family a girl with tufts of dark hair and wide eyes and the sweetest little bow of a mouth. This infant was perfect. Pain? What pain? Look at this child!

In her besotted enthusiasm over the baby and gratitude over their mutual survival, when William returned she told him she wanted to name the baby after the friend whose efforts had indirectly caused this blessed event.

"Consuelo, eh? It's a beautiful name," William said as he stood at Alva's bedside, mere inches from where he had planted the seed that resulted in this swaddled daughter in his wife's arms. "What a fine gesture."

Then he said, "And speaking of fine gestures—" He took a ring box from his pocket and gave the box to Alva, who opened it to find a wide band of diamonds. "A little reward for your troubles," he said.

"It's beautiful! I'll wear it with my pendant."

"I hope you will. I was thinking of emerald for the next one. Do you like emeralds?"

"I do—but let's not be in a rush."

"No, of course. I didn't mean . . ."

He touched one of the infant's tiny curled fingers. "She'll need her own pony," he said, then continued to stand there awkwardly, looking around the pink-striped room. "You know, William Whitney's got a fine breeding operation under way at his Stony Ford farm. I've been meaning to pay a visit, get some advice on starting my own farm. Maybe I'll drive out today."

"Today?" Alva said.

"Why not?" He gestured toward the baby. "I took the day off for this. I've nothing better to do."

Tandragee Castle, Ireland, 8 March '77

Dearest Alva,

I hope this letter will find you in a similar condition to myself. That is, recuperating from delivery of a babe—the future 9th Duke of Manchester, in my case, born five days ago in London, where my care was first-rate. (I refused to deliver here at the castle, I don't care how many Montagus were born here.) You cannot overestimate Mandeville's satisfaction upon laying eyes on his son and heir (whose given name is William, after the Duke, though tradition has it to call him "Kim"). "The title was well trusted with you," he said, to which I replied, "I'm sure Papa will say his money was well spent."

Quick though my labor went, giving birth to this frightening little creature whose wails reach every stony crevice of this place terrified me. I do hope it goes (or did go) easier for you.

Have you heard anything at all from Lady Churchill? She's gone from London without sending word to me or anyone, apparently. Rumor says her Lord is syphilitic and she's taken Winston to a house in the country to protect his health. I don't know why the British don't follow the

French example of examining whores and arresting the sick ones. You do know to look out for sign of sores or rashes, yes? Not to say that our fine W.K. is the type, necessarily. But he is a man.

What of the battle over the Commodore's will? Mandeville is still stunned by the size of the fortune! Meantime, what is your husband doing with his millions? Tell me, so I can make Mandeville seethe with envy.

Do write me with all of your news.

Ever yours,
Lady C.
(as I am now known here, and I rather hope it sticks)

New York, 20 April '77

Dearest Lady C.,
(as you like it . . .)
Many congratulations to you and Mandeville! You'll have received our official announcement by now, I hope. I was glad to get your letter and learn that you, too, delivered without crisis. We're fortunate to live in such modern times.

How remarkable that our babies are a mere day apart in age. Your namesake is proving to be a quiet, observant infant, and so precious. I am nearly over the horror of giving birth, and surprised by how gratified I feel when I nurse her (against Alice's advice—"Only common women do that." Isn't she a dear?). It's a profound feeling—and having the baby at my breast affords me time to examine her every tiny feature without provoking distress. They do howl when they're displeased! She's rarely given any chance for it, though; with the girls and my mother-in-law here so often, the baby is almost never laid down.

Regarding the lawsuit, I would rather avoid that distasteful topic. As to what William is doing with his inheritance: he's going to create an entertainment arena—there will be boxing matches, he says, and shows for breeders to compete over the finest dogs or horses, among other things. Also, he's looking into land for a hunting estate near the Connetquot in Oakdale, L.I., and for a racetrack near Coney Island. Further, he has in mind to commission himself a steam yacht like the one the Commodore owned. Corneil asked at dinner recently whether he meant to spend any time at his office. "I'm certain you have it all under control," Wm. told him. They could not be less alike.

For my part, I am again taking up the yoke of Doing Good Deeds: I have arranged for my sisters and sisters-in-law to join my new committee to raise funds for a poor children's holiday home, to be constructed somewhere outside the city—at the seaside, if I can manage it. They need fresh air and sunshine! To that end, I'll be hosting a Spring Subscription Tea at church and have invited the young Knickerbocker ladies, along with every other decent girl in town. Ticket sales are quite robust, and there is much talk of it socially. No one can resist helping children.

Your candid remark about signs of disease gave me pause. I appreciate the ways you did and still do try to take care of me. But Wm. would never consort with such women, even if he desired more frequent relations than we have, which I am certain he doesn't. American gentlemen have learned to master their impulses in ways foreign men have never been made to do.—Which isn't meant to imply that your husband behaves as Lord Churchill does. And it isn't to say that all American men of prominence are gentlemen, either.

We're taking a waterfront house in the aforementioned Oakdale for the month of September. Will you join us? I want you to tell me all about living as a Duchess-to-be. You're among the rarest of objects, you know, given there are only 27 dukedoms altogether in the peerage—and you're probably the only Lady who plays banjo.

I must close. I'm seeing a new milliner, and my sisters are coming for luncheon. I remain—

—yours truly,
Alva

X

"IT OCCURS TO me," said Lady C., recently arrived in New York from Europe, "that if little Consuelo takes a shine to Kim and he to her, you might marry her to a duke. An eventual duke, that is."

"Matchmaking already!" Alva said.

"God knows that at the rate his father spends, he'll need an heiress."

Alva was showing her friend around her home, which had undergone some improvements. Using a decorator Ward McAllister had praised as if the man hung not only draperies and wallpaper but also the moon, Alva had brought the quality of furnishings up to "millionaire" level, using—as with her wedding gown—a sublimely understated approach. This meant avoiding the garish overcrowding of tables and shelves with bibelots (no matter how valuable) that was becoming fashionable with the nouveaux riches, and refraining from overstuffing her rooms with French furniture (no matter how much en vogue) in favor of a curated assortment of objects and furnishings made of fine materials with fine artisanship. Not the *finest*—she hadn't the budget for that. Finer, though, than anyone else in her set, save for Alice, had. Alice—in confinement once again but still directing everyone and everything—had both the space and the means to do it all one better than Alva. "Do one better than Alva" seemed, in fact, to be Alice's raison d'être, second only to producing more Vanderbilt heiresses and heirs.

Observing her friend, Alva noticed Lady C. was further changed from the last time they'd been together. She was as perfect in her physical presentation as ever—hair lustrous, face smooth and powdered, form slender. Her attitude, though, was stiffer, and her Cuban-accented American English was shaded British. She smoked endlessly. Her eyes were flinty. Her tone when speaking of Mandeville was critical. Perhaps their relations were no longer as "marvelous" as they'd once been.

Possibly these alterations were no less natural for a lady in her circumstance than the evolving nature of the city's character, say. Nothing stayed the same for long. For example, thanks to the French, Madison Square now sported a forty-two-foot-high statue of a right arm and hand holding a torch—its erection there a stunt meant to inspire citizens to contribute money toward erecting all of "Liberty" on a more appropriate site. This was how things worked: forces acted upon a place or person, and that place or person changed in accordance. Manhattan had a gigantic arm growing out of its soil; Lady C. smoked cigarettes and used the word *whore*; Alva slept in a pink-striped bedroom in a millionaire's home; anything might occur, given particular conditions.

As they made their way upstairs to the nursery, Lady C. said, "I've been following the court battle in the papers—it's big news even in London. The Commodore was off his nut at the end, don't you think?"

"What, because of the Spiritualists?"

"That, the syphilis—"

"He did not have syphilis. Don't believe everything you read."

"*Something* made him batty and destroyed his innards. The papers described the autopsy findings—not one organ in his body was healthy, and why else would that be?"

"Better to ask a physician than a reporter," Alva said, irritated.

"Well, at any rate, you Vanderbilts have become quite the objects of fascination."

"At the risk of whatever social gains I've made."

"What I want to know is, how does your husband feel about his father possibly losing half the inheritance? It would mean a lot less money to hand down when the time comes."

"No one's thinking about that."

"Of course they are—and you are, too."

"I love my father-in-law."

They'd arrived at the nursery door. Lady C. said, "You'll love him even better if he can leave your husband a large share of a hundred million rather than fifty. And so will my boy here, whose spendthrift father may well leave him destitute."

"Is that true—about Mandeville?"

Lady C. waved off the question. "Look at them." The babies were sitting on a rug sharing an array of toys, their competent young nurses seated behind them. "Shall we draw up the terms now, or are you going to give her some choice in the matter?"

Alva said, "Well, of course I'll direct her interests and desires. What girl ever knows what's best for herself?"

Lady C. looked at her closely. "Am I hearing regret for *your* choice?"

"Don't be ridiculous. Besides, William was your idea for me, not my own."

"Splitting hairs."

"What is there to regret? With the exception of this ongoing nonsense about the will, my life is ideal."

"Now who's being ridiculous? No woman's life is ideal." Lady C. turned to the two young nurses. "Ellen, Bryn, tell us: are you in love with anyone?"

The girls looked at each other, puzzled by the sudden inquiry.

Lady C. said, "Come now, tell us. Is not love what every girl desires nowadays? Is it not the spice of life?"

Alva said, "I thought variety was the spice of life."

"No, I've tried that. Not sufficiently spicy for true gratification." Lady C. tilted her head and asked Alva, "How is it for you? Do you have love in *your* life?"

"We might speak of this elsewhere," Alva said.

Her friend took her hands. "Think what adventures the summer might bring!"

"For two married ladies? Really, Consuelo," Alva said, glancing pointedly at the nurses.

"Do you desire love, Mrs. Vanderbilt? Do you have love? I'm sincere. I want to know."

"This is not the time—"

"Never mind," said Lady C. She released Alva's hands. "I'm satisfied."

This scene returned to Alva's mind whenever a quiet moment permitted. As her friend had discerned, Alva's non-answer intimated her reply: she did want love, the wanting arising from the still not having. And the still not having was a disappointment, ignore it as she might; she had remained hopeful even as she'd reminded herself how unnecessary—how undesirable—love was supposed to be.

If the desire for love was in fact unnecessary, why would it persist? Young ladies were likely being sold a bill of goods where this sentiment was concerned, in order to reduce their objections to advantageous alliances. Practical, perhaps—yet how little regard was given to a lady's future contentment!

Love was not itself wrong or bad. First Corinthians declared love to be the greatest of all high endeavors. The capacity for love was among the features separating humankind from beasts. The human male desired it every bit as much as the female did—and was just as vulnerable to facsimiles of it (William being evidence of one such case). And while a person was ever in danger of being a fool when it came to romantic love, that was not reason enough to ward it off as if the plague itself were at one's door. Foolish love was to be avoided, certainly. Genuine love, however, ought to be regarded as a worthy aspiration for everyone.

Had she squandered the possibility that, given a little more time, she would have met a man with wealth and standing who would also inspire genuine love and would love her in return? It troubled her to think she might have chosen wrong in marrying William. But . . . perhaps she had chosen wrong in marrying William.

Not that there was any safe remedy for this particular mistake.

Throughout their month on Long Island, William spent his days hunting for land (for the house he wanted to build) and quail (on foot, for dinner) and foxes (with horses and hounds, for sport). Alva played hostess for the house they'd taken, a rambling Tudor on forty manicured bayfront acres that was constantly filled with the hunting crowd, moneyed young men with their young wives or their sisters. Alva had brought her sister Jenny as well, at the suggestion of Lady C.—or more precisely, Lady C.'s brother Fernando, lately arrived from New Orleans, who was also coming and had asked his sister to ask Alva to have Jenny join in. That romance might bloom here on Long Island delighted Alva, and gave every day a quiet and happy air of anticipation.

Mornings were calm, the breakfast room laid with a buffet to accommodate an irregular pace of diners and varying desires for food. Luncheon was a two-hour ladies' affair that culminated in two-hour naps. Teatime fell at four o'clock and rarely featured tea; from Lambswool and Blue Blazers on the cooler days to smashes and cobblers on the warmer ones, the conviviality started early. Dinner began at nine or so and went on for hours.

Everyone talked and talked and talked and talked. Quail. Guns. Horses. Houses. One night, William announced that he'd selected an ideal homesite on the Connetquot as well as an architect, whom he'd met at the club. Another evening, he held forth on breeding Thoroughbreds.

Hounds. Polo. Races. Oysters—there was a great deal of discussion about oysters.

A group was seated on the terrace late one evening, torches throwing shadows onto the lawn and rocky beach below, when such a conversation arose. Oysters: where to find the best ones (Boston? here? Galway? Normandy?), the best preparations (steamed? fried? butter? sauce?), the problem of getting the "bad" ones, especially when traveling abroad . . .

Listening with only half an ear while Lady C. strummed the banjo idly, Alva took in the scene—the patio's handsome fieldstone, the solidly wrought furniture with thick damask cushions, the crystal glasses in everyone's hands, the Italian wine from the cellar—and thought, *Look at me, I am a millionaire.*

That is, I am a millionaire's wife.

This life is the life of millionaires' sons and wives and daughters. Who needs to love a man anyway, if you have his money?

This is some truly excellent wine.

Aloud she mused, "I once had the most delicious French oysters, harvested from the Étang de Thau . . . This was in Paris, before Louis-Napoléon fell. Jenny, do you remember?"

Jenny was across the terrace in close conversation with Fernando. Neither was paying mind to oysters.

"Were they done in wine?" asked William, who was seated near Alva on a chaise longue. "I had some in Geneva that were astonishingly good."

From a chair next to him, Oliver Belmont said, "Alva, was the Commune justified in attempting to take over, do you think?"

William laughed. "What in God's name has that got to do with oysters?"

"It's got to do with *France*," Oliver replied. "Your wife was speaking of France."

"French oysters, not French communists."

"Oysters, communists . . ." Lady C. waved her hand, then returned to playing. Now the tune was vaguely French sounding, a lament of some kind.

Alva said, "Oliver, remind me, how old are you?"

"Nineteen."

"You're barely grown up! What do you know about the Commune?"

William stood. "Where's that maid? Who needs a refill?"

"I only know a little," Oliver said. "Hence my inquiry." William left the terrace and Oliver came to sit on the end of Alva's chaise. A bold action, she thought, given the slightness of their acquaintance. Still, he was pleasing to see up close, and he smelled wonderful.

He continued, "I do feel—as they did—that the proletariat deserves a say in its governance. Our country's democratic process is a far better form than Emperor Napoléon's—"

"Oh, ours is superior, all right," Alva said, "if one is male. For my sex, the approaches are much the same as in France, or England, for that matter: some man or other directing what we can and cannot do. Women deserve suffrage," she said. "Where do you stand on that?"

Lady C. paused her playing and said, "Oh, dear God, stop *thinking* so hard."

"Let the man speak," said Alva.

Oliver said, "Yes, do permit me to speak while I've still the facility to do so. Once Vanderbilt gets back with more wine, I won't be able to account for my thoughts, let alone my words."

Lady C. said, "I rather like no-account men."

"Anyway," Oliver said, "here's where I stand: I do agree with you in principle. Why should the Negro man be enfranchised while white ladies are not? However, as it appears the ladies mainly wish to vote down alcohol, I can't support *that*. I can see that *some* of your sex are sensible about these things"—he gestured toward Alva's glass with his own—"but too many are not."

"Oh, and every *male* in our so-called republic is sensible?"

Oliver's brother August had come over in the midst of this and now sat down on his brother's lap. "Enough of that!" he said. "There will be no more talk of politics."

Oliver pushed August to the ground. "There *is* a world beyond horses and races and the hunt, you know."

August shielded his eyes with his hand. "What world? Where?"

Alva told Oliver, "August would prefer we discuss—what? The number of hands there are in a foot?"

Oliver laughed. "A horse joke!"

"Or, let's see . . . how many feet there are in a polo field—"

"Which depends upon the number of entrants," said Oliver.

"Exactly! Very good."

The two of them beamed at each other. She hadn't had fun like this since before she was married, and never with a man! Vote down alcohol? Not a chance.

August said, "I would prefer to discuss my mare, who caused me a very poor showing at this morning's hunt because she was in a mood—as is often true about ladies, and whoops, I'm taking us back to the suffrage question. Never mind!" He leaped to his feet. "Lady Mandeville, play us a cheerful tune!"

Oliver smiled at Alva. "To be continued," he said.

"I hope so."

When Alva left the terrace that night, William had fallen asleep on his chaise while conversations went on around him. Jenny, stopping Alva while en route to her own room, whispered, "I believe I'll be an Yznaga before very long!"

Alva said, "Did he ask you?"

Jenny nodded. "We have an understanding. Do you think it's all right? Will you and Armide give us your blessing?"

"I could not wish for a better situation." She kissed her sister. "And Armide will agree. What tremendous good fortune for all of us."

She went unsteadily to her room, not bothering to rouse Mary for help to undress. Shedding her shirtwaist and skirt, she let down her hair and climbed onto the bed. How delightful, this match between Jenny and Fernando. How delightful, romance.

Alva put out the candle. Her room was lit faintly by the torches still burning outside—where Oliver Belmont was yet in conversation with the dullest young man, as far as Alva was concerned. Or perhaps her judgment was a reflection of how engaging she found Oliver. Appealing. Warm. That warmth was inside her now, a response to their flirtation, provoking her desire to slide her hand down over her stomach and lower, to that strange intersection . . .

Her mother had been so wrong. If God had not wanted a woman to be able to experience some pleasure this way, he would have made her arms shorter.

The now-promised couple announced their news in late morning. Lady C., seated beside Alva in the breakfast room, told her friend, "This will make us sisters in fact now, not just in sentiment."

Alva squeezed her arm. "Will he be good for her, do you suppose? Forgive me—I'm only playing the role my father would have done. How does he mean to spend his time?"

"He's asked William to take him on in some capacity."

Alva said, "More play than work, then. Well. He and Jenny adore each other, that's obvious."

"He's passionate about his loves, to be sure."

"Why does that sound like a warning?"

"Does it?" said Lady C. "Perhaps I was only thinking that she's so mild and tender in character." She put her hand over Alva's. "We'll watch over them and all will be well."

William asked Alva and the others to ride out with him to the land he'd settled on for their own summer house, nine hundred acres that bordered the Connetquot's Great South Bay. The entire party went on horseback "into the wilds of Long Island," as William put it, on as gentle a summer day as nature ever provided. They ambled through woods and along streams, startling deer and owls and a black bear with two cubs, the mama bear shooing the cubs up a tree before climbing up after them. The sweet scent of honeysuckle came on the light breeze. Alva, wishing she had been a little more temperate the night before, closed her eyes, letting sunlight dapple her eyelids. Times such as this, one could forget there had ever been hunger or winter or death or longing. Longing especially needed to be forgotten.

What are you, an animal?

As they came through a wood into a clearing, William said, "Here we go. This is my spot. Richard Hunt is going to draw up house plans for me. Can you see it?" he said, gesturing. "An old English hunting estate, right here on the knoll."

Oliver said, "One of those grand places with beams and ivy and such?"

"Barrels of whiskey," William said, nodding.

August said, "Muskets!"

"Muskets? My word, man, we're coming up on the twentieth century!"

"You said an old English hunting estate. I thought you meant authentic."

"Never mind authentic, I want *modern* old English, the most modern old English hunting estate money can buy."

The party rode on into nearby Oakdale, an English settlement that was said to date back to the 1600s, and it appeared that little had changed since then. As they passed a dilapidated church, Alva said to William, "You do realize that if we're to be out here, we'll need a proper house of worship."

Lady C. remarked, "I hope this sty isn't the only option."

"Indeed," said William. "Hunt might have to build us our own."

Alva studied the structure. "What would you say to my making a plan with Mr. Hunt and the church's leadership to rebuild at our expense? We'd be doing the town a good turn and serving our own purposes in the process. I could come up with a pleasing design," she added.

"What, you?" William asked.

"I like thinking about architecture. When I was a little girl, I made buildings out of sticks and books. You can leave it to me, all right? The house, too, if you like. You won't have another concern about it until it's time to move in."

"Except to pay for it," said Lady C.

"Shall I arrange it?" Alva asked her husband.

"I doubt Hunt would want you interfering."

From behind them, Oliver said to William, "It's not as if *you* want the trouble of building it. You only want to have it."

"Just so," William said, laughing.

"Well then," said Alva, "why not allow me to manage the job?"

"If it amuses and occupies you, do proceed."

Lady C. said, "One does prefer an occupied wife. Mandeville always says so."

Oliver let his horse move up beside Alva's. She was acutely aware of his shaving balm. She noticed the sure way his long fingers grasped his horse's reins. A pine needle had caught on his sleeve. She wanted to reach over, pluck it off. What did it mean, this urge to tidy him? It wasn't motherly, she understood that much. Her cheeks were hot.

Oliver said, "I am certain you'll do the job brilliantly."

"Who could doubt it?" Lady C. replied. "Alva is indomitable. And Oakdale has never seen the likes of Vanderbilt money. What good is it if it's not put to such *excellent* use?"

"Says the lady who lives in a castle," William quipped.

Alva, preferring indomitable over flustered, put aside her musings about

Oliver Belmont and thought instead of seeing her sister married to Lady C.'s brother, a tying together of families already well aligned. She thought, too, of the house she and William would build here, and of the far-off future, when William would come into his share of the money his father now possessed. Mr. Vanderbilt already spoke of how he would never put all the responsibility, the burden of such tremendous wealth, on only one of his sons. He would divide a fortune that was growing by the day. She was in no rush for this. She adored her father-in-law. Still, as her friend had intimated, the time *would* come.

"I'll help build the house and the church—and I'll build a castle one day, too. Why shouldn't I do as I please?"

She said this almost as if it were a dare.

Her Second Act

It is your turn now,
you waited, you were patient.
The time has come
for us to polish you.
We will transform your inner pearl
into a house of fire.

—RUMI

I

ALVA STOOD WITH Richard Hunt at the altar of the new St. Mark's Episcopal Church of Oakdale, the building so freshly done that sawdust still lingered in the sunbeams.

This project and the summer house had made for ideal occupation while she also created a child—a boy this time, named for his father (who'd done as forecasted and showered his wife with emeralds for the occasion—including a round, ring-set stone so large that Alva had named it the Meadow). She'd been too busy, far too busy, for frivolous thoughts. Over the months of planning and construction, Oliver Belmont almost never came to mind. Why should she think about him? He was yet a half-formed man, a flirt—her husband's friend, not hers. Why had he even come to mind now? She was short of sleep, that was all, up in the night with the baby, who was teething and had wanted comfort at his mama's breast. A new mother's mind was not always quite under her control.

Richard was saying, "This is going to be a fine place when it's all fitted out. But I do think the house is the greater accomplishment."

"For you, not for me," Alva said. "You made the house to my husband's ideal."

"Incorporating many of your suggestions."

"It isn't the same," she said. "Don't you agree? When you build from your own ideal rather than from your client's, is that not the greater pleasure?"

"I'm afraid I haven't yet had that pleasure."

Richard Hunt was a man of middle years, small in stature but great in energy. Dark-eyed and dark-haired, he had a brushy mustache that gave him an air of creative madness. Though he was American, his training was entirely French: he'd been the first of his kind to study at l'École des Beaux Arts in Paris. That alone was sufficient to win Alva's respect. Their collaboration on this church, however, the ease with which he'd accepted her participation, won him her admiration and affection, too. He had become a real friend.

She said, "What, you haven't built a house of your own? What a travesty! Do you have insufficient work, or insufficient pay for that work?"

"My field is increasingly competitive. Some of the best commissions are going to other firms."

"What are the best commissions?" she asked, envisioning great structures like the Louvre or, that being too much to hope for in New York, the new Metropolitan Museum of Art. Calvert Vaux had won that job, after he and Frederick Law Olmsted created Central Park—a project Richard had contributed to before being elbowed out. Though he didn't speak of it much, Alva knew he'd been wounded by the act. He deserved better.

Richard said, "Surprisingly, the best work is in city mansions. The margins are greater—profit margins, I mean. The men who want such homes seem keen on saying theirs is the most expensive, so it behooves the architect to satisfy such clients by billing the highest rates. I lost several opportunities by underbidding."

"When you say mansions, do you mean like Mr. Stewart's?"

A. T. Stewart had built a white marble showplace on the corner across from Caroline Astor's ordinary brownstone. The home was now said to be haunted by the dead mercantile "king," who'd been felled by what he thought was a bad cold and whose body had been stolen right out of his grave. Mrs. Stewart was certain his ghost walked the long dark halls of their home, unable or unwilling to accept eternal rest. Some said Mrs. Stewart was off her head, but Alva was inclined to believe there was something to this ghost claim. Men like Mr. Stewart had never rested in life; why should they like to do so in death?

Richard said, "Like Stewart's, yes, and others of even more elaborate design. Tiffany, Rockefeller, Lenox—they've all got building lots near where I've recently done the new Lenox Library, east of Central Park. Uptown is no longer quite the wilderness it was."

They left the church and began the drive back to the new house, which William had christened Idle Hour. It had turned out much as he'd envisioned, a Tudor lodge that outwardly resembled those old hunting estates he admired while being modern inside. It had running hot and cold water, a gas machine and built-in fixtures, and a boiler system that would pump heat into every room in the house—a remarkable advance over coal fires. The interiors were spacious and yet also warm and inviting. She and Richard had done well.

What, though, to do next? A lady's day had so many empty hours to be filled, and though the children, social luncheons, and committee meetings could take up her time, rarely were they sufficient occupation for her mind. She needed stimulating, complex projects, challenges to overcome, problems to solve. Were she to be without stimulation for too long, any manner of frivolous thoughts might vex her (about Oliver Belmont, for example—*Good Lord, get out of my thoughts!*), and who could say where that might lead? Idle hands or idle mind—the Devil had no preference.

As they bumped along a road little better than a cow path, she told Richard, "I've been thinking about what you said, about prominent men putting their stamp on the city."

"Yes?"

"My father-in-law recently settled the suit over the Commodore's will—"

"I saw that in the *Times*. Your uncle is satisfied with a single million?"

"Evidently. He seems to have been more interested in pulling Mr. Vanderbilt into the slop than in gaining a great sum. We're all glad to have the matter behind us."

She continued, "And so it seems to me that New York now needs a fresh view of who the Vanderbilts are. A Vanderbilt stamp, if you will."

Wave a wand, cast a spell.

Manhattan was heavy with late-spring humidity, the air sooty and stagnant, the street odors so farmlike that no one was impolite enough to speak of it as the Vanderbilts greeted one another and began assembling in Mr. Vanderbilt's parlor for a family dinner to celebrate the end of the litigation. Mrs. Vanderbilt kept the windows closed.

While waiting for all of William's siblings to arrive, Alva, briefly alone in the drawing room, took the scrolled paper she'd hidden in her sleeve and set it aside, then went about surveying her father-in-law's selections of artists and art; her mother-in-law's choice of fresco on the ceiling above; the fabrics of draperies and furniture; the design of the rug; the small statuary and enameled boxes on display.

Though the house design was ordinary, they'd given it fine accoutrements. These were people of taste. They recognized beauty. They were generous and well meaning and devoted to their family.

And now, with everyone present, they were serving wine, which would help allay her nerves: tonight she would announce a bold proposal that not even William was expecting.

She had dressed carefully, choosing a pale gray gown to serve as backdrop to the gems William had given her: the royal pearls; the emerald earrings; the Meadow, vivid against her white glove. Mary had embroidered the most delicate line of ivy along the outside edge of each glove, a subtle message projecting quality, art, beauty. In Alva's hair was a silver comb encrusted with tiny emeralds and seed pearls. In all, it was a costume meant to inspire in its wearer and its audience a specific and purposeful effect. The effort was not so different from the one she'd undertaken to secure William's proposal of marriage, come to think of it; she was again attempting a kind of personal salvation that would also do a greater good. Tonight, however, she was far better dressed.

Mr. Vanderbilt stood before the now-complete assemblage and said, "Though the matter took far longer to resolve than I wished, this *is* a celebration. Today we put the unpleasantness behind us."

"Amen," said Corneil. Alice put her hand on his shoulder. She was newly expecting what would be their sixth child born, fifth surviving—if the delivery went well, if nothing dire befell any of the others before then. Had Alva wanted to catch up, she would have to have triplets! And even then Alice would probably produce yet another, just to stay ahead.

Mr. Vanderbilt raised his glass. "To our collective future: may it always be as bright as my children and grandchildren. I am delighted with every one of you."

"Even William?" said Corneil, straight-faced. "He seems to have forgotten the location of our offices. Grand Central Depot, Forty-second Street."

"Even Corneil?" said William. "Grandfather never chained himself to his desk like some martyr to the gods of commerce."

"Every one of you," their father repeated, frowning at them. "Must I remind you on *this* occasion that there is no benefit to sowing division?"

Corneil said, "My apologies, Father. I meant to be lighthearted." The silence that met his statement suggested no one was convinced.

"Mr. Vanderbilt, if I may," Alva said, seeing her chance. All eyes turned to her as she waited for his nod. Her heart pounded at twice its usual pace and force, but she stood up, took a breath, and, avoiding her husband's gaze, said, "I have an announcement to make."

Mrs. Vanderbilt clapped her hands. "When is the blessed event?"

"Oh—I'm sorry, Mother V., not that kind of announcement. Rather," she continued, "it has to do with finally elevating the family to its rightful place in society."

Now she ventured a glance at William. His mouth was open slightly, but he didn't speak.

She said, "Settling the lawsuit is cause for celebration, yes. It seems to me also a call for action. For demonstration. The newspapers have sullied the Vanderbilt name, which we all know is unjust—"

"It's an outrage," said Corneil. "This family has done more for New York—"

"A lot, yes," Alva said. "But not nearly enough."

He frowned. "Your ignorance is excusable, but your tone is not. William, did you endorse this speech?"

"Ordinary philanthropy isn't sufficient," she said, giving William no chance to reply. "And frankly, not even the Vanderbilt millions can solve the problems of poverty—though of course we must all continue to address them. But we must also go beyond that.

"This city ought to be a cultural capital of the world. Yet look at the truth: there is so little to uplift the public's spirit. We've had a depression. The people are dejected and uninspired. You've all seen Paris: there's poverty, yes, but wherever one looks there's beauty, too—beauty that every citizen can see. It inspires hope. It inspires love and pride. The poorest Parisian, while he may have nothing, would live nowhere else. The same is true of Florence and Venice and Rome. But here our buildings are plain and ugly on the outside. Those who own great works of art keep them locked away from the public—"

"We have the Metropolitan Museum of Art," said Corneil.

"The new building will be so far uptown that it may as well be in Canada. What seamstress or baker or blacksmith can afford to spend their time and coin on the trip?"

Her father-in-law had tented his fingers over his ample stomach and was watching her closely. "Do you have some solution in mind?"

"I believe I know where we should start." She took the scroll from its spot beneath her chair. "New York is a little like Florence once was before the Medicis made arts patronage their cornerstone of leadership—beginning with architecture." She unrolled the paper and held it up for everyone to see. "Richard Hunt and I collaborated on this."

"It looks like a castle," Lila said.

"It's modeled on le Château de Chenonceau, which was home at one time to Catherine de' Medici and is scaled here for Fifth Avenue. This is only a sketch, but it conveys—"

"What do you purport this to be?" said Mr. Vanderbilt.

"The new William K. Vanderbilt residence."

"Alva!" William said.

"Your *house*?" George came for a closer look.

His father said, "That would be quite a statement."

"Yes, it would," said Alva. "What's more, *you* should do something in this line as well—a mansion, I mean, of whatever style you choose. And so should you, Corneil. And we'll all furnish our homes with objects of genuine beauty. The structures themselves will be works of art that anyone can admire. We'll be supporting every kind of artisan and artist—stonemasons and carpenters and ironsmiths and seamstresses, painters, sculptors—think of it, with so many men out of work."

"I like that," said Mrs. Vanderbilt.

"You may well like it, Mother," Corneil replied. "But what Alva is proposing is not viable—we must forgive her for being insensible as to the expense of such a plan."

"A considerable expense," Mr. Vanderbilt said, nodding his agreement. "Though I do admire the sentiment." He gave Alva a sympathetic smile. "Now, shall we move on to dinner?"

The family rose from their seats and conversation resumed. William came over to Alva, his expression stern. "You should have consulted with me first."

"Yes, I know, but— Gentlemen," she called out impulsively. Everyone turned toward her. "I . . . well, forgive me, I mean no disrespect, but I have to say I am astonished by your lack of vision. It's quite disappointing, to tell the truth. The Commodore must be laughing at you from his grave for this failure to recognize a great opportunity when it is laid in your lap."

"That's enough," William said, taking her arm.

Corneil was still in the fight. He said, "Grandfather would never waste money on this."

"You're wrong. His genius lay in recognizing which action to take in order to build the fortune and legacy he longed for. The fortune is made. The legacy will languish if none of you is willing to seize this opportunity."

Corneil said to William, "You had better control your—"

"Say more," Mr. Vanderbilt bade Alva, holding up his hand to silence Corneil. "You said you worked this out with Mr. Hunt. What does he have in mind?"

"A good fee, surely," said Corneil.

"Mr. Hunt thinks the corner of Fifty-second and Fifth is ideal for our house," Alva said. "The new St. Patrick's cathedral would act as a kind of architectural anchor. And he suggests that the Fifties are prime in general. Little of note has been built there so far—mainly just the Jones sisters' row houses, and as Fifth Avenue runs out at the park, we would define what uptown will be."

"Father," Corneil began again.

"I want to hear her out," said Mr. Vanderbilt. "Her observation about our legacy is not baseless." He came to stand beside her. He examined the sketch, the turrets and windows and ironwork of her castle-to-be. "How do you intend to pay for it? I'm not in favor of your husband selling any more of his shares."

She had anticipated this. "*You'll* pay for it," she said. "And for Corneil's house, too. It's not as if you can't afford it—and isn't it simply a kind of, what do you call it, a diversification of assets from stocks to real property?"

They were all looking at her as if she'd begun speaking in tongues. It was . . . rather delightful.

She continued, "Imagine what the papers will say of you: 'William Henry Vanderbilt, New York's premier patron, the man who remade Manhattan.' You'll have to act quickly, though, if you hope to upstage the others."

" 'The others'?"

"Tiffany. Rockefeller. Lenox," Alva said, repeating Richard Hunt's list. "Mr. Hunt tells me they're contemplating similar plans."

Mr. Vanderbilt's expression gave nothing away. "I must say, this is a bold proposal—"

"I'm sorry, Father," William interrupted, frowning at Alva. "It's my fault. If I had known what she was—"

"I wish I had thought of it myself," Mr. Vanderbilt finished. "The Fifties, you say?"

Alva nodded. "That's right. Yours for the taking."

"Hmm. Close enough to stroll to the park. What's more, my wife is fond of reminding me that I've long past run out of space for the paintings I've acquired. It won't do to leave them stacked against walls. Why hold on to the money like old Astor did, visiting it in its vault the way ordinary men visit with their grandchildren? You've heard me say it before: I don't intend to burden any of you boys the way my father did me."

"You could have a proper gallery," said George. "And a library."

"Indeed. All right, you've convinced me. Let's set an example for others to follow, and perhaps this city will come to something yet. I'll see my property agent in the morning, first thing."

Alva kissed him. "You are a wise and generous gentleman. Everyone will say so."

He colored, unused to avid affection. "I may even look into doing houses for the girls," he said, gesturing toward Margaret and Emily, the eldest daughters. Presumably the younger two would have to wait along with the younger two sons. He said, "Good? Good! Shall we dine?"

William caught Alva's eye. He winked.

Following the others to the dining room, she was buoyed by the pride and satisfaction of having prevailed in this contest and by the prospect of the work ahead of her. Yet beneath the surface she was limp with relief, as if she had been running from a wolf and was now safe again inside the cottage door.

William came to Alva's room later that night. She was sitting up in bed, paging through one of the books Richard Hunt had given her. *Homes of Antiquity* was a huge, heavy collection of renderings. Every Italian and French estate of note was included there.

William sat down on the bed. "That was a remarkable night. I believe it never would have occurred to Father that he could use his money in such a manner. In his mind he's still the boy whose mother managed a boardinghouse while his father was out running ferries. He couldn't stop congratulating me on choosing such a good wife."

"I suspect it was the wine," she said. Certainly it had helped her.

"I shouldn't have criticized you." He took the ribbon at her bosom between his fingers. "You always know what you're about, and you always put the family's welfare first."

She glanced at his hand. "Ladies are good for more than you think."

He gave her the sweet, crooked smile their son was beginning to exhibit when caught trying to crawl off his blanket into the dirt or after his sister's dolls. "You do admit the gentler sex is not usually interested in men's doings."

"When has a man ever bothered to pay attention to what a lady is interested in?"

"Be fair! How often have we sat at a dining table or in someone's drawing room and heard a lady prattle on about parasols or porte-monnaies? Or the exceptional qualities of her rug, her tapestries, the silver service on her last sailing abroad?"

"You like fine things—"

"But I don't go on about them in public."

"What lady would speak her true mind when, if she does, she'll be ridiculed or censured the way Corneil treated me earlier?"

"Are you telling me that in private your friends discuss the stock market and, what, Boss Tweed?"

Would that they did, Alva thought. Sometimes, at least. "I'm saying I am interested in architecture, and I mean to continue my involvement with Mr. Hunt."

"Hunt does *not* want you hovering over him as if he were incompetent." William pulled the ribbon and untied it. "He permits it because he needs the money."

Retying the ribbon, she said, "Do you know that the Wyoming and Utah territories allow women full voting rights?"

"Are there white women in those territories? I had no idea."

"Last year Congress said, 'Leave it to the states.' Yet the state of New York—and every other state but those two—refuses even to consider suffrage for women. We are more than simply decorative."

"Ah, but the decorations can be so pleasing," he said, reaching again for her ribbon. He never did this sort of thing; how was she supposed to behave?

He had his hand on her collarbone now and was saying, "Why would you want to be bothered with all that political nonsense? What's wrong with simply enjoying being a lady of privilege?"

"Ask your sisters. They want more, too."

"More recognition for their status as ladies of privilege from certain other ladies of privilege. But you!" He laughed. "You want to be at the drafting table with Hunt, saying where this column goes and how wide to make that doorway and whether the towers should be round or square—"

"Yes, I do, and why shouldn't I?"

"Because you're a wife and a mother, not an architect. You had your fun, building the church. It's time to settle into your proper place. Be grateful for your privileged life. You don't have to work, so why would you?"

"I am grateful. However, I do have a mind, and it wants to be put to purposeful use on something that matters to me."

"The children and I don't matter?"

"Do the children and I matter to you?"

"What? Of course."

"Even while you go about making horse farms and racetracks and tending railroad business?"

William raised his palms. "Let's not debate this further. What matters is that my father is ecstatic, and Hunt's got new work, and you're going to get the home of a queen."

He took the book from her lap and set it aside. He turned down the lamp.

It's worth it, she thought. This was what women did, what they'd always done. She was no different from any of them—or perhaps she was wiser: she at least was gaining in status. She was directing her fate.

Tandragee, December 5, 1879

Alva, my dear:

Am I mistaken, or did I last write you when I'd just learned I was again with child? It was such an eventful year, some of it spent at court, where I've had audiences with the prince. His set is so diverting. Even in confinement I had the company of the most entertaining ladies, who made a fine distraction for me in my discomfort.

Well, how is this for news? I am delivered of not one babe but a pair of girls, identical in every aspect, in what was a surprisingly easy birth experience, especially considering that I had to deliver twice. Do you suppose this means little Kim, who has become quite a dictator now that he's speaking actual words, will always be more difficult than his sisters? One hopes he'll be more effective in his life than his father, who did manage to arrive in time for the births but was harried and wild and thin. He kissed the babes, congratulated me, asked whether my father would reward me (and thus him) with a doubly generous cheque for my troubles, and was off again in two days. Did I imagine it would be otherwise?

I recall, years ago, seeing the Duchess's jeweled crown for the first time and thinking I'd wear it before long. How terribly long "long" has become; the old man refuses to die! And I wonder, will the crown thrill me in the least when the time actually comes? Probably it's heavy and will make my scalp ache and give me a rash.

Write me. Better yet, come see these darling girls, whose names are Alice Eleanor Louise and Jacqueline Mary Alva.

Ever yours,
Lady C.

New York, 3 January 1880

Dear Lady C.,
Happiest of New Years to you, Mandeville, Kim—and now two more at once! Many congratulations and blessings to all of you. I promise to pay you a visit when I go abroad in the spring, and hope to find you and Mandeville both in good form. Being father to three, now, might anchor him better—if not immediately, then before too long. How can any man with a heart and eyes want to be away from you?

I am currently gestating a new creation of my own, but it's not a child: it's a house like none this city has seen before. I've hired Richard Hunt again. We're also at work on a children's summertime retreat in an old home that adjoins our Long Island estate.

Honestly, I am in my glory. After tending household matters and taking luncheon with the children, I then get to spend most afternoons at Richard's offices, consulting with him and his engineer and designer, studying other structures and drawing plans for mine.

I must have been born to do architectural work. I understand the aesthetics of composition, fenestration, materials, all of it, and have never been happier than when I am putting my mind to the intricacies of a pleasing floor plan or orchestrating detail for a wall or window or stairway or hall. When Richard and I sit down for tea and discussion, I feel that I am an equal. Oh, he's far above me in training. But I tease him that I balance his superiority with my innate taste and William's money.

In April, Richard and I will be visiting auction houses in Florence, Paris, and London, to consider furnishings. I'll bring my children on the trip, and Mrs. Hunt intends to bring her younger ones. Catherine is a kind, intelligent woman, and good company. I intend to also speak to numerous artists and craftsmen regarding wall coverings, stained glass, carved paneling, and a portrait commission. I've never been properly painted, you know, and as a certain doyenne displays a portrait of herself in her drawing room, I thought I might flatter her choice by doing the same.

Will you come to London then? I want to hear all the gossip. Here's some from this side of the Atlantic: while we await Jenny & Fernando's nuptials, Julia has caught the eye of a French nobleman—a minor title, nothing like your coup, but he does seem partial to her and we are hopeful something more will develop. Maman would rejoice to see one of her swans "properly" wed. Certainly it won't be Armide, who has happily devoted herself to All the Right Causes, efforts that I gladly fund. She's well past the age any young man would look at her, even should she encourage it by dressing attractively, etc., which she steadfastly chooses not to do. Perhaps a widowed clergyman will see her merits despite herself. On the other hand, she is content.

Love to all—
Alva

II

"WILLIAM DIDN'T TRAVEL with you?" Lady C. asked after meeting Alva in the London auction house's anteroom. Dozens of well-dressed people milled about this room and in the one adjoining, where rows of chairs awaited the bidders-to-be. Today's offerings were comprised of the furnishings from two English country estates that had belonged to a now-dead baron and to a now-destitute earl, neither of whom were of particular note save for their good taste in tapestries, rugs, and furniture.

Alva said, "No, he, Fred, and Corneil are off with their father touring and inspecting all the lines, speaking with the supervisors and the laborers, that sort of thing."

"Mandeville would do well to get out and see his people in Kimbolton. He likes the title far more than the duties, such as they are. The Montagu men are a rather casual pair in that regard. Why bother to work at a thing you can't ever lose?"

"They can lose respect."

"Oh, that. I meant something that matters to them."

Alva said, "Yes, well, it's good that William had reason to be occupied elsewhere. If he were along, we'd buy twice as much."

"You'd have to simply build another house, then, to keep all the extra things."

"And anyway, the Hunts are lovely companions," Alva said, gesturing toward the couple, who'd gone into the auction room and were now engaged in conversation with a bespectacled man of very advanced years who leaned on a cane for support. A collector, she supposed, smiling at the scene; one was never too old to pursue a true love.

Lady C. said, "Catherine Hunt's not jealous of you?"

"What, because I see so much of him?" Alva shook her head. "They're completely devoted to each other."

"That is a shame."

"Why on earth would you say that?"

"You could do with a lover."

"What an odd thing to say!"

"And your last letter to me was filled with his name."

Alva said, "I could do with tea at Claridge's—New York doesn't have Devonshire cream, and no one makes scones like you've got here."

People had begun seating themselves. Richard waved to get her attention, and Alva nodded to him. "It looks as though they're about to get under way. We should go in."

As they went, Lady C. said, "What is it you're after here?"

"My decorator feels we'll do best furnishing the 'masculine' rooms from English estates. He says—rightly, I think—that William's status is best reflected by Saxon styles."

Lady C. raised an eyebrow, an expression that was just shy of being a smirk. "Indeed," she said. "Given that you're not involved with your Mr. Hunt, I wonder why you bothered to bring him along."

"He'll be invaluable in Paris—he trained there and knows everyone. Did I tell you he worked on renovations to the Louvre?"

"Listen to you—such pride! The two of you should get a little flat in Paris—"

"Will you cease this nonsense?" Alva snapped.

Her friend was taken aback. "When did you grow so serious?"

"When did you become so boorish?"

Lady C. stopped walking. "You're right. I apologize. I should keep better company—Bertie's jesters are not the refined lot they'd seem to be."

"Bertie" meant Albert, Prince of Wales, Queen Victoria's eldest son. A reputed playboy who had little of import to do while awaiting his mother's death, he'd surrounded himself with friends whose current responsibilities were something like his own. Dalliances were rumored. Alva remembered that Lady C. had written about having had audiences with him, but nothing about becoming an actual member of his set. To drop the fact into conversation so casually was a boast.

Alva said, "Keeping company with the future king."

"What of it?"

"What a *fascinating* life you lead. But do you know they call you a 'dollar princess' back home?"

"You needn't be so severe with me. I told you I was sorry."

Alva didn't reply. She went to her seat beside Richard and turned her attention to the auction. Lady C. took the seat beside Alva and for the remainder of the event made every effort to be cheerful. When Alva bid on a collection of tapestries, Lady C. praised her choice and congratulated her when she won the bid. When Alva lost out on a pair of Chinese ceramic urns, Lady C. commiserated. She spoke to the Hunts respectfully, and indeed got on so well with Catherine Hunt that at the auction's conclusion, she invited the Hunts to continue their day with herself and Alva. She suggested Claridge's for tea, and they accepted eagerly.

Alva, however, had remained out of sorts. She said, "You all will forgive me for declining the invitation. Something is not quite agreeing with me. Better that I return to my rooms to rest and rejoin you, Mr. Hunt, in the morning."

Lady C. said, "I'll call on you at dinnertime, then."

"Better not. My head is aching and I'm certain to be poor company."

"Oh. Will I see you again before you leave town?"

"I'm afraid there's no time for it," Alva told her. "We have a tight schedule."

"All right, then . . . it seems this is good-bye for now." Lady C. reached for Alva to embrace her.

Alva permitted it, stiffly. "Good-bye for now."

She left the auction house and hired a cab to take her back to her rooms at The Langham. This dark mood perplexed her. Reject teatime at Claridge's? Refuse a rare evening alone with her oldest friend? Perhaps she truly was ill—an illness of the mind. She might be at the start of a long and slow descent into madness. William would have to send her away to someplace calm and simple, where her mind would not be taxed by anything more complicated than choosing her socks. Now there was a recipe for madness, if she'd ever heard one.

She made herself reflect on the argument. Lady C. had been right; Alva was too severe with her. She should have governed her own irritation better, found high ground in both reaction and response, accepted the apology on the spot. Yet she hadn't *wanted* to accept it. Her friend's teasing had . . . what? Reminded her of how coarse Lady C. had become? Because yes, that was true, and Alva wished it were not true, wished Mandeville was an actual gentleman and hadn't affected his wife this way.

That, however, was not a sufficient explanation for her anger. Perhaps the trouble lay in her friend's ability to see in her something she did not wish anyone to see—wished was not true. No, she was not in love with Richard. She was not in love at all. She was not in love and she wanted to be and she couldn't be, and there it was, the shameful truth illuminated under her friend's knowing gaze.

Alva ordered up a cottage pie and bottle of sherry, partook of both in portions she wouldn't ever do publicly, and then went to sleep at seven o'clock. She awakened at dawn, feeling slightly less sorry for herself and a good deal more dyspeptic.

With no time to call on Lady C. in person before she and the Hunts had to be on their way to Paris, she penned a note instead:

My friend: I will leave it to Emily Bronte to express best how I feel—

Love is like the wild rose-briar,
Friendship like the holly tree—
The holly is dark when the rose-briar blooms
But which will bloom most constantly?

The wild rose-briar is sweet in the spring,
Its summer blossoms scent the air;

Yet wait till winter comes again
And who will call the wild-briar fair?

Then scorn the silly rose-wreath now
And deck thee with the holly's sheen,
That when December blights thy brow
He may still leave thy garland green.

Some time later in New York, Richard Hunt, whose usual expression was either one of polite interest or keen observation, stood before the massive front doors of the house at 660 Fifth Avenue, Alva's "petit château," as she had come to call it, unable to suppress his smile. After two years of painstaking effort by scores of craftsmen, the house was finished, the furniture and carpets and draperies installed, every surface polished and ready for her final inspection.

From the sidewalk on Fifth Avenue, Alva climbed the eight steps, every riser shortened so that climbing in heavy skirts would be easier. They'd done this with the curved staircase inside as well—Alva's own design done in carved stone.

Richard had at first balked when she told him, "I'd like five-inch risers, with twelve-inch treads."

"Five is too short. There are standards for such things."

"I read *The Building News.* I know the standards: six and a half inches is a favored one, and no one's doing anything shorter than five and a half. This is because all the architects are men. Five is ideal. Put on a half-dozen garment layers including a bustle and wool skirt and see for yourself the advantage."

"It would add expense," he told her. "Not a great deal, but I do try to avoid unnecessary—"

"It will make every lady who comes to the house very happy, I assure you. And happy ladies love to tell other ladies how happy they are. Rich happy ladies need architects to build their own new houses. You see where this goes."

He said, "I do."

What he hadn't seen until the house was nearly done was Alva's secret project: in tribute to Richard's excellent nature and talents, two stonecutters had carved his life-size likeness. After presenting it to him, Alva installed it on a peak beside the highest turret, overlooking Fifth Avenue. The whimsy of it was her particular delight.

Now Richard watched her climb the steps. As he said, "Welcome home," the doors swung open behind him.

She laughed. "Very nice touch."

She'd been here daily throughout the construction, while across Fifty-second Street the same process was under way for what would become Emily's house. Adjoining it was Margaret's, and next to this connected pair, on Fifty-first and Fifth, was the home being built for their parents. Because Mr. Vanderbilt had hired the Herter Brothers as architects, the blocky, austere design of the "triple palace," as the reporters named it, had no resemblance to what Alva and Richard had done here. Nor did the house under way for Alice and Corneil, who'd bought and demolished the buildings at the corner of Fifth Avenue and Fifty-seventh Street in order to build a redbrick Colonial.

Alva had watched her house rise from the ground four full stories, culminating in its French Gothic roof. Timbers and limestone and plaster—so much plaster! As the interior walls and ceilings were being smoothed into place, she'd been through every room to check the work, caking her boots as she went, ruining easily a dozen skirt hems. Oftentimes the plaster ended up on her gloves and hat and in her hair. Every time, she'd returned home to Forty-fourth Street smiling.

And then the stonecutters went to work, chiseling the elaborate detailing over the windows and at the base of the turrets, carving out the perimeter fence, creating the staircase, decorating the numerous arches and panels inside. Each day a little more beauty was created and revealed. Then came the furnishings, much of it thoughtfully selected by a man Ward McAllister recommended, Jules Allard, "the French king of interiors." She was watching her dream take form in the waking world, and it felt like magic. She had waved her wand over Mr. Vanderbilt's head, and this marvelous creation—a veritable fairyland of the French Renaissance—was the result.

Late that night, after William and the children had arrived at the house, after the first dinner had been served and Alva had played the first songs on the new piano, after the bedtime prayers were said, after the last of the nightcaps was drunk, Alva left her bedroom with candle in hand and went upstairs to the third floor.

The children slept in the rooms up here and would play in the gymnasium, a huge, gleaming room that stretched above the two-story banquet hall below. They had scooters and balls and hoops and a miniature sailboat on wheels that could be towed about the room. Before dinner, the two of them had taken turns towing each other. Willie was the more eager captain, directing the "wind" to go one way, then another, while Consuelo was content to sit politely and see where her "wind" might send her.

Alva went to Consuelo's door and peeked in to see her daughter abandoned to dreams—often of ponies and puppies, Consuelo would tell her in the mornings. Then Willie's room. He was sound asleep with his feet and legs propped up against his headboard. He claimed to dream of ponies and puppies as well.

She went back down to the second floor, which had a nursery and a schoolroom and an enormous guest bedroom, along with rooms for herself (*so long, pink stripes!*) and for the master of the house, who was now presumably sleeping off his generous pours of thirty-year-old scotch. He'd carried a glass around with him all evening, going from room to room and grinning like Midas on the day of his reward.

In the spacious upper hall, she did a slow waltz with an invisible partner over to the main stairway. One practically floated down its shortened steps! She was proud of her creation—the stairway, yes, but more than that, the house itself, the fact of it—much as God must have been proud after He'd looked into the vast blackness of time before time and decided, *There should be earth.*

On the first floor, to the right of the stairs, a tremendous arched doorway opened into the banquet hall, a fifty-foot-wide room two extra-tall stories high, with a fantastic stained-glass scenario on the wall opposite the doors: the meeting of King Henry VIII and King Francis I on the Field of the Cloth of Gold. That scenario was a marvel: nine panels put together to make three windows rising twenty feet high. All that colored glass cut and placed to form kings, knights, falconers, bowmen, jesters—dwarfs, even, and dogs and horses and gear . . . Not to mention Queen Claude, as well as Anne Boleyn, who there had won the attention of Henry VIII.

But nowhere in the image was gold cloth apparent. Nor was there any field—it was all castles and houses and tents and hills. Mary had asked why, then, it was named as it was.

"Well, I suppose it's because art like this is symbolic, not literal," Alva said. "Representational, not real. Do you see?" Even as she'd said it, she was thinking that there were times when she felt that none of this—the window, the paintings, the tapestries, the columns, the polished stone and wood under her feet—was real, that in fact she was dreaming it, that she might at any moment wake in a bedroom shared with her sisters, a cold wind whistling through window gaps and floorboards, nothing to look forward to, nowhere to go.

At the end of the banquet hall were the service stairs to the basement. Alva continued that way, down the dim corridor and into the kitchen, where she set her candle on the center worktable and then stood in the middle of the expansive room. It smelled of the roasted pork and yams they'd eaten earlier, with an underlying scent, still, of sawed wood and plaster and paint. The room was silent as the grave.

On the wide marble worktable was a huge wheel of cheese covered by a cloth. "Never had anything so fine," the cook had said of that table. "And these ovens and this copperware . . ." And around them, shelves and cupboards and drawers and closets and hooks and a huge icebox, everything brand new and tidy.

When the newspapers mentioned the house (which they liked to do, often), it was praised for having charm and grace—more so than its mistress, some had remarked, citing how untidy she often was when leaving the site, and what was a lady doing there amid so much mess and so many coarse men? Alva had no time for such small-mindedness. The house was done; the house was wonderful. Now she must in essence perch herself on top of Richard-the-statue's cap-covered head and see how else she might take on this city and its most snobbish inhabitants—

A noise behind Alva startled her. She turned toward the door. "My word, Mary! You'll give me heart failure. What are you doing down here at this hour?"

"My stomach's unsettled," Mary said. "So much excitement, you know, finally being here. I hoped to find a cracker—but I'm not sure where to look first."

"How do you feel about opera?"

"Opera?" Mary said. "Me? I've never heard one—but I did see two colored girls about as old as me who sang opera songs in church once. They had very pretty voices."

Alva said, "At the actual opera, almost no one pays attention to the music, except for Mrs. Vanderbilt, God love her—and she has no foreign languages, so I always have to tell her the story. And we *still* can't get a box. I think my husband should get some of his friends to form a committee and simply build a new music hall themselves. Never mind waiting for society to grant us any dearly held privilege. Take the mountain to Muhammad."

Mary lit a wall sconce and began opening cupboards in search of a cracker tin. "Mama says that's how the abolitionists had to do. No matter how right you are in your thinking, you could die waiting for some people to change their minds."

Alva nodded. "I do tire of the nonsense."

"Here, I found the crackers," said Mary, taking down the tin.

"Alice, though; she tilts her nose up and goes about her business as though exemplary living is all that's needed to erase stigma and bring society to her door. As though it's beneath her to make an overt effort."

Mary said, "You'll forgive me saying so, but you getting to the top of society is isn't exactly as important as all people being free."

"I do realize I'm not going to save anyone by besting Caroline Astor and her ilk, but I would love to do it just the same. Merely on principle."

She drew a deep breath and let it out slowly. "It's a fantastic kitchen, isn't it? I told Mr. Hunt, 'We need to make it so nice that *I'd* want to work here. That's how we'll always get the best help.' Look at this place," she continued. "We are *surrounded* by food." She uncovered the cheese and looked for a knife, saying, "I'm going to make the most of it, Mary. All of it. I'm going to beat society at its own game."

III

THE GLEAMING MAHOGANY dining table. William at one end, Alva at the other. Friends seated along both sides. French wine. Stuffed squab. Hadn't she once wished it exactly so?

Among their guests at this springtime dinner party were a slate of young, unmarried Knickerbocker ladies who wanted to take part in interesting amusements with the interesting people, whether their parents approved or not. These girls were quite attached to another of Alva's guests, Miss Sallie Whiting, despite her father being merely a wealthy merchant. Miss Whiting was as pretty as they came, but also vivid in personality. Alva had invited her on an impulse, having seen her at the Bicycle Exhibition in William's newly named Madison Square Garden. She and Miss Whiting watched a sideshow in which a pair of women demonstrated that ladies, too, could ride bicycles and really *ought* to ride in order to improve circulation, complexion, and digestion. Alva had ordered six bicycles to be delivered to Idle Hour and another six for home, and when Miss Whiting remarked, "But you're already *superior* in complexion," Alva invited her to dinner.

Tonight's party included several unwed gentlemen, too, not the least of whom was Oliver Belmont. He had been away, training at the Naval Academy and serving a year, but had changed his mind about it and come home. William quipped, "Too many boats, not enough horses," but that seemed too facile a characterization for a man like Oliver.

Certain she was now immune to the malaise that had troubled her before, Alva had seated him at her left. It was nice to see him after so long, nice to be able to admire him—platonically, of course.

Now he was raising his wineglass and saying, "To our excellent host, as fine an example of a gentleman as our Creator ever made—and still in his father's good graces! Whereas I am the bane of my father's existence. Unlike *your* older brother, Vanderbilt, *my* older brothers have failed to distract dear old dad from the harsh truth about the younger progeny: that we are gamblers and flirts—"

"And you are much too fast with four-in-hand," William said. "With all horses, in fact. I'm a good deal poorer thanks to you. This man races like the wind, I tell you. He should be driving a mail coach."

Sallie Whiting touched Oliver's arm and said, "You're very brave, I'm certain."

"Oh, very," Oliver agreed.

She shifted closer to him and asked, "Which of these is more frightening to a man: a wild horse or a wild woman?"

Could the girl be more obvious? She was throwing herself at him. It was unseemly.

Oliver said, "By which you mean, run away with herself?"

"Disregards her father's instruction—" said one of the others.

"And her mother's direction," added a third.

Sallie Whiting nodded. "Smokes cigarettes publicly, and displays her ankles when she's seated."

One of the gentlemen said, "She sounds all right to me!"

"Flirts with a man without any desire to marry him," said Miss Edith Jones, whose aunt, Mary Mason Jones, was Alva's eccentric neighbor, one of the first to build a home across from Central Park. Mrs. Jones was an aficionado of French architecture and had come over to admire Alva's house several times—a small but significant event, given that Mrs. Jones was a Knickerbocker of the first order.

William said, "Surely none of you as-yet-unwed ladies would risk your reputations by flirting that way. You should look to Alva for your example; my wife is perfection."

"I often say as much," said Oliver.

"Please," Alva said, startled by both men's remarks. "I am many things, but perfect is not among them."

Miss Jones said, "No, you truly do embody all a married lady should be. There are, however, a number of girls who have their own money and are in no rush to marry. So why not flirt if they like?"

"Think of what you're saying," William said. "They'd never be asked anywhere good. And what sort of girl doesn't want to marry?"

"Armide, for one," Alva replied. "But she's no flirt, and she doesn't smoke—or show off her ankles."

"She's dull," said Miss Whiting. "I'm sorry to be critical, but it's true!"

"Most unwomanly," William agreed, and as he said it, dessert was served—a flaming crème brûlée that had everyone exclaiming over it.

Oliver leaned nearer to Alva and said, "I'm certain your sister is excellent company, but no doubt inferior to you. Every lady is."

She laughed. "You are in your cups, sir."

"Au contraire. This is no drunken speech. W.K. is the finest gentleman I've known—and do you know how I know? I'll tell you. Because he won you."

She did not say that the game had been fixed, the trophy already engraved with his name. The portrayal was flattering, and she did not mind being flattered, even by Oliver Belmont.

Especially by Oliver Belmont.

Yes, it was true. Still true. As true as ever, why not simply admit it? Not that it mattered one whit. It did not. No, not a whit.

"And you," Oliver continued, "are impeccable. You are impeachable—no, I mean *un*impeachable. You are a peach. You are—"

"*You* are going to have to be poured into your carriage tonight," Alva said, feeling herself blush—and in feeling it, blushing harder.

He said, "You must know: if only you were—"

He stopped as their butler came in with Corneil behind him, announcing, "Sir, Mr. Cornelius Vanderbilt."

Corneil addressed the group. "My apologies for this interruption.

William—if you would." He indicated the door to the parlor. "Excuse us, please."

They left the room, and one of the gentlemen said, "What could pull good old Corneil away from his ledgers at this hour?" drawing uneasy laughter from the other men. The matters that would concern Corneil to this extent could be matters that concerned the markets, and thus affected these gentlemen's abilities to buy Thoroughbreds.

"Do enjoy the dessert," Alva said, forcing cheer. "I'm sure it's road business. It always is."

The conversation went on around her. She was less concerned with Corneil's appearance than with what had just passed between Oliver and her. She didn't dare look at him. What had he meant to say? If only she were . . . what? How did he see her? What did he imagine her capable of?

He leaned close again and said in her ear, "I must reveal something. He's *not* the finest gentleman I know—though he *should* be, the fool."

Alva said nothing.

Oliver went on, "When we travel, he often takes up with—"

"Please, stop," Alva whispered. "Would you slander your good friend?"

He looked abashed and sat back in his chair.

What had he expected? That upon hearing some terrible thing about her husband—a falsehood, probably, invented to serve his own purpose—she would take up with him? No matter how much she might desire the thrill of a love affair, indulging that desire would be social suicide.

I am unimpeachable.

I am.

"Miss Whiting," Oliver said, "do you fancy a cigarette?"

"I don't mind if I do," Sallie Whiting replied. "As long as we're waiting for our host."

"Anyone else?" he offered, holding out his case. Alva refused to look his way.

When her husband returned to the dining room, he was alone. His expression was somber and he said, "I'm afraid we have to make an early night of this. My uncle has died. I don't know much more than that. I hope you all will forgive this abrupt end to the evening." He then returned to the parlor.

In seeing everyone out, Alva avoided Oliver's attempt to catch her eye, instead watching his shoulder as he thanked her formally and said good night.

With William and Corneil still shut away, she went through her bedtime toilet absentmindedly. Though she ought to have been thinking of their poor uncle or paying attention to Mary's idle chatter, she was recalling Oliver's warm breath and voice in her ear. *If only you were—*

An immoral woman?

An unmarried woman?

My woman.

She couldn't know whether his *if only* meant he wished for what might have been, or for what he imagined might yet be.

And if she *was* his?

She felt a strange flutter in her stomach.

Stop it.

Mary said, "Is there anything else, Miss Alva?"

"What? No. Thank you. Oh—except, you'll have heard that my husband's uncle passed—"

"I was just saying," Mary told her. She tilted her head and gave Alva a look reminiscent of Lulu's. "Are you feeling all right?"

"So you know to bring out my black attire," Alva said. "Good. That's all, then."

Mary continued to look at her.

"I said that's all."

"I'm going," Mary said.

As she left, William came to Alva's bedroom door and said, "Not that it will take long for the papers to get hold of this, but I couldn't say it . . ."

Alva turned to face him. "What? It wasn't a seizure? What happened?"

"It was suicide. He shot himself in the head."

"He did not!"

"He was damned already."

"And now the rest of us are, too."

William said, "It isn't as bad as all of that."

"For the men, it isn't."

"Yes, of course, look how easy life was for Uncle C.J."

"I'm sorry for him, you know I am—but he committed a mortal sin, and some society ladies would as soon pick the flesh from my bones when my back is turned as have sympathy for your uncle's plight."

"Then don't see those ladies," he said.

"Don't see them? Think of what you're saying. That would require my never leaving the house."

❧

At the conclusion of Uncle C.J.'s funeral service, several unfamiliar men rimmed the insultingly small group in attendance, some of whom had now gathered around the casket. Each man seemed to be alone, and each wore an expression not of sadness or disappointment but of eagerness, as if waiting for a race to start. Reporters. Which of the family could they coax into speaking with them? Who was likely to provide the most sensational story about the Commodore's son's last days, last words, even his last thoughts, if any wanted to speculate so boldly? There was always more to every story, after all.

Leaving the family pew, Alva watched the men warily as she drew Ward McAllister aside. "I'm sick over this, and these men . . . Are we going to have to hire guards for our funerals?"

"It's all terrible, just terrible, to be sure. He was a much better man than many believe. I knew him quite well, before the war. We were all of us much younger then. We once spent an entire summer together in the South of France . . ."

"My husband thinks I'm worrying too much, but I know you'll understand: Do you suppose this will do us in?"

"Oh, it's beyond unfortunate, to be sure—for you and the other Vanderbilt ladies. For all her outstanding qualities, Mrs. Astor does, I am sorry to admit, take pleasure in every occasion that demonstrates the family's supposed unworthiness—it proves her right in her judgment, don't you know."

"*Unworthiness,*" Alva said. "That she still sees us in such a light—"

"The Vanderbilts aren't her only interest. Take heart. Mr. Belmont has caused a stir that's got her excited as well—though not in the same manner, I grant you."

Alva said, "Which Mr. Belmont?"

"Your husband's good friend. Named for his esteemed great-uncle, Oliver Hazard Perry, quite a hero in the War of 1812. Not too imaginative of his parents to simply tack Belmont to the end of that, I daresay—"

"What about Oliver?" Alva said.

"Oh—yes, well, apparently he's betrothed himself to Miss Sallie Whiting, who Mrs. Astor feels is too common even for a Belmont, though *Miss* Astor is Miss Whiting's good friend. And Mrs. Astor is quite persuaded that the Belmonts are secret Jews."

"He and Sallie Whiting? Where did you hear this?"

"At my club. Word is, his parents are none too keen on the pairing."

"And this rumor—"

"It's no rumor. Mr. Belmont—that is, O.H.P. himself—was there in the flesh, informing everyone. One might say he was bragging about the controversy he'd stirred. I was certain you'd have heard it as well."

"What folly!" Alva said. "He only met her the other night, at my house."

And I was the one he wanted.

"Cupid must have let his arrow fly swiftly."

"It's nonsensical. What can he be thinking?"

"His parents are wondering the same thing, he says—and he hardly cares!"

"Someone ought to stop them."

"Your concern for your friends is commendable. Who are we, though, to stand in the way of love? It's a rare enough thing; one doesn't wish to crush it."

"Doesn't one?" she muttered.

"*True* love, born not of reason but of the most genuine and passionate affections?"

"Show me such a thing."

"Better to command that of your friend!" Ward McAllister said.

"*I* don't intend to speak of it to him at all, nor to Miss Whiting. They're hardly more than acquaintances of mine. It's their affair. I have far more worrisome matters to occupy me."

What Oliver decided to do with Sallie Whiting or any other lady was not a matter she wished to spend another moment thinking about. He had shown himself to be an inconstant friend to William. He had made her uncomfortable at her own table. The sooner he attached himself to someone else, the better (though how it was that *Sallie Whiting* appealed to him so well, she didn't know).

Yes. Good. She hoped Oliver Belmont would remove himself from her scene entirely and take up instead with Miss Whiting's set. Good riddance.

Ward McAllister was saying, "Indeed you do have other concerns, indeed you do. As to your question on whether my poor friend's suicide will do you in, I say that what you need—really, the only thing you need—is to get Mrs. Astor on your side. Much as we might wish it otherwise, she still wears the gate key on her belt."

"Oh, well, if that's all I need do," Alva said. "Why, I'll simply send her a note: *Dear Mrs. Astor, you have been badly mistaken in excluding the Vanderbilts from every event with which you are involved. Please do broadcast this fact to everyone you know.*"

He took Alva's hand and patted it. "You're overly excited right now. Go home, take some brandy, have a rest, and you'll see it's not an irremediable problem. A solution will take time and thought, but I have no doubt that we'll find a way to demonstrate that despite the unfortunate actions of C. J. Vanderbilt, the rest of the family truly deserve to be ranked among the top in this nation."

"I have been demonstrating this for seven years now. Does it never end?"

"Need you ask? Of course it doesn't—not even once you've made the summit. Even a monarchy can be toppled."

Uncle C.J.'s casket was being taken to the hearse. Alva saw William beckoning. It was time to go. She made her good-byes, then joined her husband for the ride to the cemetery.

As they went, she reflected to herself on how the unmentionable Uncle C.J.'s tale—his odd habits, his poor reputation, and his gruesome end—had been written up in meticulous detail, taking almost an entire page in the day's *Times*. Now everyone knew he'd been a dissolute gambler for much of his life, that he had twice been locked up in a sanatorium, that he had used his father's name to secure credit he would not repay. They knew that he and his loyal companion, Dr. George Terry, were living in rented rooms at the Glenham Hotel; that his epilepsy had turned him pitiable in recent years; that yes, Dr. Terry knew his friend kept a revolver but never had he imagined it might be used in this manner. Dr. Terry had in fact been in the next room when his friend put the gun to his temple.

What troubled Alva most, though, was this:

> Mr. Vanderbilt always carried a revolver not from any need but from habit. He was able to leave his bed but not for any length of time. He must have arisen while Dr. Terry was absent and taken it from his pistol pocket. It could hardly have been under his pillow, as Dr. Terry would have been apt to know it if that was the case.

The statement's wording slyly suggested indecency. No doubt it had been crafted to provoke whispered speculation in drawing rooms throughout the city. Alva could almost hear Caroline Astor saying to her gathered sycophants, *It's an abomination, is what it is. Those Vanderbilts . . .*

She could not prevent the speculation. Nor could she address it directly. But she would not allow her family—her children, especially—to be tarred with that brush.

She didn't need Caroline Astor *on* her side, she needed her *at* her side, in as public a manner as she could engineer.

Alva remembered an evening in Paris, when she, Armide, and their mother had attended one of Countess de Pourtalès's salons at her Champs-Élysées apartments. The countess was known for her beauty, her taste, and her political intelligence. Some of French society's most interesting people attended her salons. Advising another woman on some matter that was lost to Alva now, she'd said, "*On ne suit pas l'exemple, on le définit.*"

One does not follow the example, one sets it.

IV

JUST AS SHE had solved the problem of the opera box and aimed to reshape New York society's music scene, Alva now intended to reshape society itself—*faire de l'exemple*: she would throw the city's most lavish costume ball ever, in the city's best residence, in honor of a visit from the viscountess, Lady Mandeville, who (Alva was certain) would condescend to grace New York with her presence only because Mrs. William K. Vanderbilt was her most cherished friend. Together they would eclipse every social event ever before staged in this city. She would invite everyone of note, *everyone*—with but a single exception.

She did not bother William with the details; this morning she simply proposed a ball and gained his consent to host and pay. Nor did she at first reveal the exception in her plan to Ward McAllister after he arrived to confer. She gave only a broad sketch, then asked, "What do you think?"

"Do you suppose Lord Mandeville would wish to put himself on display as well?"

"I'd rather he be absent; we want to maintain a certain tone."

"Ah. Well, I think it a gorgeous idea! Really, quite wonderful. Nothing has ever been done on such a scale. How marvelous: a grand celebration of everything that's good, when what society's expecting is for you all to roll over and play dead."

. . .

From the time of their conversation, Ward called on Alva weekly to assist in planning the ball. Each time he sat with his notebook at the ready, his pencil held with both hands, pinched between forefingers and thumbs. To be decided: the date, which required a mapping out and consideration of every other society event of the late winter season. Since the Vanderbilts were again in the shadows, Ward was invaluable here; he received invitations to all the significant receptions, dinners, balls, recitals, performances, and bloodlettings, as well as to most of the insignificant ones. Furthermore, he knew each of the hostesses involved, and could calculate with impressive speed their relative rank and the importance of whatever it was they were hosting. Alva did not want her ball's date to abut anything that would already have society trilling, and could only hope that no one of note would be assassinated or succumb to sudden illness in the weeks before and after her chosen date, March 26.

"Right at the end of Lent," Ward said approvingly. "When everyone is starved for good food and something lively. *Jesus has arisen; wonderful, let's eat!* We'll herald springtime's arrival with a menu of unrivaled delicacies."

To be decided: the theme, which needed to accommodate both classic and seasonal elements and provoke the most creative and elaborate costuming. Ward said, "Guests must be encouraged to outdo one another with their choices and the manifestations of those choices. I will personally put every tailor and seamstress of quality on alert for the orders that will be coming in."

To be decided: the particulars of the guest list, which must comprise every fashionable person, and all the Knickerbockers who'd deigned to notice the Vanderbilts, and Mr. and Mrs. Oliver Belmont. Oliver had married Miss Whiting in December, after his parents had attempted to break them up by sending him off to Germany for immersion in the banking trade. He'd been so unsuited to the work that they pulled him home again and consented to the marriage—though gossips were saying that not all was well with the newlyweds, who were at present honeymooning in Paris with Sallie's two sisters and their mother. *Of course all was not well,* thought Alva; the fool had married Sallie Whiting.

Not on the guest list: anyone by the name of Astor.

"Ah, the strategy of exclusion," Ward said when she revealed her intention. "A particularly effective tool for society, I daresay. Though I am not confident it will work on my dear friend."

"We know she won't come if I simply invite her." Cautiously Alva added, "If she were to learn of the strategy, it wouldn't have even a chance—and frankly, such an indiscretion would end *our* friendship."

"Don't allow a single anxious thought to vex you! It is my own dearest hope to resolve this injustice and see my great friends in harmony together. You and I are as united on this as were Grant and Lincoln in the taking of Vicksburg."

In the end, there were twelve hundred names on that list, not the least of whom was the very same Ulysses Grant of Ward's analogy, now a former President and still her father-in-law's close friend. All that remained was to order the invitations and send them out.

Ward, meantime, would hand-select members of the press to preview the house ("decorated to the hilt!") and to attend the ball as Alva's particular guests. "We'll grant a few key men early access to everything, supply them with champagne and caviar and every detail about every detail. Leave this to me; I know just the men for the job."

Too, he would direct special dance practices for the youngest of the invitees, the colorful gay unmarried ladies so reminiscent of the ones who'd intimidated Alva at the Greenbrier almost a decade earlier.

Alva said, "All of this is very good. Here, though, is where the key to my success lies: As you know, Miss Carrie Astor, who dominates this set, is said to be determined to compel Mr. Orme Wilson to fall in love with her. You should encourage her to see this ball as the ideal event for that ideal event."

"Masterful! And being unaware that no invitation is forthcoming, she could also be persuaded to join the dance practices," Ward said. "Indeed, I could give her some leading roles in some rather intricate quadrilles so that she will be stricken with horror and disappointment and, I daresay, panic, if she's not permitted to attend the ball."

"I believe you have the devil in you, Mr. McAllister."

"Oh, not a bit! Creating order is what I'm doing. Creating order. Some would call that admirable."

Miss Carrie Astor would seek her mother's advice in acquiring a costume so flattering that Mr. Wilson could not fail to find her the most desirable young lady present. Alva predicted that when this occurred, her mother would reveal that Carrie would not be attending the ball because no Astor had been issued an invitation because Mrs. Astor had, these years, continued in her determination to receive no Vanderbilt. Carrie would beg her to see Alva and, because Mrs. Astor had lost her older daughter, Emily, in childbirth almost two years earlier, Mrs. Astor would not wish to deny this daughter anything.

The woman had to feel the sand sliding from beneath her feet before she would take a single step in the right direction.

As Ward reported at their next meeting, he had been taking luncheon with Caroline Astor when the expected conflict between daughter and mother occurred:

"I thought Miss Astor quite persuasive in her argument, yet my dear friend sent the poor girl away in anger and tears."

"And?"

"Nothing further," he said. "Miss Astor is distraught. Her mother claims to be unmoved. 'The matter is one of principle,' she said. 'Relax the standard once, and before long we will have no standards at all.' I remarked that this may not be an 'everything or nothing' proposition, but she was uninterested in that view."

"Then we've failed," Alva said, distressed. "If not even her daughter can move her—"

"Did the Union toss up its hands after Bull Run? No, it assuredly did not. Show some fortitude, my dear. Have some patience. Give Miss Astor time to wear her mother down."

"Patience has not been my most reliable virtue."

A few weeks after that conversation, shortly after the invitations had been engraved and addressed and delivered, Alva went out for the first of her costume fittings and then returned home to find a satisfying number of calling cards and notes and replies on the tray, including one from Mrs. Astor's own set. Even should this plan fail, perhaps over time there would be a groundswell of good sense great enough to overwash the doyenne, clearing the way for herself and others, too.

As she was standing in the entry hall, there came a knock at the door. She answered the knock herself, opening the door to a startled-looking footman. Resplendent in the distinctive blue livery of Astor employ, the man bowed and extended his hand to deliver a card, which read:

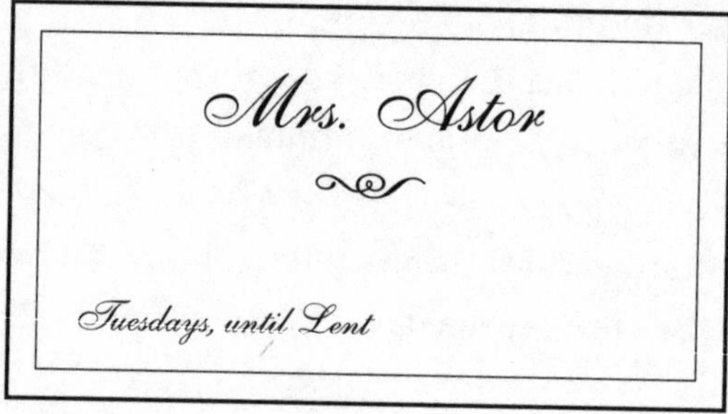

Handwritten on the back was *We would be pleased to see you.*

When the doorman turned away, Alva pressed the card to her breast, then tucked it into a pocket. Ward had been correct: their strategy was sound, they'd simply needed to wait.

At her desk shortly after, Alva took out an invitation to the ball and addressed it to Mr. and Mrs. William B. Astor and their daughters. Giving it over to her footman, she directed, "Eric, take this to 350 Fifth Avenue, first thing. That is, take it over first thing tomorrow."

How divinely sweet, the scent of success.

V

FLOWERS *EVERYWHERE*. A floral parade comprising Mr. Klunder (*le meilleur* of florists, Ward had declared) and his assistants, arms loaded with vases and urns the size of barrels, entering and leaving and entering and leaving . . . two entire days of disruption for this. Roses as big as Alva's face: the dark crimson Jacqueminot, the deep pink Gloire de Paris, the pale pink Baroness Rothschild, the King of Morocco, the Duchess of Kent, and "the new and beautiful Marie Louise Vassey," said Ward to the reporters, while leading the chosen few on a tour of the house the morning of the ball.

Then, too, came tiers of ferns, each as tall as four-year-old Willie, who was solemnly giving his nurse a tour in imitation of Ward. Palm fronds, sharp-edged and exotic, had been woven to make towering walls of green, and tucked into the green were cascades of pale orchids. The whole third-floor gymnasium was lined this way and strung with Japanese lanterns, and in the middle sat a huge potted palm tree draped in long, flowering vines of fuchsia. In each back corner was a sculpted marble fountain with its own hidden coal-fired pump. The room was done up then with dozens of small tables and café chairs—where, said Ward, his voice ringing through the house, "each and every guest will feast on the most remarkable menu of delicacies and wines, which it is my distinct pleasure to allow you to sample at the end of our tour." When he saw Alva next, he winked.

This third-floor gymnasium was where guests would dine. The banquet hall downstairs would become a ballroom, its massive oak furniture moved to the sides, calcium limelights installed around the room to take the place of the chandelier light—"Too bright!" the all-knowing Ward had declared about that chandelier. Last night Alva had watched the men run a test of the limelights, and the room had been transformed into a silvery fairyland. The stained glass had seemed to glow on its own power. Alva glowed, too.

Upstairs in her bedroom at ten o'clock, Mary and Caitlyn, Lady C's maid, were helping their ladies to dress. For Alva: the costume of a Venetian princess, drawn from a painting by Alexandre Cabanel, who, when Alva had entertained him in Paris the previous spring, said he'd just started a portrait of Shakespeare's Ophelia.

They'd discussed Ophelia's love for Hamlet, and her sad end: Ophelia, seduced and made pregnant by Hamlet, in love with him but put off by him, deranged with grief after her father's death, drowns herself.

Hamlet had toyed with Ophelia the same way supposedly upright, moral gentlemen did now with unsuspecting young ladies. Much had changed in the world since Shakespeare's day, but not how badly some men used girls, nor how too many girls walked straight into the wolf's den, singing.

"In Ophelia's place, I would have called him out and compelled him to do right," Alva had said, to which Monsieur Cabanel replied, "Ah, but with no tragedy, there would be no reason to paint her."

Mary helped Alva into the gown, with its square-cut neck and long, gold-tissue cape sleeves. The brocaded underskirt went from deepest orange to lightest canary, with highlights in white silk. Leaves and flowers were done in gold, white, and iridescent beads. A pale blue satin train was stitched with gold and lined in bloodred satin. Alva checked her reflection and smiled. "I am transformed! Though an Italian title means little, nowadays. They give them out like lollipops."

"I like lollipops," said Mary.

She pinned a jeweled cap onto Alva's hair. On the cap was a peacock brooch done in tiny multicolored gems, one of the replacements she'd bought after her mother's jewelry was stolen. The brooch cost more than a laborer would earn in ten years, and after tonight, it would get locked back in her safe, possibly never to be worn by her again—because once a lady had displayed such a piece, a second display would be considered common. Unless the piece were an heirloom; then she would be obliged to wear it frequently, which, if it was as vivid as this peacock, would be considered gauche.

Lady C. had commissioned a black velvet gown like the one worn by Marie Claire de Croÿ, Duchess of Havré, as painted by Van Dyck. With the gown, she wore a broad black hat that turned up at one side and was studded with colored gems. Three dyed-black ostrich plumes drooped in an arc from the hat to her shoulder.

Alva said, "Look at us: Dark and Light, the two sides of nature."

"Tragedy and Comedy," said her friend.

The sound of voices outside drew Alva to the window. Light from the lower windows streamed onto the street like gold, giving everything a cheerful glow.

"Come see this," she said, waving her friend over. "The sidewalks are packed full. Every stoop has got its own little gazing party."

The gazers were bundled up against the chill in overcoats and mufflers. A pack of children stood in the street at the curb, jostling one another and laughing—pickpockets, waiting to take advantage of the manifold distractions that would be created once the carriages began to arrive.

Alva put her face to the window and cupped her hands beside her eyes to see better. "What a crowd! Maybe I'll have the butler take them some wine."

"You will not," said Lady C., who hadn't come to the window. "Unless you mean to encourage them to storm the palace."

"It's a goodwill gesture," said Alva, turning to her friend. "An acknowledgment of their interest in culture and history."

"It's rubbing their noses in your superior fortune, is what it is."

Alva said, "What do *you* say, Mary?"

"Me?" Mary asked, with a glance at Lady C. "Well, some out there would love you, I expect, and some would hate you."

Lady C. smirked. "She speaks her mind."

"Well, I did ask her to. *Do* people hate me?" she asked Mary.

Lady C. said, "They despise you, Alva, and they despise me, and ever shall it be until we are all raised up as equals in the Kingdom of Heaven."

"You don't believe that for a moment."

"No, but a lot of *them* do. Anyway, none of that is relevant to your purposes tonight. Tonight you are the supreme hostess of New York, the lady who brought Mrs. Astor to heel."

"And you are my extraordinary guest of honor."

The two of them left the room, descending the staircase with graceful ease just as Alva had foreseen. They would receive their guests with William in the salon, standing beneath the portrait of Alva—apropos of Caroline Astor's tradition in her home, Ward had said. "Do this and your guests will associate your authority with hers."

"Stand beneath my own portrait? Is that necessary? I'm not attempting to be society's leader."

"You may not wish to lead, but society needs to be led. Oh, indeed, this is the manner in which you will effect the changes you desire. You mustn't pull your punches now, when you are so close to your goal."

"It's imitative. I don't wish to *be* Mrs. Astor."

Ward said, "Have I given you any bad counsel?"

"You have not."

A person might easily come to think that this ball, this house, Alva's efforts to improve culture and to beautify New York, were only about Alva wanting to elevate *herself*, with the Vanderbilt family getting the secondary benefits of her rise. One might conclude that she put personal ambition above all else in order to feed an insatiable vanity. *Well, let them,* she thought. An intelligent woman in this world takes her chances where she finds them.

The polished coaches were arriving, the costumed guests ascending her red-carpeted steps. Duchesses and dukes and princesses and princes. Marquises. Marquesses. Devils. Monks. A bumblebee. Bo-Peep. King Lear. An Old World maiden. A jester. A most ingenious lady costumed as Cat, with rows of white cats' tails made into an overskirt, and an actual cat's pelt—

head and all—fashioned into a hat. With each French or Italian princess, each cavalier, knight, or nobleman who was gazed upon by the curious people outdoors, each wonderfully outfitted guest who then turned his or her gaze upon the splendor to be found indoors, the status of the William K. Vanderbilts grew.

When the hosting trio was in place, the reception line proceeded into the oak-paneled salon, a room hung with the eighteenth-century French Gobelin tapestries. This was Alva's favorite space in the house. Cupid and Psyche frolicked on the ceiling above the host, hostess, and honored noblewoman who, overlooked by the Madrazo portrait of Alva that hung above the mantel, stood greeting the guests with warmth and pleasure undifferentiated as to whether the guest was "old New York" or new.

Which did not mean Alva noticed no difference; she was particularly amused by the obeisant curtsies and vivid smiles of some of the Knickerbocker ladies who a decade earlier would not have acknowledged Alva or any of the Vanderbilts or the former Consuelo Yznaga, even in passing. Mr. Yznaga was in trade, after all, and he was foreign—quite dark in comparison to their Dutch-descended husbands and their own Northern European complexions. Most of them wouldn't be able to find Cuba on a map, but here they were, fawning over the trio, feeling terribly important at being presented to Viscountess Mandeville, the future Duchess of Manchester.

And here was Ward, who had elected to be French Count de la Môle, the tragic lover of Marguerite de Valois, guillotined at age thirty-six for having loved not wisely, but too well. His costume was done in royal purple and scarlet stripes, with caped sleeves, pouffed pantaloons, a fur-lined feather-trimmed hat, a foil, a gold-tipped cane—and white chamois tights. How he must have struggled into those!

"Mr. McAllister," said Lady C., "how very dashing you are! Please tell me you've got a dance for me tonight."

Ward bowed deeply. "You honor me, madam."

"My evening would be incomplete if I didn't spend at least a portion of it with the most important gentleman here."

"What, him?" said William.

"Who else?" Lady C. replied.

And then came the Cornelius Vanderbilts, he clad in a white wig and bright gold brocade, she in matching bright gold, with pearl-trimmed collar and brilliant silver beading that caught the light. Alice had three of their five children in costume and corralled at her side.

Noting their presence behind him, Ward turned and said, "Good evening! A Renaissance couple, are you?"

Corneil bowed. "Not quite. Louis XVI at your service."

"Ah! Another Frenchman who, as with my Count de la Môle, ultimately lost his head. But you, my dear Mrs. Vanderbilt: you've stumped me. I haven't even a guess."

"She's Electric Light," said Corneil. "She consulted with Mr. Edison deliberately on the design. Hold up the globe," he said to Alice. She complied, showing off a gilded glass fixture attached to a handle.

"Would that he could actually light you up!" said Ward.

"Yes, well," said Corneil, "I did inquire, and Edison started going on about bulb filament instability and the difficulties of safe wiring and special containers for batteries and risk of shock or fire—"

"Say no more! I confess that I find electricity rather terrifying. A man I knew in Savannah, many years ago, was surveying his cotton fields from horseback and was struck by a bolt of lightning that came from an almost blue sky! Attempting to harness such a force, well . . ." He shook his head. "It seems unwise to me. But you, Mrs. Vanderbilt, are quite wonderful, and good for you, representing our technological future in such splendid Old World style!"

Corneil said, "She risks putting off my mother, who feels much the way you do."

"Ah, yes—that incident with the wirings! I heard all about it. Proving my point, don't you know."

With Mr. Edison's encouragement, the elder Vanderbilts' new house had been built with electrical wires inside it, along with special lighting bulbs and a steam-powered electricity-generating machine in the basement. The house was to be lighted with gas and electricity both. With electric lights being strung down by Union Square, the city's grandest citizen should have no less. Those wires were now a snarl of lines overhead, but people said, *That's progress happening before our very eyes!* Some were saying Mr. Edison was the lightning god. But when he had the Vanderbilts' system ready to demonstrate, some wires sparked in the art gallery and a curtain caught fire and that was the end: Mrs. Vanderbilt was having none of it. No wires, no boiler, no "lightning" inside her house; she would not risk her life or George's. Mr. Vanderbilt had said, "Then Morgan's going to outshine us with his new house going up on Madison." "Let him!" said his wife, as forceful as Alva had ever heard her. When the younger daughters' new homes were under way on Fifth Avenue, Mrs. Vanderbilt forbade electrification there as well.

Now Ward bent toward the children. "And don't you all look splendid as well!" The oldest boy, Bill, was dressed as an exotic-looking sailor—Turkish, perhaps, judging from his shoes. His brother Neily was a courtier. Gertrude, who was almost equal in height to Bill, was in pink tulle with a leafy green satin overdress and a white cap. "You must be Miss Vanderbilt," Ward said to her. She stared and made no reply.

Alice said, "My daughter is a rose."

"A rose indeed!" said Ward, drawing from her a slight smile.

She said, "I would rather be Sinbad, like Bill."

"Oh, that would never do! You're far too pretty." Sotto voce he added, "I wish *I* could have dressed as a rose." He obviously expected a smile of delight. Instead, he got a frown.

"Roses don't have adventures," said Gertrude.

"Ah. Quite right. Perhaps your brother will lend you his costume when he's done with it."

This brightened her. Then Alice said, "Mr. McAllister is joking. No young lady should dress as Sinbad." To Alva: "Where will we find Consuelo? I'll suppose she's dressed as a lovely little sparrow, or a shepherdess, perhaps."

"She and Willie are in the nursery with Lady Mandeville's children, all un-costumed," Alva said. "We hadn't even thought to put our children on display."

At ten-thirty, the traffic on Fifth Avenue was reportedly noseband to tailboard. Where Caroline Astor might be in the line was a mystery. Alva knew she wouldn't place herself among the first arrivals. Nor would she want to arrive so late as to miss her daughter (who'd arrived early with the other featured dancers) in the leadoff quadrille. That she might fail to come at all was an outcome Alva did not wish to consider.

Had her next guest stayed away, though, she would not have minded a bit: here was Oliver Belmont, entering the drawing room dressed in something vaguely Elizabethan. His bride and parents and brothers and their wives trailed him en masse.

"Mrs. Belmont," said Alva to the former Sallie Whiting, "what a pleasure to see you and your beloved here tonight. How splendid you look!" (Two lies.) "I'm certain you had wonderful exploits abroad. You'll have to tell me all about them later, after the quadrilles."

"You're quite splendid yourself," Sallie Belmont said with a smile so wide that Alva knew instantly it had been augmented in some way—Vin Mariani, perhaps; she had the classic glassy, giddy stare. Sallie Belmont moved along to Lady C., saying, "Oh, how much I've heard about *you*! My English friends are positively in wonder, and *so* envious that I get to meet you!" She curtsied unsteadily, then, correcting, curtsied again.

Oliver was next. William shook his hand. "Good to have you back, my friend. Running off to elope—couldn't wait to marry the little filly, eh?" He winked. "But now we can celebrate you properly."

Oliver's smile was tense. "Not at all necessary."

Alva said, "You remember Lady Mandeville."

"Yes, my memory's far sharper than my intellect, it seems. Lady Mandeville." He bowed. "You and Mrs. Vanderbilt have all the other ladies seething with envy tonight."

"We might add your wife to the list," said Lady C. "Not of seethers. Of enviable ladies."

"Oh, she seethes all right," Oliver said, and his brother nudged him. "But never mind that. Here, say hello to Perry!"

Alva watched him anxiously as the rest of the Belmonts came through. He was in obvious foul humor, not at all the amusing and happy fellow he'd been.

Not that she should concern herself with whether or not he was happy.

Still, she didn't wish for him to be unhappy, necessarily; she just wished him to be elsewhere.

Ward was again in the receiving line, this time with Caroline Astor on his arm. Alva put her thoughts of Oliver aside. *Here* was the matter of most importance, the culmination of more effort than Alva liked to recall. That one woman could have such outsize influence demonstrated all that was wrong with society, and how badly it needed reform.

When Ward and Mrs. Astor took their turn, William's face lit with his most charming smile. "Good evening, McAllister," William said as if they hadn't already greeted Ward once. "Mrs. Astor, aren't you the incarnation of beauty tonight."

"I told her precisely the same thing," said Ward. "Is her gown not the grandest, her gems not the brightest?"

"Indeed, both—but it's her great character that shines most."

Alva silently disagreed: Caroline Astor was draped in diamonds as though she were a fir tree done up in tinsel and candlelight for Christmas. Alva had never seen so many diamonds in one place. The display was in no way tasteful by old New York standards or by any standard, really, so one could only conclude the display was an element of her costume, whatever or whomever she meant to portray. Was there a mythical goddess of excess? A fabled Queen of the Extreme? Or, wait: the diamonds were meant to be stars. Caroline Astor was the Light of the Universe. In her own mind, if not everyone else's.

Mrs. Astor said, "Gentlemen, do go on."

William laughed, and gestured to the women. "You know my wife—"

"Mrs. Vanderbilt, yes, we had a good visit recently."

"We are so pleased to see you tonight," Alva said. The call to which Mrs. Astor referred had lasted perhaps ten minutes and took place while three other ladies were also present. She and Mrs. Astor had exchanged only the briefest pleasantries.

"May I present the viscountess, Lady Mandeville?"

"Lady Mandeville," said Caroline Astor, inclining her head.

"Thank you for coming. Mrs. Vanderbilt and I both are delighted that you accepted her invitation."

"Yes, truly delighted," said Alva, looking Caroline Astor in the eye. "Had you been unable to attend, tonight would've been a failure."

"So kind of you," Caroline Astor said. "Your costume is lovely. The Italians understood style." She glanced at the room around her. "Your home is lovely as well. Nothing quite like it in the city."

Ward, observing the exchange between his two friends, had let his mouth hang open. Now he closed it. "Oh, indeed. One of a kind. As are both of you. *All* of you," he amended. "You three. Sui generis."

After the receiving line was concluded, the guests assembled in the ballroom, while in the gallery above, the musicians began to play. All conversation ceased at the sight of the first group of eight dancers in the wide, arched doorway, done up as lords and ladies riding life-size hobbyhorses, each rider dressed in a red coat as if ready for the hunt. The horses had taken two months to construct. Covered in real horsehide, each one had big bright eyes and a horsehair mane and tail. An embroidered blanket hid the wearer's legs, while false legs that moved with the wearer's motion completed the illusion.

A whistle sounded and they galloped into the ballroom to an eruption of cheers.

Watching from the head of the room, Alva thought, *What a joyful scene. How intoxicating!* After tonight, all would be well. In this moment, certainly, one could not imagine otherwise.

"Ah, Mr. McAllister." Alva approached Ward in the corridor outside the gymnasium.

He swept off his hat and bowed. "My dear! Are you as pleased with this result as I am? My dinner companions could not stop praising your tastes and efforts."

Grinning, she pushed some stray hairs from her forehead and attempted to tuck them into her cap. "It's quite satisfying, I admit. Though I owe a good deal of my 'taste' to your guidance."

"You had the good judgment to be guided, so in fact it is all to your credit. Now, you must tell me: I saw you speaking with Mrs. Astor, and the two of you appeared positively passionate for each other. What did you speak of for all that time?"

They'd been on a settee in the hall outside the ballroom, with a view from there of the dancing. "Oh, so many things," Alva said. "This house, the various materials and furnishings I'd chosen, who I'd hired for the windows. The children. We spoke of her daughter's performance in the quadrille, and the likelihood of a wedding to Mr. Wilson next spring. All the sorts of matters ladies discuss with one another."

"Very good, very good! Just as it should be. Just as we hoped. Everyone here will have taken notice, and tomorrow they'll all be remarking on how Mrs. Astor has embraced the Vanderbilts. In fact, when I spot one of the newspaper fellows, I'll remark on this very thing."

Though Caroline Astor had been performing (as Alva was) for the benefit of their observers, Alva could not accuse her of insincerity or of a grudging attitude: she was attending; therefore she was attending wholeheartedly, with every confidence in the correctness of her behavior. As they'd conversed, however, she became surprisingly candid. "Leading society is a heavy yoke," she said. "A burden, at times. One does wish to sometimes share the weight."

Alva kissed Ward's cheek. "You are indispensable—and quite rakish in that getup, I might add. Thank you for all you've done. I think the only thing that could make me happier than I am right now is to be able to take off these shoes."

"You can go *sans souliers* all day tomorrow and no one the wiser," he said.

"Just now I've promised my husband a dance and haven't yet made good. Go, enjoy more of that excellent wine. Let's have luncheon together on Thursday and you can tell me all the gossip you've heard tonight."

She left Ward and went for the stairway. As she descended, Oliver Belmont came up the stairs. There was no avoiding him now.

"Alva, I'd hoped to find you," he said, meeting her at the landing.

"Are you having a good evening?"

"Dreadful," he said, swaying a little as he spoke. "One of the worst."

"You're serious? I hardly know what to say."

"Oh, do not mistake me. This ball is a tremendous success—the entire production is unrivaled in this country. In most countries, I'd wager. The food, flowers, musicians . . ." He gestured broadly, waving his arm. "And your Astor coup is all anyone can talk about tonight. There is not a wrong note in the entire composition."

"Are you ill, then?"

He put his hand on her shoulder, leaned close, and said, "I am. Sick with regret."

She stepped from his grasp, saying, "I'm sorry to hear it."

"My wife hates me." He clasped his hands behind him. "She claims I'm a brute."

"Are you a brute?"

"Possibly. I *was* provoked, but that doesn't excuse the way I raved at her and her mother."

Alva was no counselor, especially not for this man and this marriage. Eager to escape him, she said as brightly as she could manage, "Don't despair. The two of you are only getting started. It takes time to adjust to married life. Whatever's troubling you can be resolved."

"Can it? Sallie's a selfish harridan who never really wanted anything to do with me beyond my money. And I am a cold, uncaring, faithless dog because I married her knowing I'd never give her true affection."

Here came William up the stairs, calling, "I'm coming to claim my dance." At the landing, he said, "My word, Belmont, look at you—one would think you were bound for the gallows."

Alva said, "Oliver and his wife are at odds."

"Eh? So the rumors are true?"

"Everyone in my family was against the marriage," Oliver told them. "Now my father seems to almost take pleasure in reminding me that I'm rash, impulsive, and unreliable. He heard—as have others, it seems"—he nodded toward William—"that I'd taken a lover while on my honeymoon. When in fact all I took was a meander through Spain without my wife and her entourage—though with a good amount of absinthe."

"You appear well greased tonight, too," said William. He clapped Oliver on the back. "Come dance! It won't cure the disease, but you'll feel better."

"I can think of hardly anything less compatible with my mood."

William, glancing at Alva, said, "As you like. Do send my wife down before long, though. The court must have its queen." He left them, skipping down the stairs like the eager boy he had always been.

Oliver watched him, saying, "He's got all the luck, hasn't he?" He turned to Alva. "It's my wife who's found a new intimate. And now I'm told that I'm to be a father. Or I should say that my wife is with child, the two not necessarily being alike."

She could not remain unmoved. "Oh, Oliver, I am so sorry for you."

"But I've made my bed—that's what you aren't saying, though you'd be correct in the assertion. I agree with it myself."

He put a finger to his lips as if in thought—and then he put the same finger to Alva's lips, startling her severely.

"Don't—"

"Forgive me," he said. "Though I'm not sorry for the action, only the offense. Had I only been a little older, I might have been at the Greenbrier the summer that Vanderbilt proposed marriage to you. I might have had a chance of my own—would I have? Tell me the truth."

She could not look at him. "I wish only the best for you, you know that."

"I do."

"It will get better. You'll see. You two can settle in, start fresh." She moved for the stairs. "You and William can ride out sometime soon. He'll have you to Idle Hour. There's plenty for you to look forward to. Do try to enjoy the rest of the evening."

She left him on the landing. What else was there for it? He was a good man but a lost one, too. He *had* made his bed. And she had made hers—made it here inside this wonderland of music and gaiety where the seemingly impossible had finally come to pass. She could not permit herself even a moment of regret.

VI

A MAN STANDS behind Alva, so close that she can feel his body's heat on her bare neck and shoulders. His mouth is next to her ear, his breath hot against it. Surrounding the two of them are princesses and kings and knights and courtesans and court dandies and an array of dancers costumed as horses. "Alva," the man says. His lips brush her ear, sending a thrill through her body, making her catch her breath. He puts his arm around her waist and turns her to face him, pulls up her skirt and pushes his hand between her thighs.

"Alva, I want—"

"Stop," she says, pushing his hand away. Her mother will beat her if she catches them at this. But oh, how marvelous it would be—

"Breakfast has arrived, and a special treat, too."

Mary. Daylight. A dream.

Alva pulled the covers over her head. "I'm not well. Come back later."

"Oh. All right. Do you need a powder for pain? Should I send for the doctor? You ought to have some coffee, at least."

Would the girl never stop talking? "Never mind," Alva said, pushing the covers back. The dream was dissipating, as irretrievable for now as the minnows her son chased in the surf. Try again another day—that's what she always told Willie when the time came for putting up the nets and buckets and trundling back to the house. There would not be another day for her and the man in the dream, though. Besides, what was there to be gained from dreaming of such things? Nothing. Her mind betrayed her in her sleep. Perhaps she should stop sleeping.

Mary had a stack of newspapers, along with coffee, toast, and jam—though by the sun's position, it was past midday. "I hope you don't mind me having read the *Times*," Mary said, setting the tray over Alva's lap. "I was curious to see what they'd say."

She had folded the paper to display the headline:

MRS. W. K. VANDERBILT'S GREAT FANCY DRESS BALL.

A BRILLIANT SCENE OF BRIGHT AND RICH COSTUMES,
PROFUSE DECORATIONS OF FLOWERS,
AND SOME UNIQUE DANCES.

"*My* name in the headline?" Alva said. Hers, not William's. She'd accomplished more than she had expected.

"They gave you four whole columns."

"Four! Unbelievable." She would fix her mind on this, and good riddance to the dream. "Find Lady Mandeville and have her join me. If she's still sleeping, wake her."

Mary left, and while Alva waited, her thoughts (fickle mind, not at all disciplined) gravitated to Oliver, the sensation of his warm hand on her bare shoulder, the words he'd said, the way he'd put his finger to his lips and then to hers. So wonderful. So terrible.

I am unimpeachable.

But what if she hadn't been? What if she had responded to him favorably, whatever that might have entailed?

"Lady Mandeville isn't in her room," Mary announced, returning, "and I can't find her elsewhere."

"Can't find her? She has to be here someplace. She's probably with the children."

"No, ma'am. The governess has got them all in the schoolroom making drawings."

"Little Kim, too?"

"Yes. Her ladyship must have gone out."

"Unaccountable," Alva said. "Did she make a luncheon date with someone last night?"

"I wouldn't know."

"Is her maid here?"

"She says she was asleep before the ball's end, so Her Ladyship didn't share any plans with her."

"I suppose she dressed herself."

"I guess she must have."

"Well, I've no intention of dressing anytime soon. Come back when you've located our lady—and make sure you send her in."

While Alva waited, she read with pleasure—

> The Vanderbilt ball has agitated New York society more than any social event that has occurred here in many years. Since the announcement that it would take place, which was made about a week before the beginning of Lent, scarcely anything else has been talked about. It has been on every tongue and a fixed idea in every head. It has disturbed the sleep and occupied the waking hours of social butterflies, both male and female, for over six weeks, and has even, perhaps, interfered to some extent with that rigid observance of Lenten devotions which the Church exacts. Amid the rush and excitement of business we have found their minds haunted by uncontrollable thoughts as to whether they should appear as Robert le Diable, Cardinal Richelieu, Otto the barbarian . . .

There was a knock on Alva's door and Lady C. appeared, looking only a little less disheveled than Alva felt. Disheveled but beautiful. What a gift she'd been given—that deep golden hair, that sunset complexion, those deceptive wide eyes. She could hardly fail to look lovely even when at her worst.

"Come in!" Alva said. "I thought you'd wandered off into the park or left with one of the coachmen. Have you eaten? I'll send for more coffee—"

"Nothing for me. Too much wine. Not feeling quite myself this morning."

"Afternoon," Alva corrected her. Holding up the newspaper, she said,

"We've triumphed. The *Times*—look at this, practically an entire page of details. Ward McAllister may be a silly rooster of a man sometimes, but I do adore him. No one else could have helped to execute my plan so well."

"Mmm," said her friend, and went to the glass for a close look at herself.

"Wasn't Richard wonderful as the artist Cimabue? For all that he loves Paris, I suspect he may be a Florentine at heart."

"You should have married him."

"He's too old for me, and he has a wife."

"But you do love him."

"Are you on this tack again? I do love him, but not in a passionate manner."

"Who *are* you passionate over?" Lady C. said, looking at Alva in the glass. "Is there someone—"

"Please, you know there is not. You can't imagine I would risk everything I've accomplished to indulge a whim."

"Suppose you could do it without risk?"

"I *have* my riskless passion; it's not a *who*, it's a *what*, and that *what* is architecture."

"Ah, yes: Alva Vanderbilt, ever wrapped in the stony embrace of her petit château."

"Happily so."

Returning to the paper, Alva said, "Alice thinks herself so clever. Electric Light. Who dresses as an *invention*?"

"It was creative, give her that. She said she and Corneil see a lot of Mr. Edison. They intend to have their house electrified."

"William has been speaking of it as well; can't allow Corneil to best him that way," Alva told her. "Don't you think bringing the children was poor form? Alice desired an excuse to show them off *and* an excuse to leave early."

She read on. "Look: I'm described as having 'irreproachable taste,'" she said. "Oh, and there's this: 'over the chimney-piece hangs a superb portrait of Mrs. Vanderbilt by Madrazo, full of spirit, character, and grace.' That's flattering. And I rather agree."

"A bit prideful, are we?"

"Haven't I earned my pride?"

"You have." Lady C. turned to face Alva and pointed to the paper. "I can only begin to imagine how our new friend Caroline is appreciating all of this attention to detail."

"I don't think she'll begrudge me. She's had her turn. She said as much herself."

"Cobras dance before our eyes, hypnotizing us so that we're not watching for the strike."

"You are clearly suffering from a surfeit of imagination," Alva told her.

Reading on, she said, "Listen to this: 'Nothing could have been more becoming to Lady Mandeville's blond beauty than her magnificent and somber gown.' "

Lady C. was still at the dressing table, examining each angle of her face. "They've got me just right: 'magnificent and somber.' "

"Have I ever seen you actually somber?"

"Doubtful. It's bad for the complexion."

"You must have your moments, though."

"Oh, I can be absolutely black at times. Ask Mandeville."

"He gives you reason to be unhappy," said Alva.

"I'm no saint."

Alva would not call herself a saint, either. The money her husband had spent to put on last night's ball, for example, might have been put to charity had she gone to him with some proposal for that instead. Yet how extensive was her obligation to less fortunate others? Certainly her family should not need to give away *all* their money.

More to the point was the dream she was having before Mary woke her, her desire for the man in the dream, for the way he had touched her, the way she had felt. Now *here* was a question of morality—

"What is it?" said Lady C., catching Alva's eye. "Spit it out. You're no good with secrets."

Alva felt herself flush. "How can you be so certain?" she said lightly. "I might be so accomplished at them that even you can't tell."

Lady C. stood up. "Good. Keep your secrets. I'm actually dying for coffee. And a bath. And I expect the twins will be looking for me. Enjoy your triumph. You deserve it."

Only after her friend had gone and Alva was wiping the ink off her hands did she realize Lady C. hadn't said where she had been when Mary went looking for her. *I'm no saint*, she'd said. Alva had been joking about the coachman, but perhaps Lady C. *had* taken a lover. Perhaps, Alva thought, she should have looked for straw in her friend's hair.

⁂

Mrs. W. K. Vanderbilt's Great Fancy Dress Ball got written up in papers from New York to Cleveland to Chicago to San Francisco and in little towns in between. In addition to the many enthusiastic notes Alva received from attendees afterward, letters posted from all across the country began arriving as well.

—You are a fine lady of good imagination. Congratulations to you and God bless.

—Thank you for giving us this tale of wonder to lift our low spirits, as spring is late here in Illinois and we are wondering if the crops will go in at all.

—I agree with the editor that such expenditure on frivolities is immoral when so many are going hungry. You should be ashamed!

—I am a girl of fourteen years and have dreamed of moving to New York my whole life. Please send fare and I will indenture myself to you for two years if this is agreeable.

—Your dress sounds like a sweet creation and I'll bet you looked like a pare of ripe peaches. I want to put my tung all over them.

—I have recently married a man of wealth and we are going to model our ball after yours. I live in New York some of the year. We will invite you to our ball.

A note arrived marked CONFIDENTIAL and unsigned. With it was a posy of gardenias for which the sender must have paid a small fortune, having to procure them either from a hothouse or an importer. Gardenias. She could not miss the connotation.

My dear friend, I seek only one thing: your forgiveness. My intention was never to give offense. I have only the highest regard for you. Indeed, I feel it fair to name it love. Your response was appropriate and correct. I won't trouble you again with such sentiments, until and unless the Fates permit yours to match my own. In racing, such an unlikely occurrence is called "a long shot" and the bookmakers give it low odds. Those are the bets that pay the greatest return, however. Am I a gambling man? Perhaps. In all events, I trust that you will treat my regard as the highest measure of respect. I hope to keep your respect as well. You will remain dearest in my heart, and I remain yours, sincerely.

Oliver Belmont loved her.

She burst into tears.

When she had recovered herself, she began to frame in her mind a gracious but firm response. Not at all the response she wanted to give. Not the response of her heart. There was no help for it, though. None.

As she went to her desk, Mary came in with a piece of pale blue fabric draped over her arm. "I want to have your opinion of this before I go further," she said. "Are you all right? You look like you've been crying."

Alva gestured for her to come over. "It was a coughing fit. Let's see it."

"It's for the bodice of Miss Consuelo's yellow dress. I thought she might like it done this way for Easter."

Alva took the embroidered fabric and straightened it over her lap. Mary had done an array of daffodil-and-violet sprays, with the tiniest knots for baby's breath.

"This is wonderful," Alva told her.

"I thought I'd do leaves for a border here, where the waist will be. And a little yellow bird at the breast."

"She'll adore it."

"I hope she will. It was Louise, Mrs. Belmont's maid, who gave me the idea for the bird. We got to talking while the ball was going on. That's all there is to do, you know. Chatter. About how it is to work for a lady or a family, or how it is with the other servants. She had a lot to say about Mr. and Mrs. Belmont. You know I'm not one to gossip, but . . ."

Alva said, "But?"

"But, well, Louise, she traveled with Mr. and Mrs. Belmont for their honeymoon, and she said—well, I'll just tell it how she told it: Mr. Belmont was resentful of how Mrs. Whiting and the sisters were always carping or demanding things. And Mrs. Belmont kept insisting that her husband let them buy every single thing they desired at Le Bon Marché and the Bazar de l'Hôtel de Ville and Worth and Doucet. All those places."

"I could tell right away she was a frivolous type."

"And Louise says that after the wedding night Mrs. Belmont wouldn't even let Mr. Belmont near her. That's how he's so certain the baby can't be his. And his wife says she is so insulted by him accusing her that she can never spend another night in his house. So that's it. She's back home with her mama and he's suing on account of desertion."

"They're *divorcing*?"

Mary nodded. "I wondered if you knew it or not."

"I knew there was conflict. He didn't say it had gone that far."

"They only came to the ball so as to keep the whole thing quiet, as Mrs. Belmont—that is, Mr. Oliver's mother—hopes he won't go through with it. Still, the Belmont brothers aren't speaking to the Whitings, and seeing as Miss Carrie Astor is Miss Whiting's—that is, Sallie Belmont's—close friend, none of the Astors are speaking to any of the Belmonts." She took the fabric back from Alva, adding, "I thought that with Mr. Oliver being such a good friend to you and Mr. William, you should know what the facts are, before the story gets twisted who knows how many ways."

"As such stories often do."

"It's too bad, isn't it? I like Mr. Oliver."

"It is too bad."

When Alva was alone again, she had a moment in which her mind attempted to lose itself thinking, *If he's going to be free soon, might we . . .* until she stopped it cold.

No. She respected her husband, and she respected herself.

She and Oliver could be friends, nothing more. He was, of course, free to admire her in whatever measure suited him; she couldn't control such a thing—the heart will want what it will want.

One did not have to give in to unwise desires.

She wrote her reply.

My friend, you gave no offense. I am so honored by your regard, and under different circumstances might return it. That is not, however, the path my life has taken. I don't want to presume your ultimate intention, but in case this needs said: no matter your situation, my sentiments cannot change. Much as I may wish to indulge your regard, there is no scenario in which I can rightly do so; my gains over these many years are much too hard-won to sacrifice. Unlike you, I've had to battle for my place, and would lose everything if I failed to hold the line.

Reading this over, she wondered if it was firm enough. She did not wish to give him any room for hope. She was being honest is all, and "Honesty is the first chapter in the book of wisdom" according to President Jefferson. He had been wise about so many things; it could not be wrong to emulate him.

After dispatching her note to Oliver, Alva refolded his and put it, along with one of the fragrant gardenias, inside a book that she then placed high on her shelf, out of easy reach.

William came to her room that night. There in the dark, both of them were silent as he lifted her nightdress the way he always did, and climbed atop her in his usual manner. As she'd long accustomed herself to doing, she kept her head turned away, eyes open. While William moved against her, she thought of Lady C.'s remarks about taking a lover. She thought of Sallie Belmont having done so. This act, which for her was so demeaning and unpleasant, must be different for those who felt passion for each other, or why would any woman pursue it?

William finished, but didn't climb off her right away. He lay against her, not moving, not speaking. Alva, too, did not move. If not for being able to feel and hear him breathing, she would have thought he'd expired.

Finally he lifted himself off. She waited while he righted his clothing—a moment's task, usually. Tonight he took his time. Sensing he wanted to say something, she waited for him to speak. After another moment, though, he moved away from the bed and then left the room, having said not a word since he'd arrived.

This act was repeated three times over the following week, until finally Alva had to ask: "Do you have something on your mind?"

She put her nightdress back in place and sat up in bed, though the room was still dark.

William said, "Oh. Yes, well, I wanted to say thank you. For what you did, getting the Astor ladies here. The ball. All of that."

"Oh."

"You're being celebrated widely. The wives—they're all telling their husbands how much they admire you."

"That's lovely," she said.

"Isn't it. Well. Good night, then."

"Good night."

How nice of him to tell her this. How funny that he'd needed so long to do it. What a strange and unnatural thing marriage was. Though theirs did appear to be improving.

William's increased interest in her continued throughout the summer and into the fall. Thus she wasn't surprised when, in December, her monthly failed to arrive. In fact she was surprised conception had taken this long. The fact that she'd turned thirty the previous January might account for the delay, or so the doctor said when confirming her condition. "You are getting old," he added, delivering the insult almost with pleasure; apparently he had still not forgotten the trouble she'd given him during Consuelo's delivery.

On New Year's Day Alva wrote to Lady C.:

From the ashes arises the phoenix, so the story goes. I'm not only recast as society's most popular lady, I've also been given the blessing of expecting a new baby, who's supposed to arrive next July. After I gave William the news, he bought me a Russian sable coat. I wore it today when I called on Caroline Astor—a perhaps-unsubtle reminder that her husband's family money originally derived from the fur trade.

I've been reading in the papers about your Sir Francis Galton, the scientist who advocates purposeful breeding. Not one of us is inherently better than the next person, I don't care what Galton supposes is true. I might as easily have ended up being the fur puller as one who wears the fur.

VII

NEARLY TWO YEARS had passed when Alva found herself in Alice's rose-colored salon at 1 West Fifty-seventh Street trying to bear up under an unthinkable loss. Two days earlier Mr. Vanderbilt had, without warning, pitched forward out of an armchair in his own salon and was dead when he hit the floor. How stable her life had seemed in those intervening years. But stability was an illusion. Comforting. False.

Alva hated this salon. The room was so overdone with French panels and furniture and fabrics and rugs that it was as if Louis XVI himself were expected to arrive and stay awhile—which she supposed was exactly the point. What did any of it matter when death might at any moment come snatch away a beloved father or, God forbid, a child? Her new baby, Harold, her sunshiny little boy—he was as vulnerable as any. Willie. Consuelo. How contented she'd felt not long before, watching them play in the autumn sunshine, Willie "teaching" Harold how to sail their tethered skiff while Consuelo sat in the bow with a book in her lap, having been dubbed the queen—though she had protested the title. Willie said, "Who do you want to be, then?" and Consuelo replied, "A poet." "How about the poet queen?" Consuelo, thoughtful, considered it and replied, "All right, that sounds worthwhile." An idyllic day. By all accounts, the day Mr. Vanderbilt died had been idyllic for him—right up until the moment his heart seized and quit. It made no difference how good a person was. Nothing could be counted on to stay.

Alva, seated near Alice on a stiff brocaded settee, said, "I don't know how I am going to get over this. He was such a lovely man."

"You'll see him again in heaven, God willing."

"I'm no more comforted by that sentiment than Mrs. Vanderbilt was when you tried it on her the other night."

Mrs. Vanderbilt was currently upstairs in a guest bedroom with Florence and Lila, still shocked and inconsolable. Her husband had been portly, yes, and he hadn't taken to the new craze of walking for health. (One perspired so much in the doing of it, and then there was the problem of having a sufficiently comfortable shoe.) Still, he was just sixty-four years old and had given no sign of illness. Mrs. Vanderbilt had been robbed of her dearest companion, and no amount of "God's will" assurances had yet persuaded or comforted her.

Alice said, "I'm certain it's merely a matter of time."

The two of them and their daughters were waiting for the Vanderbilt men, young and less young, to finish conferring with the attorneys who were presenting Mr. Vanderbilt's last will and testament. Alva imagined the group—William and Corneil and Frederick and George and Corneil's son Bill (now fifteen)—as a somber-faced, dark-suited circle ringing the ever-faithful Chauncey Depew, each of them grieving, yes, yet also contemplating this turn in their literal fortunes. *How much? In what form? Get to the point.*

On the far side of the salon, Consuelo and Gertrude sat at a table practicing German conversation. At eight and ten years old, the pair were much alike in size and form, both of them willowy, dark-haired, pert-nosed, long-necked, well-dressed girls of best society. Consuelo was prettier, doe-like. Gertrude was more of a hawk—a beautiful bird, the hawk, but with a sharpness to it, a watchfulness, ever on the lookout for prey. Also, Gertrude had excellent posture, while Alva's daughter sat sloped, curved, almost folded into herself.

"Consuelo," said Alva, "sit up straight. You'll turn into a camel."

Alice asked, "How are you getting on with your new governess?"

"She's a fine person," Alva said, "but I've discovered she knows almost nothing of German history. What use is it for the girls to know the language if all that's being discussed is how to make a strudel? They should learn about the culture. This new German empire may figure prominently in their futures." She gestured toward the girls.

"Oh, I hardly think so; I don't intend to marry Gertrude to a foreigner."

"No? Then you're limiting her options severely."

"You would send your daughter so far away?"

"I intend for Consuelo to make the best marriage she can. Unlike you and me, our girls have the whole world as their stage."

"I made an excellent marriage. Are you intimating that you feel you did not? I grant you, William is not as industrious as he might be—"

"And Corneil never seems to enjoy himself. It seems both of them could improve their habits."

"Why, he enjoys all sorts of things. He's a vestryman, and he serves on the YMCA board and numerous other boards. His directorship at the American Museum of Natural History keeps him well occupied, as does the Botanical Society and the Metropolitan Museum of Art and—"

"My word," Alva said, "he works every moment he's not sleeping! I wonder does he sleep at all."

"Helping others gives him pleasure," Alice said primly.

"Well, good for him, then."

"I believe it is good for him. His habits should serve him better than Mr. Vanderbilt's did, God rest his soul—"

"Mr. Vanderbilt enjoyed himself, as he should have."

"He earned his leisure, of course," Alice said. "But he might have been better to abstain from—well, this will sound ungenerous, but . . . gluttony."

Alice lowered her voice and went on, "In any event, what's done is done. Now we all must manage the outcome."

"Yes, the outcome. How much does Corneil expect to inherit?"

"That's the least of his concerns!"

"Do you really think so?"

"He certainly hasn't spoken of it to me."

"No, I don't suppose he would have. You have plenty to think of as it is," Alva said.

Alice's household now included four vigorous sons along with Gertrude. And certainly Corneil was no more of a director in his children's lives than William was in his own; they were far too busy with their other employments. In this, at least, the brothers were alike.

Alice said, "I am well occupied, yes. There is always room for more joy, though, even in sad times such as this. I may as well tell you now: I've just learned I am expecting again, after all this time."

"Again! And you'd thought little Reggie was your last. My. The two of you do take the rules to heart, don't you?"

"The rules?"

Alva quoted, "'And you, be ye fruitful, and multiply.'"

"Oh. Well, yes," said Alice, "we do. 'Children are a heritage from the Lord, and the fruit of the womb is His reward.' That's in Psalms," she informed Alva. "What better service is there than to receive His blessing and rejoice in it?"

Alva was fascinated. Was that what Alice—and Corneil—believed they were doing each time he came to her in bed? Serving God Himself? Was it an every-Sunday endeavor? When Corneil was striving above her, was Alice lying there feeling virtuous? Did she encourage him? Did she enjoy his actions? Might it feel . . . good?

Suppose Alva asked her straight out: *Do you enjoy the marital act?* Suppose she asked, *Is my impiety the reason I don't?* Only three children in ten years of marriage. Alva was not doing her full Christian duty. She was evidently not serving her husband and therefore she was not serving the Lord, so what other conclusion could be drawn except to say she was serving herself? Better to spare herself that judgment.

She said, "I wonder if one day your sons—whatever number you end up with—will sit at Corneil's deathbed resenting each other because the money had to be divided into so many portions."

Alice frowned at her. "What a strange way you have of seeing things! You might offer congratulations."

"I'm very pleased for you. But don't you think that's what's going on in there right now?" She pointed to the closed door. "Not that any one of them is going to come away like Uncle C.J. did. But it's human nature, you know—for the male of the species especially—to want to get the most, to come out on top."

"Corneil isn't like that."

"Come now. This house exists on this spot because he had to have the most prominent position on Fifth Avenue that he could get."

"Mrs. Jones's house is in a more prominent spot." She gestured toward the northwest corner of Fifty-eighth.

"Mrs. Jones's house wasn't available to wreck. Mrs. Jones's house is a good bit smaller and nowhere near as opulent. She rents out her extra apartments, and has not, to my knowledge, complained that her house isn't large enough."

Without realizing it, Alva had raised her voice. The girls were watching them. Alice smiled serenely and said, "Please don't upset yourself about this. You have nothing to be ashamed of with your house down on Fifty-second."

Gertrude said, "Yes, Aunt Alva, your house is perfectly lovely. I like it very much."

"Why are the men taking so long?" said Consuelo. "I'm hungry."

"And why aren't *we* permitted to be in there?" asked Gertrude. "Why is it that men control all the money?"

"Why indeed?" Alva said. "Though it's not all, always. I expect your grandfather will have bequeathed a good deal to his daughters."

"Then why aren't they also in there?"

Alice said, "Gertrude, there are ways things are done—"

"The men are the ones who manage everything," Gertrude said. "And the boys will be able to work with Father, but I won't, not even if I really, really wish to and would be good at it. It isn't fair."

Alice said, "We have our work, too; it's different, that's all, more suited to our feminine sensibilities. Gertrude, I'd like you to recite that Goethe poem from this week's lesson. Stand up."

Gertrude, scowling, stood and recited the poem in German. Alice said, "Very nice. Now, Consuelo, you give it in English."

Consuelo looked at her mother, unsure what to do. Alva said, "Go ahead."

Her daughter remained seated. "I don't remember all of it," she said softly.

"No?" said Alva. "You translated it last week."

"It was written down."

Gertrude took Consuelo by the hand and said, "Let's go up to my bedroom and practice, shall we?"

"Do that," Alva announced before Alice had time to voice the protest she was about to make. "Go on. We'll send up for you when the men are finished, and then we'll all eat together."

When the girls were out of the room, Alva said, "I hope you have an easy delivery and a healthy, good-natured child, son or daughter, who is untroubled by whatever the results of this conference may be."

And then they waited for the men to reemerge, pretending to be occupied with their books. But Alva didn't believe for a moment that Alice was able to concentrate any better than she. The words on the page before her were rows of meaningless marks. In her mind were meaningless figures as well. She'd done calculations eight years earlier, when the figure was smaller than would now be the case, and those results had been hard to fathom. They could only be more so now.

The library's door swung open. First through the doorway was George. His cheeks and ears and neck were red. He strode past the women without remark, pursued by his brothers, who called after him not to go. A moment later, the huge front door slammed closed.

As the others emerged, Alva got up and went to her husband, saying, "What in the world—?"

William shook his head. "He's offended."

"Your father couldn't possibly have cut him out."

"No, not at all. He did quite well. About ten million. Same as Fred. And the girls."

She noticed he didn't name himself or Corneil.

William explained that George had expected the amounts to be equal—for the men, at least. Furthermore, the girls each inherited the new houses that had been built for them. Fred had already been given the old house at 459 Fifth. Mrs. Vanderbilt would keep the new one. Which left George with four hundred mostly undeveloped acres on Staten Island, where he had no desire to live. George got an ancient cemetery and an old house that had been given over to his great-grandmother until her death, a house that none of them much wanted, except for the sentimental value of it. He got an unfinished mausoleum. He got a farm.

William said, "George wanted to know why he didn't merit a Fifth Avenue house. 'Why've I been stuck with the farm?' he said. We reminded him that he's been keen on the farm operations, and that Father hadn't meant to die"—William's voice thickened, and he cleared his throat—"and so, you know, he might have gotten a house later, and the will isn't reflective of what it might've been had it been more recently done. Corneil pointed out that George seemed content to live at home. And that the house will be his when Mother's gone." William stopped and took a deep breath. Then, checking that the others couldn't hear him, he said, "Anyway, truth told, I'm a little disappointed that Bill was singled out for a million while neither of our boys got even a cent."

Luncheon was a quiet affair. Alva observed her brothers- and sisters-in-law. Every one of them was suffering the loss of a dear man, an excellent father who'd loved them actively. Their affection and grief was plain on their faces. Along with that, however, was this: every one of them was now a multimillionaire in his or her own right. Personal wealth was nothing new for Corneil and William, but for the other five at the table—and for the girls especially—their lives had taken a profound turn. Alva didn't yet know that William's had, too.

Later that evening, in the privacy of their home's salon, William put his feet up and leaned his head back, looking up at the whimsical figures in the fresco overhead. "Father valued you a great deal, you know. Truth told, I believe he thought more of *me* because of you."

"That's flattering," she said. "But I know he appreciated you for yourself."

"At any rate, Corneil hasn't said a word against him, but I suspect he's as surprised as I am at the way Father structured his will. I don't know . . . perhaps you didn't influence this at all, but, given how Corneil has made the business his life's work while I have been—shall we say—less devoted, I really don't see any other reason I've come out so well."

"And how well is that?" Alva asked. Her expectation was that Mr. Vanderbilt had settled perhaps twenty million dollars on William. More than the others received, less than Corneil's share. Given Corneil's responsibilities, this would be just.

William said, "You are ever direct, aren't you?"

"Would you say the same thing to a man?"

"Of course not. In a man, directness is a good trait."

"Then pretend I hinted at the question coyly."

This made him smile. "All right. The remainder of Father's estate beyond what went to Fred and the girls and George—and a good amount for Mother's keeping, of course, and many gifts to charity—is to be divided equally between Corneil and myself."

"Equally?"

"Well, except that Father made a token bequest of two million more for Corneil, to indicate that he should be considered the head of the family."

"Two million dollars is a token?" Alva said.

He nodded. "Comparatively. Depew says my portion is in the range of . . . Well, it's sixty-five million, or thereabouts."

Alva blinked. She blinked again. "You're inheriting sixty-five million dollars?"

"It's . . . startling, I know."

She did a quick calculation. "Your father must have *doubled* what he inherited."

"In only eight years," William said, nodding. "It seems Father was very good at his work."

And William need never give work a thought again.

He did not say this. That he believed it, however, would become plain before long. Alva would not have guessed the effect exceptional wealth could have on an already very rich man.

When one inherits so much money that publishers create and sell to the public booklet reproductions of the last will and testament from which it came, so much money that it seems there is no limit to it, so much that it can't possibly be spent by oneself, so much that barring a complete catastrophic collapse of one's country's economy, it can't even be lost, one must, it appeared, commission the largest yacht ever made for personal use. Or at least this was William's first action.

If one were Corneil Vanderbilt, now head of the House of Vanderbilt (as it was said), one reenlisted George Post to figure out how to double the size of one's Fifth Avenue mansion, acquiring and demolishing whatever neighboring real estate necessary to accomplish this (and, not incidentally, open its view to Central Park). His new child would eventually need a bedroom of his or her own, after all, and because he and his wife had so many children, it would be so practical if the laundresses lived in, and with Gertrude only a few years away from her debut, a larger ballroom was going to be required. Or at least these were the reasons Alice gave.

If one were an offended party (legitimately or not) and youngest son, in possession of more than enough but still far less, one was given the ceremonial duty of laying the cornerstone of the building that would arise due to one's father's half-million-dollar bequest: the new College of Physicians and Surgeons, at Tenth Avenue and Fifty-ninth Street, a bequest made so that the cause of medical science could be advanced and perhaps fewer men would topple over dead at age sixty-four, inadvertently offending such a son in the process. The admiring crowd's cheers would lend this son a sense of importance, a connection to the greater good being done. Sufficiently lifted, he would go out and buy a yacht as his reward—a small one, to simplify his travel to Bar Harbor, where he would buy himself a house. His most impressive gesture would come later.

If one was none of these men—if instead one was on the other side of the gilded gate, a hardworking member of the Knights of Labor, perhaps—one read the flyer sent around in the midst of the May 1 strike, and on May 3 grew horrified and outraged by the police firing on strikers at the Chicago McCormick plant, killing two men. And on the fourth of May, gathered with others at the Haymarket to demonstrate support for those two dead men and for the enforcement of an eight-hour workday, when the bomb exploded and the shooting followed and men lay bleeding and dying in the square, one ran for cover, because what else could one do?

And if one was a lady who'd married for money, who had aimed high but had never imagined she would be seated with the gods?

Alva went about her days as usual. Still, she was ever aware that with this incredible fortune now underlying her life, there was almost nothing she couldn't have, almost nothing she couldn't do. She had greater resources at her disposal than any other woman in the world except perhaps Queen Victoria, and Alice.

What more might she do than she was doing already? Already she'd been helping the less fortunate in myriad ways. Teas for orphans. Balls for maternity care. Auctions for veterans—homeless or limbless or helpless or all at once.

What else might she acquire? Already she had built a beautiful city château and a summer home. Already she traveled wherever she liked—traveled in high style, no less. Already she ate like a queen. She attended concerts and operas and musicales and plays, garden parties, flower shows, dog shows, fashion shows . . .

On a spring day when she was strolling in Central Park while cherry blossoms fluttered like fat pink snowflakes on the breeze, it came to her: What she could do was relax. Everything was settled now. Her life was ideal.

Lady C.'s words came back to her: *Don't be ridiculous. No woman's life is ideal.*

"Mine is," she said aloud. To think otherwise was to insult every poor woman, every woman who rose before dawn and worked until night, who made do with the barest minimum. Every seamstress and laundress and cook and shopgirl and farmer and nurse and teacher. All of them, the women whose labor allowed women like herself to be turned out in perfect style, to have her children looked after, to sleep on pressed sheets in clean rooms, to eat dainty cakes and savory roasts, to keep herself as distant as possible from the unsanitary, unpleasant facts and features of the body. A woman changed Alva's babies' diapers. A woman washed those diapers, along with Alva's bloody pads, her stained bedsheets and underclothes. Those women would rightly see Alva's life as nothing short of heavenly.

Yet she understood a truth she could never say aloud: this ideal life was still deficient. She was not wholly content. Perhaps she should be, but contentment, she had learned, lay beyond money's considerable reach.

Inside a book high up on her bedroom shelf was a note and a pressed gardenia.

A 285-foot three-masted barque-rigged screw steamer with a steel hull, William's yacht *Alva* was delivered in October. In return, he'd paid six hundred and fifty thousand dollars, and that was merely the beginning of the expense. Yachts such as this were remarkable for many reasons, but especially for the way they demanded perpetual cash outlays for docking, for cleaning, for coal, for spare line and sailcloth, for brass polish, for harbor fees, for supplies like water and food, and for a well-qualified crew. Alva thought of this and put it aside. It was not her money, after all. And her husband had named the yacht for her, just as he had once said he would.

The *Alva* was as luxurious a vessel as anyone could desire. Included between bow and stern was a paneled library with fireplace, a plush music saloon, a dining room, a humidor, a flower-filled ladies' lounge, a stateroom each for William and Alva plus seven more for the children and guests. Electric lights throughout. Carpets and crystal and gilt-edged panels. A grand piano. A four-foot-wide globe "for geography lessons," William said. Fine china, exquisite silver, perfect linen. Incidentally, the *Alva* was also painted a vivid yellow, easily spotted against waves or sky. As William had requested of her maker, the *Alva* was a home away from home, a far better alternative to sailing on the passenger liners.

Her crew would grow to more than fifty, but only a dozen or so were on staff for the family's short demonstration cruise from the Sixtieth Street dock to Newport Harbor, where they would put in for a few days' stay with Corneil and Alice at their newest house, the Breakers. This so-called cottage was a Bellevue Avenue ivy-covered Queen Anne they'd acquired from tobacco king Pierre Lorillard—who'd decided it would be more fun to make a men's playground called the Tuxedo Club in the Ramapo Mountains not too far from Manhattan with the help of Caroline's nephew William Astor, who had plenty of millions of his own. Everything in the Vanderbilts' world was thusly connected. They and their friends existed on a joyous merry-go-round of wealth.

Cool air, gentle seas, and sunshine greeted them the morning of their daylong cruise. The trees along the riverbanks were vivid orange, gold, and red. At the mouth of the North River they saw the new Liberty statue, which was finally finished and would be dedicated in a few days.

William bade the captain to approach it slowly so that the children could have a close look. "Do you know," he told them as they stood together at the rail, "more than one hundred thousand citizens sent in money so that the statue could be raised here?"

Alva said, "And our friend Mr. Hunt designed Madame Liberty's pedestal. Imagine, won't you, how people who are arriving from far-off places will feel when they come into the harbor and see her after days and days at sea. Especially poor people who've lost their money and their homes and have come here to start anew."

"It's the people's statue," Consuelo said, looking up at Alva for approval.

"That's right. You must always remember—you, too, Willie—"

"And Harold," Willie said.

Alva smiled. "And Harold, when he's old enough—that God made us equal and it's man who creates the imbalances, the unfairness, the arbitrary rules meant to keep power in the hands of—"

"Don't trouble them with politics," William said.

"Did you not just tell them how the statue was funded by the people?"

"Merely to educate them."

"Which is my aim as well."

"All right. But let's enjoy the day."

"I was enjoying it, until you reprimanded me."

William signaled to the captain to carry on, and Alva forced down her irritation. Perhaps he'd been right to scold her. This wasn't the time for lectures. It was a perfect day on a perfect yacht—a perfect yacht named for her. Lest she forget.

Watching her children while they watched for whales, Alva thought of her own early voyages. Her mother had stood at the rail beside the children, proud and confident of her decisions to shape their experiences, direct their destinies. What might she think of Alva if she could see her now?

Maman had been as shortsighted about "lesser" people as Caroline Astor was before Alva's coup. She had disdained the "merely rich." She said that wealth, while desirable, could be as impermanent as love; if the money went, so went everything else. What's more, a wealthy man could discard his wife if he liked and leave her with absolutely nothing, whereas a discarded nobleman's wife could not be made to give up her title ever, nor the benefits that title conferred, money (if there was any) being the least of it. "A title gives you status," Maman said, "and it gives you purpose. Or the right ones do, at any rate." Even a marriage as unhappy as Lady C.'s would by this measure be superior to most.

Alva's mother might be fond of William, his family, even his money. She might credit Alva for her social coup. She would adore the grandchildren without question. There would, however, always be some disappointment that Alva hadn't found a way to do better. To do best.

But never mind that. Maman was gone. That life—if it had ever been possible—was not Alva's life, and look what had come instead: this unbelievably luxurious yacht; this gorgeous day with its sunshine diamonds glinting off the water; a new niece to coo over; a dinner party to officially close the Newport season; a winter of opera and Christmastime festivities and balls ahead. If William never had a reason to discard her, she needn't ever miss the security a title conferred. She had done well enough.

"Ahoy!" Willie yelled to a pair of men as the family arrived in Newport's harbor and eased up to a dock that was not quite long enough for this record-setting yacht, but would serve. Beside Willie, Consuelo waved and grinned. One of the men saluted smartly. The other caught Alva's eye, turned, and spat on the dock.

Consuelo turned to Alva. "How terribly rude of him!"

"Never mind," Alva told her. "He's got a bad taste in his mouth, that's all."

When debarking a few minutes later, she paused near the man and said,

"You might show some restraint around my children. It isn't their fault any more than your circumstances are yours."

He looked her over. "Spare a dollar, might you?"

She gave him one, then pointed at his stained, scraggly beard. "Diseases can live in there, you know. You should get a shave." Then she gave him another dollar. "Can you read? Good books can improve your mind and your opportunities."

He pushed the money back into her hand. "Didn't ask for a sermon."

That night's dinner was a formal affair that included Ward McAllister, whom Alice occasionally consulted for advice on whom to see for draperies and rugs and fine art and flowers. She had brought in all of the fashionable people. No Astors, as they were in mourning for their patriarch, John Jacob III, who had died in February. But she had a Van Alen. An Oelrichs. A Belmont (Perry, not Oliver, who was who knew where). Two Roosevelts—including Lydia (now Mrs. Harry Brook), who was seated next to William and was, as much as Alva could tell from her end of the table, holding him in thrall. An act of politeness on his part, she was certain.

Seated beside Ward, Alva turned her attention to the others at the long table—thirty of them in all. "Is that gentleman across the table one of yours? He's not familiar to me."

"Mr. Sargent, yes, a portraitist. Marvelous gentleman—I met him through Mr. Wilde, the writer, when I was in London. Excellent reputation. He's seeking new commissions, you know, and I recommend him with utmost enthusiasm."

"I've already got an agreement with Mr. Chaplin to do the children—"

"An excellent choice, of course," said Ward, though his tone belied his words.

"He was favored by Empress Eugénie."

"Yes? Well, that *is* an impeccable recommendation, I must say."

This was why she had selected Chaplin above other qualified artists; even now, *especially* now, there was no one she admired more than the empress. Beyond Eugénie's humane statement about Alva and her sisters, Alva respected her accomplishments. The empress had involved herself in the

Second Empire's politics. She had advocated for women's equality. She had loved her husband deeply, had been a consultant to him and even at times been his regent. *Envy* was too tame a word for Alva's sentiments. She would have liked to step right into Eugénie's shoes, even if only for a day. She wore her pearls at least once every week just on principle.

She told Ward, "I'll bear Mr. Sargent in mind. Now, that adorable fellow there, beside my sister-in-law: Is he one of yours as well?" The gentleman was as smooth-cheeked and youthful as her nephew, Bill.

"That's Mr. Harry Lehr. I'll introduce you after dinner. The most entertaining young man to cross a Newport threshold in many a year, I don't mind saying. Plays piano, sings like a lark, tremendous sense of humor—"

"Not to mention style," Alva said. In contrast, Bill was obviously a fraternity boy (Yale, in his case) who was yet playing at adult sophistication. Bill was sweet and warm and confident and coddled. Mr. Lehr seemed nervous, insecure. But she told Ward, "He's very well turned out."

Ward said, "He is, indeed. I sent him to my tailor earlier this summer. His edges were the slightest bit rough in spots, don't you know. Family troubles when he was young. Younger, that is. He's all of twenty! Looks up to me like a favorite uncle, I daresay."

"What else is occupying you? It's been an age since we had a proper sit-down."

"Hasn't it?" His expression was wistful. "That's because you're beyond needing me—flown the nest! As it should be. Yes. As it should be. I flatter myself that you've flown even higher than you might have, had I not been the one bringing you fish."

"And you're correct. You have my enduring gratitude."

Ward said, "You are a dear, dear friend. So I don't mind telling you this: Believe it or not, I've been tucked away writing my memoirs! Indeed, I have a publisher already, and you'll see the fruit of my labors in October."

"Truly? Well, I'll look forward to that. That is, I think I will. Should I?"

"Not one of my dear friends need make herself or himself anxious. Discretion is my creed! The book is anecdotes sans identities, and framed to serve my broader goal, that being to educate those who desire entrée into our social world as well as those who, though they can't hope to ever enter, look upon it with fascination and seek to imitate. The account is amusing, it's instructional—I give many examples on the correct forms for social occasions, for correspondence. What a stroll along memory lane it was, to write it." His expression was wistful. "Energetic as I may seem to be, the truth is that I'm in my golden years. But not yet in my dotage!"

"The book will be highly valued, I'm certain," Alva said.

"My publisher agrees! Such guides usually come from authors whose knowledge is far slighter than my own."

The sound of silver against crystal got their attention. At the far end of the table, Corneil had stood and was preparing to speak.

"Another summer full of God's bounty has come to an end. Our cook has labored to bring you the freshest and most sumptuous examples of His offerings direct from Vanderbilt farms—here in Portsmouth as well as the Staten Island operation, now being run so ably by my brother George."

George stood and made a half-bow. Everyone applauded.

Corneil then said, "As you know, last year was a somber one for us, a year of mourning my father's passing. We missed being able to host occasions such as this, to have so many excellent old friends around us—and to make new acquaintances. So as the season ends, as the days grow short, as we return to our routines in the city and the activities that occupy us so thoroughly there, I make this toast: to bounty and to friendship. May we always have a surfeit of both."

"Hear, hear!"

Ward murmured to Alva, "A man with his worth has got nothing to fear in that regard. Your husband, too."

She smiled. "Tell me again when your book will be published."

"October twenty-first!"

"And will there be a fete?"

"A modest gathering. Perhaps fifty in all. Invitations forthcoming," he said. "I do hope you'll be able to come."

She said, "I wouldn't miss it for the world," and very nearly meant it.

VIII

ON THE MORNING before Ward's party, Alva received a copy of his book and a note of gratitude for her friendship. The book was slim but handsome, done in brown leather with gold embossing. The front cover featured the McAllister coat of arms. Inside the cover was a page bearing a space for a handwritten number, with this copy bearing the number 4. Below that was Ward's signature, a swirl of pen strokes as florid as Ward himself.

His "modest" fete would take place at Sherry's that evening, a restaurant that had gained great favor with New York society in recent years, and was timed to celebrate the expected laudatory notices.

William came into the parlor holding up a section of the *Times*. "Did you read this?"

Alva said, "No, I haven't seen the papers yet. I'm still catching up on my correspondence."

Among the letters was one from Jennie Churchill which mentioned, among many other events, a visit by Oliver Belmont, who she said had attached himself to Randolph Churchill at Royal Ascot in June and was eager to hear all about Tory policy. *Whisky, cigars, and politics well into the night,* Jennie wrote. *Churchill adores him.*

She'd also written, *Mr. Belmont says he'll never marry again. Isn't that sad?* Despite knowing she ought to agree, Alva felt the opposite.

William set the newspaper on the table beside her. "You can't possibly go to McAllister's party tonight."

"Of course I'm going."

"They've eviscerated him. Read it."

As she read, her spirits fell. The review was long and quoted from the book liberally, every instance made to paint Ward as not only pompous but ridiculous, too. His intentions were ridiculed, his actions were ridiculed—all of it served up as droll entertainment for the paper's readers, drawing itself to a point with this:

> When a man of mature years betakes himself to organizing tea parties and dances as a career he becomes an interesting object. The first requisite for success, as in so many other things, is intense moral earnestness. No suspicion that he is making a continental laughingstock of himself must disturb his mind or interfere with the singleness of his devotion. It would be fatal to him. In this volume there is no trace of such a suspicion. The degree of fervor that the author puts into undertakings that adults commonly leave to adolescents is really wonderful.

They did not mean "wonderful" as a compliment.

> In writing this remarkable book, he has produced a social document of considerable interest, for he not only illuminates himself, but he sheds a somewhat garish light up the "society" whose leader he is.

As Alva laid the paper aside, William said, "You see why I can't permit you to attend."

"*Why* must they do this? Why could they not let him have his happiness? What harm has he ever done? A great many people in this city have benefited from his influence—"

"Himself among them."

"Why shouldn't he benefit? And why are you not taking his side?"

"You have to admit it: he is ridiculous."

"That never troubled you when it was your cause he was advancing."

"Times have changed. A wise fellow would never have written that book, or at least he wouldn't have put it out for review. He could have had it printed up and distributed to the five people who might truly want to read it."

"He's beloved and admired by thousands."

"And now he's a laughingstock to thousands more—and in particular, to people whose opinions I care about. Which is why you won't be attending his—"

"I'll make my own decisions on what I attend, thank you." As she spoke, she had a glimpse of a figure in pale pink outside the doorway. She said, "Consuelo, come in here."

Her daughter emerged from behind the door.

"Won't you show your father that essay you wrote for Mr. Rosa?"

Consuelo brightened. "It's about the Punic Wars," she said, coming to take him by the hand.

William said, "That sounds terribly interesting. I'd like to see it. Have you left it upstairs? Let's go have a look."

When Alva was alone, she picked up the newspaper, read the piece again, then laid it down in disgust. William was correct. She was wiser to not go, lest she be derided herself. There were always reporters at such functions nowadays. Even should Ward show his displeasure by keeping them out, they'd post themselves nearby to keep account of the comings and goings. They'd manufacture even more controversy simply out of spite or sport.

Still, she meant what she had said about Ward. He was a good man. He didn't deserve such mistreatment.

Suppose she went anyway. Faced the inevitable derision. How bad could it be? As she often told her children, a person should stand up for what he or she believed in. Set the example for others. How could she expect them to do so if she didn't do it herself? Yes, it was decided. She was going.

When evening fell, Alva called Mary to her room to help her change for the party. "What's a triumphant color, do you think?"

"Red?"

"It's bold . . . but I'm thinking 'celebratory.' Bright blue?"

"Yellow."

Alva nodded. "I think you're right. The new Worth gown. With my pearls."

Mary retrieved a yellow dress done in raw silk. Along its neckline she had embroidered asters and anemones with delicate branches and leaves, a design that took nearly a month of nightly work.

As she helped Alva out of her day dress, she said, "I feel so bad for him."

"Word does get around quickly!"

"I know a lot of people who admire him and who always like reading about the dances and committees and things. Some people, they need those lessons. Colored folks haven't had much high society before—their own, I mean. Nobody likes to look ignorant."

Alva said, "There you go! He's a treasure. How else does one learn correct forms, if not through expert instruction?"

"I only know so much because Mama taught me, and she knew because Mrs. Smith got her trained by a French maid."

"Every occupation requires training—and society *is* an occupation, let there be no mistake about that." Alva held out her arms while Mary buttoned her into the yellow dress. "The critics may laugh at Mr. McAllister, yet every paper has featured his activities—and the activities of all of us in society—for more than fifteen years. They do love to play both sides."

"I guess so they can say they're more high-minded."

"We want high-mindedness in journalism! That's why this review angers me so much—in ridiculing him they have abandoned a standard. Mr. McAllister's guidance and assistance has brought real joy to many lives. He has served a public good. Overseeing charity balls is a service: those balls are what compel stingy rich people to part with their money."

After adding jewelry, hat, gloves, and cape, Alva went downstairs. With each step, she was sure William was going to call her out at any moment. Yet she managed to get out the door without interference. Evidently he'd thought about the matter further and changed his mind.

As Eric prepared to hand her into the carriage, she told the coachman, "Sherry's, please."

"I'm sorry, ma'am," he said, not meeting her eyes. "I'm unable to take you there."

"If you don't, you'll be unable to keep your position here."

"Yes, ma'am. But you see, Mr. Vanderbilt says I can't keep it if I do."

"Oh, for the love of Jesus," she said. "Can he be so determined?"

Alva stepped back from the carriage. Her options now were to walk fifteen blocks down Fifth Avenue or to get a hired cab. Either choice would excite attention. Why was Mrs. William K. Vanderbilt going about without her own carriage? Without any carriage? The speculation would be carefully framed, of course, much as Uncle C.J.'s companionship with Dr. Terry had been, and would result in ever more reputation-damaging gossip, gossip that would be amplified with discussion of her having gone out *sans carriage* in support of the now-disgraced Ward McAllister. *My goodness! Has Alva Vanderbilt lost her mind?*

Such poor judgment.

Yet she takes herself so seriously!

She's the only one who does, to be sure.

Behind her, William and the children came out the front door, all of them dressed for dinner. Alva said, "What's this about?"

"Corneil's having us in, didn't I tell you? He sent word this morning. Mother and George are back from another foray in the North Carolina mountains and he—George, that is—has something to announce." He ushered the children into the carriage, then stood beside Eric expectantly, waiting for Alva to get in, too.

She said, "The carriage, when you could simply walk up the street?"

"Willie turned his ankle this morning while dismounting after our ride."

The blatant lie surprised her. The withholding of information about tonight's plan surprised her. Perhaps he had also wounded her, but she was not about to let that show.

She remarked coolly, "Did he? This is the first I've heard of it."

"Everyone is waiting on you. Won't you get in?" Though his expression was mild, she sensed he was warning her against making a scene here on the street, in front of the children and servants and any passersby. He said, "I'm only helping you, Alva."

"Of course," she said, and she complied.

George Vanderbilt was a month shy of his twenty-eighth birthday. Unlike his three older brothers and a couple of his brothers-in-law, he had no role in the operation of the New York Central, no particular interest in railroads or locomotives or the business of transportation. He enjoyed books. He enjoyed art. He liked to travel and, while traveling, buy books and art.

He remained the companion to his mother that he had become when his siblings all left home, taking her along on most of his journeys, keeping watch over her when she was ill—which she was more and more often. Consumption. Heart ailments. A slow fading of the energies she'd once brought to her activities, though she was still able to enjoy her children and grandchildren.

He had taken her to North Carolina for the reportedly healthful climate, as well as to consult with one of the nation's foremost specialists in conditions like hers. Tonight, as she stood near the hearth in her son Corneil's dining room, she appeared to have benefited from their three-month stay: her face had color; there was vitality in her posture; she was laughing at something Gertrude said as Consuelo and little Gladys, Alice's youngest, looked on.

Alva had warmed to the occasion (if not to her husband), though her anxiety at letting Ward down persisted. Still, she must make the best of it. She approached the group, saying, "I believe I've found the heart of this party." She kissed her mother-in-law. "Welcome back. I think George has confused his seasons, though; isn't autumn when one wishes to leave New York for the South, if possible?"

"And miss Christmastime with these darlings?" said Mrs. Vanderbilt, drawing the girls to her.

Gertrude asked, "How long was the trip?"

"I'm not certain. At my age, one doesn't count the hours."

George, joining them, said, "Twenty-nine hours, in fact."

"I would *die*," said Gertrude. "Especially if I had to travel with Reggie."

"I would love it," Consuelo said. "Nothing to do but read."

"Reading is all well and good when your little brother will leave you to it," said Gertrude. "Why Mother hasn't sent *mine* off to school yet is a question for the ages."

"Now, be kind," said George. "I'm a younger brother. A youngest brother, in fact. A youngest *child*." He tapped Gladys on her nose. "It isn't as easy as you might guess, is it?" he said.

Gladys shook her head. "I am the youngest of *everyone*."

"Just as I used to be," he told her. "And see? I have survived it. So will you."

"I am in the middle and it's awful," Gertrude said.

Alva said, "George, not that having you two home isn't reason enough to celebrate, but the rumor of an announcement has all of us excited."

Presumably there was a young lady connected to this announcement. If so, he would be going straight from a walk to a gallop, as he'd never, to Alva's knowledge, been sweet on anyone, nor had he indicated any desire to satisfy his sisters' urgings to find himself a suitable wife or let them find him one. They often said that if he waited too long, his nephews would take the best girls from under his very nose.

George clasped his hands. "I'm excited as well. Perhaps we can get our host to invite everyone to the table so that I don't burst from it."

The children laughed and Gertrude said, "I'll go find Papa."

Alice came over. "I was admiring your dress," she said. "The embroidery is exquisite. That isn't *your* handiwork. Did you buy it that way?"

"Mary did this."

"Mary?"

"My maid."

"The Negro girl did that?"

"She's quite good at all her work—as I told you she would be, if you'll recall."

"And you don't mind what the other ladies say, I suppose. Though I confess *I* do; I don't have your . . . outlook. I'm traditional. Corneil says I need to be more tolerant of our differences—yours and mine—and of society's whispering. And I *am* trying."

Alva said, "I don't know if I mind, because I don't know what they say. Will you enlighten me?"

"Oh, well, merely that your insistence on employing a Negro to be your lady's maid is in terrible taste, though it may have been looked upon as a generous act at first. The South lost the war, after all, and slave-owning went with it—"

"For God's sake, she's not a slave."

"Please, your language."

"Then don't provoke me!"

"You asked what's being said."

"Mary is an intelligent, talented woman and impeccable in her work. Am I not always turned out in such ways that I exemplify excellent taste? Credit Mary for much of that."

"You needn't attack me."

"If you would stand up to those slandering fools—"

"You know I prefer to demonstrate my position through example."

"Who would have thought we were so much alike?" Alva said before turning to go. "That's my approach, too."

When everyone was seated, Corneil began his usual orating. The mantle of power had aged him little; he was still lean and angular, the way his grandfather had been. No matter the subject, he spoke with the righteous authority of a man who believed he had earned his place when in fact he had been given it.

While he spoke, Alva imagined the scene that must be in progress at Sherry's. Ward would notice her absence and wonder about it—or perhaps he'd believe he knew why she stayed away. He would be hurt and probably angry as well. He would never allow either emotion to show, however. The consummate gentleman, consummate host, he might this minute be standing before his own gathered darlings (whichever among them had shown) delivering his own oration. Even hurt and angry he'd be more entertaining than Corneil, who was saying something about mountain air . . .

". . . the healthful benefits of which are evident. And now, in order to prevent some kind of terrible bursting incident I was warned about, I give you George."

Alva hadn't spoken to William since leaving their house. How content he looked, seated between his mother and Consuelo. And why not? He had every benefit the fattened New York Central could possibly confer, with no real responsibility. If he spent more than ten hours in his office each month, Alva would be astonished. Nor did he use the remainder of his time tending to new business ventures—unless breeding and racing Thoroughbreds could be considered "business." He did make money doing it, but it was a rich man's hobby, existing entirely for the benefit of other rich men.

George began, "As you all know, Mother and I have been spending time in Asheville—"

"A village of ashes?" said Reggie, ten years old and, as Gertrude had alluded to earlier, irrepressible. "Who wants to be *there*?"

Corneil said, "Son, if you want to be allowed to stay at this table—"

"Sorry, Papa."

"As you know," George began again, "Mother and I have once again been in the North Carolina mountains—in a town named after one of the state's governors, Mr. Samuel Ashe, A-S-H-E. We've met a great many lovely people there. It's a fine place! Not at all the remote outpost you might have imagined it to be."

"No savage natives?" said William.

"Some savage trout, that's the worst of it."

"You mean the best of it."

Everyone laughed, and George said, "Well, yes, the trout are fantastic. What's better still is that I have been acquiring those trout en masse by acquiring a large stretch of the river they inhabit, the Swannanoa, as it travels through the land I've bought. And I have acquired an architect—who is also fantastic—to build a house on that land."

Corneil said, "You've mentioned that you might build there. A fishing lodge, then?"

"Eh, something a bit more ambitious than that. I've been consulting Fred Olmsted on what we might do to take advantage of the geography there, while Richard Hunt's been working up plans for me and—"

"Your bride-to-be?" Alice finished hopefully.

"My . . . ?" George shook his head. "Goodness, no. Is that what you thought I was going to . . . ? Corneil, I told you we ought not to make a production of this dinner."

"I said only that we were celebrating your return and that you had some news."

"Tell us more," said Alva. "About the house."

"Rather than tell you very much, I invite you to see it."

"You've brought drawings?"

He shook his head again. "Hunt has commissioned a detailed model. It was delivered to his office today—with a great amount of attention from the press, which I expect will manifest in print tomorrow."

Alice said, "Why so much attention?"

"Well, due to the house's size and design, the model is . . . rather large."

Corneil, who had begun to look concerned, said, "Why is that necessary?"

George had an air of authority Alva hadn't seen in him before now. He seemed taller. Firm. Quietly forceful. "The house—a French Renaissance design, as Hunt did so well for Alva and William—will be some three hundred and seventy-five feet across and have two hundred fifty rooms, give or take a few."

Alva said, "Goodness."

"On how much land?" said Corneil.

"In the range of one hundred and twenty-five thousand acres. I'll have a dairy, a church, a school, a farm. We're considering a forestry effort, as well. The Germans have advanced it as a science, and I like what I've heard."

As they all took in these details, no one spoke. Then Corneil, now looking severe, said, "That's not a house, George. That's an actual castle."

William said, "And you want to put it in the North Carolina wilderness? What possible sense can that make? You're nowhere close to being married. Mother needn't be there year-round, and we're all here in the Northeast."

Then Alice: "I don't understand. Why do you wish to . . . ? That is, why not someplace nearer to here? Along the Hudson or in New Jersey, say? Or Vermont, like Lila's planning."

"This is not responsible," Corneil said. "You might build it, all right.

The expense of *keeping* it, though—have you considered staff, maintenance, supplies?"

As Corneil went on, Alva watched George's face. He looked strangely pleased, as if this severe response was the reaction he'd intended. Let his brothers and sisters follow in each other's footsteps around the Northeast, making themselves indistinguishable one from the next. He was nothing like any of them—never had been, had no desire to be. Corneil might be the patriarch, but it was he, George, who was going to show everyone what it was to be a Vanderbilt.

Farther down Fifth Avenue, the man who had been instrumental in polishing that name was seeing his own tarnished irreparably. As the papers would gleefully note, not one of Ward McAllister's top society friends had shown up to his party—though there were second-tier friends aplenty. Those grateful mamas and daughters who under his tutelage had risen a few rungs were delighted to celebrate with him. Those gentlemen of comparatively modest means who had found in Ward a willing guide to improving their dress, their vocabulary, their habits—they'd turned out as well. He hadn't been left alone with a room full of uneaten food and unoccupied waiters—a comforting salve to Alva's guilty conscience. When she set down her note of apology to him, she wrote only that a family obligation had interfered, and she would call on him sometime soon.

The next time Alva saw Caroline Astor, who, like Alva, had been featured in the memoir in flimsy disguise, Caroline told her, "Mr. McAllister has shown himself to be a wolf in sheep's clothing. We can have nothing more to do with him."

They were at a reception for some German baron's wife who was visiting New York as a first stop on her tour of America. All the usual ladies were in attendance, none of them especially interested in the German baroness, who sat, prim and upright, in an armchair with the hostess at her left, both of them smiling thinly and saying little as the others stood or sat, gathered in their usual cliques.

Alva said, "You mean to say we should cut him permanently?"

"He knows the rules better than anyone. You would be well to remember them yourself. Ward McAllister sold us out for his personal gain—and did a poor job of it, at that. To put one's friends up publicly, *for profit*, as objects of gossip and derision, is unforgivable."

From Caroline's perspective—a perspective likely shared by all the ladies in the topmost circle—he had callously allowed their priorities, their very existence, to be mocked and diminished, judged as useless and insipid. The only way for these ladies to reject such a judgment was to pretend that it did not apply and had never applied to them. To pretend that Ward McAllister had never mattered and was absolutely not their man.

Though Alva felt certain that Ward had intended to flatter his friends, and in the doing, flatter himself, she could not disagree with Caroline. There *were* rules. There *were* consequences for breaking them so egregiously, even if he had not intended the effect. Ward's die was cast.

Alva made some mental calculations. Then she said, "I do wish he'd have thought better. Have you met his protégé Mr. Harry Lehr?"

Caroline raised an eyebrow. "Mamie Fish brought him around, yes. He's lively and bright."

"The jester shall now wear the crown, I suppose."

"Indeed. You know, I admire you, Alva. I don't like you very much, but then I don't really like anyone."

Alva raised her teacup. "It's mutual."

Ward had sent no response to Alva's apology, nor did he call. Alva, occupied with holiday planning and her children and so many social events, never seemed to have the time to seek him out. She knew that in a certain light this would appear hypocritical of her. In another light, it would look like self-preservation.

Alloy

I never see a baby's eyes,
So innocently bright,
I never hear the cooing voice,
Full of a sweet delight,
But thoughts will come of future years
Of sorrows, blent with joy;
For every life, however bright,
Has something of alloy.

I never hear a baby's cry
Of either fear or pain,
And hear the joyous, sipling laugh
That follows quick again,
But thoughts will come of bitter tears
On some far distant day,
And of the laugh that then will strive
To hide the grief away.

—JENNIE L. LYALL

I

ALVA RECOGNIZED THAT something was amiss at home the moment she debarked from her coupe. When her doorman greeted her, he was stiff in his manner. Her housekeeper, Mrs. Evelyn, saw her as she was coming in the door and scurried off down the corridor before Alva could speak. Alva went upstairs to her bedroom, where she rang for Mary, intending to ask for information—and one of the housemaids showed up.

"Ma'am?" said the girl, giving a quick curtsy.

"What's this? I rang for Mary."

"Yes, ma'am. Only Mary isn't able to come."

"What do you mean, isn't able? Is she ill? Injured? Has she gone out?"

The housemaid said, "All's I know is Mrs. Evelyn said I'm to assist you."

Alva pressed the button to summon Mrs. Evelyn, and told the girl to go.

"End this mystery," Alva said when Mrs. Evelyn appeared. "Where is Mary?"

"I suppose she's still upstairs in her room, as she hasn't yet returned her key or given leave." She sounded disapproving, though whether of Alva or Mary, Alva couldn't say.

"Given leave?"

"You did say she was to be let go today."

"Let go? Have you lost your mind? I said no such thing."

Mrs. Evelyn, flustered, said, "What I mean to say is that Mr. Vanderbilt said you requested I let her go. So I did."

"Why in heaven's name would I do that?"

Now Mrs. Evelyn looked miserable. "It's not my place to ask."

"No, of course. Where is Mr. Vanderbilt?"

"He went out, probably an hour ago."

"Of all the . . ." Alva muttered, leaving her room for the servants' stairway.

As she reached the landing outside Mary's bedroom, Mary was coming out the door dressed as if for church, hat and gloves on. She carried a suitcase in each hand. Alva said, "Stop. Put those back. I didn't discharge you. My husband was mistaken."

Mary stopped. "Mistaken? You don't want me gone?"

"Goodness, no!"

"Because, well, I just thought why on earth . . . ?" Mary paused. Then she said, "So, all right, I'm relieved to hear this. But . . . I think leaving may be best just the same."

Alva steered her back into the bedroom. "I don't know what compelled him to do as he did, but whatever it was, I'll correct it. Unpack your things. I can't even imagine trying to replace you."

"I'm kind of glad he did it," Mary said. "I mean, I don't *want* to leave; you're almost like my own sister. But . . ."

"What is it? Tell me."

"I could ignore it, mostly, so I never made a fuss. When you're a black-skinned girl, you get so it's hardly more than noise, like when I hear the elevated." She was still holding the suitcases. "Sometimes it's the other servants saying things—like how it's not right for someone like me to keep a position that ought to be done by 'someone who's better suited.' And now Mr. William has been making remarks, too."

"Never mind him," Alva said. "You unpack, and I'll put things to rights."

"He put his hand on my cheek and told me, 'You're much too pretty to be where white men have to watch you. Girls like you used to be the masters' pets.' "

"*William* did this?"

Mary simply looked at her.

"Was there . . . That is, did he—"

"No," Mary said, shaking her head. "Not yet. It's best I go, before it can get worse."

"Perhaps it is."

Alva wanted to cry. Mary had been a feature of her life for as far back as she could remember. And William—what could he have been thinking?

She said, "What will you do?"

"Miss Armide can use me, with Mama nearly blind," she said. "You'll come see us. And I'll do any needlework you want."

"What if . . . I don't know, suppose you were to open a little shop where you could sell your goods? Your work is exceptional. Every woman I know would pay handsomely for it."

"Not from me, they wouldn't. You know, it's funny, we all thought that since the North wanted slaves free, we would all be equal here. I guess they do want us free, just free to keep to ourselves."

"Suppose we get you a white girl to mind the shop. Or an Italian who's still got her accent. They'll all go for that. She'll say all the goods are imported from the best needle-mistress in Italy."

"I expect I can find shops that'll buy from me wholesale."

"I'll make the introductions, then. You have to allow me to help. It's only right."

They walked downstairs together. At the service door, Alva told Mary to wait a moment, then came back and pressed fifty dollars into her hand. "So you can get settled in. And I'll see to it that Armide gives you a salary."

"You come see us Sunday afternoon."

"It won't be the same," Alva said.

"Here's my advice: get yourself an ugly girl to replace me."

"An ugly . . . ?"

"So he isn't as tempted. You don't want it going on in your own house if you can help it."

Alva opened her mouth to argue that *William wouldn't ever*, then closed it. She didn't actually know what he would or wouldn't ever do. She would not have predicted that he would obstruct her desire to attend Ward's party the way he did. She would not have believed him so graceless as to take up with another woman, and especially not with Mary.

"I don't know what's gotten into him," Alva said. "He hardly even likes to . . . well, you know what I mean. Your room is right above mine."

"Mmm. He is away a lot."

"Are you saying—"

"I don't know what he does, Miss Alva. Maxwell, he doesn't talk. But you said you don't know what's gotten into him, and what I think is that a change in fortune doesn't change who a person is. It reveals your true self, the one you were maybe hiding away. Now Mr. William doesn't have to hide anything anymore."

"You think he's *always* been selfish and conniving and immoral?" Alva said. "That makes no sense. He's been very generous to me, you know he has."

"Because it makes him feel like he's best. Think about it. He's always been someone who would rather put himself first. We know that."

("*Woo him, Alva. Flatter him. Do you understand?* Be *the prize.*")

Alva could not deny Mary's insight entirely. She said, "And so, by your theory, now that he's *so* rich, he can do what he likes without consequence."

"Consequences that matter to him," Mary said.

Hasenpfeffer tonight, with a delicate herbed stuffing and an array of spring vegetables. Discomposed as she was, Alva could hardly taste the food—which aggravated her further. She was seeing her husband with new clarity, and she did not like what she saw.

The two of them were alone, so they used the smaller dining table in the morning room. She loved this oak table, which was inlaid with maple stars as constellations, and she loved this room. The light was particularly good in here throughout the day. The art pieces on the walls were some of her favorites. None of it pleased her now, though.

"The strangest thing happened earlier," she said to William from across the table.

"Oh?"

"I'd been out, and when I returned, I was told that Mary had been dismissed at my direction. This was very odd, since I'd given no such direction, and it was odder still that you'd conveyed the message on my behalf. Perhaps you dreamt that I asked you to have her dismissed?"

William set down his fork. "I wish you wouldn't try to be clever."

"I wish you wouldn't—well, where do I start? Lie to the servants, for one, and make me look bad in the process. Then there's the trouble provoked by your lie. Thanks to you, I'm now without as good a lady's maid as has ever had the position. Suppose I went and dismissed Maxwell for no cause and without your knowledge or consent?"

"Maxwell is ideal for his position. Your girl shouldn't have been in hers to start with. No one of our class uses Negroes in the house, not even as scullery maids."

"This never made any difference to you before."

"I've been made aware of the problem only recently."

"By whom?"

"Others in society. My brother—"

"Corneil."

"He has mentioned it, yes," William said, his tone as friendly and even as ever. "But it makes no difference who said it. It is a fact. As is the family reputation being diminished by your having had that girl on staff. Apparently Alice brought this to your attention several times in the past and you refused to take action, giving me no choice but to remedy the matter myself."

"There have been small-minded ladies taking this position since '75, and it has made no difference whatsoever."

He made no reply to this, instead taking another bite of rabbit.

Alva said, "Suppose she had permitted your advances."

He set down his fork. "I beg your pardon?"

"If Mary had encouraged you, would you have been so troubled by 'society's' concern?"

"I can't think *what* it is you're talking about. A problem was brought to my attention, and I remedied it."

"By pretending the order came from me," Alva said.

"A man uses the most effective means for the task at hand."

"You wanted her to believe *I* wanted her gone."

"Alva, she was no asset to my household and therefore she has been removed from it. I believe that's all that needs to be said on the matter."

Alva turned to the butler stationed behind her and told him, "Please have my meal sent to my bedroom. I'd much prefer to dine alone."

In her room, though, she left the food untouched. She left her food untouched!

The following day, William was as sunny as ever when he stopped in the parlor on his way in from wherever he'd been. Riding, by the looks of it; he wore jodhpurs and carried a pair of cowhide gloves. His hair was in wild disarray.

"Fancy this," he said. "I was at the Union earlier—do you remember the Astor girl, Charlotte, who married James Drayton?"

Alva set down her pen. On the desk before her was her list of the qualifications she was seeking in a new lady's maid, which Mrs. Evelyn would take to the agency while the family went to Paris for their annual spring trip. Alva had conscripted one of the housemaids in Mary's place, with low expectations. For now it would be enough to have someone to pack and unpack and pack again, to fetch and steam and iron. The rest she could do for herself.

She said, "Of course I remember Charlotte Drayton. She only went to New Jersey."

William took an apple from a bowl on the desk. Polishing it against his lapel, he said, "Well, she's been having a flaming love affair with Hallet Borrowe. Drayton threw her out, her father won't see her, and now Drayton has challenged Borrowe to a duel. Marvelous, isn't it? We can't get theater like this at the theater!"

"Where is she living?"

"Who knows?"

"Are her children with her?"

"I'm certain Drayton has them, don't worry."

"And now he proposes to put himself in front of a bullet? That hardly seems responsible for a man who would be his children's sole parent."

"I can't see why this should make you angry."

"It doesn't. No—it does, but I was angry already. What you did yesterday—"

"Now wait," he said, coming to sit in a chair near hers. "Have we not spent God only knows how much money and a great deal of effort to put ourselves at the top of society?"

"We have. But—"

"You are one of the most admired ladies in this country, Alva, but where that maid was concerned, you were blind. I only wish I'd realized the problem sooner. If Alice couldn't reason with you, I certainly had no hope of doing so. My duty is to protect you, to protect your reputation and that of our children—just the way Drayton is doing by facing off with that fop, Borrowe." He reached for her hand. "Understand, you are . . . well, you're just what they say: an angel in the home. And you're an angel to me. You're clever and determined, and you have made all the difference for the family socially. If I have to stand in front of a bullet to protect you, I will. If I have to risk insulting you to protect you from your own soft heart, so be it."

He let go of her hand and stood up. "Paris-bound tomorrow," he said, moving for the hall. "I'd better make sure Maxwell got my new togs packed . . ."

Alva sat in stunned silence while he bounded up the stairs. He'd managed to talk his way around her bringing up again his advances to Mary. And he had just called her an angel. *His* angel.

Was it all an act?

London, April 27th, 1891

Alva, dearest—

I'm afraid I was correct all along about how little value I would find in becoming the Duchess of Manchester when the time actually arrived. It isn't the crown that gives me headaches, though. It's my husband's poverty of both spirit and purse. He's sold off almost everything to pay his debts and gives his time to the habitués of places no lady would be found.

Therefore, I've taken a somewhat shabby but pleasant home in Great Cumberland Street. The situation with His Grace has become untenable and our parting is for good and all. Perhaps I might have held out a little longer; he is dying of consumption, it's confirmed, and I could have spared myself the attention this separation has produced. My sympathy wore out long ago, however—timed, I suppose, with my father's loss of fortune and my husband's subsequent complete disinterest in me. Yet <u>*Bertie*</u> *still considers me a prize and has said he wished I could have been a real prospect for him! The irony of being adored by the man who will be king and discarded by a bankrupt duke is quite terrible and quite funny, at once.*

It is difficult to keep one's chin up at such times. But I must do so for the children's sake if not my own. You should see them, Alva. They are so beautiful and so good. I do worry that Kim is at risk of becoming like his father—who now takes him about and shows him off and God only knows what else; he's fourteen, you know. And he loves the attention and admiration he gets from the twins' friends whenever he's home from school, so it's likely his father is initiating him into that wonderful wide world of easy companionship that comes with having a title of note (or from money, though not in this case, la!). Such companions don't know that the Duke's wife and daughters are destitute and dependent on a meager allowance and the generosity of friends. Or perhaps they do, but don't care so long as they get to make a duke-shaped notch on their belts.

Forgive my tone. When you sail next, put a London stop on your tour.

——C.

II

ON AN EARLY July afternoon in their leased Newport cottage, William called Alva into the parlor, where he'd spread a plat map on the table.

"For some time now I've been thinking we should have our own place here, *and* you have a significant birthday coming up, so I've acquired this parcel of land"—he pointed—"on Bellevue. It goes all the way to the sea. This one next to it on the north side is Astor's. We'll be about halfway between Corneil's, here, and Fred's, here." He pointed to the locations of the Breakers and Rough Point, about a crow's mile apart.

The significant birthday on the horizon was Alva's fortieth. Though still two years out, it blinked at her as steadily as a beacon at the shoals. *For-ty. For-ty.* Not that there was any way to steer clear of it except to die first, and that hardly seemed a reasonable response to middle age.

William said, "What do you think? It's a prime location. You and Hunt can do another showplace."

"I can build anything I like?"

"It's only four acres, so you can't fit something like George's folly. But yes, generally, you can build whatever you like."

"Why?"

"What do you mean, why? I told you."

"Why now?"

"I told you that, as well."

His expression gave nothing away, yet she sensed there was more to this offer than what he claimed. He had, in fact, become increasingly opaque in general. In her most generous thoughts, she attributed this change as a natural result of his altered circumstances and not evidence for Mary's theory, a theory she preferred to believe was well meaning but not sufficiently informed. In her dark moments, of which there were blessedly few, she regretted her choices, resented the circumstances that had led to them, and worried that William was playing her for some kind of fool.

He continued, "I thought, if I don't acquire this property, some rich upstart's going to get it, and who's more deserving of a new cottage here than my wife?"

"I've been content with this house—but I would very much enjoy building again." The intensive occupation would only do her good.

"It's too bad Mandeville isn't as good to *his* wife," William said, rolling up the map. "What do you hear from our friend the duchess? Aren't the two of you due for a visit?"

"I had a letter from her right as we were leaving the city. She and Mandeville are on the outs, but she's spending a lot of time at court. She's one of the prince's pets, you know."

"Is she?"

"Nothing gossip-worthy about it, if that's what you're imagining."

"I'm not imagining a thing. It's only as I say: that it's unfortunate she didn't do better than Mandeville."

"She always lands on her feet," Alva said. As William prepared to leave the room, she added, "Does Corneil have something in the works? Are they expanding the Breakers, or—"

"Not that I'm aware of. Have you heard something?"

She shook her head.

"Their place is good, certainly, for what it is," he said. "You'll come up with something far more impressive, though, I've no doubt. If you want to work with Hunt again, you should secure him as soon as possible. Between George's place and now Belmont's, he's already well employed."

"Perry's hired Richard? Or do you mean August has?"

"Neither. It's Oliver who's at it. He's getting ready to build down near the end of Bellevue, on the west side."

"When did this arise? I haven't heard a thing."

William shrugged. "I saw him at my club the other day and he told me he was arranging it."

So Oliver was here in Newport, to stay—a dismaying development. It had been much easier to not think of him when he was thousands of miles away. This did, however, explain William's sudden desire to build here. If Oliver Belmont was going to have his own Newport cottage on Bellevue, William had better get one, too.

She said, "I thought he was determined to stay abroad. Has he eloped with a local girl?"

William laughed. "It does seem the sort of thing he'd do, doesn't it? No, it's nothing as dramatic or entertaining as that. He's decided he should put himself back into American society, is all. Resume his place—and with old Belmont dead, now he's got money to spend. He was away for almost seven years; it's about time, wouldn't you say?"

Alva would not say. Better that he had remained anywhere else.

William said, "Now if you'll excuse me, he and I are meeting some of the other chaps at the Casino for doubles." He pretended to swing a racquet. "You might come down and watch us."

She considered the scene and rejected it immediately. Watching Oliver play lawn tennis, or for that matter, stand still and breathe, held more appeal than she wanted to admit, let alone indulge.

This ongoing attraction: *Why* did it persist? What did it say about her that she had not been able to put it to rest? Perhaps it was only a matter of—what did they call it? Animal chemistry? Or something of the sort. A physiological response to specific stimuli. Nothing at all to do with an individual's character or will. She'd learned about it at a lecture by a noted naturalist last January. Many speakers came through New York in wintertime, knowing that people who could pay three dollars apiece to relieve their boredom would gladly do so. And then in April she'd gone to hear the author Mark Twain. Most of society snubbed him, having found in his book *The Gilded Age* a displeasing mirror. Well, she supposed any bug caught so securely *would* hate being pinned that way, but there it was, sometimes people had to face facts.

She took a book of European architecture from a nearby shelf and held it up so William could see the title. "I've got to get to work if I'm going to have my present on that birthday. Have a lovely time."

❧

Having brought the children into town to see a magic show, Alva was helping Harold out of the carriage when Richard Hunt emerged from a shop before them.

"Ah, Richard! Just the man I need to see. Say hello to Mr. Hunt," she directed the children.

As she spoke, another man rounded the corner. "There you are," Hunt said to Oliver Belmont, who stopped beside him. "I thought I'd lost you."

"I was waylaid. Why, Alva Vanderbilt, hello!"

The sensations hit her all at once: happiness; excitement; annoyance at feeling happy and excited. Really, it had been so much more convenient for her to have him elsewhere. Out of sight, out of mind—she had taken this adage to heart. One couldn't suffer the effects of animal chemistry so long as the offending animal was out of range.

But oh, just look at him. He really did not offend.

He appeared not older so much as more mature, more confident, at ease with himself and his situation. Impish. Handsome. Intelligent. Happy. Perhaps there *was* a lady involved. If so, good for him. Yes, good for him; he deserved happiness if he could find it.

And good for herself that she and William would be spending a piece of the summer taking the children to Lisbon.

"You remember Mr. Belmont," she told the children.

"I don't," said Harold.

"In fact, we've never met." Oliver bent down so that he was at Harold's level. "Oliver Belmont at your service." He put out his hand, and Harold, giggling, shook it. Then Oliver stood and faced Alva. "The boy is as handsome as his mother is lovely," he said cheerfully. "It's wonderful to see you again."

There was nothing in his manner to indicate there'd ever been an awkward moment between them. He was past it, then. All right. She would endeavor to be past it, too.

She said, "William tells me you and Richard have a project under way."

"We do indeed," Richard said just as a very tall, dark-skinned man joined the group. He was dressed exotically in a Zouave jacket and had a fez for a hat. Neither Oliver nor Richard paid him any notice as Richard went on, "And it turns out that Mr. Belmont is very much a man of stubborn ideas, as with some other client who shall remain nameless."

Alva smiled. "Is that so?"

"Hunt was at odds with my desire to integrate the stables into the ground floor of the house. They've done it all over Europe."

"When economy made it necessary," Richard said. "You've got the space and the budget to build them separately—but," he said, holding off Oliver's retort, "as I learned when working for Mrs. Vanderbilt, not to mention her brother-in-law, the client's wishes are paramount. *My* task is to accommodate those wishes with style."

Pretending Richard couldn't hear him, Oliver said, "This is how he gets so many rich clients."

"I'd like to believe the quality of my work is what recommends me."

"If all one wants is quality," Oliver said, "one can hire Post or Codman, or White and his fellows. You, Mr. Hunt, have an artist's soul. Either that or you have an exceptional tolerance for eccentric clients and their vanities. At any rate," he said to Alva, "I will have horseflesh under my quarters—"

"Just as when you ride," Willie joked, reminding Alva of that night on Long Island when she and Oliver had made their own horse jokes. Youth and summertime had laid soft hands upon all of them. How long ago it was, and yet the memory felt freshly made.

Harold tugged on Alva's sleeve. She turned to him. "What is it, dearest?"

He was staring at the strange man, who had stationed himself far enough away to be respectful but close enough that it was clear he intended attachment. Harold stood on tiptoe to be nearer her ear and whispered loudly, as children do, "Why is that man watching us?"

Oliver spoke up. "That giant fellow is my manservant. Come," he said, beckoning the children over. "This is Azar. He's Egypt-born. We had some adventures together while I was away exploring, and he decided to return with me."

Azar bowed. "Greetings, children," he said in a deep and accented voice.

Harold bowed and said, "Greetings, sir."

"Did anyone else return with you?" Alva asked Oliver lightly. "William alluded to the possibility of your having made a new attachment."

He shook his head. "Nothing like that."

Richard said, "Unfortunately. As I've told him, a lady's influence would benefit the cottage."

"Well. In due time," Alva said. "Come along, my chicks. I'm afraid we have to be about our business. But, Mr. Hunt, if you have space in your schedule tomorrow, I've a new project to discuss with—"

"Meet us at the site," Oliver said. "Nine o'clock? We're getting ready to break ground and I would love to have the benefit of your eye in case we've made some grave error. While there's still time to remedy it, you know."

"I beg your pardon," Richard said.

"Nothing against you, Hunt. Measure twice, cut once—isn't that the saying?"

"My morning is full," Alva lied. "Nor would I want to jeopardize getting Mr. Hunt's cooperation in building my own cottage by insulting his judgment on yours."

Richard said, "I'm not at all sure whether I should attend to Mr. Belmont's doubt or Mrs. Vanderbilt's praise."

"You should come see the magic show," said Willie.

Richard patted his shoulder. "One has to admire how he sees straight through to a situation's best merits. It wasn't so long ago that I was bringing my daughter. She thinks she's too grown-up for it now."

Alva said, "If we delay further, my daughter will be old enough to protest, too. Will you come for luncheon tomorrow, Mr. Hunt?"

He nodded. "I'll look forward to it."

Glancing at Oliver, Alva said, "Good day then, gentlemen," and herded her children into the theater.

After getting them seated for the show, Alva excused herself to the ladies' lounge and there found Alice, who said, "Oh, hello. I didn't realize your children were coming. I'd have offered to bring them with Reggie and Gladys."

"No Gertrude?"

"She's gone driving with the Hunt girl."

"You say that with distaste."

"I'm sure Miss Hunt is perfectly fine in her own circle. But I don't like her latching on to Gertrude the way she's done. I've said as much, but Gertrude won't hear me. 'I ought to be able to choose my own friends, Mother.' Her tone! Esther Hunt is only attracted to my daughter's position—"

"Her position? She's not a princess."

"She's the wealthiest heiress in the country, possibly the world. You should be mindful that Consuelo might be used similarly—though she's probably safe as long as Gertrude's encouraging all the leeches herself."

"My, you're in rare temper."

"That girl is at the Breakers *constantly*, and I can't very well forbid it; Mr. Hunt was a pleasure to work with when we expanded the house in New York, and of course George has him now. I like Mr. Hunt well enough. I'll suppose it's Mrs. Hunt who's to blame for not teaching her daughter better."

"Does Gertrude enjoy her company?"

"They're thick as thieves! This is what I have been saying."

"Then I don't see the harm. The Hunts are a perfectly respectable family—"

"He's only well off because he's made so much money from his rich clients."

"And *we're* only well off because we have a monopoly on all the rail lines going to and from the shipyards, and because investors are willing to pay so much for New York Central stock."

Alice adjusted her hat. "I'd better get back. I can't leave Reggie untended too long."

Alva watched her go, glad to have had a few minutes of Alice's discomfiture to distract her from her own. In sight, in mind.

July 28th, 1891

My dear Duchess,

Apologies for my lapse in correspondence. It's been a full summer. I write you from the "Alva" somewhere on the Atlantic, where I've been entertaining myself by sketching plans for our own Newport cottage. I have in mind something like the Petit Trianon at Versailles, Louis XV's intended gift to his mistress Madame de Pompadour. She didn't live to see it finished. I do hope I fare better.

We've just spent a week in Lisbon. It's a marvelous city, even the children thought so. Wm. already plans for us to ship out again in October—to Italy and the Mediterranean for the winter, returning home in May. I want to visit the great auction houses—the cottage will have themed rooms (Renaissance, Gothic, etc.), and as you know, all the best, authentic things are in the Old World.

Some society news to amuse you: my current Newport neighbor is Mrs. Hermann Oelrichs—the former <u>Miss Theresa Fair</u>. Yes, our red-haired Greenbrier maiden, the one I thought Wm. might choose. She is so besotted with Hermann that one can't help but adore her.

Hermann, being such a terrific athlete, has provided great amusement for the ladies this summer as he challenges all the fellows to contests of swimming and riding and wrestling. He absolutely insists that the man-eating sharks of Jules Verne's imagination are entirely that: imaginary. And to prove it, he had us, his wife, newlyweds Alice and Teddy Roosevelt, Oliver Belmont, the Fishes, the Goelets, and several others out on "Hildegard" for a cruise when he announced he was going for a swim. "Definitive proof that sharks will not attack man!" he proclaimed before descending the ladder and then diving into the depths. Everyone crowded the rail—I thought his wife was going to faint. The men were making wagers (Wm. bet against him) and yelling out to Hermann, but then we saw shark fins and everyone went mute. Imagine it: there we were, anchored miles offshore, the boat rolling on five-foot swells, a stiff breeze whipping the ladies' skirts about their legs, all of us with our hearts in our throats—well, some of the ladies turned away, thinking a scene of horror was imminent, but I kept my eyes on the water. I actually believed he would succeed. And he did! He thrashed about as if he were Poseidon himself, and the sharks swam away!

I don't mean to leave your last letter unremarked upon . . . When I began this reply, I thought, "I'll cheer her with cottage details and amusing stories"—and perhaps I have. Yet all along I sit here thinking of you in that shabby London house, and of how much I admire you for telling the truth about your circumstances. It seems truth-telling has gone well out of fashion here, if in fact anyone ever did it.

What is it that drives some men to such poor behavior? Mandeville never deserved you. And Pierpont Morgan—he has built his mistress a house near his own and goes there with impunity. Mrs. Morgan is forced to act as if none of us knows and she doesn't either. These men must believe themselves completely beyond reproach! And, well, why wouldn't they? Wives permit all of it. Because of course if we're to believe what we read in the Lady's Book, the True Woman is completely fulfilled by her domestic duties—her home, her children, her charity functions. The True Woman understands that men have needs of a different kind.

But I don't believe a word of it. We accept their behavior because of what would happen if we didn't.

Here is one of my truths:

Many years ago, on the day after our '83 ball, you asked me if I had a secret. I didn't. Not exactly. But I was keeping something to myself. There was a gentleman who was in love with me. I rejected him completely that night, and that put an end to it. We didn't see each other for a time. He was abroad, and our paths never crossed. I heard about him from time to time, of course. Enough to know he was in good form, and to know that although he was well occupied, he hadn't taken a wife, nor did he seem inclined to. Now this man is again in circulation and I see him with some frequency. Despite my rejection of him, I was powerfully attracted to him then and remain as attracted as before. It's maddening.

I have never acted on this attraction, and I'm so glad of that, as it is clear that he did as I requested and put his feelings for me behind him. But to you I confess it with chagrin: I dream of him sometimes, and in my dreams we have a passion that I have never experienced in my waking life. And when I wake, I carry with me a yearning that is heightened whenever he is nearby. It's ridiculous for a woman nearing forty years old to feel this way, and in no way appropriate for any lady. That's what I tell myself. Pathetic is what it really is, as there is nothing to be done about it. Oh, the gods are laughing at me now.

I will close and address this to you before I lose my nerve. We are a pitiable pair, are we not?

—Alva

London, Sept. 12, 1891

Alva, my brave and honest friend: for all that I should be mourning my circumstances and yours, I am actually laughing. Think of the way the two of us used to be so certain of ourselves, so convinced that we knew exactly what we were doing and that what we were doing was going to absolutely lead us to contentment for the rest of our lives. Is this the curse of youth, or the blessing of it?

I am sorry for your situation. Not as sorry as I am for my own, though, because you have a cloak of cash to protect you somewhat from life's storms. Whereas I get soaked through to the skin.

Or is that overly dramatic? Yes. Yes, it is. I'm comfortable enough. I do, after all, benefit from my friends in high places.

You might consider making new friends. Or making more of old ones.

Send your agenda for the winter trip when you know it, and we'll meet up somewhere along the way. Would you like another invitation to court? On second thought, I'd rather have you to myself. Come to

Tandragee. We can sit before one of the great hearths and drink hot wine in quantities sufficient to both warm us and make us forget that we aren't still those headstrong, self-sure girls smugly plotting advantageous matrimonies and everlasting satisfaction.

Until then, I remain yours truly,

Lady C.

III

AFTER WINTERING IN Italy, Alva and the family returned to New York to find their coachman waiting at the dock with the news that Corneil and Alice's oldest son, Bill, had died a week earlier. For a moment, the family stood in shocked silence. Then William said, "What are you talking about?"

"The typhoid, sir."

Consuelo began to cry.

"Typhoid? Are any of the others ill?" Alva asked.

"No, ma'am. He came from Yale already quite sick."

William said, "But . . . how can he have died from it, for God's sake? Typhoid is curable."

Eric had no answer.

Alva said, "Have we missed the funeral?"

"I'm afraid so."

William said, "Take us straight to my brother's home."

In the coach, Alva sat between Willie and Harold with her arms around them, her eyes on her daughter—as if her fierceness and attention could protect them from harm any better than Alice's had done for Bill or for little Alice.

Alva's pleasure over the stimulating and enjoyable things they'd done during the trip withered in sympathy. While she had been watching her elder son run across the Champ de Mars to the Eiffel Tower and stand beneath it with his arms stretched overhead in joy, Alice must have been begging the doctor to please do something to bring down her son's fever, to reduce his pain, to stop the vomiting and hemorrhages of the bowel, to *cure* him, damn it! Why wasn't he recovering? Most people didn't die from typhoid anymore, and certainly not when they were receiving the best treatment! Certainly not when they were young and strong. Certainly not when they were poised to be among the most influential and important men in the world. His parents were God-fearing and devout.

While Alva had been at Tandragee with her dear friend, the two of them alone in a cavernous room seated in wing chairs before a roaring fire, drunk on laughter and mulled wine, Alice was likely sitting on a chair beside her unconscious son's bed looking upon his fever-pink face, certain that if she lost him as she'd lost her sweet daughter, she would never have cause nor energy to smile again.

Corneil and Alice, who through extraordinary good luck possessed every advantage life on this earth could bring, had for the second time buried one of their children. Alva would not insult them by asking how it was they put so much store in a God who would treat them—treat their *children*—thusly. She would not openly question their faith. But she did wonder why and how it was that they did not.

For weeks, the papers ran lengthy and lavish accounts of kind young Bill's promising life and remarkable funeral, and of the Vanderbilt men and their money. As a result of the attention, Alva and William received letters like this:

> *Mr. William Vanderbilt,*
> *I hear you are a good man. My family is hungry. With your sons death there is now more money to share with others. Please 10 dollars will be fine or more if you as a Christian sees fit.*

—though it was not their son who'd died.

And this:

Mrs. William Vanderbilt,
I suppose you are now heiress to many many millions and can help out a poor soul like me. Send whatever you can afford. My husband is out of work and we have six to feed plus my father and my husband's two brothers who are lame from the war.

—though it was not anyone's father who'd died.

The facts of who had died and what relation he was to the rest of them were of no matter; they were Vanderbilts, and there was money to go around. All of them received these begging letters by the scores. Alice and Corneil, bereft, would read none of them. William read a few and then instructed the butler to burn any more that arrived. The heartlessness, the presumption, of all these strangers—where was their compassion? A precious, beloved young man was dead and his family was grieving! The Vanderbilts were more than newspaper tales and cartoons meant to inflame or entertain the public. They were human, and they were hurting.

Still, knowing how it was to feel desperate and hungry, knowing that she and the children needed to *do* things to help assuage their grief, Alva ordered an assortment of dry goods and food, then took the children over to St. Bart's to help assemble packages the church would distribute to the needy.

When they returned home in the carriage that day, they saw several people waiting on the stoop outside the front door. Two were women holding babies. All the people looked careworn and exhausted.

The coachman yelled, "You lot! Out of the way, now!" They moved, but not far. As he climbed from his bench, the people called to Alva, visible in the carriage window:

"Help us out, ma'am, won't you?"

"Please, we've no work. Surely you can spare a few dollars?"

"There's no jobs. How am I going to feed my baby?"

"*My* baby has the croup. We need money for a doctor."

A well-dressed gentleman unfamiliar to Alva was walking past. "Get out of here!" he scolded the group. "You've no cause to trouble this lady with your complaints. You want help, go to city hall."

A hatless young man with dirty hair said, "That one horse there costs more to feed than my whole family." He pointed to the coachman. "If they can put their servants in velvet jackets, sure they can throw some cash our way—bet you can, too. All of you up here, I bet you wipe your asses with dollar bills."

While the men continued to argue, Consuelo said, "Mother, we *have* to help. I have a few dollars here." She indicated the small purse she carried with her now that she was receiving a regular allowance.

"Your impulse is good, but we can't give handouts this way or we'll have every poor person in the city lining up at our door."

Harold peeked past his sister to see better, then sat back again. "I don't like those people."

Willie said, "Don't be scared. They're . . . well, they're sort of like pirates who've gone off duty."

"I'm scared of pirates."

Consuelo took Harold's hand. "They're all perfectly nice people, they're just hungry. You know how you get cross sometimes when you're hungry."

"That's right," Alva said, and knowing there was nothing for it but to get on with her day, she climbed out to the sidewalk. Turning to the children, she said, "Come on, now. Just keep your eyes on Eric, he's holding the front door for us. Straight in," she warned Consuelo. "I know it's hard, but there you go, sometimes life is hard."

"Please, Mother? I'll tell them it's just this once."

Alva looked at her daughter. She looked again at the people on the stoop, reduced by circumstances to being beggars.

"Yes, all right, just this once," she said, opening her own purse.

They decided to leave for Newport as soon as the *Alva* could be refitted for the trip. The children needed a release from their sadness at losing a most-admired cousin, time to roam the fields and climb the cliffs and swim and sail and run and ride. The new house there—which while it was being built had been dubbed *the marble house* for its liberal use of the material, and then simply Marble House—was done but for some of the small touches, and ready enough for their summer stay. Alva would turn her attention to that.

As they motored down the North River, they waved to the people on the Manhattan shore and to the passengers of other boats. It was a fine June day, hardly a cloud to be seen—a perfect day to be out on the water. Alva's heart lifted for the first time in weeks.

Was Captain Morrison preoccupied when he steered them toward a cruiser in the water ahead? Was he reading a magazine? Chatting up the children's governess, perhaps, who liked to visit the bridge and talk with the engineer? Whatever it was, he had them on a collision course if something wasn't done—

"Morrison!" William yelled as he ran for the pilothouse.

"Move!" Alva said, pulling the children away from the rail to the center of the deck. They instinctively crouched and grabbed the nearest line.

In another moment the yacht was veering sharply, barely missing the cruiser's port side—then came a thump and the sound of splitting wood and someone screaming.

"Stay put," Alva said, moving to the rail to look behind the yacht. As she did, she felt the yacht slowing, while, in their wake, the flotsam of what looked to be a rowboat held a struggling half-submerged woman. Some yards away from the woman was another figure who was going under.

"Stop!" Alva yelled to Morrison. "Turn around!" The crewmen were at the rail now, too. Everyone was yelling. Still, though they were slowed, Morrison didn't attempt to turn. The woman disappeared beneath the water. The other person was gone.

Alva rushed to the pilothouse. "For God's sake, why don't you turn us?"

"There's no use," Morrison said. "By the time we manage it, they'll have either swum to shore or gone down."

"They're down already," said one of the mates from the doorway. "No sign at all."

William and the captain looked at each other. For a long moment, the only sound was the engine's low rumble. Then Captain Morrison said, "Carry on." William made no reply. Morrison said, "Believe me."

"Yes," said William. "All right. Carry on."

"I'll cable Depew as soon as we put in at Newport."

Alva said, "William, we can't—"

"This is none of your concern," he said. "Tend to the children."

Fortunately, the children had seen nothing. Taking Consuelo's hand, Alva told them, "We hit a rowboat with two people on board. Pray for them."

The next day's newspaper story about the incident told every detail about the man who had rented the rowboat for an outing on the river, and about his companion, who was his housekeeper. It told how the rowboat was "cut in two," and how the man had tried and failed to catch hold of the *Alva*'s bobstays, and how the woman had been thrown aside, then had found and clung to a piece of wood, then lost her hold. Both had drowned. It accused the *Alva*'s crew of failing to throw out life buoys—which may have been true; Alva couldn't say.

The story, though it identified the yacht as belonging to William K. Vanderbilt, made no mention of whether he or any Vanderbilt was traveling on board.

Alva was sickened by the subterfuge.

Alva was grateful for the subterfuge.

She could not reconcile her outrage and her gratitude, so she threw herself into arranging the details of Marble House. The precise positioning of every rug, each piece of furniture, the tapestries, the paintings, the sculptures, the lamps, the planters, every little bibelot, the folds of the draperies, the height of the grass on the lawn that ran from the rear veranda's steps to the blue, blue, blue water (*no, don't think about water*). She gave a great deal of thought to the green lawn, the trees, the flowers—all of it so bucolic in the summertime sunshine. She scrutinized the children—Harold, always a love, eight years old and quick with a silly joke; Willie, almost fourteen, sprouting dark blond hairs on his upper lip, a horse lover, keeper of two fillies he liked to race; Consuelo, fifteen, slim as a reed, hair like a cascade, her lithe self ever curled into a sofa with a book open on her lap. Sloping shoulders and spine, even when she walked—

Must tend to that . . .

The doctor prescribed a rod and straps: one strap at the waist, one at the head, two hours' use every day to strengthen the abdomen and encourage a permanent habit. "I know it feels uncomfortable," Alva told her as she buckled the forehead strap. "It's only for a month or so. You'll thank me one day." Her daughter's answering expression bespoke betrayal and hatred. Oh, her tender firstborn . . . How would such a girl survive in the world? She needed to be toughened up for her own good.

Their days in Newport had a comforting rigidity; when one doesn't have to think of what to do with one's time, one doesn't have to think. Up for breakfast; dress for breakfast; eat breakfast. Dress for riding; ride. Change for a trip to the Casino to watch tennis; watch tennis; have a look in the boutiques. Take luncheon with friends in one's own home or theirs. Change to bathing costumes for ladies' time at the beach; take ladies' time at the beach; change again and go see the gentlemen play polo. Take the phaeton out to pay calls; home for tea, then nap, then dress again for whichever event was occurring that night—mourning a nephew allowed for attendance at small birthday dinners, engagement parties, receptions for visiting dignitaries. No time for reflection, for introspection, for questioning the sense of it all. They had *killed* two innocent people. Lovers, probably, taking a boat out for a day of sunshine and sandwiches and poetry. Maybe she liked to sing. He might have had a guitar. And then came a great yellow yacht, bearing down on them—

Alva simply could not allow herself to dwell, or else she would conclude she was a monster, and she was not a monster. Was William? He might be. Or not. He'd made a practical decision, a choice that protected himself, yes, but also her and the children. Besides, what else could have been done? Bad luck. Bad timing. God's will? But they hadn't even *attempted* to go back. In her pew at St. Mark's, the church she had designed and built, a space she had made for herself and God, Alva bowed her head and did as she had bade her children do, and then added a prayer for herself.

. . .

What William did: came and went throughout the summer while developing (with Oliver, God help her) a plan to create an exotic animal park a few miles from Bellevue Avenue, in Middletown. They incorporated their company as Grey Crag, ordered their livestock, and took the boys out to the property daily to watch the carpenters build stables and pens and fences. Then Alva and Consuelo joined them to see the delivery and release of emus, camels, an elephant, peacocks, gazelles, a pair of giraffes.

Harold especially was beside himself with delight. "My own elephant!" he beamed. "No one else has an elephant." *No, probably not just yet,* Alva thought. *But give it time.*

Try as she might, she could not be easy in William's company, which he must have noticed though he made no remark. But when the family picnicked at Grey Crag Park on Independence Day, Oliver was there, too, as if William was attempting to use him to influence Alva's opinion. As if he were saying that since Oliver knew about the accident and Oliver was still his friend, could she now cease her silent judgment of him and put the trouble behind her?

The children took camel rides and fed peanuts to the elephant and climbed those gray crags to get eye to eye with the giraffes, while the peacocks strutted and screeched and, as night began to fall, flapped into the trees.

Thinking she was alone while the others were off building a fire to bake clams as evening fell, Alva stood watching a peacock situate itself on a branch with enviable grace and contentment, its feathered train trailing behind it. Imagine, she thought, after a day of preening and strutting one could just find a quiet limb and settle there, not a care in the world. "I envy you," she said.

Then she heard a step and Oliver came up beside her. He said nothing, just caressed the back of her neck briefly and then continued along the path to the fire site.

Alva stood very still, facing the peacock but not really seeing it. What had Oliver meant by touching her that way? Had he meant anything at all? Was it merely a friendly stroke, such as he might give a favored sister?

Was it meant to assuage the loneliness he'd perceived? Did he know how she had struggled all summer to be good, to be mindful of her children and friends and duties, to believe that there was no way they could have prevented that tragic accident? None of them had spoken of it, not once. But it had happened. And William was indifferent. And Oliver was around all the time. And she had not had a moment's peace in her mind or heart all summer long.

Her throat tightened. She should not feel confused and lonely and sad; she should feel coddled, spoiled, admired. She should definitely not succumb to the yearning that Oliver's touch provoked.

Here, alone in the fading light, with the sensation of his touch lingering, she succumbed to that yearning. For a minute only. Perhaps three minutes. All right, five, but that was all.

She stayed there envying the peacock until her tears had dried, and then she joined the others. In the twilight, with the fire crackling before them, no one in the party noticed her red-rimmed eyes. She could go on pretending that all was well. She must go on pretending that all was well.

With her husband and his brother Fred off with friends on the *Alva* to visit George in Bar Harbor, Alva invited Mamie Fish for luncheon at Marble House with her and Armide. Mamie, whose husband Stuyvesant Fish made his fortune in banking and Midwestern railroads, was a forthright woman unafraid to say what she thought. They'd been loosely acquainted for years but hadn't made friends until this past spring, when Mamie asked Alva to work with her on the Friends of Chinese Orphans Ball. "Nobody else would do it," Mamie had told her after she accepted. "They don't want to think about malnourished Chinese babies—but they'll go to a benefit ball for anyone or anything if the guest list is good. So I thought, Alva Vanderbilt's got what I need for this: gumption and pull. Are you offended?"

Alva had laughed. "I should be."

"But you're not."

"No, I'm not."

Today's meal would begin with bouillabaisse, made with fresh seafood brought in that morning, accompanied by a *boule* made from imported French flour—all the more *authentique, oui*? And champagne, which Alva had discovered was a good medicine for her symptoms.

The three ladies had shared two bottles on the veranda before being seated in the dining room. As the first course came out, Mamie said, "Alva, I have to tell you, the house is marvelous, but I am unnerved to have your King Louis, there"—she pointed at the portrait that hung at the table's head—"watching me eat my soup. He looks as if he might invade at any moment, and this soup is simply too good to give over or leave behind. I'll have to defend myself." She called out: "Can someone bring me a sharp knife?"

"I find him fascinating," said Alva. "Let the Sun King live!"

"He had as many mistresses as Versailles has rooms," Armide remarked.

Mamie said, "Speaking of: Alva, I must say I respect the restraint you've shown—" She stopped midsentence.

"Yes?"

"Well, I'm only saying that if Stuyvie brought one of those harlots into *my* home—"

"What are you talking about?"

Mamie looked at Alva, then went back to her soup. "Oh, never mind me. I misremembered. It was someone else's husband. Gossip! Manna to idle minds."

Armide said, "Someone's husband brought a loose woman to their home?"

"It's only a rumor," Mamie replied. "Maybe it didn't even happen."

Alva would not let it go. "Where? Whose husband?"

"No, no, I won't credit it by repeating details no one has verified. What I do want to say is that I respect how you chose to imitate the Petit Trianon when you might rather have gone for Versailles."

Alva drained her glass and signaled for more champagne. "On four acres? I couldn't have, even had I wanted to."

"Did you want to?" asked Mamie.

"I try not to want what I can't possibly have."

As Alva spoke, the butler brought a telegram. She read it, then laid it on the table. "Good lord," she said.

Her companions looked at her inquisitively.

"My husband has sunk his yacht."

On the veranda that night, torchlight dancing over the wide, sun-warmed stone, stars above, tide high, surf shushing against the rocks, William told the story of his sinking to an eager crowd that included his travel mates, along with Armide, the Oelrichs, and the Fishes—but not Oliver, who might have been out at Grey Crag watching the peacocks while her husband was holding court as if he were the Sun King, untouchable and untouched.

Alva was not so unaffected. The yacht had been rammed by a freighter. It was a wonder that no one was killed.

"We were still asleep," William was saying. "Last night was a late one, you know, all of us sitting out on the foredeck under the stars, Fred passing around some excellent Scotch that George'd brought home from Scotland. The boy knows his whiskeys!"

"That boy knows his brothers," Fred quipped.

Hermann Oelrichs asked, "When's his North Carolina mountain castle going to be finished?"

"Half past eventually," William said. "George has got Hunt and Olmsted turning somersaults to get every detail just so."

"We might hire Hunt to build us a cottage here on Bellevue—Tessie has gotten quite fond of you lot, and I wouldn't deny her a thing."

"Excellent," William said. "I'll write your letter of introduction—"

"Or Stanford White," said Mrs. Oelrichs. "He's quite good, and, well, I don't want anyone to feel we're being imitative."

William said, "Yes, White's a fine choice. Now do you want to hear this, or don't you?"

Stuyvesant Fish said, "Carry on!"

"Carry on!" said Mrs. Oelrichs.

Carry on.

Alva watched her husband with detached fascination as he continued telling his tale. He was so cheerful! Did nothing ever affect him?

"Morrison had put out anchor very early this morning to wait out a pea-soup fog, and then next thing we knew, we were all jolted from our beds. The noise was absolutely terrifying—I thought we were done for on the spot. It was only luck that the *Dimock* missed the staterooms when she rammed us."

Fred added, "Another ten feet toward the bow, and . . ." His wife reached for his hand.

William said, "We all rushed on deck. The crew got the lifeboats rigged and we were safely off in a matter of, I don't know, fifteen minutes, and on board the *Dimock* shortly after. *Alva* listed a bit, then started going down. I guess she's underwater a good ten feet, now. Morrison cabled to say all that's in sight are her masts."

"She just stays there like that?" said Armide. "I thought that if a boat sank, it, well, *sank*."

"Would that it did! It'd save me the expense of attempting to salvage the thing!"

"I guess insurance will pay," said Hermann.

"Ten percent was all they'd insure, for a premium that was nearly that much! I didn't bother. We'll get a crew out next week to try to raise her, but I don't hold out much hope."

"Will you replace her, then?"

"I can't think why I wouldn't."

Later, when they'd all retired, Alva knocked on William's bedroom door.

"*Entrez*," he called.

He was in pajamas, sitting in an armchair with his feet up on the windowsill and a glass of scotch resting on his stomach. The window was open to the night breeze. If he was the least bit traumatized by the morning's events, he was disguising it beautifully.

She said, "Forgive the intrusion, but there's something I wanted to ask you. About the house."

"Don't tell me: You want to add a wing."

"Something simpler, fortunately. Remember how you said this house was your birthday gift to me? I'd like you to turn over its title. If it's mine, it should be *truly* mine."

"What's mine is yours."

"But it isn't. Imagine that everything in your life, from your shirt cuffs to the blocks of stone around you, was yours to use but belonged to someone else. It could all be taken away from you at any time."

"My dear. I was not brought up to cast aside a wife and leave her to perish. You can't think I would ever treat you in such a way."

"Yes, all right, but suppose you'd been killed—"

"Alva, I wasn't even bruised—"

"This time. Put yourself in my place. I'm not like your sisters, with their inheritances. No matter what happens to them, they've got the means to carry them through life comfortably. I am at the mercy of circumstances I can't affect. I feel—well, as vulnerable as you were this morning anchored there in the fog."

"You needn't worry so much. But I'll prove my word is as good as my checks. I'll have Depew get the papers drawn up and Marble House will be yours."

"Do you mean it?"

"Do you doubt me?" he said, standing up and going to his writing desk. "I'll write to him this minute. I won't have you thinking I'm anything less than I say." He penned a note, folded it, and handed it to her. "Here—see that it's sent, so you'll know without question that I've ordered it."

"That's not necessary."

"I desire it. This house *is* yours, Alva. You put your soul into its planning; you deserve to own it outright."

"Thank you."

They faced each other. Their eyes met. He reached out and put his hand on her shoulder. She held as still as she could manage and kept her eyes on his.

William squeezed her shoulder, then let go and reached for his scotch. "It's been a hard summer, but things are looking up. Say, I'll bet Maxwell can get that message cabled yet tonight, if you catch him before he turns in."

"I'll do that."

He sat down again in the armchair. "Sleep well, dear."

"You, too."

After giving the note and instructions to Maxwell, Alva rang for a bottle of brandy and two glasses, then went up to Armide's room.

Oliver's hand on her neck. William's on her shoulder. Mere moments of intimacy, sharp reminders of what she wanted and shouldn't want, couldn't have and didn't deserve, would never have and would always wish for, reminders of what she shouldn't even desire if she were a decent woman.

What exactly did she desire, anyway?

Not the sex act, or at least not as she knew it. Might it be simple affection she longed for, the uncomplicated pleasure of being held in a loving person's arms? When had she last been embraced that way? William had never been one for such displays. Willie and then Harold had outgrown their urges to wrap their arms around her when kissing her good night. And now Harold was beyond even allowing her to hold his hand. Occasionally Consuelo would put her arm around Alva's waist if the two were standing together and she was particularly contented (less and less often now). Willie was at the handshake stage—a curious development Alva hadn't anticipated, but Mrs. Vanderbilt said all the boys got that way, and Alice had concurred.

Alva knocked on Armide's door. "It's Alva," she said, and waited for her sister to let her in.

"You're still dressed! I thought you'd gone to bed." Armide closed the door behind them.

"I might have been widowed today."

"But you weren't, so all is well."

"That is what I tell myself." Alva poured brandy for both of them and handed Armide a glass. "I don't like leaving so much to chance, though, so I took some action to protect myself and the children. I've persuaded William to give me this house outright."

"Good for you!" Armide said. She pointed to a magazine lying on the bedcover. "I've been reading the most startling story," she said, getting back into bed. " 'The Yellow Wallpaper,' it's called. An anxious new mother has a rest cure forced upon her, and the lack of stimulation is driving her mad. *Actually* mad. Her husband thinks he's so solicitous, but in fact he's imprisoned her. You should read it, really. I'm so glad I never married."

"Marriage has its benefits," Alva said.

"But at what cost?"

Alva drained her glass in one long go, then put it aside and climbed into bed beside her sister. "I don't want to talk about the costs. You weren't concerned about them when I married William."

"I didn't press you into it. There were alternatives, but you wouldn't hear them."

"I had to marry him—or someone with means. We'd have starved! I only wish . . ."

"What?"

"Nothing. Never mind. Here," Alva said, lying down and tucking herself up against Armide. "Put your arm around me like you used to when I was a little girl. Don't you miss having someone perfect and trustworthy and warm beside you every night?"

"I can't say I ever thought of you in quite that way."

Alva heard the smile in her voice. "Let's pretend you did. Let's pretend we're children again, in our pretty Paris flat."

Armide put out the light and curled up behind Alva. Her hand stroked Alva's hair. "You had all those dolls . . ."

"*Mes petits bébés.*"

"You were rather a tyrant to them."

"Shhh."

Armide said, "I'll give you this: you get things done."

Tandragee, Aug. 19th, 1892

Dearest Vanderbilts,

As of late yesterday, I am now officially a Dowager Duchess. George Victor Drogo Montagu, Duke of Manchester, known as "Mandeville," as "His Grace," as "Father" (for however little he deserved it), is dead of tuberculosis. A little later than predicted, but no less dead for the waiting. I didn't cable because I don't want you to trouble yourselves to come for the funeral. I won't have you undertaking a trip to "honour" an honourless man. Kim, Alice, and May are bearing up well enough; it's not as if they saw much of him when he was alive.

Love to you and yours,

~C.

Newport, 31 August '92

My dear Lady C.,

I offer our sincerest condolences, if not for Mandeville's death then for the troubles he caused that led you to more difficulties. I pray you and the children will find peace and happiness in days to come.

But for a small measure of luck, I might have been widowed recently myself. The Alva *was hit and sunk with William aboard, and he and his friends escaped unharmed.*

As I write, he is en route to Liverpool to meet with new shipbuilders across the river in Birkenhead. I've cabled him your news and asked him to please pay you a visit if his schedule permits.

We send our love—

Alva

IV

"IS PAPA COMING with us?" Harold asked Alva on the morning of the annual Coaching Parade, held in Central Park on what usually was a mild spring day of sunshine and flowering trees and warm breezes. Today, though, was chilly and overcast. Harold's mood matched the weather, as evidenced by the way he was dressing at a snail's pace and scowling as he did it.

Alva said, "He's away, you know that."

"I thought he might have got home while I was asleep."

"Well, he didn't. We're going with Colonel Jay and Mrs. Jay and the girls."

Harold sat down on the floor and crossed his arms. "If Papa isn't going, I don't wish to go."

"The Jays are expecting us. Stand up. You're too old for this nonsense. Your hair needs combed and Cook's got your breakfast waiting."

He looked up at her. "Is Willie going?"

"He has other plans. Get up *now*."

Reluctantly, Harold complied. "Papa always lets me ride. May I ride?"

"No," she said, herding him from the room. "We'll be in the Jays' coach."

"Why does Papa have to be away?"

He didn't have to be. Once again, he'd chosen to be. Alva didn't say this. "The shipbuilder needed him to come back to oversee some things."

Things that were taking a very long time. He'd been there since February, and now it was May.

"Will the new yacht be bigger than the *Alva*?"

"She will."

"When will she be done?"

"Soon."

In fact she was built already, though not outfitted. William's most recent letter told what Alva had already seen reported in *Town Topics* and the *World*: the *Valiant*, as he had named this yacht, had been launched in a ceremony at which Alva's namesake was given the christening honor. *I asked Lady May Alva Montagu to do the honors in your stead*, he wrote. *"Valiant" is a nod to you, my dear.*

She would have been far more pleased about this had he at least given her the opportunity to decline an invitation to launch *Valiant* herself.

Too, the papers regularly had reports that placed him in Cannes and Berlin and Geneva and Paris and Budapest, usually at gambling tables, sometimes on yachts. His name was ever amongst numerous others—playboys and noblewomen and the occasional minor prince. Alva didn't wish to be among them; she was not seeking what thrilled that set. Yet each time she read that he was part of a group celebrating someone's birthday or a substantial win at roulette, she felt resentful. *Her* days were full with the tediousness of household management and society luncheons. She'd had to do the round of opera balls and dinners unaccompanied. She had put off her annual trip to Paris, William having told her to wait until he returned with the new yacht. And then he had not returned with the new yacht.

As William was not here to represent the family today, she had initially refused the Jays' invitation, until Lucy Jay reminded her that the parade was a good opportunity for Consuelo to be displayed. "All the best young men will be out, and as you know, it's never too soon to encourage their hopes. Really, Alva, it's your duty as her mother."

Whereas Consuelo's father's duty was only to pay for Consuelo's silk organdy dress and plumed hat, and the embroidered gloves and shirtwaists Alva had ordered from Mary. After all, Consuelo's father need do nothing more than exist, being that he was America's second-wealthiest man. Short of him committing murder publicly, almost nothing would diminish his standing with the public or his peers. He had already done everything he was obliged to do, including marrying a woman who could and would do the rest.

Following Harold to the kitchen, Alva resolved to let this go. She shouldn't be so cross. William had named the yacht for her. She was valiant.

The valiant woman was installing her son at the breakfast table with his organdy-clad sister when a maid came into the room. "Ma'am, Mr. Oliver Belmont is here to see you."

"Uncle Oliver!" Harold said, rising.

Alva put her hand on his shoulder. "Stay here and have your eggs."

"I want to see him."

"That's quite enough from you, unless you'd like to spend the day doing schoolwork."

"Yes, ma'am," he muttered, and took up his fork.

Alva hadn't meant to be so sharp with him. He was an enthusiastic, inquisitive child, much the way she had been. Valiant or not, she found William's cavalier absence wearing. She told the maid, "Send Mr. Belmont in."

Seating herself, she poured coffee and took a piece of toast, though she'd had breakfast earlier. Best to have some occupation in hand when he was nearby.

Oliver strode in, saying, "Greetings, Vanderbilts! Are you ready for today's excellent promenade in the park?" He kissed Consuelo on the crown of her head on his way to shake hands with Harold.

"You're far sunnier than the day," said Alva.

He told Harold, "Don't tell your mother, but I had candy for breakfast."

"That would make me cheerful," Harold said.

"A chocolate croissant, that's what would cheer me," said Consuelo, though she'd evinced no displeasure before his arrival.

"And you?" Oliver said, looking at Alva.

"Would you like coffee? Or I can ring for something with better nutrition than your previous meal."

He sat down opposite Harold. "I'm fixed for food, thank you. What I would like, however, is to accompany you to the parade. I had a cable from William suggesting I stand in."

"Are you riding?" said Harold. "I'd rather ride."

"I am. We should all ride. It's good for anything that ails you."

Alva said, "Thank you, but the Jays have asked us to coach with them. It is a *coaching* parade. Besides, it might rain."

"Suppose it does?" said Oliver. "What would happen then?"

"We'd get wet," Alva said.

"And then?"

"We might catch cold."

"Have you ever? Caught cold from being wet, I mean? Think of it. Every time you've had a bath, you've been wet."

Harold said, "Please, Mother? Please, please? Riding is so much better. It's good for anything that ails you."

Consuelo said, "I'd far rather ride."

"The Jay girls will be disappointed," said Alva.

"I'll make it up to them," Consuelo said. "I'll propose a picnic just for them in Newport next week. May I? We're going Tuesday, yes? I'll have the picnic on Friday."

Alva glanced at Oliver, who watched the exchange with a half-smile. He knew he was making trouble for her, and he liked it. She liked it, too, God help her. And the children were right: riding was so much better than sitting in a coach, even one as good as the German-made landau Colonel Jay had just acquired and was eager to show off today. Even when the sky threatened rain.

Oliver said, "If it rains and you get wet and catch cold, I will personally make chicken soup for you."

"You can cook?"

"I am a man of myriad abilities," he said.

Harold looked at Alva expectantly. She nodded, and he announced, "We accept!"

"I'll send Mrs. Jay a note," she said, already knowing the note wouldn't mention Oliver but would pin the change in plans on Harold's desire to go on horseback—which would not be untrue. There was an art to these things. She hadn't reached society's apex by accident. William had named the yacht for her. *Valiant.*

As spring gave way to summer and long, languid days in Newport, Oliver made it easy for her to accept his offers to accompany them wherever William might have otherwise gone. He was sweet and relaxed and amusing, and if she felt in any way uncomfortable in his presence, well, that was a side effect she would bear.

William, meanwhile, wrote to say the yacht was getting its carpets, its chandeliers, its carved paneling, its grand piano. *Expect me in July.*

Alva wrote back, *July is good. The children miss you. I do, too.*

She told herself this was true, and chose not to dwell on the fact that with Oliver as her escort to social events, she was enjoying them more than she'd done before. He was such good company. He treated her with the familiarity and affection he would give a sister. He spoke of William regularly and fondly, without criticism or envy. Every now and again, when Oliver wasn't present—when she was, for example, lying in her bed at night waiting for sleep to come—she had the oddest sensation that he was thinking of her. Intimately. Yet he behaved so circumspectly! The contrast was maddening—or it would be if she allowed it to madden her, and so she refused to allow it.

She did miss William—she told herself she did, insisted it, in fact. Said it out loud to anyone who mentioned that William had been away for a long time. Alva replied, *Yes, we miss him. I miss him. The yacht is going to be truly incredible. We'll have you on for a sail.*

No one said (to her, at least), *My, you do spend a lot of time with Mr. Belmont!* That observation was left to *Town Topics*, the small but powerful society gossip sheet run by an opportunist named Colonel Mann, who had a keen eye for rich men's vulnerabilities and the temerity to exploit them unless he was sufficiently "encouraged" not to. In a relatively innocuous report, the paper remarked that—

> Since Oliver Belmont shaved his mustache away, he looks so much like Mr. W. K. Vanderbilt that when driving with Mrs. W.K., which he does frequently, one is easily led to believe that he is the lady's husband.

No one was led to believe any such thing. But then Mann had not intended his words to be taken at face value. And so Alva paid a call to the *Town Topics* offices with a message of her own.

"Thank you for seeing me," she told Mann as he offered her a chair.

Known for his dapper suits, his silver hair, and the quality of his cigars, when seen at close range, he appeared worn and wary. He had small eyes in a saggy lined face. A thin scar stretched from his right jawline to his nose.

"Ever a pleasure, Mrs. Vanderbilt. What can I do for you today?"

With dead seriousness, Alva said, "Well, having read your latest, I was compelled to come help you recall who my husband is."

He smiled. "We were having a little joke, that's all that was. You read us. You know we have a sense of humor and we expect—or we hope, anyway—that our readers do, too."

"You may recall that my husband—that is, William K. Vanderbilt—inherited some money from his father."

"Mrs. Vanderbilt, I see that you're displeased—"

"Do you recall the figure? Sixty-five million dollars. The value has increased since then, of course. How much money do you have, Colonel Mann?"

"That's my personal business, and not at all relevant to—"

"How interesting that you mention 'personal business' and 'not at all relevant.' I feel precisely that way about *my* affairs, as I expect Mr. Belmont does, and certainly my husband feels that way as well." She stood up. "Though I don't know the particulars of your finances, I am confident that you would profit from thinking about how far my husband's money would go if he were to pursue a libel suit against *Town Topics*."

Mann stood and escorted her to the door, saying, "We've got something in this country called free speech. I don't need even a dollar for that. Good day, Mrs. Vanderbilt. Give your husband my best."

"Oh, I will," Alva said, confident that despite his bravado, he had gotten her point.

As July neared, Richard Hunt and Oliver were well into the final stages of construction of Oliver's house just down the road from hers, the project having been delayed after Oliver's mother fell ill. Alva worried that Richard was overextending himself. In addition to Oliver's and George's homes, he was now simultaneously employed in building a replacement Breakers cottage for Corneil and Alice after the original had caught fire and burned to the ground.

The new Breakers was, of course, in every way better than the old—and twice the size of Marble House. Where Alva had two stories in stone, Alice had three. Alva had used gilt in her Gold Salon, and her Rose Dining Room had a good dose of it as well. Alice, though, was using it liberally in every public room. Alva, being married to William K. Vanderbilt, had as impressive a house as Newport had seen up to now. Alice, being Cornelius Vanderbilt II's wife, was making certain hers was even more impressive. Indeed, she couldn't have it otherwise, or what would people say?

Oliver liked to be on site the way Alva always did, overseeing the overseer, catching the mistakes before the plaster could dry. He admired Alva's Gothic Room and wanted advice on incorporating the style into Belcourt (as he was calling his house). He played polo with the other gentlemen, took the children and her to Grey Crag, persuaded Hermann Oelrichs to put Harold at the wheel of *Hildegard* for regular lessons, took Willie to the races at Sheepshead Bay. Consuelo and Oliver took turns reading aloud from *The American Claimant* by Mark Twain. He escorted Alva to balls and dinners and picnics, where often they would put themselves into a quiet spot and converse.

At one such dinner party, Tessie Oelrichs took Alva aside and said, "I have to ask: What's going on with you and Mr. Belmont?"

"Conversation," Alva said.

"Oh? Do tell."

"Well, we were speaking about President Cleveland and the problems with having an administration that's lent so much power to men in families like the Belmonts and Vanderbilts. An oligarchy is *not* a representational government."

"Alva, you're so funny. What did you *really* talk about? He's making love to you, isn't he? Tell me—it'll be our secret."

Oliver was definitely not making love to her. His attitude toward her, though affectionate, continued to be free of the sentiments he'd expressed in the past. This was a relief in that it allowed her to spend time with him without awkwardness or guilt. If it was also a strange kind of disappointment—well, she had to live with that. *I know it's hard, but there you go, sometimes life is hard.*

Alva whispered in Tessie Oelrichs's ear, "Free silver."

"What?"

"Monetary policy. It's true. Ask him yourself."

Tessie Oelrichs laughed. "All right, you've convinced me. There's not even a hint of romance in that."

Alva didn't tell her this, but she disagreed. Talking politics with Oliver was terribly romantic; what could be more endearing and stimulating than to have her intelligence and viewpoints taken seriously by an attractive, interesting man?

Alva also didn't tell Tessie, nor would she tell William, nor would she ever tell Oliver that, much as she had been trying to deny the portent and ridiculous as it seemed, Oliver's proximity made her feel vivid and alive. It made her feel *desire*. By contrast, William had only ever inspired a mild warmth in her breast and nothing at all in the nether region. The situation was preposterous. Untoward. Wrong. Still, she wanted to see Oliver all the time, had basked in his company even knowing her feelings were unrequited.

Mustache, no mustache, no matter: Alva could never mistake this man for the other.

Come late July, she sat on the broad Marble House veranda and stared out across the lawn at the ocean's deepening blue. A pitcher of julep sat in an ice bucket near her elbow. William had cabled that he would be home "Thursday next," and now, on this Thursday next, she was deciding not to think overmuch about the length of his absence nor the infrequency of his letters while he was away.

From this well-padded chaise, with its setting and its view, one might find it easy to also not think about the country being once again in rather dire straits. To not notice the Treasury crisis. To fail to recall there'd been a run on banks that forced many to close. High unemployment. Low wages. A shortage in the cities of healthful housing. Increasing crime. From here on the veranda, a marriage, the country—indeed, the world—was bucolic and secure, peaceful, even bounteous if one considered the lobster and crab traps set not far offshore, the generous abundance of blackberries in the nearby shrubs, the lush garden Cook tended on the east side of the house, its rows fat with tomatoes and cucumbers and cabbages, herbs, peas, and the young trails of vines that would produce pumpkins later in the season.

There was nothing to be gained by confronting William about why he'd stayed away so long, leaving his children (not to mention his wife) to attach themselves to a different clean-shaven man. He would be home and they would resume their usual routine, and perhaps Oliver would grow his mustache again. She could not right the nation's troubles. So she would drink julep and let the breeze cool her and eat her peas with a knife and honey if she pleased.

The sun was low now in the western sky. The house threw a wide, square shadow over the lawn. Beyond the lawn, the ocean heaved and sighed, heaved and sighed. From the house came the faint sound of voices. She'd instructed the footman to tell Mr. Vanderbilt where he could find her upon arrival, and it seemed he'd done just that—

She heard William's step, but didn't turn. "Welcome home," she said.

He came to face her, holding *Town Topics* in front of her and pointing at a circled passage. "Explain this." It was the article about Oliver.

"Oh, that's old business," Alva replied, pushing the paper aside. "How was the journey? Is *Valiant* more seaworthy than her predecessor? You look well."

He was prettier than ever. Middle age had given his face a degree of character he'd lacked in youth. *Someone ought to drape him in ermine and crown him,* she thought.

"Depew says people are talking."

"You were gone a long time. Of course people are talking. That's what they do when a lady's husband goes abroad indefinitely."

"Clearly *talking's* not all *some* people do."

"Quit being so dramatic. Anyway, Oliver looks nothing like you."

"Do you deny that he drives with you frequently?"

"*Often* would be more accurate," she said, refreshing her drink. "Would you like to join me?"

"You're *my* wife, Alva. I won't have it."

"You told him expressly to stand in for you, and so he did. *Socially.*"

William sat down in a chair adjacent to her. "Are you saying you're not in love with him? The two of you aren't involved?"

He was jealous! How marvelous.

She said, "My goodness, William. Oliver and I are not *involved.* He's good company, just as he always has been." She tapped the paper and said, "I told Colonel Mann that this nonsense must cease or you will bring him up for libel."

William reached for her julep and downed it quickly, then refilled the glass and downed that, too. "All right," he said, exhaling heavily. He returned the glass, then pressed his palms to his thighs. "Very good. I should have known you wouldn't—"

"Yes, you should have known," she said calmly. The liquor was doing a fine job of keeping her keel even.

"I apologize. You've been nothing but a credit to me all these years."

"We are in agreement there."

"I do appreciate that Belmont is a true and steady friend."

"As you should."

They sat peacefully for a few minutes, listening to the *shush* of the surf. Then Alva said, "Tell me about the *Valiant.* Is she worthy of your effort and expense?"

William smiled. "She's unbelievable. There's nothing like having a fresh beginning, you know?"

"It's too bad it's not so easy to fix everything else that's sinking or sunken. The situation here in the New World has gotten rather grim during your absence."

"Then let me take you away from it for a while. A real first-rate trip—someplace new and fascinating. Further the children's cultural education. I've got some connections to Viscount Lansdowne in Calcutta. I'm sure he and his wife would be delighted to have us. I'll write him tonight and get it all under way."

"What, India?"

"He's the governor general. They have a palace—it wouldn't be any hardship. We can start in northern Africa, cruise the Mediterranean, use the Suez passage to the Red Sea and then out to the Arabian. I'll have *Valiant* fitted up for it, we'll set an itinerary, and we can sail in November or December, when the climate is favorable there."

"William, you just got home."

"No matter." He waved off her concern. "You merit a great adventure. We could end the trip on the Continent, spend next summer in Paris—you'd enjoy that. It'll be good for you, Alva. Good for *us*."

"Us."

"We should get reacquainted. We aren't the children we were twenty years ago. To think—our own daughter is nearly old enough to be brought out." He sat forward in his chair and reached for her hand. "A fresh start, all right?"

"William—"

"I'm forty-three years old."

"So?"

"So . . ." He studied their hands. "I don't know. Something. This can't be all there is."

She considered his statement for a few moments and then said, "All right."

He looked up at her. "Yes? You want to do it?"

"I do want to. A fresh start, yes."

She would get away from the familiar, away from society, from the unpleasant conjoining of her friendship with Oliver and marriage to

William—because although her body had been faithful, her sentiments had not, and those sentiments were wrong, and she would be far happier if she was rid of them.

In her eagerness, Alva did not think to wonder about William's motivations. Nor did she reexamine his selfish acts. Going abroad for the better part of a year with this apparently devoted, ever-prettier version of him could, she hoped, aid her in building a new regard for him and, even better, cure her of Oliver for good.

V

ON THE OCTOBER morning the William K. Vanderbilts were to begin their world cruise, Consuelo and Harold trailed their father up the gangway like sullen prisoners, their sullenness deepened by Willie's having been spared the journey because he was at St. Mark's School in Massachusetts. Another yacht, another voyage, another trip "to see the world," another absence—nine months or more, this time—from their friends, from Idle Hour, where they'd grown accustomed to spending the still-warm autumn days, from their schools in the city. This time they would see Egypt and India. They would escape a simmering cauldron of unemployed men, of hungry women and children, people sitting on their steps hoping for handouts. They would have their whole existence upended, though none of them knew that yet.

Alva followed her daughter over the gangway. Consuelo's slender shoulders, her graceful neck, the narrowness of her waist: she was grown now, there was no denying it, no discounting her as merely a child. Which was not to say the girl had any wisdom about her. She was still as naive as a first-day fawn.

After getting the children settled in their staterooms, Alva gave them leave to roam and went to the salon to read a Henry James novel while awaiting the launch. George had recommended she read James, who was a good friend of his. She'd chosen *The Portrait of a Lady*, being sympathetic to its premise of a young woman of small means having her life changed by an unexpected windfall—an *anti*-marriage plot, it was. Already, though, Alva was impatient with the young Miss Archer's inability to see what was going on around her, the ways she was being deceived. However, that did make for good drama: When would the girl get wise?

Before long, the sound of men's voices coming from the saloon assured Alva that William's companions were aboard now as well. He'd invited several gentlemen who either had no wife or were bringing none. Alva had invited Armide, but Armide was inclined to spend her holidays with Miss Crane in Boston. Alva's companions would be Consuelo, Harold, and Miss Harper, the governess. Mary would have been a welcome addition, and Alva might have invited her, had William not put Mary off him for good.

When Alva had been shopping in the flower district with Mary and Armide the previous week, she told the two of them, "Being away changed William. He's more considerate now. I believe he regrets his poor behavior of the past."

"Did he say so?" Armide asked.

"He said he wants to make a fresh start."

Mary pursed her lips.

"What?" Alva asked. "Tell me whatever it is you aren't saying."

"What I'm thinking is, a leopard can't change its spots."

"A man is not a leopard."

Neither woman replied.

"Do you think he's beyond rehabilitation?"

"Miss Alva," said Mary, "that man always has done and always will do whatever it is he thinks suits him best."

"You don't know him," Alva insisted.

Armide glanced at Mary. "We want whatever is best for you."

"Then we're in agreement," Alva said. "I'll write you with news of how mistaken you are."

Now Harold appeared in the *Valiant* salon's doorway. "Come on deck, Mama. It's time." Sweet child. Once aboard, he was as excited to sail as ever.

"I may need your assistance," Alva said, extending her hand. He came and took it, and she let him pull her up.

"Will we see any whales, do you suppose?"

"Humpbacks and blues, if we're lucky."

"I'm feeling quite lucky," he said.

He opened the door to the deck and as they went outside, Alva saw the party gathered at the bow. The gentleman Alva didn't yet know she should worry about was thirty-one-year-old playboy Winthrop Rutherfurd. And then there was Oliver Belmont.

Gibraltar and Tunis and Alexandria. A side trip up the Nile in a flatboat. Through the Suez Canal. Into the gulf, then the Red Sea.

"Isn't it wondrous?" William asked, standing at *Valiant*'s bow with his arm crooked through Alva's. Before them were Egypt's dry, dun-colored hills and mountains so barren and stark that it seemed nothing could live in such a place, making a sharp contrast to water so luminous and blue.

Oliver, standing on Alva's other side, said, "One can see why Moses needed God's help here."

Alva wondered whether if she went overboard the sea would part or swallow her up.

Onward they went. Cities explored. Sights seen. How could Alva concentrate on what she was seeing, appreciate its significance or beauty, when she was so vexed by her situation? Once, when she was a child, she'd had a delirium that made her feel as though she were swimming through a haze of heat and light and sound. This was something like that. At each day's end, when she retired to her cabin the first moment she felt she could politely go, she sat on her padded vanity stool and leaned in close to the glass, looked into her eyes, and cursed herself, cursed God, cursed fate, cursed Oliver for coming, and of course cursed William for blithely adding Oliver to the manifest without having said he was doing so.

—Not that she could have protested either man's action without giving herself away. She might have been able to prepare herself, though.

—No, she would not have been able to. The way Oliver affected her was unalterable, because she was flawed. She was the very sort of woman her mother had warned her about becoming, a woman driven by selfish, shameful desires. An animal.

"You deserve this twist of fate's knife," she said to her reflection, embracing the melodrama of her situation. She blamed Henry James for exciting her imagination. If only his titular lady could free herself from her injudicious heart! If only Alva could be kidnapped by pirates!

—No, they would just hold her for ransom and William, devoted as he was, would pay for her safe return.

So wealthy, such a social success, yet so discontent. Married to one man but in love with another. Trapped by circumstances she should have known better than to accept. How terribly tragic! What would she do next?

The woman in the glass had creases in her forehead. Her lips were downturned.

Stop frowning!

How very long ago it was, that day at the Greenbrier. What would the duchess think if she knew Alva had gotten herself into such a state?

"My God," Alva told her reflection. "She would laugh you out of town. Now hitch up your stockings, girl, and forget all of this nonsense before you embarrass us both."

Heading to India, they sailed into an unfriendly Arabian Sea, the yacht rolling over the swells beneath low gray skies. Alva had seated herself at the deck lounge and was finishing the novel. The ending left her somewhat perplexed. Was this Mr. James's intent? Isabel Archer's willful ignorance, her rigid morality, her inability to see her way clear of a situation that only made her miserable in the end—had he meant for all of that to be redeemed or not?

Consuelo sat nearby, a volume of Wordsworth at hand. How lovely she was! How vulnerable, just the way Miss Archer had been.

Alva was still unused to her daughter being so grown up. Consuelo's skirts were long, her hair was coiffed, her posture was perfect, she enjoyed her studies—if the girl had a flaw, it was her gentleness. Who, though, could truly consider this a fault? Yet it endangered her: she would not be able to live in her safe cocoon of poems and ideals forever.

Consuelo was giving more attention to the sea than she was to the pages in front of her. She put the book aside. "I think I'll have a stroll."

"A stroll?"

"Yes. I'm tired of sitting still."

"I'd hardly call this sitting *still*," Alva said, meaning to make a joke.

"No, I suppose you're right," said Consuelo, taking her mother seriously. Yet she remained in her chair, indecision plain on her face.

"Ahoy," called Winthrop Rutherfurd as he and Oliver approached. "Fine sailing, eh?"

Consuelo laid her book aside and stood up. "I will have that stroll," she said, and left as the men arrived.

Alva wished she were free to disappear as well. She made herself sound cheerful, saying, "One last week of this, and then we're in Bombay. I think my daughter is ready to stay on land for a while."

Oliver dropped into the chaise beside her. "I know I am."

Winthrop Rutherfurd—who liked to be called Winty—said, "Yes, the sea gets tiresome after a while. That's why I haven't bought my own vessel. Put me on the back of a horse, that's where I like to be! Running up the turf, you know, mallet in my hand. Yes, land is best. Remarkable vistas at sea, though." He went to the rail and stood there for a moment, then, after glancing in the direction Consuelo had gone, went off the opposite way.

Oliver said, "Not so subtle, is he?"

"No, but he imagines he is." She kept her gaze outward. The horizon dipped and rose beyond the railing. "I don't know what William was thinking when he asked him along—he's known for being 'fond' of heiresses. But sixteen is much too young in general, and certainly too young for our Winty here, even if I didn't already know about his other special affection."

"Oh? I'm afraid I'm not current on Rutherfurd's tastes."

"Rich married women who've found themselves possessing the time, desire, and opportunity to enjoy his company." She'd heard that he liked to keep several on a string at once, the better to play one off another, the goal being to gain a new suit or a new horse or passage to some playground or other. His familial allowance never seemed to stretch quite far enough.

Oliver said, "Shall I go put him overboard?"

Alva laughed. She wanted to resist her enjoyment, but she enjoyed him too much to resist. She said, "'*Mr. Rutherfurd suffered an unfortunate accident while at sea on W. K. Vanderbilt's astonishing new yacht.*' You'd be a hero, even if known only to me."

"It's a difficult thing, isn't it, figuring out who to marry a daughter off to."

"Especially when that daughter is an heiress. She hopes his attention might indicate true love—you can see it in the way she looks at him. Those wide, admiring doe eyes."

"We can't fault her," Oliver said. "She's completely naive."

Alva warmed to the conversation. It was always lovely to talk with him. "Even supposing his attentions were genuine," she said, "what sort of life would a man like him offer her? She'd be a very pretty, very useless doll, bored senseless, her quick mind and innate curiosities shriveled from disuse while he spent all his time riding and dining out and having new suits made on William's dime. I intend to spare her that, at least."

"I fear you describe too many of our friends," Oliver said.

"Yes, I do. Consuelo is too soft to battle with a husband, too unsure of her opinions and talents. He'd squash her as surely as Miss Archer here"—she pointed at her book—"was squashed by Gilbert Osmond. One has no idea, in youth, how false an appearance can be."

"And then in maturity one knows, but often can do nothing about it. Naiveté is better, it seems to me."

Alva said, "Willful ignorance can sometimes suffice, I've learned."

Consuelo's and Rutherfurd's paths had crossed somewhere out of Alva's sight, as she'd suspected they would, and now the two unsubtle lovers were making a slow and unsteady promenade along the rail. He'd offered Consuelo his arm, and she held on to it tightly. Alva watched them as Oliver said, "You seem to have constructed an ideal existence."

Something in his tone put Alva suddenly on her guard. Cautious, she said, "I've been fortunate."

"You live by deliberation, by design."

"Yes, well, the effort has been worthwhile."

"Oh, certainly you've got every material thing and an elevated standing in the world. But what about happiness?"

This made her even more wary. "Why would you ask me that?"

"Because I know you," he said.

Now she was uncomfortable. His remarks probed a wound she'd believed no one could see. "Perhaps I'm not who you think I am," she said, an attempt to reinforce her defenses.

"Forgive me, but I would submit that you're not who *you* think you are. Or at least not who you'd have everyone believe. I know what you keep hidden behind that faultless façade."

She blanched. Had he known all this time how she felt about him? Was he criticizing her, or worse, pitying her?

"You'll excuse me," she said, rising quickly and moving from the lounge. "I . . . I need to remind Winty that the impressionable young lady's mother is watching him."

"Alva—" called Oliver.

Let him call. She would not turn, would not see him one more time if she could avoid it. (If only she could avoid it!) The boat, still rolling, made her feel like a drunk lurching about. She was barely out of his sight when she reached the rail and vomited over it.

"Mama?" Consuelo called, hurrying over.

Rutherfurd approached as well. "I'm seasick," she said. "Give me your handkerchief." He did. Wiping her mouth, Alva told him, "Be advised: I'm watching you," and stuffed the handkerchief in his pocket before leaving the startled pair staring after her. This trip could not conclude soon enough. Thank God they'd be parting ways with Oliver and the others for a while as soon as they reached India.

Consuelo found Alva in her stateroom a little later. "Are you feeling better?"

No, the matter is hopeless, I am pathetic and miserable and I want to go home.

Alva said, "I'll be fine, thank you. It's sweet of you to look after me. Come in."

Consuelo closed the door behind her. "Mr. Rutherfurd said he was perplexed by your remark—that you're watching him. He wonders whether he's done something wrong."

"He might wonder directly, don't you think? A man of his age? Rather than put you up to asking."

"Oh, he didn't. I—I wondered it as well. *Has* he done something?"

"He's paying keen attention to a young lady half his age."

Consuelo blushed. "He doesn't mean anything by it."

"You think he doesn't?"

"He's a grown man, and I'm only a girl."

"But you'd like it if I were correct that he's making love to you."

Consuelo's blush deepened, and she gave a small shrug. "It's flattering to think so."

"Sit," Alva said, directing her daughter to the vanity stool. She faced her toward the glass and took the pins from her hair. Loose, it extended past the seat.

Taking up a hairbrush, she began brushing Consuelo's hair in long strokes. "Flattery is lovely. You're going to receive a great deal of it in the years ahead. But it isn't all. Take your time," she said.

"At what?"

"At everything."

Consuelo sighed. "That's so easy for you to say. You already have all you could desire."

Alva stifled a rueful laugh. Let her daughter be innocent for as long as that innocence could last.

Their British hosts in Calcutta were the Lansdownes. Vicereine Lansdowne's sister had been married to (and then divorced by) the late eighth Duke of Marlborough. Viceroy Lansdowne was, in addition to being governor general, a marquess. Government House, the enormous marble-halled Calcutta palace in which they lived and were served by silent, proud-seeming native men and women in red silk livery, highlighted Lansdowne's prominence. There was not a higher-ranking Englishman on the subcontinent, and few anywhere else. He served at the pleasure of the queen.

The palace atmosphere was at once exotic and properly British, as if the governor general had (at least in this astonishing marble compound) found a way to subdue the uncivilized and disturbing elements that existed in areas outside its extensive walls. Alva would like to forget some of what she'd seen from the train windows as they'd trundled from Bombay overland and along rivers, sights that included the burning of bodies on funeral pyres and infants being tossed as offerings into the water—to bring on the rains but prevent floods, one of the guides claimed. "Please, you do not worry. Baby is dead already."

Alva mentioned this while taking tea alone with Lady Lansdowne in the Yellow Drawing Room, surrounded by paintings as significant as any the National Gallery or Louvre had to display. Bassano and Titian and Watteau and Rembrandt were among the artists represented just in this room. The palace was an oasis of refinement in a land of so much dust and chaos.

She said, "Your Excellency, allow me to say how impressed I am by your treatment here. Even in the English court, I've never seen such deference."

"It really is more civilized here, I agree."

"I'd expected the Indian people to be somewhat primitive—and in parts of the country they are." Alva described what she'd seen, then said, "One fears for their souls! But in the markets, I've haggled with some of the loveliest, most intelligent women, who speak of you and the viceroy with reverence. And your servants here are impeccable in their habits and speech."

"It is a country of contrasts, to be sure."

Alva said, "*Are* those babies dead before they're given over to . . . to the rain gods, or what have you?"

"They are, yes. You must understand, however, that to the traditional Indian, our custom of *burying* the dead is horrid and cruel, as it traps the soul for all eternity."

Alva took her point. "I've always believed one's situation has everything to do with one's circumstances. And yours here is extraordinary. Her Royal Highness might have me put in the Tower if she heard me ask—but living so remarkably well as you do, do you feel like a queen?"

Lady Lansdowne smiled. "An accidental one, perhaps."

"How is it for your children?"

"Our sons are at Oxford, of course, so we only see them at holidays. Our eldest daughter is lately married to the Duke of Devonshire. Our youngest was here with us originally, but she's being finished now in London. One really can't bring a daughter out in Calcutta."

"No, I would imagine not. And truthfully, New York City isn't much more ideal."

"But your daughter should have her choice of the entire field."

"Oh, she does. It's the field that's the problem. I intend to bring her out in Paris this summer. Perhaps your son, Lord Henry, will be spending time there?"

Lady Lansdowne arched one eyebrow. "I do appreciate American directness."

"I don't mean to suggest there's any rush to pair her off. But I can speak to you so directly because I know a mother of daughters will have, as you call it, the proper perspective."

"Then I should be plain as well. The British—by which I mean the public—are not pleased to see their noblemen marrying Americans, even when badly needed capital for diminished estates is involved. It disrupts the proper order of things."

"Well, if the public prefers to see those estates crumble and the lands and villages fail, they should by all means reject the practice."

Lady Lansdowne dipped a chocolate biscuit into her tea before taking a bite. Then she said, "My Henry is already quite attached to a young lady, but you should consider a London visit to meet my sister, Lady Albertha Spencer-Churchill."

This seemed an odd change of subject, and one Alva was not especially interested in pursuing. Jennie Churchill's brother-in-law, the eighth Duke of Marlborough, had divorced Lady Albertha some time after having fathered a child with a married woman, whom he later put aside in favor of Lillian Price, a New York millionaire's widow. It had all been rather messy and sordid.

Alva said, "Ordinarily I would be delighted to meet her. I can't say, though, that a London visit will fit our itinerary."

"Her son's estate, Blenheim, is one that unfortunately is at risk of the fate you described and therefore in need of bolstering. And my nephew the duke is beginning to consider potential wives. He's an excellent young man. The Spencer-Churchills are well regarded by the queen—despite the late duke's poor judgment," she added, having perceived Alva's concern. "He had the good form to die and tidy things up that way."

"Ah," Alva said, "I suspect I can make time in the schedule after all."

"Very good. Your daughter is a poised, well-spoken, beautiful young lady. I would be surprised if she didn't appeal to my nephew. And if she did, the British public would, I'm certain, find it difficult to resist such an addition to the peerage. Incidentally, his is the only dukedom with a female-as-heir line, meaning there's less of that ghastly pressure to produce a son."

Though Alva saw the advantages in meeting the young duke, the image of her daughter fulfilling a wife's duties sobered her. "She's too young to consider anyone seriously just yet."

"Sixteen is old enough. Wait too long and you risk her being passed over for the younger ones."

"And she's too inexperienced. We've already discovered that she's bound to favor anyone who purports to favor her."

Alva had spoken to William about Rutherfurd, and they had agreed that William would warn him off when they rejoined the men later, in Nice. Better that Consuelo learn about the vagaries of the heart now, this way.

Lady Lansdowne said, "Then get her some experience, and in the meantime, secure a promise for her yourself. If it turns out she despises the gentleman, whoever he may be, you can reconsider and call it off. Didn't your mother choose for you?"

"She would have, if she hadn't died first."

The meeting left Alva hopeful for Consuelo's prospects. If her daughter could win the approval of Lady Lansdowne, she would easily attract the best prospects from all the good countries. If the Duke of Marlborough proved undesirable for any reason, they would choose some other titled gentleman, some amiable young man whose responsibilities extended beyond keeping a polo pony fed and groomed. Someone with a sense of history. Connections to a deep and abiding past. Someone whose prominence and stature were not determined mainly by his wealth. If Consuelo were to fall for someone, why shouldn't it be someone with all of this to recommend him?

With this crystallized mission in mind, Alva was cheered immensely. She had purpose. She had direction. She would do whatever it took to prevent her daughter from becoming just one more vapid society matron who fretted over the skin color of some other lady's lady's maid.

The family left India, bound for France and a rejoining with the other gentlemen of their party. Alva kept the prospect of Charles Spencer-Churchill to herself for now; Consuelo would not be able to hear about any other man while she still swooned over Rutherfurd, and she was unlikely to cease her swoon while she still anticipated his company. Alva could wait. There would be plenty of time to reshape her daughter's desires later.

By the time they put into the harbor in Nice, Alva had formed a strategy. Regardless of the offers of marriage that would undoubtedly be made in Paris, they would proceed to London and explore the possibilities there. Though Alva and William would select the best husband for her, Consuelo needed to see for herself the variety and quality of gentlemen who were available to her, and how Rutherfurd was diminished in comparison.

After a visit to the local market and a stop at the post office to retrieve their mail, they boarded their train for Paris. William's companions were there as well, all of them seated in the parlor car.

"How lovely to see you gentlemen again," Alva said as she and the family filed in. She did not look at Oliver.

The governess continued with Harold into the next car while William said, "I trust none of you has acquired anything undesirable during our separation—no infections, no arrests, no wives, no tattoos."

"No tattoos," Oliver said. Alva glanced his way. His face was browner than when they'd parted, making his blond eyebrows and green eyes stand out. How had he spent the last few weeks? Lounging in the coastal sunshine, perhaps? She hoped he had forgotten their last exchange, hoped she had somehow mistaken it, hoped he did not know what he must know.

"No wives or any of that," said Rutherfurd. He did not move toward Consuelo, but the pair exchanged an easily deciphered glance. It was almost sweet, this puppy love Consuelo had for him. Almost.

William asked, "Who'll join me for a cigar? We've got a smoking car down the way, so as to not offend the ladies."

Alva indicated the sack of letters in her hand and said, "Do go on, gentlemen. My daughter and I have to tend to all of this correspondence, anyway."

"No cigars for me," said Rutherfurd. "The smoke irritates the eyes, you see."

Consuelo said, "Might I do that later, Mother? I'm interested in seeing the locomotive."

Could the child be any more transparent? Alva said, "Are you? Then get Harold and go ahead. He'll love a chance to talk to the conductor."

"He needs to rest. That is, didn't he say he wanted to?"

Alva resisted the urge to smile. "I'm certain he did not."

"Oh. Well then, good. I'll get him." Consuelo left the car, going forward to where the family parlor was hitched while the men, Rutherfurd included, exited to the rear, toward the smoking car attached behind the dining car. Alva now had this parlor to herself.

She sorted the mail. Near the top of her stack was a thick envelope from the duchess, who was to meet up with them in Paris after having taken her girls to see relatives in Cuba—"a charity trip," she'd written in her last correspondence, travel she undertook to satisfy an aging aunt who might look upon them favorably both before and after death, if sufficient effort was made. This letter would, Alva thought, be a recounting of that trip. She could not have been more mistaken.

London, April 17th, 1893

Alva, dearest—

Fortified with bourbon, I am putting pen to the page and have promised myself I won't cease, nor will I flinch, because you are the dearest and truest of the friends I've had in this disappointing life of mine. I owe you the same fidelity.

When my husband died, I expected to feel released. I would soar on the satisfaction of his having suffered at the end, as I have suffered all these years. As he weakened and shrank and wheezed and coughed and spat blood (out of my sight for the most part; my mother-in-law was the one to nurse him), I dined with friends and took the children to the country and sang pleasing songs to myself. Soon, la, la, la, soon the Duke will die, la, la, la, and then I shall celebrate the world having one fewer sorry soul in it—make more room for the rest of us!

Well, he died, and I waited for that soaring, and it didn't come.

Instead, I felt cheated. Cheated, I tell you—because he escaped the slop he made of our lives and left me mired in it, knee-deep and flailing. Yet I had to do and say all the proper things for the children's sakes, and observe all the correct forms of a Duchess in mourning, and see to all the procedures required for Kim to take the title, and it nearly drove me mad.

Then one day I got a cable from an old friend who was coming to England. A man for whom I'd had some affection long before, as he had for me—though little had come of it in previous times. Short dalliances for diversion, really, no one the wiser. He was coming, he said, to meet with boat-builders. He was in need of a yacht. A supreme yacht, better than anything anyone had sailed before. Better than his last, the Alva, *which had been sunk.*

Alva gasped and read it again, disbelieving.

William.

Dalliances.

No one the wiser.

The forward door opened and her daughter came in, saying, "I've changed my mind." She didn't even glance at Alva before seating herself in a chair that faced outward. She sorted through some magazines, settled on one, and began reading it.

Alva's face burned. She blinked back her tears. She could not believe the words she'd read, what they meant. The deception. The betrayal.

Mindful of her daughter's presence, Alva read further:

It was loneliness that caused it, this time. Perhaps every time. And I knew how you felt about him. You confessed you had a love if not a lover, and so I reminded myself there was no harm. Again. I didn't expect it to be more than a night or two. Perhaps it would run a week and then use itself up.

It was so easy to let things continue, though, when he returned a few months later. The girls adore "Uncle Will," who is quite the lamb with them.

We were careful, he and I, but as you know, rumors are currency and they spend well in society. Colonel Mann, with his ubiquitous spies, got word and had his <u>*Town Topics*</u> *column set to run, intending to scandalize everyone involved. But he was "kind" enough to alert William to the impending disaster. Your husband's "contribution" of $25,000 persuaded Mann to reconsider, thank God, and when the boat was fitted out, I ended the affair for good and all. I hadn't meant to let it go so long. I don't love him, never did love him. Ending it was a relief, or at least it was for me.*

He was angry, and didn't seem at all contrite when I spoke of the immorality of our actions, of feeling guilty for betraying you. Why should he be contrite? He is a man—a very, very rich man.

Perhaps I was stupid to not accept the role he offered me—or I should say the cash that would have come with being his mistress permanently.

—No. No, I was not stupid. It's the whispering voice of avarice in me that writes those words, and I can resist it now, just as I resisted the offer.

I, the real I, the good I who has been buried alive for too long, will be bereft if I should lose your love, Alva, love that I could not hope to deserve to keep unless I bared my soul to you, as I have now done. Until I hear your response, I will keep away—but whatever else you feel you must do, please, don't leave me in suspense.

And don't fear that there will be further trouble. You can be certain I'm shut of him. My loyalty and my love were always with <u>*you*</u>*, but I didn't realize until after I'd betrayed you so thoroughly how deeply true that statement actually is.*

Perhaps you won't forgive me, and my confession will have served no one except myself—and even then it will be a chilly ease in my soul. So be it. Or embrace me as the genuine friend I have always tried to be. You've never loved Will, but you have always loved me.

One more thing, as long as I'm going this far: That day you referred to in your letter last year—the day after the ball, when I asked if you had a secret—I had spent the morning hours in Will's bed. I'd seen Oliver Belmont with you on the stairs that night, so obviously in love with you, and I was jealous. Jealous of that, of you, your new house, all that money, your being society's belle. So I sought out the man who'd long before offered to marry me—the man I'd turned down because he had no title—and I allowed him to seduce me.

Alva, men are either pit vipers like my husband or self-satisfied playboys like Bertie and Will and too many others I've known.

Does love exist?

~C.

Numbed, Alva folded the letter and returned it to its envelope, then put the envelope in her satchel. The train was moving now, chugging into the countryside, the snow-topped Alps visible out her window. The men might rejoin them at any moment. It would be another two hours until they'd all go to dinner. Even longer to get to Paris. How was she to survive and not make a scene, or even give herself away?

"I want off this train."

Consuelo said, "Did you say something, Mother?"

This life! What had she done, bringing a daughter into such a trap as every man laid for women like them? Good, dutiful women, women who could be counted on, who could be trusted. Even they could be horribly misused.

"What?" Alva said. "No. Talking to myself."

How long did she sit there, swaying with the car's rhythm, unable to act, unable to think beyond the words she had read? That she'd been so thoroughly betrayed by the two of them was a blade in her heart. Surely her blood was draining out of her body, and in another moment or two she would slump to the floor, freed from her horror and embarrassment.

William, devoted to her. His angel, he had called her.

Being away changed William. He's more considerate now. How stupid she'd been! Stupid in every way. And her friend, giving Alva her handoffs and then taking them back for amusement whenever it suited her—and now claiming to love her. Oh, yes, *love* had compelled her to reveal this tawdry scenario. *Love* had compelled her to reject William's offer of conditional support. Alva hoped the duchess didn't love all her friends so well!

The sound of the door opening ended her trance. William led his friends into the car, the lot of them reeking of cigar smoke. *Look at him,* she thought, *so self-satisfied, so assured of his privilege, his command of the world in which he lives.* Who had better horses, a better yacht, more attractive children, a more accomplished wife? Whose grandfather and father had been among the richest men in the world? Whose family dominated Manhattan's and Newport's most exclusive avenues with the most impressive homes? Who was still as fit and well turned out at forty-three as he had been at twenty-three? He had all his hair. He had his choice of horses and wines and women and friends and occupations, and his days were completely his own. If he wanted to go roaming for months on end, he went. If he wanted to betray his wife with her best friend, he did it. The cost of any and all of it was merely money, and he had more of that than he could ever spend.

As the men approached, Alva said, "I'm going to take a walk." Then she stood up and left the car's opposite end.

Standing on the gangway, she peered down as the train sped onward, the ground a blur of rocks and rail. She could throw herself out, right here between the cars. Say nothing to anyone, be gone long before anyone thought to wonder why she hadn't returned. Become merely a body beside a track. A tangle of skirts and gravel. Blood, too, she supposed. End her humiliation quickly, all at once. Wouldn't William and his two-faced whore be sorry then?

"Probably not," she said.

Remembering she still had children to raise, a daughter to marry into something better, please God, she stepped across the coupling and into the next car.

Alva paced the string of cars, once, twice, and back again, and then, when everyone went to dinner, hid herself in her berth proclaiming a headache. When the train arrived at Paris's Gare de Lyon, she pretended exhaustion, said little except *au revoir* to the men. She avoided Oliver's questioning gaze and herded the children into the hansom, curtly bidding William to stay behind with the governess and other servants, to make certain all their trunks were accounted for. "It's late. The children are tired. We'll see you at breakfast."

They *were* tired. Harold let his head droop against Alva's shoulder and was asleep moments later. Consuelo leaned her elbow on the bench's arm, chin in hand, and yawned mightily before closing her eyes. Lulled by the sway of the cab and the sound of hooves on bricks, Alva allowed herself a few minutes' rest, too.

The Hôtel Continental's views of the Tuileries brought to mind childhood nights when she'd watched the beautiful carriages as they rolled along the rue de Rivoli and had imagined herself grown up, a fine lady with the glossiest carriage, the best horses—a matched team that would toss their manes as they pranced, lamplight making their flanks gleam. Everyone would see her, admire her, recognize her as one of the great ladies of Paris. How easy it had all seemed then. How fulfilling such a life would be.

Alone in her room, she stood on the balcony. To her left, Notre-Dame. To her right, Eiffel's Tower—lighted, Monsieur Eiffel had said when he gave them a tour, with ten thousand gas lamps. "Already it is a technology of the past," he said. "One day they will be replaced with Mr. Edison's wires and bulbs. Man ever desires what's newer, more vivid."

The Duchess of Manchester was not newer than Alva. She was, however, more vivid. By certain measures, anyway.

Inside, Alva took the letter from her satchel and spread it over the desk. Her once-dear friend's handwriting was small, tidy, as precise as a good artist's line work.

Fortified with bourbon, I am putting pen to the page and have promised myself I won't cease, nor will I flinch, because you are the dearest and truest of the friends I've had in this disappointing life of mine . . .

This was no impulsive note. She had considered it as carefully as she had written it.

"Selfish," Alva said. "Confession aids only the sinner."

Her heart felt heavy inside her breast, as if it had filled with sludge and swelled four times its size, crowding her lungs, making it difficult for her to breathe. Her stomach, empty, roiled anyway. Her mind raced from memory to memory, recasting so many conversations and situations in this new garish light. She had not even suspected. God, how they must have laughed at her!

And all the while, she had been *scrupulous* in her own behavior.

Alva clutched the chair's arm as if it were a dagger. William, an adulterer. A liar and a cheat even as he had harassed Mary and run her off, claiming to be protecting the family's interests—protecting Alva's own interests. So righteous and honorable, that was him. Ha! The joke was on her.

She was not going to let him get away with this. She would do . . . something. Kill him, perhaps. Really, it was so much wiser to kill *him* than herself. Courts across the land were acquitting justified murderers every day.

Or, though she might derive less satisfaction from the act, she could divorce him. His blatant infidelity gave her legal cause in New York.

In either case, the details of his infidelity would be made public by papers across America with lip-smacking pleasure. A widowed American duchess whose best friend was the wife of her millionaire lover—the playboy Vanderbilt, the one everyone knew let his brother do all the work. A duchess who'd helped the friend overtake New York society in the legendary '83 costume ball, whose namesake was the friend's daughter and whose own daughter was named in part for the friend whose own husband had been a dissolute womanizer and died in ignominy. The whole situation was tangled and sordid. Damage to Alva's own reputation aside, the resulting scandal could hinder or even ruin Consuelo's chances to make the right marriage, and would certainly destroy the twins' chances, damaged as they already were by their own father's behavior.

Too, Alva had to think of the consequences her actions would have on her own future, and her sons'. She might lose guardianship of her children if a judge felt she ought to have done what every other good, God-fearing wife did—that being to stop complaining and just let the poor husband have his fun. And it was one thing to feel righteous in the face of social scorn, but quite another to be poor and to be cast out of society. She would have to sell Marble House and budget the proceeds for the rest of her life.

What sad irony it would be if in rescuing her pride, she ended up no better off than if she'd never married into money. Henry James would give such a character just that end.

"I won't allow it," she said to herself.

"Oh, won't you?" her self replied. "How do you imagine you'll prevent it?"

"Make a separate life," she said. Live apart from William in London, say, or Paris. He probably wouldn't protest. He would keep paying the bills. She would carry no overt stain on her reputation.

Still, everyone would know they'd separated. Much would be made of her absence from New York, and speculation would be rampant. She would be blamed. *She* would be blamed! Because no right-thinking lady could possibly wish to leave an amiable gentleman like him. She'd have money and all its accoutrements, but she'd have neither respect nor self-respect and would die a lonely, sour old woman.

Or . . . she could do nothing at all about it, simply carry on as usual.

"No, I can't," she said.

She was damned in some measure no matter which path she took. "That sounds like a Mr. James story, too." She gave a wry laugh that was a half-sob. "He does understand society."

The sound of someone trying the doorknob made her nearly jump out of her skin. "Who's there?"

"It's William. Will you let me come in?"

"Your room is across the hall."

"Alva, open the door."

She ignored him.

A minute later came the sound of a key in the lock and of William's voice saying, "*Merci beaucoup*," as the door opened.

"What's going on?" he said, closing the door behind him. "You claimed to be exhausted, and yet here you are still up—not even dressed for bed." His tone was terse. "Oliver and I had a drink near the station. 'What's the matter with Alva?' he asked. 'Is she ill? Should you send for a doctor?' He was quite solicitous of you."

"It's late," she said. "We can speak in the morning."

"The two of you are always conversing," he went on, ignoring her. "What do you discuss? You don't give a fig for horses—"

"I enjoy riding," she said, seeing little choice but to play this out. Did he imagine that somehow her odd behavior today had to do with Oliver? Was he jealous again?

"Riding, yes, but not racing or breeding, which is all he ever seems to want to discuss with *me*. So what is it?"

"I told you. Horses."

"Alva."

"The Belmont Stakes," she said blithely. She would not make this easy for him. "August can't seem to breed a winner. Different feed for the mares might help."

"You expect me to believe that's the extent of it."

"All right, I confess: that is not all we've discussed. We've also spoken about architecture and building materials and furnishings, and national monetary policy, and whether he and Perry will ever agree on the merits of progressivism; Perry is just so wed to the past. We've talked about the children."

"What about me?"

"You?" Alva said.

"Does he talk about me—claim I'm involved with other women, for example?"

Now this was an interesting turn. Alva said, "Why would he?"

"Because he's in love with you—not that he'll admit it, and feeding you lies about me would help his case. I expect he would say anything. The worse the better, for his purposes!"

"Oliver Belmont is not in love—" Just then, Alva understood something, or thought she did. "Wait," she said. "Oliver knows?"

William's infidelity must have been what Oliver had in mind when they'd spoken that day on the yacht. Hearing her remark about how willful ignorance could suffice for naiveté, he must have thought she'd found out and was pretending ignorance, the way so many wives in her position did. With her own guilty conscience, she had mistaken his query about her happiness.

But wait—he knew about William and yet never raised the subject with her? All that time when William was away, not a word! Escorting her everywhere—to keep her occupied and therefore distracting her from any suspicions. Protecting his friend, no doubt—until her remark about willful ignorance gave him the impression she had found out.

How dare he question her apparent decision to pretend happiness when he was part of the deception!

He was part of the deception. Oliver, a liar.

Well, she'd wanted a cure for her stupid, desperate feelings about him. Now she had it.

William said, "Oliver knows what?"

"About you and the duchess. I have her confession in a letter."

William got very still for a moment. Then he said, "I'd like to see that letter."

"It's put away for safekeeping."

"Well, whatever she said, it isn't true. She's distraught—perhaps even disturbed. Mandeville left her in trying circumstances. I did see her briefly, as you know, but there was nothing to it. You can't trust her, Alva. She gambles. She's in debt—"

"She could have no possible reason to state the things she did in the way she did unless they were true." Alva's throat tightened as she spoke. "If you have any regard for me, any honor or self-respect, you'll end this charade."

William dropped into a chair and put his hands to his face. Then, lowering his hands, he said, "It didn't mean *anything*."

"How ironic. To me, it means everything."

"Why should it? I have given you every single thing you've desired. Men have . . . well, we have ongoing . . . needs, you see, and I couldn't burden *you* with . . ." He trailed off. His face was red.

Alva said quietly, "She was my closest friend. Whether she was willing or not, couldn't you at least have gone a bit further afield?"

William made no reply.

"You have betrayed and insulted me," Alva said, "but worse, you have failed the children—ours and hers. It's unconscionable, the way you put the girls' futures at risk. If word gets out—"

"It won't."

"You had better pray it doesn't. Because if it does, our daughter's prospects are *ruined*. The stain on her reputation will be permanent. And considering how the twins' circumstances are reduced already—"

"All right, yes, it was ill advised! But I didn't exactly do it myself. She—"

"If not for the girls, I'd parade both of you before the courts like the criminals you are. But I know what it's like to have to compromise on a husband, and I won't put that on any of them."

"You're saying I was a compromise?"

"I am, yes," she said. "I might have done better."

"What, like Consuelo with Mandeville? Look where that got her."

"Yes, look. Poor thing. Had she only married *you* when she had the chance, an *American* gentleman could have betrayed her. So much better for her."

"I *gave* you Marble House! I didn't have to do that—or any of the other things I've done for you. I am as decent a man as there is, and any other woman would be grateful."

She said, "Grateful to be betrayed? Suppose I had done it to you?"

"Your moral superiority—"

"Is correct and earned! Can you honestly claim it isn't?"

For several moments he didn't reply. Then he said, "I suppose it is."

He raked his hair. He stood. He walked the room from end to end and back. "I'm actually glad to have this out. It's finished—did she say that?

I wanted to end it cleanly, but I felt morally obliged to offer support. I hope you'll be able to forgive me."

"What, as easily as that? I don't know yet what I'm going to do."

"Do? What is there to do? I've told you that it's over, and I'm sorry. What more could you need?"

Alva stared at him. He was sincere.

She said, "I need time to consider everything clearly."

"You can't be thinking about divorce," he scoffed. "That would be ridiculous."

The presumption in his remark was too much to bear. "You *will not* tell me what I can or cannot consider." She got up. "Quite honestly, I've had all I can stand of you just now. Get out of my room. Now."

"My dear," he said, reaching for her.

"Don't," she said, moving away from him. She was trembling. "If I thought I could get away with it, I would pull your heart right out of your chest and feed it to your dogs."

He put up his hands. "All right. But tomorrow—"

"Get out."

"You're correct in your anger. But—"

"Go!" She grabbed the first thing in her reach—a plate still piled with cherry wafers—and threw it at him. It hit the mantel and shattered.

If she had not been so upset, she might have laughed at how he bolted from the room.

Alva locked her door. Then she picked up a pillow, put it to her face, and screamed.

When she was calmer, she went again onto the balcony to lick her wounds. She did not like to feel sorry for herself. After all, here she was in the best hotel in Paris. The hotel's safe held on her behalf a strand of pearls that had belonged to the empress whose palace had been right across this street. She had borne three children, all of whom were alive and healthful—as she was herself.

Yet she was feeling pitiable—and did she not deserve to? She was a queen of society, an angel in the house, a benefactress to those in need, and *still* her husband had betrayed her. His best friend—who had once claimed to love her—had been complicit in the deceit. And her own best friend was the mistress in this sordid affair. Perhaps the worst part of all was that in her pain she could not turn to the one friend who had been her comfort and confidante all these years.

And why? Why had this happened to her? She had led an exemplary life, damn it.

She yelled out across the rue de Rivoli, across the Tuileries, out to the Seine, to the Left Bank, to all of Paris, to everyone everywhere, "I have led an exemplary life!" Only now it wasn't a lament, it was a warning.

VI

ALVA COULD NOT afford right now to dwell on her heartache, on the horror of being so deceivable and so deceived. Nor was it profitable to think further, for the moment, on murder or divorce. Extreme action of any kind (exhibited publicly, at least) would not aid her agenda; Consuelo's betrothal must now happen as soon as possible. Alva had spent most of her life perfecting the art of good behavior; let it serve her for at least a little while longer.

Consuelo's society debut was to be at a *bal blanc* being thrown by the Duc de Gramont for his daughter. She would follow that event with an appearance at Countess Mélanie de Pourtalès's evening salon two days later—rare events, these salons, now that the countess was up in years and less inclined than she'd once been to entertain at home.

"My mother got us invited to the countess's salon a time or two," Alva told her daughter on their way to Worth, where they would order Consuelo's white gown. "I once dreamt of becoming a regular. To attend is quite an honor, you know."

"Why is it?" Consuelo asked.

"Because it means the countess recognizes one's value or contributions."

They were on rue de la Paix, a street Alva had tread many times on her way to the shop. Worth's black marble facade was the only significant mark on an otherwise nondescript street. The plainness of the setting was in stark opposition to the wonders one found inside the shop.

"Contributions to what?" said Consuelo.

"To society and culture."

"I would think it more important to contribute to the public good in some manner. The wealthy have a responsibility to avoid decadence and corruption."

If only your father thought so.

Alva said, "Indeed we do. What you'll learn, though, is that in order to gain the power to do significant good, one must first manage to not only survive in the snake pits but *succeed* in them—the French court, the English court, wherever you eventually find yourself. Countess de Pourtalès and Empress Eugénie and others like them throughout history all understood that in order for a woman to find meaningful occupation, she has to be political, even cunning. Otherwise, what is any woman of wealth and prominence but a decoration? And for only a little while, at that."

She continued, "You're going to be a truly beautiful woman. You'll have years of admiration and adulation. What you have to consider is what you want for yourself afterward."

The child looked bewildered. Well, she would learn soon enough. Alva would continue to try to illuminate the path for her, to interpret and explain and, if necessary, pull her out of harm's way, prevent catastrophe. How much simpler it was to raise sons!

As they were about to enter the shop, Consuelo said, "Why must I debut here instead of at my own ball at home, as Gertrude will?"

"Because Gertrude's mother is satisfied with the prospects there."

"I know some very fine American gentlemen."

"Do you, now?"

"Yes."

A shopgirl held the door open and greeted them in French. "Madame Vanderbilt, Miss Vanderbilt. We are so pleased to have you with us again."

"A mutual pleasure," Alva replied. "My daughter needs the perfect white gown, and I'll want to order some items for her trousseau. I'd love to see Monsieur Worth. Is he in?"

"Sadly, no. His health has been poor. We see him rarely."

"Please convey my warmest wishes for his return to health." To her daughter she said, "Monsieur Worth did Empress Eugénie's trousseau."

In English, Consuelo asked, "Why are you buying mine now?"

"We won't be back before next spring," Alva said. She didn't say they might not be back at all—or Alva might not, that is, if her outcome made her too poor to travel to Paris let alone be dressed by Worth. She added, "And who knows what will have developed for you by then?"

She and Consuelo were shown to a settee to await a display of prospective gowns. She asked her daughter, "Do you have a particular gentleman in mind? You said you know some fine ones."

"What? No, no one in particular."

"Then you might stop fretting about your debut geography and consider *les jeunes hommes* you're going to meet at the ball, *s'il vous plait*."

"I don't know if I do please. Papa is so cross lately, and you've been . . ."

"What have I been?"

"Miss Harper likened you to an ox. She said sometimes you just put your head down and push until you get where you wish to be."

Miss Harper was more observant than Alva would have given her credit for. Alva said, "I suppose I do."

"Doesn't it bother you, having her say such a thing?"

"It's a compliment! Whether she means it to be or not. Listen to me," Alva said, turning her daughter's face so that they were looking directly at each other. "This is important: no person's good opinion of you matters more than your own."

Shortly a trio of young ladies appeared in all-white gowns of varying style. Each girl and each gown was attractive. Consuelo pointed at the second girl. "I like hers," she said.

Alva shook her head. "No, the ruching at the neckline is all wrong for you. Next!" she called, and the girls disappeared into the dressing room, returning soon after in new selections. Again Consuelo pointed out one she thought was appealing, and again Alva dismissed all three. When the girls made their third appearance, Alva told the shopgirl, "There. The last one. We'll have one like that, but I'll want the sleeve modified." She stood up and went to the model, then directed the assistant in the alterations she wanted done.

When Alva had finished, Consuelo told her in a low voice, "But I didn't care as much for that one."

Alva ushered her over to the dais to have her measurements taken. "It will show you to your best advantage. That's the objective."

"They're all white gowns, and I'm the same in any of them. How can it make that much difference?"

"That you're asking the question demonstrates how little you understand such things. Which is why I'm making the decisions." Alva moved so that the seamstress could begin measuring, then continued, "Dressing for occasions is an art. For now, I am the artist and you are the canvas. Together—with Monsieur Worth's designer's assistance—we'll create a portrait of a modest yet remarkable young beauty, and then on the night of the ball we'll see who the true aficionados are."

The seamstress smiled at Alva's remarks. Consuelo was not as entertained. "But you just said it's *my* good opinion of myself that matters most."

"Yes," Alva said, "and I meant it. But you haven't learned yet all the factors that make up the basis of that opinion. You're a month past seventeen! I haven't finished training you."

Consuelo muttered, "I'm not one of Papa's hounds."

Alva forced herself not to smile at this remark. So her daughter was finally gaining some strength of character! This was another good sign—though expressing it at this precise moment was perhaps less than ideal.

Alva said, "If only it were so easy as training dogs! Children require far more work, and you're hardly more than a child. Be grateful! Consider what I've done for you already."

"What do you mean?"

"Which languages do you speak?"

"English, German, French, and some Italian and Spanish."

"What have you studied?"

"History, literature, art, mathematics, geography—"

"And you've traveled extensively."

"Yes."

"How are you spending your days here?"

"At the museums, and the Théâtre-Français . . . oh, and at Saint-Sulpice on Sundays, especially to hear Monsieur Widor play the organ. He's an incredible talent. And Miss Harper and I read in the Tuileries Garden . . . Sometimes I drive in the Bois—"

"Do you hear yourself? What stimulation! What culture! I've made sure you had an education as good as any gentleman ever got. Further, you sit a horse as well as anyone, can drive your own gig, know all the dances, and are able to comport yourself equally well with porters as with presidents. Would you not agree that I've done a good job with you so far?"

"Well, yes, I suppose you have."

"You suppose. Good. Well, then, suppose you trust me to continue the job for a little while longer, all right?"

Alva had imagined this night many times over the years. Her daughter, ever so elegant in white tulle, being escorted to the dance floor again and again, every worthy young man in Paris lining up to take her by the elbow and attempt to dazzle her in a quadrille or with a waltz. Consuelo was having an experience Alva had longed for but never got.

Much had to occur in the space of a single dance, because at a ball such as this, there was no allowance for conversation before or after. Purity, the only commodity an unmarried young woman had some control over, the one thing of value she could offer regardless of her station or her appearance, was what was being advertised here. Behind the scenes were all the political machinations: the conversation and consideration of alliances that might be made if the young lady was in fact everything she ought to be (or if she or her family could persuade everyone that such was the case when it was not).

In Alva's own youth, the politics of the debut hadn't mattered to her at all. She had been fixed on the romance of it, the mystery and excitement in wondering which, if any, of the gentlemen who would seek her out would win her father's approval.

And her daughter—well, Consuelo was fixed on Winthrop Rutherfurd, who was gone to Spain to watch bullfights. If she found tonight romantic, mysterious, or exciting, she was not letting on. Just before they'd left the hotel, Consuelo had said, "How late must we stay?"

From the perimeter, Alva watched as Consuelo greeted each gentleman with a modest smile and then followed all the correct forms throughout the dance, parting with the same modest smile. Those gentlemen who wished a further hearing (which was every one of them, so far) then came to speak to Alva. William was in a salon or drawing room somewhere in the house talking horses or yachts or cigars or racetracks or dogs with another of his set.

This method of bringing a girl out was very different from the approach being enacted for Gertrude. Alice was determined to open the gate to every American heir whose family name sounded good to her ears. Already she was allowing Gertrude to ride out with groups of friends without supervision—much the way Lady C's mother had once permitted her to do. And look at the results: young and vibrant Miss Consuelo Yznaga had allowed William (and who knew how many others?) to "sample her offerings," one might say, and then went on to marry just the kind of man who was attracted to just that kind of girl, leading to much unhappiness, infidelities, and at least one egregious betrayal that ruined a lifelong friendship and probably a marriage as well. Alva was not going to release her daughter onto that pathway.

William reappeared at Alva's side. "She's the most beautiful girl here," he said.

Alva said nothing.

He said, "Her mother is beautiful, too."

Alva left him to stand by himself.

They had one week left in their Paris tenure. London was next, and in London, a dinner with Lady Albertha Spencer-Churchill and her son the duke—and likely another twenty assorted visitors and friends. Here at the salon of Countess Mélanie de Pourtalès, though, came the possibility of seeing Consuelo's lustrous dark hair supporting a *royal* crown, for among the countess's guests was—

"Prince Francis Joseph of Battenberg," said the countess. "Many consider him the lesser of the four brothers. But with sufficient capital to underwrite his efforts, he may well rule Bulgaria in due time."

Alva, seated at the countess's side, assessed him. Tall and lean, with fine, upright posture, thick hair, handsome features . . . She said, "Battenberg—isn't one of them married to the queen's daughter, Princess Beatrice?"

"That would be Henry. Yes, Victoria consented to a union with the family, bringing great status to all the relations."

Warming to the possibilities, Alva said, "It's just as I told my sister-in-law a few years ago: learning German history and language is going to be a genuine benefit to the girls. Her daughter is two years older than mine, but nowhere near as prepared for a position of significance."

Alva was loosely acquainted with the Battenberg family's situation. Beyond Henry's marriage, she recalled that the eldest brother had ruled Bulgaria a decade earlier, but after clashing with Russia and his own government, he'd been forced to abdicate.

She said, "Who is Bulgaria's monarch now?"

"That would be Prince Ferdinand of Saxe-Coburg. The queen is not delighted with the selection," she said. Alva waited for her to elaborate, but the countess said only, "This one's quite pleasing to look at, isn't he?" The countess gave her famed foxlike smile. "Think of how beautiful their children will be."

"They've spent less than a minute in each other's company and you've got them producing heirs!"

"Experience," said the countess. "He'll try for her, you'll see. I like the Battenbergs. They're going to amount to something."

Consuelo and the prince sat in conversation for much of the evening. The prince was obvious in his desire to remain at her side. As for Consuelo, Alva noted her flushed skin; having the undivided attention of such a man was a heady experience (and a good comparison to Winty). Alva remembered being in the company of men like the prince, in the days before she was old enough to be considered for anything more than conversation. She remembered how she had glowed in the light of such sophistication, much the way her daughter glowed now. She remembered how her pithy remarks won admiration from such men and won, too (she felt certain at the time), a favored spot in each man's heart, such that when she was a little bit older—*not much longer*, she would tell herself, *not long now*—one of them (the best one, whoever he might be) would come to see her father with an offer of marriage.

Alva said, "If not for my mother—"

"You might have worn a crown? Perhaps so. We all felt sad for your sisters and you. Yet you have prevailed! You rule the premier citizens in America, no? You can buy yourself a crown as impressive as any you might have received."

"I may lead, but I don't rule. And should I buy a crown, I still can't buy a title," Alva said. "I can't purchase the status and prestige the top houses have—though I will say, I've learned that a title is no guarantee of superior character."

"Do tell," said the countess.

"England's Manchester."

And his wife.

"Ah, yes. One must choose carefully, if one can choose."

"At any rate, it's youth that truly rules in America. With few exceptions, older ladies may as well not exist. One of the many things I so admire about the French is that a woman of power and grace like yourself never loses her power."

"Not unless she squanders it," said the countess. "Or lets it go."

"No risk of that with you."

"None at all. Nor will you lose yours, if you make the correct choices." The countess's gaze was on Consuelo and the prince. Alva, though, thought of William.

Much as Alva had been ignoring her husband and the trouble he'd made for her, what the countess said stayed with her into the small hours of the night.

She did not wish to lose everything she had worked so hard to gain. Yet what she would preserve by inaction would be polluted by her knowledge of what had happened.

Was polluted luxury better, though, than being poor and ostracized?

The answer had been so clear to her younger self.

. . .

After spending a sleepless night imagining what women like the countess and the empress might do in her place, Alva sent William a note inviting him to breakfast in her room. She chose a conservative blue serge dress and pinned her hair close to her head. Face powder, to hide the evidence of her sleeplessness. Single pearls at her ears.

Thus costumed, she had the breakfast brought in on a cart and now she waited, sitting up straight at the small table, breathing deeply, ready to put on a show once again.

William arrived and took the chair across from her. "I trust you're well this morning," he said as he lifted lids from platters and began filling his plate.

Her head ached. Her stomach was knotted. She said, "Very well, thank you."

"Are you not going to eat?" he asked, noticing she had only her coffee before her.

"I've decided: I am going to sue for divorce on the basis of infidelity."

He had a bite of sausage. "No, I don't think so."

"I'm not asking your permission."

"What you said that first night, about protecting our daughter and the Montagu girls . . ." He bit into his toast, chewed, swallowed. "There can't be any divorce. Besides which, I don't want a divorce. We're managing. We'll manage even better if you'll try."

Alva said, "Let's try this. After the children and I leave for London, you're going to hire a woman here in Paris to pose as your mistress. You'll get her a flat in a nice building, with staff, and meet her there regularly. You'll take her to the races. You'll make certain your friends see the two of you together. It needn't last long. Or if you like each other, keep her. I don't especially care. When the news of your behavior breaks, I will make a visible show of outrage and then have my attorney proceed. Our settlement will include a cash award, along with sufficient funds for running Marble House and a new place in the city—you've ruined our home, so it's yours. The settlement will also include support for the children, who'll remain in my charge." She pushed a folded sheet of paper across the table. "Here, I've outlined the details for you."

William stared at her. She sat as still as she could, straight-backed, impassive. Her head throbbed.

He said, "I'm to stage an infidelity so that you can get a divorce."

"No, you're to stage one so that you protect the girls' reputations."

"But I can do that by doing nothing. Why would I agree to your plan? I told you, I don't wish to be divorced."

"Well, I don't wish to be married to a man so duplicitous that he could carry on with my best friend while naming his yachts after me."

"Alva, she means nothing to me. You're the one I—"

"Don't you dare say *love*. Don't you perjure yourself just to save some money and a little pride."

"Whatever I say, it's not going to make any difference."

"Finally you're seeing me clearly. Good."

"Yes, I see that you are willing to undo everything you've accomplished these twenty years just to soothe your own pride."

"I prefer to think of it as retaining my self-respect."

"And for that you'd willfully spoil your own daughter's chances to marry well."

"*You* are the one who caused this. I am mitigating the scandal. This way you look merely stupid instead of evil, heartless, and cruel. Divorce in this circumstance won't be so troubling for her. One of her better prospects is the son of divorced parents himself."

"How righteous you sound."

"And why do you suppose that is? Now, I'm due at Maison Doucet in twenty minutes," she lied. "Do I have your commitment to follow this plan?"

"If I refuse?"

"Colonel Mann will gleefully report my affirmation of your trysts with the duchess. It will be an even better story than the one he had intended to print before you paid him off."

He had another bite of sausage, shaking his head as he chewed. "You won't do that to the girls."

Coldly she said, "I would rather not, it's true. But if you once again do only what *you* desire, imagining, as ever, that you can yet get away with it, I will expose you."

She watched his face. Did he believe her?

He said, "I don't know why you can't simply let it alone."

"No, it is quite obvious that you don't."

He took the folded paper and put it in his breast pocket. "I'll consider this." Saying nothing further, he left the room.

Alva remained in her chair feeling deflated. The headache now came full on.

He would consider it. He would consider it, because he could.

Prince Francis Joseph called on Consuelo the following afternoon. Alva sat at the far end of the suite's drawing room pretending to be occupied with her correspondence while keeping an ear on the conversation, which had evolved into a monologue by the prince.

"Sofia, seat of Bulgarian rule, isn't Paris, of course. I did spend many pleasant days there, though, before my brother was abducted and forced to give up the throne. The weather is very fine. I won't trouble you with the political claptrap required for my election to rule. Very likely it will all be accomplished peacefully . . ."

Consuelo's expression today was not the flattered and flushed ingénue of the previous evening. As the prince went on about his schemes, she wore a smile and gave the appearance of genuine interest in all the prince had to say, but in her eyes—perhaps not obvious to the prince but clear enough to Alva, who could guess her thoughts—was apprehension.

Alva, too, was apprehensive. Though some of her courage to coerce William had been drawn on the possibility that the prince would propose marriage, was this man, attractive and exalted as he might be, good for Consuelo? What's more, the continual arranging and rearranging of political alliances *in* the Balkans and *with* the Balkans could mean that even if Prince Francis Joseph succeeded in his plan to unseat Prince Ferdinand, he might face incursion himself. The risk of instability and upheaval had to be balanced against the benefits Consuelo would derive from a royal title, a royal life. Few young women ever got such opportunities.

". . . and therefore," the prince was saying as he stood, "I must reluctantly take my leave. Thank you for your hospitality. I have enjoyed our acquaintance and hope to continue it."

Consuelo nodded and extended her hand. "The pleasure was mine."

Alva saw him out. When she returned to the drawing room, Consuelo was absent. Alva found her at the desk in her bedroom, readying a pen with ink.

"Pressing business?" she asked.

"I'm writing down some of my thoughts. Gertrude keeps diaries. She says it helps order her mind. I thought I might try it."

"He's an excellent gentleman, isn't he?"

"Yes, quite."

"If he succeeds in his plans, he'll be powerful in his little corner of the world."

"He said he's been reading the Greeks. It's good that he does that. Read, I mean."

"The countess is eager to see you two paired."

"He told me. Yet it seems so . . . That is, she knows me so little."

"You make a good impression," Alva said, leaving aside the matters of political allegiances and the intricate webs tying together generosity and self-interest that informed the countess's opinion.

She changed the subject. "Won't it be lovely to have an evening to ourselves? Harold has said he's ready to challenge you in bezique."

"Will you play with him?" Consuelo asked, turning back to the desk. "I'm in no mood for it."

"He'll be disappointed, but I will, yes, if he'll settle for me."

Alva, too, was in no mood for bezique (though she would pretend for Harold's sake). Challenging William in a game of far higher stakes hadn't brought her the satisfaction she thought it might. Nothing was clear. She felt like an ox trudging through mud in a rainstorm.

The prince's proposal of marriage came three hours later, relayed to Alva along with a note from her husband giving his consent, if Consuelo desired it. Leaving Harold to eat his dinner with Miss Harper, Alva took

Consuelo to a quiet table in the ladies' dining room and, once they'd gotten their wine and their soup, presented the prince's note to her.

"It seems you've dazzled Francis Joseph of Battenberg more than sufficiently. What do you think of that?"

"I—well, I am terribly flattered, of course . . ." Consuelo's wide brown eyes were even wider than usual, and her expression conveyed fear as much as excitement. She put her hand to her mouth to stifle a nervous laugh. "It's an honor, isn't it?"

"It is exceptional. He has his choice of all the young ladies."

"But it could very well be Papa's money that impresses him most."

"We know your being so well fixed is almost always going to be some consideration," Alva said as their dinner was presented. (Roasted duck, with stuffed figs and sliced carrots and a lovely frisée surround. If she failed with William, she would dearly miss eating so well.)

She continued, "There are very, very few men who would be on equal footing with you as regards money."

"I do think he likes me."

"I believe he does."

"And he's quite handsome."

"He is."

Consuelo clutched her hands. "Suppose he's the only one who will ask? If I turn him down, I might end up like Aunt Armide."

"There will be others. There already have been."

"What? Which others?"

"Several of your partners at the Duc de Gramont's ball. They put their proposals to your father and me, and we thanked them and sent them on their ways."

"Several?"

"Rest assured that if you turn down the prince, other offers will follow."

"What if I had wished to consider one of the ones you rejected?"

Alva tried the wine, then said, "I promise you, they weren't worth considering. This wine, however, is lovely."

"What of Kim?" Consuelo asked, referring to the duchess's son. "That is, the duke."

"You and Kim? That's only ever been a joke. Besides, he isn't right for you."

"You always say I should have a title."

"I would see you married to a footman before I would consider young Manchester. Please tell me you aren't serious in your interest."

Consuelo shook her head. "No. I only wondered what you would say. Will we see the twins, at least? I thought they were coming to Paris."

"Their plans have changed."

Alva thought of the letter, which was beside her in her satchel. She had it with her at all times, as insurance, but had not replied to it. Nor did she intend to reply.

She stayed quiet while Consuelo pushed several carrot slices from one side of her plate to the other.

Consuelo said, "What does Papa think? Of Prince Francis Joseph, I mean."

"He thinks this one is worth considering. Obviously I agree."

More carrots were relocated, and then Consuelo said, "He's very nice, but I feel . . . I feel as though I could be almost any sort of girl and it wouldn't make a difference to him, as long as I was well mannered and my name was Miss Vanderbilt."

"Many of history's great unions have begun on similar terms."

"Am I wrong to wish to be desired for myself?"

"No, but you need to recognize that such regard often comes later, when the acquaintance is deepened by time and experience."

"Then you think I would be wrong to refuse him."

Alva paused before answering. Certainly there was a tremendous advantage in deferring risk and arranging Consuelo's marriage now. Still, the larger goal was to ensure her daughter a future that was both happy and secure. The Duke of Marlborough would offer much more in that regard. If he offered. Which he might not do. Or he might. And if he did, Consuelo would live in England, not Bulgaria, and no one would attempt to overthrow her husband and there would be no risk of (she could hardly bear to think of it) the kind of angry mobs and guillotines that other queens had faced. Not that this was likely. But then, wouldn't Marie Antoinette have thought the same?

Alva said, "As your mother, I would feel much better if he were already Bulgaria's beloved regent."

Consuelo was visibly relieved. "Then I should refuse. I should wait for an offer I like better."

"Yes," Alva said, praying neither of them was making a mistake. "We'll put this situation to rest and carry on with our London trip as planned."

The morning of their departure, Alva received a note from William asking that she meet with him in his suite at eleven A.M.: *We should finalize things before you leave.*

He was ready to agree to her terms, then. Good. The sooner all of this was behind them, the better.

She arrived at the appointed time, saying as she entered, "All right, let's be quick about this—"

She stopped. Corneil was standing to the right of the door. His arms were folded, and he wore a pained expression. "Hello, Alva."

William said, "He's hoping we'll permit him a hearing on our difficulties."

"You might have told me he was coming."

"Please," Corneil said. "Let's sit down. Would you like anything? We can order up coffee, some pastry—"

"Nothing, thank you," Alva said, seating herself in an armchair. "Be brief. The children and I leave on the train to Calais at three and there's still packing to do."

The men sat, and Corneil began, "I came as soon as William cabled me. He is greatly distressed by the turn of events—"

"What do you want?" Alva said.

"To preserve your marriage. There's no need for this misunderstanding to end an almost twenty-year union."

"There is no misunderstanding. The facts are clear. Has William not made them out to you? He and Lady Mandeville were lovers for all of those years, a situation made known to me only because she saw fit to confess it. Do we all understand now?"

The men glanced at each other. Then Corneil replied, "I misspoke. Yes, my brother behaved badly, and he's sorry for it."

"I believe he is."

"Then why do you delay your forgiveness?" Corneil said. "He's made a very, very good life for you, Alva. What's more, you made a vow to God. You must not take that lightly. There are consequences to breaking it—"

"I'll go to hell, you mean? What a convenient argument! A man may do as he will as regards his vows, but if a woman should break them, *she* faces eternal damnation."

"My God, you're hardheaded," William said, getting up to pace the room.

Corneil asked, "Alva, what would you gain in obtaining a divorce? No respectable woman will receive you. What kind of life will you have? And think of the effect on the children—and on my mother, whose health is increasingly poor. You're angry. I understand. But William will reform," he said, beckoning William back to his chair. "He'll make it up to you, and you can resume your lives as before. How can you claim to be offended by his betrayal if you don't even love him enough to forgive him? To divorce under these conditions is a wholly selfish act."

Alva focused her gaze on her gloves, on the delicate embroidery that Mary had taken such care with. Corneil was correct. She couldn't argue with a single point he'd made.

And she had no actual leverage to get her way; her threat to expose William was a bluff. If he called her on it, that would be one more humiliation she would suffer at his hands. If she also lost her lawsuit, that would put an end to her for good and all.

How much easier it would be to capitulate than to fight.

She could simply agree with Corneil, let all of this go, and then make a separate life for herself the way the duchess had done. Yes, that, too, would mean that William had won yet again, but perhaps that was the price she deserved to pay for having sat in the Greenbrier's garden that night long ago and falsely secured his proposal.

How clever she had thought herself. How charming, how persuasive. Heroic, even. Her troubles were over forever.

She had fooled herself, then. Was she fooling herself this time, too?

Alva looked up at Corneil. She said, "You're absolutely right."

"I am so glad to hear this. William, didn't I tell you she would come around?"

What self-satisfied expressions the two men now wore as they looked at each other. How accustomed they were to having their way! Thus it was with great pleasure that Alva said, "Your gloating is premature; I haven't finished. I agree with all you said *and* I am going to divorce your brother. It's time some woman set an example, or this kind of treatment will never end."

"Unbelievable!" William said, launching himself from his chair. "You seem to think you're entitled to *everything*."

"No, merely respect."

Corneil said, "I implore you to reconsider. The example you should be setting is one of Christian forgiveness. Otherwise you will have to answer to God."

"Which I will gladly do." She looked at William. "I won't ask you again: do you intend to be honorable and carry out our plan?"

"*Your* plan."

She waited.

He said tersely, "As I've always told you, I am a man of honor. I'll make the arrangements."

"Wise decision," Alva said. "You might also inform the duchess of these developments. She'll want to know that her letter has had good effect."

When Alva was clear of the room with the door closed behind her, she stood for a moment in the hotel's corridor and turned her gaze to the ceiling.

She had won.

Better than that, William had *not* won.

Some time ago, she had attended a lecture at which Victoria Woodhull argued that God was female. Today was the first time Alva thought the argument could be right.

VII

LONDON IN AUGUST was no great pleasure. The sky wouldn't commit to full-on sunshine, lending the days a halfhearted haze of indifference that Alva hoped would not follow them into the country, to the house she'd let near Marlow. She'd taken the house on an impulse, preferring not to wait in Newport for William's public infidelity to play out. In Newport, she would have to see Alice and submit to reiterations of Corneil's damnation declaration. Or, if Alice was as yet in the dark on this matter, Alva would have to pretend that nothing unusual was afoot. Better to while away what was left of the summer on the banks of the Thames, where Lucy Jay and her daughters would join them. Willie and his tutor were due there as well.

First, though, Lady Paget would dominate their schedule. One of Bertie's favorites at court, the former Minnie Stevens had been part of Alva's set in the early '70s before marrying an English lord's son. She had become a sharp-eyed quick wit whose opinions were both sought and celebrated. She would not only act as ambassador for Alva with Lady Albertha and her son the duke, she would also see that Consuelo was, as she'd put it in a letter to Alva, "rigged up" for the rest of London society so that regardless of the duke's response and inclinations, Consuelo would make the strongest possible impression on every gentleman who met her and on the public besides.

Alva brought her daughter to meet Lady Paget at her Belgrave Square home. Buckingham Palace Gardens was just down the street.

"She's pretty enough," Lady Paget said upon seeing Consuelo. "But her style is far too innocent for this scene. You absolutely must put her in satin for our dinner party Thursday evening. See that she shows more of that marvelously milky skin. Gloves past her elbows. A ribbon at her neck." She inspected Consuelo as if she were a mannequin standing before them.

Alva said, "Satin? She's got nothing in satin. We'll have to get a seamstress—today."

"Do. He won't be able to resist her, turned out like a true sophisticate."

The "he" of her statement was Charles Spencer-Churchill, the duke. Also present would be his mother and his aunt, Jennie, along with Jennie's son Winston, who was on leave from the Royal Military College. Jennie had written that Winston was "positively obsessed" with being in the cavalry, as he'd been a poor student in his previous school and was determined to make something worthwhile of himself. Two years earlier, he'd nearly died from injuries he sustained after falling from a bridge, so Alva was pleased to know he was getting on. She hoped Jennie did not see him or his younger brother as prospects for Consuelo; the duke was the prize here.

Consuelo had kept her gaze straight ahead throughout the discussion. Now Alva said to her, "I expect you're bored by our chatter. Did you want to stay and have tea?" Consuelo gave a quick shake of her head. "All right, then. Lady Paget's man will put you in a cab for the hotel. You might have Miss Harper go over English history and geography with you. I know you've studied it, but a refresher will give you confidence when we're at dinner."

When Consuelo had gone, Alva and Lady Paget discussed the duke. He was twenty-three years old but appeared younger, she said, as he was blond and boyish in his features and build. Born in India during his father's post there, he'd gained his title upon his father's death two years earlier. He was educated at Trinity College.

Lady Paget said, "He's not especially passionate about anything, really."

"That will be a relief after Prince Francis Joseph."

"Perhaps she'll bring out his passions," said Lady Paget with a wink. "We should encourage her to try."

"Please. This is my daughter we're speaking of."

"It works. Proven successful by yours truly, and of course our Duchess and Lady Churchill. Why didn't you marry in?"

"No money."

"Oh, yes—one forgets, what with how well fixed you are now."

Lady Paget said that Blenheim, the duke's estate, was much as Lady Lansdowne had described. "The stepmother and her money brought electricity and a heating system, both of which have done wonders in making the palace habitable. The house alone covers something like seven acres. That's a lot of stone. Quite impressive. Its town, Woodstock, is a charming place. Lots of history there."

"Consuelo will like that," Alva said.

"Who wouldn't? We'll get Sunny—that's what we call the duke—to tell her all."

"Is he sunny? In temperament?"

"It's for Sunderland. He's Earl of Sunderland. I don't actually know if I've ever seen him smile."

Having procured the correct dress and accessories, on the night of the dinner a more sophisticated-looking Consuelo sat with the young duke to her right and his cousin to her left, and from Alva's perspective appeared to be delighting in their conversation throughout the meal and afterward as well. A few glasses of wine into the evening, Alva told Lady Paget, "Sunny is shining on my girl," causing her friend to snort with laughter.

Too, Alva observed that although her daughter was well aware that the duke was a prospect, she seemed to forget this in the course of the evening and was simply enjoying herself.

The months ahead were going to be difficult; Consuelo in particular was going to be upset by the gossip and subsequent divorce. She revered her father—and why wouldn't she? He was her very own king, ever kind to her, ever the golden boy of his youth. For now, though, she was reveling in the attention of two engaging young men, finally having a taste of what adult life could bring her. Alva was certain her daughter would only grow prettier and more confident. She would make a significant marriage that would, Alva hoped, become a love match. She would have everything Alva herself had been denied.

Lady Paget told Alva, "I do believe you're off to the races. How marvelous you must feel about everything. What a life you've made for yourself!"

"Haven't I just?" Alva said.

The *World* got hold of the story first. William K. Vanderbilt had been seen in Paris repeatedly in the company of a Miss Nellie Neustretter, a comely American of perhaps thirty years. Eager detectives ferreted out the details: The object of Mr. Vanderbilt's open affections hailed from San Francisco but was enjoying her time on the Continent. She was installed in a fashionable apartment, where the servants had been observed wearing Vanderbilt livery.

The first reporter to spot Alva in New York rushed up to her on the street outside the Fifth Avenue house, where she'd been staying only to keep up appearances. The marvel of her home was lost on her now. She roamed it the way Mr. Stewart's ghost roamed his mansion, dismayed that a once-excellent existence could be ruined so abruptly.

"Mrs. Vanderbilt," the reporter called as he approached, "do you have any comment regarding Miss Neustretter and your husband?"

"I'm beyond outrage," she said, quite truthfully. "He should be ashamed of himself. Don't you think so?"

The reporter removed his hat. "Yes, ma'am."

"For the sake of my children's pride and my own, I won't allow this insult to stand. You may quote me on that."

Now Alva could proceed.

She met with her attorney, Mr. Joseph Choate, evidence in hand: the *World*'s report and three others like it, along with a cable from William in which he stated, *I regret that I am able to confirm the reports.* Additionally, she had produced with care a document that specified the terms of the settlement to which William had already agreed: she would receive two million dollars, custody of all three children, and one hundred thousand dollars annually for each of the children's upkeep, money that would later continue to be apportioned to each of them as they came of age. She would relinquish the Fifth Avenue home in favor of a new, more suitable townhouse on East Seventy-second Street.

She gave over the documents to Mr. Choate, a tall man with thick gray hair and a waxed mustache. She said, "This should suffice for the judge, wouldn't you agree?"

He examined the papers. "It's without question. Also without question: your right to feel aggrieved. However, I really must advise you, Mrs. Vanderbilt, that taking this action will result in a terrible disservice to your class, and therefore I recommend you don't pursue the lawsuit."

"What on earth are you talking about?"

Leaning back in his chair, he lit a pipe and said, "If we view topmost society as a piece of fabric, we can think of each member as a thread in that fabric. Part of what holds it together—weaves it into a thing of strength such that each of us is clothed, protected, by that fabric—is the concentration of assets and power in the hands of particularly accomplished men, your husband being such a one. These men see to the care and well-being and material needs of their respective families, resulting in societal harmony—or let's say a fine overcoat that covers everyone, keeps you safe and warm. If you persist in your suit, you divide Mr. Vanderbilt's assets, thus weakening the fabric. Your example could plant in other ladies' minds the notion that they, too, can take their offenses to the courts, resulting in further subdivision and thus further weakening. The coat is moth-eaten and worthless.

"What's more," he continued, "ladies have no capacity for managing assets. A household is nothing like a portfolio of investment holdings. The money you and others would win will invariably be misspent, wasted—weakening the fabric further, as you'll become destitute and unable to give proper care to yourselves, your children, your homes. I'm certain you are intelligent enough to see where this could lead."

Alva said, "Your concern is admirable. We certainly don't want to be the architects of society's downfall."

He nodded with satisfaction. "Then you understand me well."

"Oh, indeed, I understand you very well. And your theory is quite interesting. The trouble with theories, however, is that one can't know what is true unless the theory is tested empirically. You may be correct that if I pursue my case, moral society's overcoat will unravel to strings and leave the lot of us exposed to life's harshest elements; I'm quite curious to know. So please do file the lawsuit and send all further correspondence and inquiries to me at the Seventy-second Street address."

"Madame—"

"Shall I seek another attorney whose theories won't hinder his ability to do the job I'm paying him for?"

He said, "I entreat you: This is no game. You might satisfy yourself, all right, but would you wish for other ladies to ruin their families?"

"I would like gentlemen to stop provoking in their wives the desire to divorce them! Perhaps that is the lesson our esteemed friends will take away from this parting of one of our 'great men' from so much of his money."

Alva was back at 660 Fifth Avenue for perhaps twenty minutes when Alice arrived with Mrs. Vanderbilt, who was thin and pale and shorter, it seemed, than the last time Alva had seen her.

She took Alva's hand. "William didn't mean anything by it. He's always been a little impulsive, a little less serious than Corneil. It's his nature."

Alva helped her to a chair in the parlor. "Respectfully, I've lived with William for twenty years, which, given his time away at school, is longer than he spent with you, and much more recent. I know precisely how he is. I'm sorry for the distress this is causing you. But you must see how my action is necessary and correct."

Alice sat next to their mother-in-law. "I'm afraid you're deluding yourself. What we see—what everyone sees—is an angry, bitter woman selfishly lashing out because she was offended."

"It isn't anger, it's passion, and I am entitled. William has embarrassed me, misused me, betrayed and disrespected me. I deserved none of it."

"There, you see?" said Alice. "Anger."

Mrs. Vanderbilt said, "He didn't mean to harm you, surely you know that. That Paris woman, she's nothing more than an amusement."

"So he's excused from consequence?" She turned to Alice. "*This* is what we want our sons to emulate?"

Alice said, "To forgive is divine."

"Then William can get his forgiveness from God directly," Alva said, sitting down across from them. "I don't mean to be glib. I really do want you to understand: If these men never suffer for their wrongs, they will never change their ways. Why should they?"

Alice said, "I don't know that they can. It's men's nature to—"

"Does Corneil have lovers?"

"Of course not! He's not that kind of man."

Alva asked Mrs. Vanderbilt, "Did you ever suffer this kind of humiliation?"

Mrs. Vanderbilt shook her head.

"Then it isn't *men's nature*, is it? They *choose*. Neither of you has the first idea how this feels."

"I'm reluctant to say this," Alice began, "but . . . perhaps if you had been a better wife to him, he wouldn't have strayed."

Alva clenched her fists. Now she was angry. "Has the Vanderbilt name blinded you to simple right and wrong?" She pounded one fist on the table beside her, saying, "*I* am the offended party."

Alice stood up. "Come, Mother V. We've wasted our time here."

Mrs. Vanderbilt rose with difficulty. Alva approached her and took her hands. "You have always been a kind and reasonable woman. You *must* be able to see my viewpoint."

Alice pulled Mrs. Vanderbilt's arm to forcibly move her away from Alva toward the door. Mrs. Vanderbilt, though her expression was one of sadness and distress, made no reply, nor did she resist being shepherded away.

Alice said, "I fear for your soul, Alva. Nothing good will come of this. God's wrath is just and mighty."

"What did *you* do to incur it?"

"Pardon me?"

"This wrathful God—what sin did you commit to bring that wrath down upon your innocent children?"

As the words were leaving Alva's mouth, she knew she'd gone too far. Alice's horrified expression only confirmed it.

"I'm sorry. I didn't mean that. I know it isn't your fault—"

"You are no lady," Alice told her, pausing at the door. "I always felt it but hoped I was wrong. May the Lord forgive you."

❧

On the evening before Willie was due to return to St. Mark's for the start of autumn term, William arrived—from Paris, presumably, though Alva didn't ask and he hadn't said when he'd cabled her to expect him.

She and Consuelo were in the library when he came in. Consuelo, who had chosen willful disbelief when Alva told her and Willie what their father had done, sprung from her chair. "Papa! Welcome home."

Embracing Consuelo, William said, "You're a sight for these weary eyes."

"It's 'sore' eyes, and I'm glad. Not that they're sore. Or weary. I'm glad you're pleased to see me."

He laughed. "I understand. Tell me," he said, releasing her, "are your brothers at home, too? I'm afraid I have other business later this evening, so I can't stay long."

"You've only just arrived," Consuelo said.

Alva told him, "They're in. Shall we do this right now?" When he nodded, she called them down.

Consuelo said, "Do what right now?"

"A little family conference," William told her.

The boys hurried in, happy to see their father. If she didn't think about what the papers had reported, didn't allow herself to remember the confession, didn't indulge her disappointment, she could find this scene heartwarming. The five of them hadn't been all together since last Christmastime.

With greetings done, William said, "Everyone take a seat." Then he turned to Alva. "The floor is yours."

"*I'm* doing this?"

"It was your idea."

He and the children watched her expectantly. She said, "All right. Well, I'll get straight to it. Due to the . . . situation, which could not be resolved by any other action, your father and I are divorcing. You'll continue to live with me, but not here. I've taken a house for us east of the park. It isn't far."

The older two wore expressions of shock. Harold said, "What is *divorcing*?"

Alva said, "It means we won't be married any longer. We'll live apart."

"Then . . . who will be my father?"

"I will," William said, going to sit next to him. "A divorce isn't anything to do with children, only adults."

Harold still looked confused.

Alva said, "We are still your mother and father. We just won't be wife and husband to each other."

He said, "Oh."

Willie stood up. "You'll excuse me." Without looking at either of his parents, he strode from the room.

Consuelo was on the verge of tears. She said, "Why are you doing this?"

Alva said, "You know the source of the trouble."

"I thought it was a lie."

Harold said, "What was a lie?"

"Daddy?" Consuelo said, and William shifted his gaze away.

Alva told Harold, "She thought it was a lie that your father and I have had a falling-out. We have, that's the truth, and we've agreed to divorce because of it."

"Your mother insisted," William said.

"Is it true?" Consuelo asked him. "The . . . the reason?"

"William," Alva said. "Answer your daughter."

He said, "I made a mistake."

Consuelo looked stricken and Alva said, "We can talk about this further another time. What we want you to know—all of you," she said, gesturing toward upstairs, where Willie had gone, "is that nothing else need change in any significant way. We'll continue to care for you as we always have, but you will spend time with us separately."

William said, "This Christmas, for example. I'm going to take the three of you to Palm Beach."

Alva's mouth dropped open. He'd said nothing about this previously. Now he looked her way and smiled, as if daring her to protest.

"You see?" she said brightly. "Won't that be lovely? You'll have a grand time."

Consuelo's gaze was on her lap. "I can't believe you would do this to us." She looked up at Alva.

"I know it's hard," Alva began, but Consuelo was on her feet and moving for the doorway before Alva could finish the sentence.

Harold, still seated, was crying. William said to him, "Let's go find your brother, shall we? I heard a joke I want to tell you both."

As they were leaving the room, he looked over his shoulder at Alva. "Well done," he said.

Mamie Fish saw it her way, at least.

"They'll be fine," she said, after hearing Alva's account of the scene with William and the children. She'd come to see Alva's new townhouse, now that Alva was getting settled in. Mamie said, "Nobody died."

"You wouldn't know it from the way Consuelo mopes about."

"She's too young to see how you're a warrior for the Woman's Cause. You should tell her she's lucky you didn't take a more old-fashioned approach and shoot him dead."

"I have considered it—shooting him, I mean. I might fare better in society if I did," Alva said.

Now that word of the impending divorce was out, almost no one would receive her. The women were cowards, the lot of them, afraid to be seen in her company lest they subject themselves to Alice's scorn.

"It isn't too late," Mamie said. "I've got a gun. I'll even teach you how to use it."

"You are a good and generous friend."

Mamie poured bourbon for both of them. "When do you have your day in court?"

"Not until next spring. I suspect the attorneys and judge imagine that if they drag this out, I'll become remorseful and change my mind."

"The ladies are saying you will."

"I admit, the thought crosses my mind now and then. One tires of pushing a boulder up a hill only to have it roll back down. But then I remind myself of what you said—I'm a warrior. I am a warrior." She went over to the stairs and called, "I am a warrior, Consuelo!"

"Come to the Maternity Charities committee meeting at Laura Davies's house next Tuesday," Mamie said. "Show them what you're made of. It'll do everyone good. Four-thirty o'clock."

"I'm not on that committee."

"I just put you on it."

On Tuesday, Alva arrived for the meeting wearing a modest green suit and one of her simplest hats. Her jewelry was equally modest. She would behave just as modestly: listen actively; speak only if her opinion was invited; offer her time or money, whichever was requested. In other words, she would be a drone. A polite, smiling, appreciative drone. Not forever, just as a way to demonstrate that she was as considerate and cooperative as any of them. Observing this, they would be reminded that she was a reasonable person and, as such, must be justified in her actions regarding divorce. They needed to *see* her being the example they could follow if need be. They would thank her for her leadership. She would be respected not for being Mrs. William K. Vanderbilt but for being herself.

A maid answered the door and took her coat, then ushered her into the parlor. After a moment, as her presence was noticed, the buzz of conversation from the gathered ladies ceased. Ten powdered faces turned toward her in surprise.

Mamie, she noticed, hadn't yet arrived. Still, she knew every one of these women, had known them for much of her life. Those who'd given themselves the chance to think about it must be grateful that she had hacked a path into the jungle for them to follow; none of them was obliged to stay locked in a gilded cage any longer. Each of them could and should claim the respect they deserved. Perhaps they all could discuss the matter once the business of the meeting had concluded.

"Good afternoon," Alva said, aiming herself toward the hostess.

Laura Davies turned her back to Alva.

The others stared and then, after a moment, turned away from her as well.

"Come now," she said to this sea of collars and shoulders and hair, though her voice was not as robust as she'd intended.

She tried again. "Surely—" she began, her face growing hot. Not one of them moved, nor, she now understood, would they move, nor would they speak. Today's queen bee had issued the directive and no drone would risk her ire.

"You are all making a mistake," she said. "I'm not the one who's in the wrong. I'm helping your cause, every one of you."

Nothing.

Alva returned to the hall and asked the maid for her coat, keeping her back to the parlor as she waited. The murmuring had begun already. She had betrayed her children and destroyed her family. She was greedy, selfish, immoral, low. All she had ever wanted was Vanderbilt cash, and it was a shame that William had gotten hooked by her. Why on earth would she leave him? She must be unbalanced—after all, even her own attorney, Mr. Choate, had discouraged the action; he'd told their husbands all about it.

My God, Alva thought, *women can be hateful creatures*. She knew what Mamie would say: she had hoped for too much, too soon, just as on the night she and William attended their first Patriarch Ball; had she learned nothing in the intervening years?

Ah, thank God, here was the maid.

Alva put on her coat, left the house, and got situated in her carriage before she allowed herself to cry.

Snow was falling on Christmas Eve, great fat flakes that coated the ground quickly, with no sign of letting up. Alva, dressed in galoshes and fur, was just going down her steps en route to the park when a carriage pulled to her curb and a man called out, "Hello, hold up!"

In the darkness, she couldn't make out the man's features in the carriage window. His voice, though, was familiar, and unwelcome. Oliver. As the carriage door opened, she continued past, calling out, "No, thank you, I prefer my own company."

He was beside her in a moment. "Holiday blues? I've had them myself."

She stopped and turned toward him. In the lamplight, with his fur-collared coat and glossy beaver top hat, he was a Dickensian image of the ideal gentleman. She said, "I'm quite all right, thank you."

"I won't have you spending this evening alone. Are you off to the park?" He gestured ahead of them, across the street. "It's a marvelous scene, isn't it?"

"It is, and you're spoiling it. Do go away."

He was taken aback. "You're serious in your rejection of me."

"You can't really be surprised. I'd counted you among my true friends! Your betrayal was almost as terrible as theirs."

"Do you mean because I haven't lent you my support before now? I've been away and the news didn't reach me until—"

"Please, don't pretend ignorance. Give me that much respect."

Now he appeared confused. "I am in fact ignorant. How did *I* betray you?"

"By withholding your knowledge! A true friend wouldn't have let me go on unenlightened, more a dupe with every passing day. The entire time you were standing in for him—"

Disgusted, she turned and continued westward, hardly pausing at the corner of Park Avenue before striding across. Oliver followed, matching her stride but not speaking. When they'd gone another fifty feet, Alva stopped and faced him.

"*Go away.* I want to have a walk on what is an otherwise wonderful evening, yet you persist in spoiling it for me. Will you please leave me to it?"

"I'm trying to understand you, but you're not making sense. He didn't take up with that Neustretter woman until last summer."

"I refer to the Duchess of Manchester."

Oliver said, "William and *the duchess*?"

His expression was guileless. She said, "If you're pretending innocence—"

"This is no act."

"You honestly didn't know?"

He shook his head. "When—?"

"While *Valiant* was being built," she said as this new information settled into her mind. He had not betrayed her?

He had *not* betrayed her.

She said, "Before that, too, on occasion. For *years.* Tell me you didn't know about any of it."

"Not of your friend. But there were others—and I did attempt to tell you, once. You had no desire to hear it."

"I was stubborn."

"You were honorable. *He,* however, is a low-down son of a . . . How did you learn of this, the two of them?"

"She confessed it in a letter that awaited me in Nice, when we were on the trip to India."

"My God. So *that's* what had you so upset."

She said, "Do you remember our conversation on *Valiant* when you asked whether I valued being happy?"

"I do."

"If you didn't know about them and therefore hadn't concluded that *I* must know, why did you ask?"

"Because I knew you weren't. You'd been out of sorts for the entire cruise. I was concerned about you."

"That's all?"

"That's all. But you're saying you didn't learn of the affair until Nice?"

"I read her letter on the train."

"Yet you were discontent before then."

Because you were there. Because you have always been there and always out of reach.

She shrugged. "I may have sensed the trouble before I knew its cause."

Oliver walked to a nearby bench and sat down. "I can hardly believe what I'm hearing." He looked up at her. "He admitted it to you?"

"She did not invent it," Alva said. "Though I don't know why I should sound as if I'm defending her. Yes, he admitted it."

She sat down next to him. He smelled of the shaving balm he'd always used. He smelled of *Oliver.* Her friend who had known she was unhappy and had cared enough to challenge her about it.

She said, "I assumed you knew everything and that was why you disappeared. We didn't see you once here in New York or Newport."

"I've been traveling, as I said. Political endeavors. I'm still trying to comprehend all of this: he then went and insulted you further with that Neustretter woman?"

"Only for show. I made him do it." She explained the situation, and then said, "No one but Corneil knows any of this. William may have informed the duchess; I can't say."

"Then you haven't seen her?"

"Nor written," Alva said. "I can't bring myself to do it. And listen, for the girls' sake you must keep all this information to yourself."

"You can count on me." He leaned so that his face was before her. "Do you hear me? I mean it: you can—I want you to—count on me."

Her heart, in its old habit, rose in hopeful response to his words. She pushed it down.

"Thank you. I've been quite low, I confess. Righteousness has brought me only cold comfort these past few days when the house has been empty and what few friends I've kept are busy with their lives. I have my sisters' support as well, but only Armide is nearby, and I don't like to be a bother." She stood up. "Let's walk, shall we? I want you to tell me how you've been."

As they went, they encountered other couples, old and young, along the park's snowy paths. Pairs of ladies. Men remarking on the ongoing depression and its effect on their wealth. Children chasing one another, throwing snowballs, making snow angels and snowmen on the open lawn.

Oliver told her he had recently founded and made himself publisher, editor, and writer of a progressive weekly paper he named *The Verdict.* It was a way to promote his beliefs and desires for the direction of the country, he said. In it, he pilloried business leaders and politicians, taking on corruption, imperialism, corporate greed—the ills that sickened society for the common man. No one was spared the point of his pen.

"I used to play tennis with these gentlemen. They used to have me to their homes. Do you know Andrew Carnegie? He's come around to my side, at least. More than I can say for my own brother, August. He won't speak to me."

"I'm spurned by all the Vanderbilts. We have to draw strength from our convictions."

"While they are all doing the same."

"Yes, but we're right." She laughed.

They'd reached Cleopatra's Needle, the obelisk behind the Met. Alva said, "William's father paid to have this installed here after the Egyptian government offered it, did you know? One hundred thousand dollars, just so that all the people of the city could be exposed to a glimpse of ancient Egypt. He was a good man. He would *not* be pleased with his son."

"I remember that he admired you very much. As do I. 'Though she be but little, she is fierce.' That's Shakespeare."

"Fierce. I like that."

"Joan of Arc."

"Now there is someone truly fierce," Alva said.

"I'd rather not see you burned to death, however."

"I *am* a social heretic. It could yet be my fate."

Having returned to her street, Alva asked, "Will you be seeing your family tonight?"

"Yes, I'm driving up to Perry's next—though I may need the sleigh to get there. Will you join us?"

"Thank you, no. Armide and her friend Miss Crane are coming for mass, then we'll dine here at my house. My house," she repeated. "How good that sounds. Mine."

"You earned it."

"I believe I did."

He extended his hand to her. "So then, friends?"

She shook it and said, "Friends."

Though his presence tonight had not proved to be any kind of Christmas miracle, it was without question a gift.

Outside the church in the lamplight, snow still drifting down, Alva saw a familiar form among the stream of people climbing the steps. She told her companions, "You go ahead; there's someone I need to speak to."

She made her way over to the man who had caught her eye. "Merry Christmas," she said.

Ward McAllister turned his head, then stopped in place. His expression was wary, but he was as finely turned out as ever. "Why, Mrs. Alva Vanderbilt, as I live and breathe. I daresay. Is it a good Christmas for you?"

"It has improved greatly, and is, I hope, still improving—or it will do so if you'll permit me to apologize to you."

"Ah, the spirit of Christ has overtaken you this evening!" His tone edged on sarcastic but didn't tip over—saved, perhaps, by the hopefulness she was herself attempting to convey.

He went on, "Well, never let it be said that Ward McAllister was unable to rise to such an occasion! No, indeed, seeing this unexpected olive branch quite inspires my charity."

"I'm glad to know it. You'll have heard that I've had some difficulties—"

"Please," he said, holding up a hand. "If you're coming to me for aid, I am not at all certain my goodwill is prepared to extend that far."

She shook her head. "No, nothing of the kind. I just wanted to tell you, I regret the way I treated you. I had been going to come to your party despite the bad press. Honestly, I was all set to go—I still remember it, I wore bright yellow on your behalf. I was actually out the door when my husband prevented my leaving.

"But after that, I had no excuse. I was thinking only of myself. I put far too much store in society's good opinion of me when the good opinion of good *people* is what I should have cultivated most."

Ward smiled. "Well. You have always been accomplished with a speech."

"I am sincere!"

"Oh, indeed, I can see that you are, yes, I can see that very well. And I, too, failed; my pride prevented me from calling after I received your note. Though I do still say yours was the greater offense. I wish to be big enough to overcome small-minded behavior; therefore, apology accepted. We have both been humbled by troubles we didn't deserve. This is the danger of excellence, don't you know: it invites scorn. Yet we must not permit ourselves to be any less than we are."

They had by this time drawn an audience. He held out his arm. "Walk in with me, won't you?"

Alva said, "Yes, I will."

VIII

ALVA JOINED THE small group that had assembled, on this March day, in her drawing room, where every surface held a vase (or two or more) of roses that had been arriving at the house throughout the morning in honor of her daughter's eighteenth birthday. Consuelo's friends were showing their affection for her in the manner that had become the fashion (and quite a boon for florists). Alva was pleased to see it, as it showed that the children of those who yet shunned her were not shunning her daughter. The boys' social lives seemed similarly vigorous. But for the formal hearing to grant Alva's divorce, everything was in its new order and all of them were adjusting well.

Harold, who waited with Consuelo and Armide to go bicycling, said, "What took so long?"

"I had to change my dress for these." Alva referred to her bloomers, a remarkable invention she'd discovered at last week's Madison Square Garden Flower Show, where two women had a booth and a bicycle and were demonstrating the comfort and ease of the silly looking garment.

"I have never seen a lady in pants."

"This will be merely the first time," Armide told him. "I plan to buy some, too. Before you know it, all the ladies will be as sensible about their clothing as your mother here."

Consuelo said, "I wouldn't wear them, ever."

Alva laughed. "You didn't see the demonstration! If they turn out to be as ideal as the ladies who sold these made them out to be, I might burn all our skirts."

As the group descended to the entry hall, the doorbell rang. Alva anticipated another flower delivery, but no: when her footman swung the door open, there stood Winthrop Rutherfurd whom Alva had not seen in some time, with an armful of red roses.

"Good afternoon! I've come to convey my regards to Miss Vanderbilt," he said. Looking past Alva at her daughter, he added, "Happy birthday to you!"

All the other friends and admirers had let the flowers be the extent of their involvement in the day; they knew that the family would be sailing tomorrow for France and there was no time for a formal birthday celebration. How interesting, then, that Rutherfurd felt he should act differently from the others.

Consuelo, delighted, stepped into the doorway and accepted the roses. "Thank you! We're just about to go out riding bicycles." She gestured to where theirs waited on the sidewalk.

"Are you? How lucky, then, that I've been wheeling about on my own."

And indeed, after Consuelo gave the flowers over to a maid and the group went outside, Alva saw that there to the left of the door was one more bicycle. What an astonishing coincidence.

Consuelo said, "Won't you ride along with us?"

"It would be a privilege."

"Is it all right, Mother?"

According to the newspapers, Rutherfurd had been in regular attendance at the same events Consuelo attended over the winter. This bit of trivia had meant little to Alva when she read it. Consuelo had given no indication that she was yet under his spell. Now, though, it was obvious that a secret romance was afoot. The child was cagier than she would have guessed.

So that she might see the extent of the romance for herself, Alva told the cagey child, "By all means."

Across Central Park and over to Riverside Drive they pedaled. Though the scenery was still winter-barren, the day was mild and windless and smelled of damp earth. Alva spoke with Armide and Harold of inconsequential matters while keeping an eye on the pair of sweethearts, whose distance from Alva, Harold, and Armide increased bit by bit until they were well out of earshot. Alva watched with interest when the pair stopped well ahead of them. Rutherfurd was obviously making some kind of speech or plea; Consuelo glanced back toward Alva and then spoke in turn. Eager happiness radiated from the child.

Armide said, "You do see what's going on there."

"William made it clear to him that she was off-limits."

"Clearly he's a poor listener."

"Yes. And I doubt that his appearance on her eighteenth birthday is coincidental."

"Do you think he's asked her to marry him?"

"Look at her."

Armide said, "What will you do?"

"For now? Take her to Europe. And watch the mail."

What a poor liar Consuelo made, even without Alva inquiring about Rutherfurd or challenging the statements Consuelo offered explaining how he'd only wanted to talk to her about her father ("He didn't want to offend you by saying so when you were nearby") and about a mutual friend ("She's quite sick over a rejection from the gentleman she's set her heart on") and about her cousin Neily ("He's seeing a girl Aunt Alice and Uncle Corneil disapprove of")—in this last case, a truth-based excuse, as word was out widely of his being involved with Miss Grace Wilson, a young woman who had once been attached to his brother Bill. Mamie Fish reported that the Corneil Vanderbilts had forbidden their son from seeing Grace and threatened withdrawal of all support as well as disinheritance. "Bad blood happening there," she'd said. "It never pays to tell them it's forbidden. They just try harder and hate you more."

Where Consuelo had radiated happiness on her birthday afternoon, during the trip across the Atlantic and as they made their way toward Paris, she radiated anxiety and guilt. Alva remarked on none of it, allowing her daughter to carry on unimpeded (for now) by debate or any overt effort at deterrence. The child believed herself to be in love.

It was a baseless, artless love, a love brought about by flattery and attentiveness from a lover who was skillful at appearing to be sincere but would only do real harm in the end. This love was a temporary state. Alva would make certain of it.

European gentlemen who had interest in Miss Vanderbilt cared not at all about her father's divorce so long as he still retained his tens of millions of American dollars. Thus Consuelo's spring proceeded much the way the previous year's had, with shopping and parties and dinners and balls and offers of marriage, some of them from the dullest, most tendentious men. Alva relayed to her daughter the story of each man's request, until Consuelo, growing increasingly disillusioned, complained, "Am I no more than prime horseflesh?"

"To some of them: no, you are not."

As far as Consuelo knew, "Winty" had failed to write even the briefest response to her letters. Neither had he shown up at any of the places she might have expected to see him. She said nothing about it; her demeanor, though, revealed her frustration. Rutherfurd never received Consuelo's letters because they'd been intercepted. Consuelo never heard from him for the same reason. The two never met up because Alva gave strict notice to key hostesses that if Mr. Rutherfurd was expected, Miss Vanderbilt would be unable to attend.

Alva had begun to wonder whether the Duke of Marlborough would prove himself an exception among his untroubled-by-divorce European counterparts—that is, titled gentlemen in need of money—when his note arrived: *I've been traveling this spring but am hoping to see Miss Vanderbilt at Blenheim.*

Alva and Consuelo were in Luxembourg Garden when Alva relayed his message. The weather was fair, the trees thick in leaf. A light breeze made ripples across the *bassin.* Songbirds chased one another from tree to tree overhead. It was said that Marie de' Medici's ghost lent favor to young lovers who visited the park; Alva hoped that favor would also extend to lovers who *ought* to be together and that having merely one of the pair present in the park would do the trick.

"I'm not inclined to go," Consuelo said. "His interest last year was merely polite. He didn't seem to like me beyond friendship."

"Isn't this evidence that he must?"

"I don't see how it is."

"He wishes to impress you. The others just come around and say, 'I'd like your consent in marrying your daughter,' whereas the duke isn't presuming you have even the least bit of interest in him. He understands he has to win you over."

"Has he said so?"

"Logic says so."

"Logic says he needs money, since the stepmother no longer underwrites the estate."

Alva said, "What a cynic you've become, and at such a young age."

"Am I incorrect?"

"The estate could benefit from Vanderbilt money, that's a fact. So then, why doesn't he pursue Gertrude instead of you? Her father's wealthier and her parents have no scandals attached to their names."

This gave Consuelo pause.

Alva continued, "And there are many other heiresses whose family names may not carry the cachet yours does but whose fathers would quite willingly trade millions to get their daughters this title. If the duke was actually indifferent to you, he'd pursue one of those blatantly eager girls."

"I suppose you're right."

"He may not win you over," Alva said, "but aren't you curious to see Blenheim? It's a genuine palace. And Oxfordshire will be quaint."

"If you're so eager, I suppose I don't mind going."

"What else have we to do with our summer?" Alva said, nonchalant. "The English countryside is as fine a place to spend it as any."

. . .

No one approaching Blenheim could be unaffected by its sheer size and grandeur. One thought of Versailles, minus the gilded accents.

Consuelo's remark upon her initial view of it was "Oh, my."

Alva, seated beside her in the carriage, said, "Could you see yourself here? I could."

"I would never presume . . ."

"He's going to marry someone," Alva said.

After greeting them in the broad stone courtyard, Marlborough said, "Would you like some refreshment first, or a tour?"

"A tour," said Consuelo.

He offered her his arm. "Allow me to be your guide."

Alva hung back so that she could walk behind them. The duke was slightly shorter than Consuelo, but impeccably presented. From his neat hair to his crisp jacket and pants to his unscuffed shoes, he was a model of the "refined country gentleman at home."

He was saying, "First, the overview: In 1704, the first Duke of Marlborough, John Churchill, beat the French in the Battle of Blenheim. As a reward, Queen Anne granted him this land, a great deal of cash, and her consent to build a palace. And as you can see," he said, "he took the direction very much to heart. I should add that this is the only non-royal palace in all of England."

Consuelo said, "You're right to be proud of it."

He led them inside. "You can see, too, that my father wasn't the steward of it that he might have been. The windows need glazing. We have leaks," he said, pointing at a water stain on the ceiling of the hall in which they stood. "I would love to restore it to its earlier glory. *Your* homes are quite impressive, I'm told, so I would imagine you understand the pleasures of fine things well kept."

"We do," Consuelo told him. "My mother is somewhat of an architect herself."

"Yes," said Alva. "We take these things quite seriously."

Marlborough smiled. "Excellent."

They spent the entire day seeing the house and gardens, Marlborough an affable guide, Consuelo an eager tourist. And while Alva would not have characterized the pair's relations as anything more than companionable, when Marlborough remarked that he intended to come see the United States that summer and, yes, he would be pleased to stay with them for a time at Marble House, Alva thought companionable might well be sufficient. Whether or not her daughter saw it similarly was quite another question.

Kimbolton Castle, Mar. 18 '95

My dear Alva,

When word came last year that you were in London, I was distraught about the affair and how terribly I'd wounded you, so I decided not to approach you at all. You were right to shun me by sending no response to my confession and making no effort to see me in person. Word has it that you are again nearby, and so I hope this letter finds you soon, and well.

Last year I was denying the necessity of telling friends that May had been ill. No need to alarm anyone—nor did I wish to make it seem as if I deserved to be pitied. I, who had wronged you and jeopardized so much. My silence was hope that my suspicion of consumption was wrong—and indeed, she improved and seemed delicate but well.

That hope was extinguished four days ago, when, during our stay in Rome, my sweet, beautiful girl collapsed and could not be revived. Alva, she is gone.

I can't say whether it is worse for her sister or for me; Alice is her twin and, while they inhabited two identical bodies, they've seemed to always have a single heart. Alice, though, has only her loss to endure, whereas I have loss and horrifying guilt for my failure to protect May or heal her, my failure to be the upstanding mother she deserved to have.

As I have spent these days numbed by the horror, unable to sleep, unwilling to see anyone other than my Alice, who, now that we are home again will not leave her bed, I read of your receiving your divorce on the terms you commanded. The London papers gave every detail. Of course you're made out to be a demon, and dangerous for setting such an example. If ladies can seek divorce and win not only custody of the children but millions of dollars, too, the whole of society will eventually fall into ruin.

I say, let it. Like the phoenix, you will rise. Perhaps one day I will, too.

We bury Lady May tomorrow, here at Kimbolton. I wake and breathe and eat only for the sake of my surviving daughter. God keep her—and you, and yours—safe and healthy.

Yours—
Consuelo

Alva read the letter with one hand pressed to her mouth.

The horror of it. The wrongness.

No mother should ever have to outlive her child.

Through her tears, she went for paper and pen, then sat down and wrote,

Consuelo,

We were abroad, so please forgive the tardiness of this reply. Your letter was long delayed, as we had already departed London when it must have come to the hotel . . .

My heart could hardly be heavier than it is at this moment. For all that I have steeled myself against you and sworn I would not give you the satisfaction of hearing from me again, I cannot let this terrible news go unanswered. I am so, so sorry for you, and for your Alice, and for May's suffering.

I have wanted to ask you, yet could not do it, why you misled me in believing you were a true friend. Or, if you yet believe yourself my friend, how you could lie and betray and lie and betray again and again. If you disdained me so much that you could use me so badly, then pretending friendship (though you claim yours was always true)

Alva stopped writing and set down her pen. This was not the appropriate time to address that trouble, nor could her mind even begin to organize itself around that difficult subject just now.

She took a new sheet of paper and tried again. Again, she was unable to offer her condolences without also straying into her justifications for not having written before and trying to litigate all of that. It was as if in opening her heart in a display of sympathy, she could not keep its other needs reined in.

Yet she could not leave this letter unanswered. Finally she took fresh paper and wrote:

New York, 28 June 1895

Duchess Consuelo Montagu and Miss Alice Montagu,
The children and I wish to extend our most sincere condolences on the loss of Lady May. We are heartsick for you. Lord grant her peaceful rest and a place at His side.

With sympathy,
Mrs. Alva Vanderbilt, Consuelo Vanderbilt,
Willie Vanderbilt, and Harold Vanderbilt

IX

"WE TRULY ENJOYED our time with the duke," Alva told Lucy Jay, having returned to Newport for the summer.

They were at a ball being held by one of the newer families in society, a coal-money family far more concerned with currying Alva's favor than with judging her choice to divorce. To those on this rung of society, a Vanderbilt was a Vanderbilt, and all that mattered was getting one (any one) to one's party, ever after being able to claim a connection. Probably Ward had recommended the strategy. For Alva's part, she was willing to indulge any good family, and especially those bold enough to risk Alice's disapproval. Alice, whose rebuilt house was almost all anyone could talk about.

Alice was reportedly reveling in the attention, despite the fact that Richard Hunt, having been ground to a nib by both Alice and George, was at this moment lying weak and debilitated in his bed, seeing no visitors. His wife, Catherine Hunt, had admitted to Alva that the end was near. "He wanted me to tell you how grateful he is to you. Not only for your business but your friendship."

Alva said tearfully, "I was challenging."

"Not as bad as the others." She smiled. "He loves and admires you."

"And I him. Tell him, won't you?" Wiping her eyes, she'd left the Hunts' home refusing to believe she might not see him again alive.

Now she watched from the periphery as Consuelo danced with one of the hostess's sons in an overcrowded dining-room-cum-ballroom. He was a tall young man, a law student said to be good at polo and friendly with Harry Whitney, Gertrude's new fiancé. He planned to defend the poor and indigent, and was obviously entranced with Consuelo. If Marlborough didn't come through, Alva might encourage his interest.

She said, "Blenheim was remarkable—better than the Breakers, I'll wager—though the palace does need an influx of cash, and soon."

"Was Consuelo impressed?"

"Oh, quite. Though she played it down afterward."

"Let me guess: Mr. Rutherfurd?"

"She is tenacious," Alva said. She took a glass of wine from a servant's tray and walked toward the windows, to get some of the breeze. "Still, I could tell she thought the entire place was marvelous. Being there was like being inside English history! The past dukes are entombed there. The rooms are furnished with the spoils of wars. There is an enormous bust of Louis XIV atop the south portico as if to display the man's head on a pike for all the populace to see."

"When will the duke be here?"

"Late August, he says."

"Will he ask her to marry him?"

"I wish I knew!"

"Do you think she's expecting a proposal?"

"I think she expected one while we were there, and when it didn't come she was surprised and disappointed. She wouldn't have accepted it, honor bound as I'm certain she is to her dear Mr. Rutherfurd. She wants to be flattered, though."

"Who doesn't?"

"Indeed," said Alva, whose thoughts turned for a moment to the man whose flattery she always desired. Oliver was away again, stumping with Nebraskan transplant William Jennings Bryan throughout the Midwest on Bryan's presidential campaign. Oliver posted letters to her from towns she'd never heard of. Osceola. Baraboo. Milan, an Illinois township on the Rock

River that said its name *MY-lan*, to differentiate it from the Italian city of the same spelling—though, as he'd written,

> *There is no danger of confusion for any who've seen both! They are fine people, however. Farmers, mainly, plus a few Sauk Indians in peaceful coexistence. Bryan is a great friend to the native peoples. We've had no trouble. The corn and beef here are the best I've had—but none of this is any improvement on your company. I trust you are well. Please write with assurances c/o Chicago general delivery.*

Lucy said, "Consuelo has no idea you've been keeping them apart?"

"None at all. I had hoped she would lose patience with him while we were abroad, and then Marlborough would propose to her and she'd accept out of spite as much as desire. I went so far as to order a wedding gown with this scenario in mind. But she didn't, and he didn't. Which is quite all right; she ought not marry anyone unless she believes thoroughly in the merits of the situation—and is correct in that belief, of course."

As Alva was speaking, she turned back to watch the dancers and caught sight of Winthrop Rutherfurd, who had joined Consuelo on the dance floor.

Lucy said, "Did you know he would be here?"

"I had been assured he would not."

Momentarily paralyzed by her daughter's expression of joy, Alva remembered herself and went straight to the pair, taking Consuelo by the arm and steering her away from Rutherfurd while telling him, "Do not follow us."

"Let me go," Consuelo said as Alva towed her into the entry hall.

Alva called to the footman stationed at the door, "Get my coach."

"You're being horrid," Consuelo said. She tried to turn back toward the ballroom, but Alva held her tightly.

"That man will ruin your life."

"He will not. He loves me."

Alva led her outside. "Yes, of course he does. He also loves his mount and Kentucky bourbon, and the prospect of boasting of the ultimate conquest at every club he'll get to be a member of after snaring a Vanderbilt heiress."

Consuelo said, "Then why did he not pursue Gertrude?"

Alva towed her daughter up to the carriage door. Consuelo climbed inside and Alva followed. The silent coachman closed the door.

Neither of them spoke during the short ride back to Marble House. When they alighted from the carriage, Alva told her, "Upstairs."

Once they were shut into Alva's bedroom, Consuelo said, "Nothing you do will make any difference. I will marry him. We've been engaged for months."

"The engagement is off."

Consuelo glared at her. "Why are you so determined to ruin my life?"

"Me? It's Rutherfurd who'll ruin it, unless I stop you or stop him."

"He told me he was in Paris *and* London. He said he tried to see me. He said he never got even *one* of my letters. How could you be that cruel?"

"How? Because if I were not, he would have taken you off to elope."

"I am an adult. I get to choose my husband."

"Do you want to become nothing more than a pretty line of credit for a man who could not care less about you?"

"You don't know him. He loves me!"

"All these years while you were curled up in window seats reading poems and philosophy and history books, I was hearing of his exploits. He's made no secret of trying repeatedly for only rich young ladies' affections until their fathers put him off—all the while carrying on with married women who've treated him like a pet. No sensible person takes him seriously, Consuelo. That's why he is still unmarried. That's why he's preying on a girl like you—you are so perfectly naive that he nearly got away with his plan."

"He told me you would do this. I don't care what you say. That's all just gossip."

"My God. You really won't see it!"

"He said you're jealous of me because no one ever loved you and that's why you're keeping us apart. You don't respect me. You don't believe I can think for myself."

"The husband you think you want will make you miserable. How can I possibly allow you to do that to yourself?"

"Aunt Alice didn't tell Gertrude who she can or can't marry."

"No, they are doing that to Corneil; Gertrude is far too sensible to choose someone her parents disapprove of."

Consuelo cried, "You insult me at every turn!"

Trying to remain calm, Alva said, "You are confusing an insult with a fact."

"Do you deny that I have the right to lead my life however I choose?"

Alva said, "If you elope with that man, I will personally get a gun and hunt him down and shoot him dead. I mean it, Consuelo. If you cannot see your way clear of him, I will solve the problem once and for all!"

Consuelo, horrified, turned and left the room.

Alva rang for the butler, her hand shaking as she pressed the button. When he arrived, she told him, "My daughter does not leave this house without Miss Harper. She will not send a letter or accept a caller unless I approve of it first."

"Yes, ma'am."

He withdrew, and Alva went to the window. Her chest felt tight and she was sweating. Almost without knowing she was about to do it, she vomited into an urn. Doubled over and panting, she fought another wave of nausea as she moved to ring for a maid, who then found Alva still crouched at the windowsill, now clammy and scared. This had happened on the *Valiant*, too; perhaps there was something terribly wrong with her.

"I'm sorry for this," Alva said, indicating the urn. "Send for the doctor and have Mrs. Jay come in."

"Am I dying?" she asked the doctor when he'd concluded his examination. Lucy Jay stood nearby, looking as scared as Alva felt. "My father had heart ailments. He never really improved."

To say the least.

"You have suffered a severe strain on both your heart and nervous system, but if you rest and avoid further upset, you should recover." The doctor produced a bottle of laudanum, instructed Alva on its dosage, and then left with a promise to return the next day.

Lucy saw him out, saying, "What a relief."

"Yes—if he's correct."

"Of course he's correct. You already look much better."

"Don't tell my daughter."

"Don't tell her? She's worried about you."

"Let her be worried, for a while longer anyway."

After a few hours of medicated rest, Alva felt more herself again. The tightness in her chest had eased and the nausea was gone. Even so, she remained sequestered with her curtains drawn and had Lucy enforce a quiet household. Now she would wait for Consuelo to make up her mind.

On the second day of this, about a half hour after Consuelo was permitted a brief visit in Alva's dim room, Lucy came in to report, "She asked if I thought you would ever relent, and I told her there was no possibility of that."

"Good."

"I said, 'And if your mother is provoked like that again, she could suffer a fatal attack. I doubt you want that on your conscience.' "

"That's dire." And, Alva hoped, an exaggeration of the risk.

"It is dire, but, well, when needs must. And it was effective!"

"Yes? Tell me."

"She directed me to send word to Mr. Rutherfurd that she would not be marrying him."

"Oh, that is excellent news," said Alva. "Did you send word?" Lucy nodded, and Alva continued, "I hope she made the decision based on the merits of my argument rather than your threat. Or mine. Still, I'll take what I can get and be glad of it."

The Duke of Marlborough arrived in Newport late on Saturday on the last weekend of the month. Traveling with a small entourage of servants and a larger collection of trunks, he was installed at Marble House before the public had the opportunity to set eyes on him—a situation distressing to society until it was remedied when he appeared with Alva, Consuelo, Willie, and Harold at Trinity Church the next morning.

The austere setting, acting, as it did, as a governor on the public's excited reaction, gave Alva the opportunity to tell Mamie Fish in a voice easily overheard, "I'll be holding Marble House open beginning at three o'clock this afternoon. The duke is quite eager to meet Newport's citizens."

"I am, quite," said Marlborough. "Such a charming community."

At 3:05, the house was so full that Alva's footmen and the Newport police had to turn away the remaining crowd.

It was at a time such as this when Alva missed Ward McAllister most.

Ward had been dining alone at the Union Club in late January when a waiter returned to his table and found him upright but dead. He had been enjoying rib roast with potatoes, peas, and truffles, with a glass of a red wine he'd brought himself. Evidently he had simply . . . expired. It was not a bad end, and indeed, many said he would have approved of going this way.

In the past, when Alva had been faced with the kind of social intricacies she was weaving now, she and Ward would be in his home, or, later, in the parlor of 660 Fifth Avenue plotting strategy while upstairs the children played or napped. She could trust him to speak plainly and thoughtfully. She could reveal her anxieties without fear of being seen as selfish or grasping. He had been her friend.

Perhaps due to the current hour being so late, or to the strain she was under, or to the effects of the drink or the laudanum she'd consumed, Alva could almost persuade herself that Ward was beside her on the settee, his notebook opened on the table in front of them, his pencil gripped by thumb and middle finger of both hands in that way he had . . .

Now, let's set down the goal of your campaign, he would say.

To see my daughter truly finished with Mr. Rutherfurd and engaged to marry Marlborough.

Is Rutherfurd still a threat?

I am keeping my daughter isolated; that's all I can say for certain.

Ward would say, *Very good, then. You've planned a ball with the duke as the guest of honor, yes?*

I did. I'm billing it the way we did when the Duchess of Manchester was the esteemed guest.

He would hear the bitterness in her tone and say, *You mustn't continue to haul that anvil around on your back, my dear. See how it bends you under its weight! No. That's in no way useful to you.*

"Useful" has had no part in my reasoning.

I fail to see evidence of much reasoning myself.

I haven't invited you here to lecture me on forgiveness.

I haven't begun my lecture! Nor will I, he would add, recognizing that she was nearly at the end of her tether as it was. *Tell me about this ball.*

She would describe the extensive preparations being made to Marble House, as well as the favors she had bought, the food she would serve, the guest list she had made—she had included even those who yet refused to receive a divorcée, hoping that their desperate desire to be among those who would speak or dance with the duke would countermand the "rule" to snub her. Later they would justify this with statements claiming Christian tolerance for Alva's sin. The scenario amused her.

She had not, however, invited any of the Vanderbilts, whose decisions to side with William she could not excuse. Her heart ached over it, but so be it. Sometimes life was hard.

I've asked Oliver Belmont to receive with me—

Ah.

"Ah?"

You ought to have named him *on your agenda as well.*

Oliver is not an item on my agenda.

And why is that? You'll fight to engineer the duke's commitment to a girl whose mother is supposedly out of top society. You'll fight to regain your place in the order. But you won't fight for your chance at happiness?

Those first two things will result in my happiness.

Ward would say, *Pah. Social standing never brought that, not to you—you've got more depth in your little finger than those shallow ladies possess in their entire bodies.*

(A flattering judgment to put in his mouth, she admitted.)

Leaving that aside, she would say, *neither is a man going to bring me happiness.*

Ward would smile sardonically. *Please. Oliver Hazard Perry Belmont isn't "a man."*

It doesn't matter. He's only a dear friend, nothing more.

Enough of this nonsense, thought Alva, ending her wishful conference and ringing for her maid. She needed some rest. Tomorrow and the following day and the days after that were all filled with the activities she had devised to entertain and impress and inspire the duke, as well as to give her daughter numerous opportunities to share his company.

Taking a page from Ward's guide, she had also invited the press, guaranteeing breathless coverage of every event. She would win the duke for Consuelo if it killed her.

Everyone attended the ball.

On a fine September afternoon when all Alva desired at the moment was a quiet hour in a sunlit alcove, the duke invited Consuelo to join him alone in the Gothic Room. Ten minutes later, Consuelo came running to Alva.

"The duke has asked me to marry him." She was breathless.

Thank you, God, thought Alva. She said, "Is it what you want?"

Consuelo nodded somberly. "It is."

"Are you in love with him?"

Her daughter tilted her head. "No," she said. "No, it doesn't feel like that, exactly."

"I think that's for the best; to imagine yourself in love now would indicate mere infatuation. Genuine love will occur later."

If it occurred at all.

Neither of them said this.

"I've enjoyed his company a great deal," Consuelo said. "He's intelligent, and he seems to truly like me."

"I have observed that as well."

"I'm confident I'm going to love being the mistress of Blenheim, and I'm eager to serve the Oxfordshire people. It will be such good occupation for me."

"Then . . . shall we cable your father and then make the announcement?" Alva asked. When Consuelo nodded, Alva stood up and hugged her. "Congratulations, my darling girl. I suppose it goes without saying, but I approve heartily. I'm proud of you."

With fewer than sixty days standing between the promise and its culmination, Alva began assembling the wedding plans as quickly as she could, all the while praying that neither the duke nor her daughter backed out. There was no reason they should. But she had learned that trouble did not heed reason.

The press treated the news as if it were as important as the presidential campaigns now forming for next fall's election. And while most reports were fawning accounts of the budding romance between the heiress and the duke, there were a few that claimed Alva had denied her daughter her true love and *forced* her to marry the duke. Perhaps Rutherfurd was getting his revenge.

In response, letters arrived with remarks like this:

> *Mrs. Vanderbilt: Not only did you cause harm to a good man by divorce, now you are harming America by selling your daughter to a foreigner. Vanderbilt millions belong to this economy. If these dukes and earls and such are so important, let the Brits find their own funds.*

And this:

> *Miss Vanderbilt: I saw the newspaper story on how your terrible mother is forcing you to be sold to that short duke. I am more handsome, and taller, and have loved you from afar. Send a kind word and I will rescue you from this sad and awful fate.*

And this:

People like you deserve to be choked to death.

Alva hired extra guards and sent a note to *Vogue* magazine's editor in chief, Mrs. Josephine Redding, inviting her to tea. During their meeting, Alva said, "We've had some troubling press about my daughter's impending wedding to the ninth Duke of Marlborough. I could use your help in getting the story out correctly. Will you trade true and favorable coverage for exclusive details on the items in her trousseau?"

Alva did this with other publications as well, offering exclusive information or access or an invitation to the wedding, whichever suited each one's particular strengths, desires, or audience. All of them were happy to horse-trade this way. A Vanderbilt heiress! The most eligible of England's dukes! They lapped up every detail, buckles to bows, like cats with milk.

Alva was exhausted.

Whatever it takes.

In the meantime, she attempted to prepare her daughter for what she might expect on her wedding night and afterward. Alva used neither "peg" nor "plank" in her discussion, which took place in Consuelo's room one evening over wine and cake. She did not want to ruin for her daughter the possibility that she, Consuelo, might find the act less odious than Alva had. And so she described with unprejudiced language the steps Consuelo should expect to take whenever the young duke approached her for "intercourse of a sexual nature, which should be looked on without dread. It's a natural act and a necessary one."

She outlined the probable scene, then said, "You'll be embarrassed—and that's appropriate. He'll likely be embarrassed as well, though he will do his best not to show it. Men are instructed in the specifics. Let him lead you. His . . . erect organ is made to fit into you between your legs, into the opening there—"

Consuelo's eyes had never been larger.

Alva had to laugh. "It sounds absolutely absurd, I know. This is the way of it, though. He's required to move himself in and—" (Good lord, this was much more difficult than she'd expected!) "So, then, after a few moments of . . . that, he'll have a kind of small convulsion and then withdraw. The convulsing is the method that expels the fluid necessary for you to conceive. All right? Will you look at this cake? My word—chocolate cream layers! Cook's very good to us, isn't she?"

"It sounds horrid!" said Consuelo. Alva knew she did not refer to the cake.

She said, "So does blood pudding, but you're very fond of that. Here now, don't fret over it." She refilled her daughter's wineglass and her own. "After the first time, it will be of no consequence at all. Just another part of your routine."

During this period of preparation, the duke intended to take in amusements throughout the region and down in Kentucky at the horse farms. Oliver, who after working with Bryan was hearing a call to office himself, took time away from politics to tend the duke. "You need someone looking after your interests," Oliver told Alva. "I won't call myself a chaperone. 'Ambassador,' that's the thing. He's a self-important chap; he'll like that."

America hardly knew what to make of the self-important chap, who could be charming or imperious and was often both. He was not tall, not strapping, not dashing or athletic the way American heroes tended to be. He engaged in no sport outside of bicycling (though he sat a horse as well as anyone)—in short, he was not in any way "clubbable," though to be sure no club existed that would refuse him membership if he desired to join.

The press trailed him adoringly, while his representative stayed behind in New York to negotiate terms with William. Marlborough returned to New York in early November, looking forward to having more than two million dollars with which to restore his heritage, as well as a personal allowance of $25,000 quarterly, matching what his future father-in-law would also give the bride. All was well. It was very well, indeed.

On the morning of November 6, St. Thomas Church filled its pews with wedding guests pressed hip to hip and full of self-satisfied pride at being among the invitees, especially given that some five thousand less fortunate but no less avid onlookers thronged the streets outside. Police lines and barriers held back the most aggressive of them—handkerchief-waving young women who wanted nothing more from life on this morning than a glimpse of the bride-to-be's angelic face.

Alva, still tending to the last of the details inside the church, took stock of the scene there: Duke. Bishops. Flowers. The organist and choir. The Astors. All that was missing was the bride and her father, who was charged with bringing her to the church.

The appointed hour arrived. No bride.

Three minutes passed.

Five.

People were murmuring. Alva went to her seat. Consuelo and William would arrive at any moment. Of course they would. She sat in the first pew beside her sisters while the groom moved into position at the foot of chancel steps. He wore a tight expression and glanced at Bishop Littlejohn, who returned a smile of encouragement.

"I shouldn't have left her before William got there," Alva told her sisters. But she'd had to be here to oversee things directly. With such a crucial event as this, nothing could be left to chance.

Armide said, "I'm certain she will be here presently."

"I wonder if one of the horses took lame." Or perhaps Consuelo had a fit of pique and was balking at the gate. Or perhaps, knowing Alva was off to the church, she had waited until the moment she was alone and then run off with Rutherfurd, gleefully punishing Alva for engineering all of this when her heart was now and had ever been his. Perhaps William was now in pursuit of them and hadn't had time to send word.

The organist played on. Five more minutes elapsed. The murmuring increased.

Alva began, "I'm going to go—" when she saw Marlborough and Bishop Littlejohn come to attention. A cheer was rising outside.

After a minute the chapel's doors swung open. The "Wedding March" from *Lohengrin* began, and up the aisle came Consuelo's bridesmaids, four of them filing to the left of the chancel, the other four moving to the right, exactly as they had rehearsed. The fifty-member choir lifted their voices to God, and in the bridesmaids' wake came the bride and her father—she, veiled, he, somber-looking, both *there.*

Alva swallowed a sob.

Throughout the lengthy ceremony, her eyes leaked in a steady trickle that at the pronouncement of marriage briefly became a stream.

She had done it.

It was done.

Her daughter was forever protected from fortune-hunting playboys, from seeing opportunity pass her by while her friends went off gaily to (sometimes) better fates. Consuelo Vanderbilt had in the space of mere moments, in a single sentence uttered by a man she might never see again after today, been transformed into a living piece of history.

Alva spent the remainder of the morning in a daze. Certainly she left the church, boarded her carriage, traversed the avenues and arrived at her home, where she hosted the wedding breakfast, accepted congratulations, talked, laughed, ate. Her awareness of it later, though, was a scene as viewed through fog. How suddenly came the time for the newlyweds to go. How rapidly the duke and his just-anointed duchess were exiting the house in a shower of rice, off to Italy and Egypt.

Alva watched from a window. Consuelo waved to her. Alva waved in return. Possibly in this moment both of them had the same thought: What in heaven's name did I just do?

X

ON A COLD day shortly before Christmas, Oliver surprised Alva by appearing on the Marble House veranda, where she'd been standing with her face tilted up to the sun.

The last she'd heard from him, he was with Bryan taking meetings in Cincinnati, where he had also been to the zoo "visiting Harold's elephant," he'd written, the Grey Crag partnership having been dissolved in the wake of William's poor behavior. Oliver had placed many of the animals at the zoo in Cincinnati.

Though she had wished for him to stay nearby after the wedding, she couldn't begrudge his purposeful travel. In fact she was proud of him. He might easily have done as most of the men in their class did: use all his resources for his own amusements (cf. William K. Vanderbilt). He might have taken a pretty young wife. Why hadn't he taken a wife? Theories ranged from his being irreparably broken by Sallie's dismissal to his being secretly in love with a society matron with an unrhymable first name. Alva was aware of the speculation as regards her role in his drama. How nice it would be if those gossipy ladies were correct, for a change!

He had, however, remained steadfastly platonic in their interactions. Whatever had once motivated his love for her was gone. He said now, "Mrs. Evelyn told me you'd run away and joined up with Barnum's circus."

"And so I did," she said, turning toward him. "Trapeze. But when

Mr. Barnum put us on holiday hiatus, I thought I would benefit from a little time here."

"Very sensible. Quite the year it's been."

"Quite."

"Last year this time, you were convinced I was the enemy."

"And would have remained convinced, had you not been so thoughtful as to come see me on Christmas Eve."

He said, "How are you now, having conquered society on both sides of the Atlantic?"

"I'm well," she replied. "My world has been righted after all—though getting it there took everything I had. I'll confess, though: this year I'm a little forlorn with my daughter away in England and my boys off with the rest of the Vanderbilts to see George's new estate. Biltmore, he's named it."

"The house is done, then?"

"Sufficiently enough to allow visitors, William says. Richard's sons took it over to finish the job. I hear it has a bowling alley and a swimming pool *indoors*. No wonder it gave Richard fits."

"Not unlike my having horses living in Belcourt."

"Belcourt was no chore to build, I'm certain."

They stood side by side, squinting out at the whitecapped water. Alva said, "What are you doing up here, anyway? I thought you'd closed your place for the winter."

"I told you before: I don't like to think of you being lonely. You weren't in New York and I was worried about you."

She laughed. "You truly are as mad as they say."

"Madder, probably; how does one appraise these things? That said, I am not the one who has been standing *outside* of a perfectly good, warm house on a frigid day."

"If I had any manners, I would invite you *inside*."

"I am hopeful you have none, because then you'll more easily forgive me for this," he said, then put his hand on the back of her head and kissed her. She could not have been more surprised if he had sprouted wings and lifted himself in flight.

The kiss was tender at first, then forceful. When they parted, both of them were breathing hard, their commingled breaths making a cloud around them. "There, I've broken my promise," he said, "and I am not sorry in the least."

Alva couldn't speak.

"What's more," he went on, "I am determined to do it again."

And he did. When he released her, she said, her voice full of wonder, "But I thought you didn't—that is, that you had ceased to—"

"Oh, no, I do. I always have. And dare I hope that your response suggests a mutual affection? Unless I am badly mistaken, in which case I offer my most ardent apology. I'll go right now, straight back to the depot—"

"No! No, you're not mistaken. It is mutual. It always has been."

"I felt it was! Despite everything. Though you hardly indicated—"

"How could I?"

"No, of course. Yet it was always there. An affinity. A kind of chemistry between us. The tether of gravity, I would say, no less powerful than the moon to the earth or the earth to the sun."

Alva had to laugh. He was quite pleased with himself.

Really, this was impossible to fathom. Even had she attempted to conjure such a scene, she would not have known to make it so *joyful*.

So *this* was love.

She said, "A man of science *and* a poet now, are you?"

"A man of all interests and trades. A man of the world. Alva's man, now, if she is so inclined."

"I hardly know what to think! Except that I think we had better get warm and, I don't know, discuss this further, I suppose."

They went to the Gothic Room and seated themselves near the fire. This room was his favorite, just as it was Alva's. It was more austere than the other rooms, more intimate. A space for quiet reflection—though what was happening inside her mind was very much the opposite. Oliver Belmont had kissed her passionately! Everything was different and strange. What came next? What were his intentions? She might as well be a virginal maid of fifteen for the tumult going on inside her. Was one never beyond the capacity for feeling so desperate and ill about love?

Oliver said, "So you aren't scandalized by my actions?"

"Scandalized? Me? You'll have to try much harder than that."

The one maid she kept on staff in winter brought in a tray with coffee and biscuits, then discreetly hurried out as Oliver was saying, "When you and Vanderbilt separated, for the first time I thought my long shot could actually pay. It has been difficult to bide my time. I have been dying to take action."

"I'm delighted the action occurred to you at all."

"Oh, I am full of such occurrences," he said.

He poured coffee for them and handed Alva her cup. She liked his hands—the length of his fingers, the tidy squares of his fingernails, the calluses on the pads of his fingers, a result of so many years holding reins. Was there a tremor in his grip as he handed over the cup? She concentrated on keeping her own cup steady, letting the heat warm her palms, thinking only of that and not her rabbit-fast heartbeat. Not the recollection of his lips against hers. His warm mouth. Oh—she was thinking of those things, wasn't she? She was thinking of those things and of the sensation in her center, a warm and urgent feeling she had rarely addressed, and never without some shame.

She was beyond that shame now—or if she wasn't, she was determined to be.

She said, "Am I awful to admit I suffered and wished that you suffered along with me? I was thoroughly committed to my marriage—foolishly, I know now—and yet I still—"

"Yes, awful. Irredeemable, in fact." He stood up and extended his hand to her. "Therefore, no harm in indulging every level of corruption. Is anyone besides the maid about?"

"Only downstairs," she said, taking his hand.

Now her heart was pounding so fast she feared she might collapse or faint or who knew what before she saw this through to wherever he meant it to go. Ridiculous! She was too old to be so fearful, giddy, eager—except that she was, in fact, all of those things and therefore must not be too old.

Oliver kept hold of her hand, leading her up the staircase and to her bedroom where, once inside, he closed and locked the door.

"Now," he said, backing her against the wall.

She attempted to gather her wits. "Oliver, I'm . . ."

"What?"

"Not so young as I once was."

He looked at her severely. "Do you want me to kiss you?"

"And it's been a very long time since—"

"Will you let me kiss you?"

She laughed. "I will."

And he did. He pushed against her. Their breathing grew ragged.

"How many years?" he said, putting his mouth against her neck. His teeth grazed her earlobe. His tongue traced higher. "So many years, waiting for this."

"Yes," she said, to all of it.

He stripped her gloves from her hands and dropped them at their feet. Then his hands were on her shoulders, her neck, her breast. Undoing her hooks and buttons. Shedding his coat and jacket and shirt. Pushing her bodice off her shoulders, stroking her bare skin. Unbuttoning her skirt, pushing it down. Unhooking her corset and tossing it aside. Pulling her toward the bed and then down onto it with him.

He asked, "This is no accusation: Has there been anyone other than William?"

She shook her head. "And it was never . . . That is, I didn't . . ."

He shifted so that he was leaning on one elbow. "Let's begin here," he said, moving her chemise strap off her shoulder. "I intend to spoil you in ways I suspect you haven't even imagined. You deserve to be spoiled."

"I don't know what to do," she whispered. "Suppose I let you down?"

"Then I'll toss you back like a cankerous fish."

This made her laugh again. "Fair enough."

He said, "In some parts of the world, young men are trained up to put the desires and pleasures of their partner before their own. This has always seemed to me not only fair but wise. Happy companionship using every capacity God has given us. I've read up on this a good deal."

"Oh, you've read up on it," Alva said.

Kissing her forehead, he said, "You are the only woman I've ever truly wanted."

He pushed the strap farther down and his mouth followed his hands. Then his hands found her waist, her ribs, her breasts. He stroked her neck, loosened her hair and combed his hand through it. He kissed her jaw, her chin, her mouth.

When he said *Kiss me*, she did, and when he said *Touch me*, she did that, too, and when he put his hand where she'd once been forbidden to put hers, when he murmured, *Just allow yourself to feel it*, she was no longer nervous or scared. His fingers stroked her, he pressed his hips to her thigh, desire plain, and when she cried out, he moved onto her and she pulled him in. "I want this," she said, looking up at him.

He smiled. "And you shall have it."

The sensation was familiar and yet so strange. He was deliberate, kissing her, watching her, asking, as he shifted her leg or his, pushed up from her or pressed her down, *Is this good?* It *was* good, and it went on, and intoxication overtook her, her mind so full of this, of him. He moved sensuously, his mouth at her ear, his words praising, enticing, encouraging her. And then she was gasping, then calling out, and after he did, too, she burst into hard, happy tears of surprise and gratitude and wonder.

"Will you marry me?" she said.

Oliver laughed. "Finally! The lady comes to her senses."

He raised himself up to look at her. "I'm going to run for the U.S. House. Would you want to be a congressman's wife?"

"Only if you want to be a congressman."

"Do you feel the children will approve of our pairing?"

"They have always loved you. I think that will bear out."

"Then I accept. Be my wife and partner in all things, Alva. The world will be our oyster."

"Feed me," she said.

The day after their marriage in January, she and Oliver went to dine at Sherry's, and there in the foyer saw Laura Davies and her husband. Laura Davies, the selfsame woman who had turned her back on Alva at the charity meeting two years earlier and hadn't acknowledged her even one time since, was saying now, "Why, it's Mr. and Mrs. Belmont! May we offer our congratulations? What happy news."

Alva said, "You may. And I am so very happy about it myself that I won't remark further." She nodded to the maître d'hôtel to show them to their table. There she said to Oliver, "That woman snubbed me for two years."

"For two years, you weren't married. Now all is right again. Everyone is in her correct place."

"Well, I can't disagree with that."

Not long afterward, Willie brought the news that after a round of stubborn fighting with Neily about Grace Wilson, Corneil woke the following morning, ate breakfast, went to his study, and slumped over in his armchair, completely insensible. The doctors said it was a stroke.

Alice blamed Neily. Neily married the girl just the same, and Corneil didn't die from the insult.

While Corneil was recovering, Alva and Oliver went to Long Island to buy a home site in East Meadow, on which they would build a new house. Already they had Classical, with Marble House; with Belcourt, they had Gothic; why not try Colonial Revival this time around?

While the new house rose, Corneil's health worsened. While Alva was gaining the trust and friendship of Oliver's man, Azar, and overseeing alterations to Belcourt so that it would better accommodate a married pair, Alice, having seen Corneil through a second stroke, was reacquainting herself with strong, efficient nurses whose job it was to get her husband out of his bed, into his wheelchair, into and out of the bath.

While Alva was in England seeing her first grandson born, while she was in Newport encouraging Willie to court and marry Tessie Oelrichs's youngest sister, Birdie, while she was on the Upper East Side of New York City scouting locations for the townhouse she and Oliver wanted to build near Central Park, Alice was fretting over Corneil's decline. Alice was being awakened, early one morning, by her husband calling out from his bedroom next to hers, "I think I'm dying!" He then proved himself correct.

While Alice was donning the black she would wear for the rest of her life, Alva was starting hers over again. She was very sorry for Alice, but she was not otherwise sorry.

❧

"Will you help me with this chain?" Alva asked Mary. She was seated at her vanity table, dressed and nearly ready for the night's festivities. One of the great pleasures of this new life had been the chance to fully cultivate Mary as a friend.

Mary came to stand behind her and took the necklace from her hands. "I do like that now you have to ask."

The necklace was simple in design: a silver chain with a cameo of Oliver in profile. Alva had it made especially to imitate the buttons they would distribute to every guest at tonight's New Year's celebration—and not an ordinary one: tonight marked the final hours of the nineteenth century.

At the button's top border were the words *For Congress* and at its bottom, *Oliver H. P. Belmont*. A photograph of him in profile filled the center of the button. He looked distinguished. Congressional.

"There, all set," Mary said.

Alva put her fingers to the cameo. "My Oliver is handsome, isn't he?"

"He is. It's a shame women can't vote."

"A shame for so many reasons," Alva said, standing. "Look at you! You are a beauty yourself."

Mary, who showed her age only in the lines around her eyes, stood before the cheval glass and smiled at her reflection. "I am rather fine. Which doesn't mean your other guests are going to be thrilled to have us here."

The *us* of Mary's reference consisted of Mary and her husband of three years, Caleb Taylor, an attorney whose practice was in San Juan Hill.

Alva said, "If they aren't thrilled, they're not Oliver's voters—and they're not friends of mine, and they can leave."

"You've made an art of cutting your losses, I have to say. I always knew you *could* do it, I just wasn't ever certain you would."

"May the burning of my bridges—if indeed any more are burned—light the way for others!"

"Alva, you do know it's only me here."

"I'm rehearsing," Alva said.

"For tonight? I thought it was Oliver who'll be speaking."

"For eventually."

That Alva had found love and was so wholly content did not mean she was going to spend all her days eating éclairs and reading stories by Edith Wharton, say (though the stories were quite good). Alva commended her old friend, the former Edith Jones, for taking action with her talents. She did admire women who took action—which was why she could not spend all her time reading. They had a campaign to launch and a House seat to win, and if it was unfortunate that the only way she (or any woman) could do this was through a man—well, every tree had to start from a seed, did it not?

She and Oliver had hired a ten-piece orchestra, as well as the new chef from Delmonico's. They would have three hundred revelers in attendance. Now Alva found Oliver standing before the orchestra as the men warmed up their instruments. He faced them, his hands clasped behind his back. On his head was a shiny tin crown.

"King Oliver, I presume."

He turned. "Ah, my lovely queen!" He assessed the fruit-and-flowers garland she wore, and grinned. "You look delicious."

"For shame, sire; our guests will be arriving any minute. The Taylors are here already."

"Yes, Taylor went into the salon for a cocktail. Isn't that a marvelous word for a drink, *cock-tail*? How far up the pole must someone have been to equate a cock's tail—or perhaps a cocked tail—with mixed liquors?"

Caleb Taylor, who was in his fifties and was graying at temples and chin, had joined them, drink in hand. He said, "How far up the pole must a rich man be to seek office on a progressive platform?"

"Some would presume I am drunken all the time."

"And how many friends will you lose simply by having my wife and me as guests here tonight?"

Alva said, "May the burning of those bridges light the way for others! . . . I'm practicing."

"And many are already burnt in our paths, to be sure," said Oliver. He kissed her, for emphasis.

Mary joined them, tin crowns in hand for herself, her husband, and Alva, who said, "Will you look at us? Four people of exceptional quality and intellect, three of whom began life as the property of wealthy white men. Not to say that our situations were equal. I just mean to demonstrate that all sorts of societal wrongs *can* be improved." She took glasses of champagne from the sideboard for herself and Mary, adding, "And it all starts afresh with a new century, French grapes, and New York's Representative-to-be Oliver Belmont, my husband."

The ball proceeded much as balls did. The arrival of guests. The exclamations over a lady's gown or brooch or fur or hairstyle. Julia arrived with her husband, the French count Charles Gaston de Fontenilliat (a dandy, as one might expect), dressed in a pure white polar fox coat. There was champagne. There was music and dancing and conversation on every topic—from what a "lovely little war" they'd just had with Spain, to the gunslinger Pearl Hart (a woman!) robbing a stagecoach out in Arizona, to the hurricane that had wiped out every estate and all the rum production on St. Croix (where several of the guests had interests), to the recent opening of the Bronx Zoo. (Harold and Alva had already visited five times—and he'd only been home from St. Mark's School for two weeks.) A good many of the white guests (though not all, by any means) engaged in conversation with the Taylors. Mary found Alva at one point in the evening and said, "I'm not certain I've ever before seen white people working so hard at being polite."

Harry Lehr arrived at 11:45, escorting Mamie Fish, and Alva found herself standing there in her ballroom, staring at the pair of them. Harry was not Ward McAllister. Mamie was not Caroline Astor. Yet in the moment, Alva felt as though time had stood still. Were none of them important or unique? Was each of them nothing beyond a fresh player taking over a fixed role in a never-ending production of a single play?

Oliver put his hand on her arm. "Come with me?"

"Where are we going?"

"To the terrace."

Outside on their roof, the night air was sharp. There was no moon, and the stars were vivid against their black backdrop. Oliver put his arm around Alva's shoulders.

"It's awfully cold, I know. But I wanted you all to myself for a minute or two at least."

Beyond them, Central Park was a dark and barren landscape, its skeleton trees faintly visible, the lake a slick mirror of the sky above.

"It's so much quieter out here," Alva said. "I don't mind the cold."

"We have an anniversary coming up. Four exceptional years. How should we observe it, do you suppose?"

"Only four! How odd it is—I feel as if we've always been together and all those things in my past are imagined, or I read them in a book. And yet not three minutes ago I was watching Harry Lehr and Mamie Fish and feeling as though nothing was different from that old life. Time behaves very strangely."

"I remember the first time I saw you. Florence Vanderbilt's debutante ball. I was, what, sixteen years old—a skinny, reluctant boy masquerading as a gentleman. My father made all of us attend, in deference to the old Commodore."

"You noticed *me*?"

"You were wearing a green dress, and you seemed uncomfortable—not in the dress; rather, at the ball."

"I hardly knew anyone there. I was barely out of mourning for my mother." Consuelo Yznaga had made her go.

Oliver said, "I wished to talk to you, but I couldn't work up my courage. You wouldn't have thought twice about me then."

"Let's imagine it, though. Say you did speak to me, and I liked you as well as I know I would have, and we'd begun our life together that night with a fast friendship that would become a romance in due time, and marriage."

"And then all these years later, we would stand out here at the balustrade getting frostbite on the ends of our noses, waiting for the end of the century."

"And for the beginning of the century."

Oliver turned to face her. "I didn't used to believe in love. It's all very untoward, you know. No dignity in it. Who wants to be a sentimental sap? Well, as it happens, I do. Thank you for changing my life."

"The sentiment is mutual," she said.

They kissed, and then Alva said with some reluctance, "I expect we had better go back in. Doesn't this remind you of that day you came to find me at Marble House? Only, this time you've got a rather different sort of speech to give. Are you ready to become Candidate Belmont?"

He stepped away from her, unbuttoned his coat, and hooked his thumbs under his suspenders. After clearing his throat theatrically, he began, "I believe that Man is good. I believe that we stand at the dawn of a century that will be more peaceful and prosperous than any in history . . ."

"Such an optimist!"

"Unfortunate, isn't it? Political life chews up my sort and spits us out, all mangled and useless. But . . . I don't know how to be any other way." He pulled Alva against him. "It got me here, didn't it?"

"Precisely where you ought to be."

There in Oliver's embrace, Alva looked beyond his shoulder into the night, at the lights in the buildings bordering the park at Fifty-ninth Street, at Alice's enormous house, the swelling city behind it. The joy Alva felt tonight would not endure forever. Hardships always waited in the wings. Right now, though, she was a beloved woman on a rooftop terrace under the stars, wrapped in the arms of a man she adored. Right now, she was.

Constellation

Up then, fair phoenix bride, frustrate the sun;
Thyself from thine affection
Takest warmth enough, and from thine eye
All lesser birds will take their jollity.
Up, up, fair bride, and call
Thy stars from out their several boxes, take
Thy rubies, pearls, and diamonds forth, and make
Thyself a constellation of them all;
And by their blazing signify
That a great princess falls, but doth not die.
Be thou a new star, that to us portends
Ends of much wonder; and be thou those ends.

—JOHN DONNE

I

WHEN THEY ASKED her about the Vanderbilts and Belmonts, about their celebrations and depredations, the mansions and balls, the lawsuits, the betrayals, the rifts—Alva said nothing is ever quite the way you think it's going to be: Once there was a woman who married for money and had some regrets about that. Then she was betrayed, so she cut her losses and went on to marry for love. Now it was 1908. Springtime. She was fifty-five years old, unburdened, expecting to see the fruits of her cultivations ripen further.

"Do come out to the meeting, won't you?" Mrs. Kitty Mackay asked Alva, the two having met up by accident one April day at the excellent new Plaza Hotel, where Alva and Armide were having afternoon tea on the finest gilt-edged china Alva had ever seen in a restaurant.

Kitty had been among Consuelo's school friends, and according to Consuelo's recent telling, had just founded the Equal Franchise Society. She was dividing her time between Manhattan and Long Island, where she had her primary home, a husband, children, and numerous philanthropic endeavors. Consuelo had indicated a possible involvement between Kitty and her husband's doctor, as well. Whether or not that was so, the young woman was pretty and earnest and had the energy of a terrier, it seemed, because she kept on speaking despite seeing that Alva and Armide were engaged with a delicate tower of cakes and sandwiches.

"It's at the Colony Club tonight, eight o'clock. We need women such as yourselves to bolster the cause. You *do* want women to have the vote?"

"I always have," Alva said.

"Then come! We have a very distinguished panel for the lecture. Mrs. Carrie Catt, Mrs. Ida Tarbell—"

"She's the one who made all the trouble for John Rockefeller," Alva told Armide. "I read her book." To Kitty she said, "All right, count me in. I'm interested to see what sort of muck these ladies are raking up."

"Marvelous, simply marvelous," Kitty said. "I told the duchess last time I wrote that I'd find you and rope you in, and here I've done it. Excellent. Good day! See you soon!"

Armide stifled a laugh. "How long would she have stood there yapping had you not consented to go?"

"Shhh," Alva said, bringing a delicate circle of brioche topped with caviar to her mouth. "I want to enjoy this." She enjoyed another one after that, and then a third for good measure. She did like to measure well.

At the Colony Club that evening, the ballroom was still only half filled when the event began. The ladies in attendance were not all familiar to Alva, but they were almost exclusively of her generation. Kitty was one of only a handful of younger women present.

The first of the speakers, Mrs. Mary Ellen something or other, spoke so softly that Alva found herself leaning forward, trying to make sense of "benefit of having a say . . . poor, no means of . . . democratic . . ." to the point of nearly falling from her chair into the ladies seated in the row ahead.

The next speaker, a Mrs. Aubrey or Audrey, read from her notes in a monotone: "Every person whom God saw fit to bring into this world here in this wonderful country of bounty and plenty when times are good should have a say in his or her own governance, and by this I include all white women but not Indian women who deserve no rights for the crimes of warring with the United States government. Nor do I feel it is best to include the Negress in this otherwise sweeping statement due to the Negress being inferior in her intelligence even compared to the male of her race—"

Alva interjected, "This is not so!"

"Shhh!" said a woman next to her.

"She is in error," Alva said. "Negro women are no less intelligent than you or I!"

Mrs. Aubrey or Audrey, startled, remained silent for another moment. Then she looked again at her notes, running her finger along the page until she found her place, and resumed her oration, an event lasting seventeen more minutes (Alva timed her), during which some of the ladies who'd been nodding along nodded off.

Another three women spoke, all of them more competent but none of them inspiring, and when the thing was concluded, Alva was no more enlightened than she'd been at the start.

On her way out, she thanked Kitty and said, "That was very nice," just to be polite. The girl had been so earnest, after all.

"Then you'll come again?" Kitty said brightly.

"I'm afraid I'm leaving for my house on Long Island, and then I'll be away most of the summer in England. Good luck to you, though."

"We'll be ongoing in the fall. Can I count on you to join us then?"

"My dear, your persistence is admirable. However, unless you and the other ladies in your organization put that energy into the program itself, you'll only ever get the same already-converted bunch coming to hear you—if that. I didn't learn a single thing that wasn't said fifty years ago."

"Our mission is to educate—"

"*Stimulate*," Alva said. "That's what you need to do. Give ladies your age a reason to miss their bridge games and piano recitals. Get yourself a firebrand speaker—the equivalent of Christabel Pankhurst, that English suffragette who keeps getting herself arrested. Use a meeting to organize a march on the Metropolitan Club in Washington; the congressmen are more likely to be there than in chambers. Make posters. Write letters. *Do* things."

Kitty smiled as politely as Alva had done a minute before. "I'm sure we appreciate the advice."

"You know, for an intelligent woman, you are not very sensible."

By the time Alva arrived at home again, her mind was already onto other matters. She and Oliver had a date for cards and cocktails in the parlor with their new bespoke Edison phonograph and a stack of ragtime records. The sound quality with this new machine was so good, one could almost believe the band was in the room.

Oliver was mixing the cocktails when Alva came in. He had Vess Ossman on the phonograph and *The Bon-Vivant's Companion* at hand for recipes. He said, "How was the meeting?"

"They would do a lot better if they followed *this* sort of program."

Oliver handed her a rum cocktail called the Knickerbocker—a little joke of theirs. He raised his own glass and said, "Everyone would do better if they followed this sort of program."

"I've got a bit of indigestion," Oliver told her one night in early May after they'd arrived at Brookholt, their Long Island mansion. They'd eaten a dinner of cold chicken, then followed it with a nightcap and were now getting ready for bed. He put on his robe, saying, "I'm going to have a walk around the house."

Long Island was enjoying a marvelous spring, and they intended to make the most of it before going to England for the summer. Making the most of things was rather their way, now. For example, though William Jennings Bryan had lost to William McKinley, Oliver won his bid for Congress and did what he could to advance his agenda against a conservative majority. When McKinley died in '01 a week after being gut-shot by an anarchist, Teddy Roosevelt took office, putting the country in progressive hands and leaving Oliver content to return to their habits of fine wines, excellent food, leisurely travel, visits to the Belmont track, and nights that ended with the two of them lying in bed together, Oliver behind her with his hand resting on her hip. If Alva had a single regret, it was that she hadn't divorced William sooner.

Lately, Oliver and Willie, who had grown into a serious driver of fast motorcars, had been planning an automobile racecourse on Long Island, their progress interrupted only by Willie's world-record-setting race in Daytona. Harold was now studying law at Harvard, but his real love was, as ever, sailing. Neither boy had much interest in working for the family business, even with William now at its helm—though in truth he was little more than an overseer himself. And Consuelo—well, Consuelo had endured a great deal of change, and Alva was impatient to get back to England and help her daughter continue to sort things out.

Now Oliver put on his slippers and told Alva, "You needn't wait up for me."

"No, but I will."

She was sitting up in bed, sketching plans for a conservatory, when Oliver returned some forty minutes later. Standing inside the doorway, he said, "I must say, I don't get tired of this."

"Of indigestion?"

"No, that's better. Of having you in my bed."

She laid the sketchbook aside. "Prove it."

"All that fresh air does me in," Oliver told Alva one evening in the middle of May, when they'd been outdoors since not long after breakfast supervising and assisting with alterations to the gardens. Moving topsoil and shrubbery. Pulling up stones from new paths. She was in her bicycle bloomers and a shirtwaist. Oliver wore dungarees. Both of them were smudged and dusty and badly needed to bathe.

He stretched out on one of the drawing room's divans. "Maybe I'll rest here before coming upstairs."

"You smell to high heaven."

"Then I'll have to smell a while longer."

His tone was unusually sharp. Alva tilted her head. "What is it you're not saying?"

"Can't a man have a lie-down without being interrogated?"

"Have whatever you wish," Alva said, and left him there.

But it was so unlike them to provoke each other. A little while later she returned to the drawing room to smooth things over. He was still on the divan, curled on his side, asleep.

He woke her the next morning with a freshly cut rose and an apology. "My stomach was hurting a good deal, but I didn't want to say so. Forgive me?"

"Are you all right now?"

"A bit off my feed, but the pain's better."

"I didn't know pain made you snappish."

"Neither did I—which I suppose is fortunate. Blessed with good health all my life so far. I'll have to mind my temper if it happens again."

"Better to find the cause of the pain, and resolve it before we sail."

"I'm fine. Probably offended a muscle when I was helping to move those rocks." He raised his arms, stretched, then flexed his biceps. "Impressive, am I not? Tell me the truth: you've never seen a finer man than the one standing here before you."

"He *looks* very appealing. His scent, however . . ." She pinched her nose shut.

"He's quite astute, too. He knows that if he pushes this button here"—he pressed it to ring for a maid—"hot water will soon appear in his bathtub. He is a problem-solver extraordinaire."

"I believe I read about his skills in the newspaper."

"And experienced them firsthand." He waggled his eyebrows. "He is the lover all ladies long for, but only she could win his heart."

In late May, after a meal that involved (as so many of theirs did) several savory courses and a bottle of excellent wine, Oliver, hand on stomach, said, "I believe I overdid it."

"Are you in pain?"

"Some," he said, coming around to her side of the table. "I'll stay in my own room tonight. I would say, 'I'll miss you,'" he said, kissing her forehead, "but I fear you won't be the first thing on my mind."

"I don't like this."

"I like it even less, but it's nothing to worry over."

But when the night and then the next day and then another night passed and his pain and nausea would not abate, he agreed it was time to seek help.

After consulting his local physician, he told Alva, "Mystery solved: It's a liver irritation. I'm to eat only mild foods, no imbibing at all, and he's given me some pills. So you see? Nothing that won't be remedied in short order."

"We can change our tickets, if you need a little more time—"

"I'll be in fighting form in a day or two. Don't think twice about it."

But on June 1, when he couldn't rise or even move without wincing, when his color was terrible and he said he felt feverish, Alva said, "I'm cabling our New York doctors."

Drs. Bull and McCosh arrived on the afternoon train. After examining Oliver and consulting with Dr. Lanehart, the trio brought Alva into Oliver's room and delivered the bad news to them together:

"While the liver may well be implicated as Dr. Lanehart observed," said Dr. McCosh, "it now appears to be trouble with the appendix, which we hope may yet resolve with treatment. Mr. Belmont will take morphine for the pain, calomel as a purgative, Ichthyol for nausea. We'll bring a nurse in to tend to him and apply poultices to his abdomen for further relief."

Oliver looked at Alva. "It appears we may need to rearrange our trip after all." His tone was confident, but his expression was anxious and he was breathless as he spoke. Alva remembered sounding something like that when she was in the midst of childbirth.

She sat at Oliver's bedside throughout the evening, reading while he dozed. The poultices and morphine had eased his pain. When the nurse came to check on him, she told Alva, "The doctors are hopeful that rest will allow the organ to repair itself."

"Is that usually the way of it?"

"Well." The nurse paused. "I have seen it happen."

Alva went to Mrs. Evelyn and asked, "How many saltcellars do we have?"

"Two, I believe."

"Send someone into town to get two more. No, four more. Fill them all and bring them to the room Mr. Belmont's in."

"Ma'am?" said Mrs. Evelyn.

"They go beneath the bed—to harbor healing spirits or some such. We have to try everything, don't we?"

Mrs. Evelyn drew Alva to her for a hug.

When after another two days of all these treatments Oliver hadn't improved further, the doctor sat beside his bed and told them there was no longer any question: he must undergo surgery.

"And if I don't?" Oliver asked. "Not that I fear it," he added. "I'm certain you gents are as skillful as they come. It's the recovery time I'm thinking of. We're supposed to sail next week."

Alva told him, "My love, that's hardly a concern. England will be there."

"You've been waiting months to see Consuelo and the boys as it is."

He asked Dr. McCosh, "We could give it a little more time, don't you think? Just to be certain?"

The doctor said, "I understand your reluctance. But let me be quite clear: If the appendix is not removed, it's likely to become increasingly swollen with infection, which would then cause it to rupture. The resulting illness and pain will frankly be more horrible than you can conceive, and you will certainly die. I've sent for my assistants and supplies, and we'll undertake the surgery in the morning, first thing."

He left them, and Oliver told Alva, "Humorless bastard, isn't he?"

"It *is* a rather serious matter."

Oliver reached for her hand. "I'm very sorry about this."

"Please shut up," Alva said, fighting to keep her voice steady.

"Well, at least this will resolve the trouble so that when we do go abroad, I'll be fitter than ever."

"Maybe I should have my appendix out as well, prevention being the best cure."

"Solidarity," he said, smiling wanly.

In the morning, Willie, Birdie, and Harold came to sit with Alva during what felt like the longest day of her life—though she was unable to sit. She paced the hall outside the guest room McCosh had selected for the surgery, favored for its southeastern-facing windows. A glimpse into the room as nurses came and went with buckets of hot water showed a scene of bloodied linens beneath and around Oliver as he lay unconscious on a table. The odor took her back to 1874, to that day at the tenement where she and Armide discovered the dead girl. This odor, though, was worse. Blood, and a putrid scent like spoilt, rotting meat.

"The organ is septic," a nurse explained. "That's why it smells that way. Try not to worry. They're cleaning him out."

Alva turned toward the children. "They're 'cleaning him out.' Good lord."

In late evening, Dr. McCosh finally emerged from the bedroom. "We've completed the surgery and Mr. Belmont is stable—a remarkable testament to his fortitude; we discovered upon opening his abdomen that the appendix had already ruptured."

He shook his head in wonder, then went on, "Bacteria had infiltrated the abdominal muscles. The peritoneum—that is, the interior of the abdomen—was itself filled with it. We excised the diseased appendix and scraped the peritoneum, douching with warm water to cleanse the walls thoroughly. This is all we can do."

Alva said, "Is he conscious?"

"Not yet."

"Is that normal?"

"Ether's effects can be slow to diminish. We'll know more in a little while."

"I want to see him."

The room smelled now of cleanser and gauze. The bloody surgical field was gone, and Oliver had been moved onto the bed. His face was ashen. Had Alva not been assured otherwise, she would have mistaken him for a man lying in state.

"My brave darling," she said, kissing his cheek. "You were splendid.

The doctors anticipate a full recovery." She had no idea whether or not this was true.

Hours passed. Alva sent the children to bed and stayed with Oliver so that she would be there when he awakened. Periodically the nurse would attempt to rouse him, getting nothing better than a murmur in response.

At dawn, Dr. Lanehart came to check on him, asking Alva to wait outside the room. "I need to examine his incision." When he let her back in a short time later, he said, "The wound looks good, but Mr. Belmont's vital signs are weak. It's incumbent upon me to warn you that if he doesn't revive soon, his condition may be terminal."

"Do you hear this, Oliver? Open your eyes, dearest. Prove the doctor wrong."

Oliver stirred, and then his eyes opened slightly. "First . . ."

"Yes?"

"First," he said again, and winced.

"What do you want first?"

"First time I've had sympathy for McKinley," he finished, attempting a smile.

Alva laughed. "That's my Oliver."

He closed his eyes again. "Stay," he said, lifting his hand to invite hers.

"Always."

The newspapers followed the course of Oliver's crisis closely. Having first reported that the situation was dire, the next day they reported his rally and declared that he was now expected to live. Their next reports said he'd taken another turn. Later: a rally. Four long days this went on. Four long days Alva held Oliver's hand, spoke softly to him, saw her hopes rise and resisted their fall. She ate little, slept less; there would be time for that when he was in the clear—and it wouldn't hurt her a bit to be slimmer, as Oliver certainly would be. And they would stay here at Brookholt until fall, when he was strong again, spend their days sitting in the sunshine reading to each other, eating jam made from their raspberry bushes atop shortbread she'd bake herself.

On the fifth day following his surgery, Alva, who'd been dozing at Oliver's bedside, woke with a start. The sun was just up. Wrens and cardinals chattered outside. No one was in the room but Oliver and her. Perhaps the nurse had gone out just then and that's what awakened her? Turning toward Oliver, she heard him draw a short, shallow breath.

Then . . . nothing.

Outside, the sun rose higher. Birdsong went on unabated.

Alva refused to be one of those widows who keened piteously. Yes, her eyes and nose were raw behind her black veil; she had cried a lot over the past few days, sometimes when she wasn't aware, at first, that she was doing it. But Oliver wouldn't approve of hysterics, even were she inclined toward such behavior.

Quiet, vigorous grief he would approve of heartily. If at the funeral's conclusion she stood there in the church with her hands on the edge of the open casket fighting the impulse to climb inside and close the lid, no one around her could tell. If while sailing to England to stay with Consuelo she stood at the ship's rail in a similar state, she didn't give that state away. But perhaps Oliver knew she was lost. Perhaps he knew she was quietly frantic at the permanence of the situation. She hoped he knew. She wished she could tell if he did.

II

"WHAT'S ALL OF this?" Alva asked her daughter. "I've never seen it so crowded, even on a Saturday."

London's streets were nearly impossible to navigate going from the docks to Consuelo's current home, Sunderland House in Mayfair. Carts and automobiles of every size and condition packed the roadways in all directions. Consuelo had retrieved her in a new chauffeured Siddeley, an auto that was capable of going at a pace of something like a hundred miles an hour, yet they hardly moved faster than an infant could crawl.

"I'm so sorry, Mother. This is why I made the boys wait at home. I had no idea it would be so bad or I'd have suggested you wait for the next crossing."

"Don't distress yourself. I have nothing now but time." She gave a rueful laugh. "Listen to me. My God, I'm maudlin."

"You're entitled to be maudlin."

"He would scold me for it." Alva turned her gaze back out the window. "Is there some event?"

"Do you recall the paper I sent you about woman suffrage here, *Votes for Women*? Its publisher and the WSPU organized a 'monster meeting,' they're calling it, for tomorrow in Hyde Park. Today's *Times* said *hundreds of thousands* will attend. I'd been going to speak, but then Oliver . . . Well, I thought it best to beg off, under the circumstances."

Alva hadn't seen Consuelo since right after her separation from Marlborough two years earlier. The couple had tried their best. They had two sons, a much-improved palace, and tremendous popularity amongst both the public and the peerage. The trouble was that as Marlborough had grown in importance, serving as paymaster general and then undersecretary of state for the colonies, he'd gotten stiff and pompous, while Consuelo, recognizing the pageantry of their world as an elaborate game of dress-up, became less serious. Oh, she was as sincere as ever about the responsibilities of her station and her efforts to improve the lives of working-class women and children. She followed the intricate rules of the court and observed all the forms and customs. But to do the latter required she keep a sense of humor about it all.

Consuelo found Marlborough's attitude grating. He found hers American. They both found "amusements" outside the marriage, if one could credit the gossip. Divorce for two such as they was all but impossible: Marlborough would have to prove adultery or Consuelo would have to prove physical cruelty or desertion. So they'd worked out an agreement to separate. Alva had come here to lend Consuelo an extra bit of strength to pull against the tide. And now here she was again, allowing Consuelo to do that for her.

This tide, oh, it was like nothing Alva had felt before. This tide swirled and wrapped and dragged. It brought the unmitigated black of helpless anger and faithless grief, a darkness so black that it blocked out all light. Mausoleum black.

"We should go to the meeting," Alva said, shaking her head to clear it. "They might fit you back into the schedule."

"Please, don't give it a thought."

"What I mean to say is that going would occupy me. I need to be occupied."

Consuelo nodded. "All right, then. I'll see that we get reserved seating. Emmeline Pankhurst will be—"

Alva knocked on the window that separated them from the driver. "Stop!"

"What, here?" said Consuelo.

"We can walk faster." Alva reached for the door.

"Mother, wait. I'd like to, but— Well, we'd be waylaid constantly. Everyone recognizes me here."

Alva sat back. She looked down at her daughter's shoes—blue silk pumps with silver buckles—and said, "Those aren't the shoes for it, anyway." She thumped the window again. "Continue on!" she called.

"Tell me," she said as the car resumed its slow progress, "would you do it differently? Would you trade all of this for some other life if you could?"

"No, I wouldn't."

"You didn't even think about it before you answered!"

"That's because I already have thought about it, a great deal. Oh, I know I behaved as if you'd ruined everything I cared about, and I was entirely sincere. To my inexperienced heart, Mr. Rutherfurd was the most gallant, marvelous figure. I did believe myself in love with him. But becoming the Duchess of Marlborough opened the world up to me. I've found great satisfaction in civic service, in addressing children and women's needs in particular. I would not change anything, truly, except Marlborough's personality. If he wasn't such a *prig*—" She laughed. "I love that word. *Prig.* Having that word in my vocabulary is benefit enough."

"I am rather impressed with us," Alva said. "Two independent women of the world."

❧

On Sunday, Alva woke early to the sound of an insistent wren outside her bedroom window. The sky was only beginning to lighten. There would be no more sleep, she knew this from recent experience. A few hours a night was all she managed lately anyway. Enough to keep exhaustion at bay. Not enough to feel well rested. Her mind, once stimulated into wakefulness, then went roaming with impunity into every recess of her memory while sleep sidled away, a reluctant but obedient slave to the power of the past.

A wound could not heal if one kept touching it. So if she did not want to dwell—and most often she did not—she got out of bed and found distracting occupation. Doing this in her daughter's house at five A.M., however, was not good form, so although the first thoughts that came to mind this too-early morning were of her former friend the Duchess of Manchester, she remained where she was. Perhaps the wren would distract her sufficiently. Perhaps her mind would then find a new tack.

It was to be expected that the London environment would prod her memory in certain directions. In fact it happened every time she was in the city. Her old friend the duchess was here, somewhere. She'd stayed on even after losing her other daughter, Lady May, to tuberculosis eight years ago, now.

Alva always thought she might happen upon her by chance and was ever on the lookout, anxious about how she might behave if their paths were to cross. It was a festering wound but a small one, and not in plain sight, so she had left it untended. Oliver had supported her choice to leave things lie. When he had presented her with a statue of Joan of Arc, a marble likeness five feet tall that they'd given pride of place in Belcourt's Great Hall, he said, "Like Joan, you've always known how to choose your battles."

The wren's call sounded farther from the window, and then farther again, and then Alva couldn't hear it anymore.

She and the duchess were both widows now. Both firmly in their middle age (unfirm as it increasingly was). Neither was likely to find new love, nor could Alva imagine wanting it; she'd been spoiled irreparably. And so they had in common the potential of a long stretch of years ahead, years that wanted to be filled with meaning.

Perhaps she'd been wrong to leave things lie. Perhaps she had been wrong to believe there was nothing to be gained by facing whatever might arise. She had loved Consuelo Yznaga. She might love her again.

Alva sat up in the bed. The sky was lighter now. Another bird's song was audible—a pigeon this time, cooing companionably from a windowsill nearby. Her day ahead would be full, but after that? She would inquire into the current whereabouts of the Duchess of Manchester, who along with Alva had once been a hopeful, willful young lady with great adventures in mind. She would send her old friend a note. Perhaps they could find a restaurant with a pleasing view and Devonshire tea.

. . .

Alva and her daughter joined a procession that would march to Hyde Park from the Victoria Embankment. Six other processions had formed at other locations. In all of them, women from every part of England carried placards and banners naming their districts or declaring their views. The women were in almost every case dressed in white, some with accents of purple and green in their hats or on sashes. There had been so much demand for white clothing that the city's shops were stripped of white fabric as thoroughly as a forest could be stripped of its leaves by a multitude of locusts.

Consuelo said, "As you can see, the WSPU has declared its colors: purple for royalty, which Mrs. Pankhurst claims is in every right-thinking woman's veins. The white is for purity of heart and purpose. Green is emblematic of hope, renewal, springtime."

"Good for them," Alva said. "No army should go into battle without colors to fly."

"I don't like thinking of it as a battle. Rather, it's an ongoing negotiation, don't you agree?"

"A negotiation requires negotiating. There's no evidence of that from the government side. I think Mrs. Pankhurst is right to invoke customs of battle; she knows what she's about."

Consuelo said, "Then you approve of her daughter's having been arrested for disruption and provocation while promoting the cause? Never mind—your expression gives me your answer. And yet you insisted we children behave so well!"

"Circumstances make all the difference."

"Mother, she went to *jail*."

She and Consuelo marched near the head of their procession, which would take them past the prime minister's residence at 10 Downing, then onward into St. James's Park, along past Buckingham Palace, the Wellington Arch, and finally into Hyde Park. As they walked along a route lined with onlookers—older men, most of them, some of whom scowled or spat—Alva said, "I do feel rather liberated wearing a color other than black. Black is so severe—it drains one of vitality. Why should one appear as if one's own death is imminent? The armband suffices."

Alva may have been favored by her white dress, but Consuelo was a vision in hers. Consuelo was a vision in any color. Alva thought she had never seen her daughter as beautiful as she'd become at age thirty-one. Her features had the quality of having been arranged by angels. Her coltishness was gone, and in its place was the slender confidence of the gazelle. That doctor who'd prescribed the rod and straps, medieval as the contraption may have been, had known a thing or two about looking to a lady's future interests.

Consuelo said, "We do restrict ourselves with so many stringent social rules. Men restrict us further, and will, for as long as we allow it."

A woman beside them cried, "Hear, hear!"

Alva said, "When Oliver was in Congress, I gave a dinner party at which the sisters behind *Woodhull & Claflin's Weekly* were my secret special guests. Victoria Woodhull once put herself on the ballot for U.S. President, did you know? I was, what, nineteen at that time? I hardly paid it any attention; I needed a husband, I didn't care who lived in the White House! Anyway, she and her sister gave us an engaging lecture in favor of women getting the vote. The congressmen were quite put out at being confronted this way—which may be why I thought it was a marvelous evening."

Consuelo laughed. "Have you always been a rebel?"

"Yes and no. I did try to conform. I was never very good at it, though."

"I'm not comfortable being aggressive. I'm more like Papa."

"You think your father isn't aggressive?" Alva said with a laugh. "I suppose with you he's still some combination of St. Nicholas and a basset hound."

"At any rate," said Consuelo, "all of this . . . passion . . ." She gestured around them. "It makes me anxious. Why is it necessary? We've been making progress—"

"My entire life, Consuelo. That's how long women have been patiently speaking on this subject to one another and to the men in charge—who take advantage of our habits of being polite and cooperative while censuring every opposite behavior. Men only respect power. So we must be powerful."

Again the woman near them shouted, "Hear, hear!"

Alva said, "I count myself among the guilty. I've given little more than lip service to suffrage before now. You're making a good example—as is all of this."

All of this—that is, their procession of hundreds—was impressive to be certain. But the sight that greeted them as they arrived at Hyde Park made Alva catch her breath. Hyde Park in June under ordinary circumstances was a vast verdant space not unlike New York's Central Park. Today was not ordinary. Today, the open spaces were aswarm with all manner of persons. Women mostly, but children, too, and a good many sensible men, all of them come to impress upon the English government their support for women getting their due. There was not a patch of grass in sight. Along the sidewalk were food carts and numerous tables featuring pamphlets and assorted items done in the battle colors. Nearby, a brass band played a march.

Alva was heartened by the display. As was true with American women, for more than fifty years Englishwomen had been petitioning for equal rights, and for more than fifty years they'd been told that catastrophe would befall society if men permitted those rights. *Permitted!* As if rights were kept piled in bank vaults and men got to distribute them only as they saw fit.

The older Alva got, the more ludicrous the situation seemed to her. She had more wit and intelligence and capability than almost any man she'd ever met, and while she could not say that *every* woman she'd known would do a better job running things than the men who adjudicated their lives, they certainly wouldn't do worse. If England changed its laws, other countries might well follow suit. She hardly knew an American gentleman who didn't revere his English counterpart and want to be like him.

Alva said, "Those roasting nuts smell heavenly. Shall we get some? And look—there's a cart with sausages. I've hardly eaten since . . ." Gazing up into the vivid blue sky, she said, "There, I'm hungry. You needn't worry I'll waste away."

"Mother?"

"The sausage might be a bit of a mess to eat. Just the nuts, then." She left her daughter staring after her, though whether in concern or amusement she didn't know. Well, either was fine. Let any of them judge her as batty; until they'd lost their own loves, they couldn't know the comfort of conversing with ghosts. Which was not to say that she wholly believed in ghosts herself, only that she didn't *not* believe, and in fact she rather liked the way the impulse to converse with Oliver had struck her just now. It felt as though he were there keeping her company, much as he would have been if they'd made this trip as they'd planned.

Distributed throughout the park were twenty platforms, each of which would host notable figures of this country's woman's suffrage movement. It was the stage that was soon to feature Emmeline Pankhurst, however, that most interested Alva, and this was where she and Consuelo went. Five rows of folding chairs designated for special guests and dignitaries had been positioned before the platform, cordoned off and tended by bobbies. As they found their seats, Consuelo introduced Alva to several distinguished women who, like Consuelo, had been giving their time to the women's rights cause. Behind them, the crowd pressed ever closer as the appointed time for Mrs. Pankhurst's speech approached.

Alva knew a little about the woman. Mrs. Pankhurst was five years younger than Alva. She'd been widowed after a happy marriage to a progressive gentleman. Her involvement in this effort dated back some thirty years, but in losing patience with the slow pace and ineffectual tactics of her colleagues, she'd broken with them to form a new, more assertive organization, the Women's Social and Political Union or WSPU, as Consuelo had referred to it. She was tough-minded and unafraid.

A group of bobbies surrounding several women moved through the crowd toward the platform at stage left. From the group, a woman of Consuelo's age (but with none of her gracefulness) ascended the steps to the platform and put her arms up, then stood waiting for the crowd to quiet. Pinned onto her white dress at the breast was the same green, white, and purple ribbon many of the others were wearing.

"On this historic day," she shouted, "I am privileged to introduce a woman whose tenaciousness and wisdom will forever mark her as superior. Her indefatigable effort and commitment to our rights make her an example to us all. I give you Mrs. Emmeline Pankhurst!"

As the crowd cheered, Emmeline Pankhurst replaced the young woman and stood before the sea of people with a calm, matter-of-fact expression on her face, her hands clasped before her. She wore a sash that read *Votes for Women.*

Calm though she was, her face had a magnetic, dramatic quality more often seen on women of rank. She had a long, patrician nose and deep-set eyes, with chestnut-brown hair upon which she'd pinned a gleaming white hat. Her white dress gleamed as well. She let her hawklike gaze sweep the crowd: women in Sunday dresses, women in torn, stained clothes; in hats and hatless; hair blond, black, brown, red, silver, white. Women with babies in their arms. Women with daughters leaning against their legs. So many women tired of having no say in their government but not too tired to use the one day they had off from whatever work they did to come here and stand for hours in Hyde Park until this singular woman took the stage. Now they cheered Mrs. Pankhurst as though she would deliver them from their bondage the way Cyrus delivered the Jews from Babylon.

Alva tilted her head and looked skyward. The sky was so crisply blue, so unusual for London. A person could dive into it and drown.

Mrs. Pankhurst stepped closer to the front of the stage. The crowd quieted.

"Deeds, not words!" she yelled.

The women cheered, louder than before. They stamped and screamed. Alva stood up so that she could see them en masse. Tears filled her eyes and spilled onto her cheeks. So much passion. So much righteousness. Because they were right!

What if she could inspire such passion? What if she could invigorate the American women's suffrage fight, be a force to help win that war? Wouldn't Oliver be proud of her. Wouldn't she be proud of herself!

She was no Emmeline Pankhurst, but she had other tools: connections and political experience and lots and lots of money. *Money's no fix*, she had once been told, a truth she had learned repeatedly. Fortunately, she had more than money. She had ideas and talents. She had ambition and passion. She had time.

All her life, she had so often tried to make things different. Society loved her when she was advancing its causes, then castigated her when she was advancing her own. Yet, were not the two ever entwined?

Life was contrast. Light and dark. Comedy and tragedy.

She looked out across the crowd and thought she saw a familiar face . . .

Alva Smith and Consuelo Yznaga. Alva Belmont and Consuelo Montagu.

End. Beginning.

Author's Note

From the moment Alva Smith Vanderbilt Belmont was first inspired to devote her considerable resources to the American women's suffrage cause, she was unstoppable. She went on to form alliances with the movement's leaders, and when she grew frustrated or impatient with the practices of some of those leaders, she formed her own organization: the Political Equality Association (PEA), opening her headquarters in Manhattan and establishing satellite locations throughout the boroughs, including the only such office in Harlem. She was one of just a few suffragists who very deliberately encouraged and included African American women's involvement in the fight for the vote. Although Mary Smith Taylor is an invented composite character in this novel, she demonstrates Alva's real experiences with and concerns for African Americans at a time when many people (including those within the suffragist movement) and most states were pushing for the formalization of racial discrimination through Jim Crow laws.

Alva's association sponsored lectures on a wide variety of subjects, all aimed at educating women so that they could be empowered to make choices that were good for themselves and their children. It also operated a Department of Hygiene, wherein women took classes about health that included information on reproduction and contraception, which they could not get from most physicians in that era. The Department of Hygiene sold everything from cosmetics to devices for treating uterine prolapse—a common problem for women who had multiple pregnancies over a short span of time. Alva also created a farming work-study program at her home, Brookholt, on Long Island for women who had an interest in rural-based occupations. She was determined to improve the lives of working-class women in every way she could think to do it.

Among the accomplishments of her years working for passage of the Nineteenth Amendment is the stage play *Melinda and Her Sisters*, a satire she wrote that was staged as a fundraiser in 1916. Emulating the efforts of Mrs. Pankhurst and her daughters, she commissioned a variety of Votes for Women products produced at low cost and sold to the public to raise funds for the cause. She wrote essays and letters of opinion for publication in newspapers and magazines nationally. She hired a lobbyist and met repeatedly with lawmakers to encourage both a state (New York) and a national women's suffrage amendment. She secured a building in Washington, D.C., so that the National Woman's Party (NWP), which she had cofounded with Alice Paul and Lucy Burns, could have its headquarters there. The Alva Belmont House, now the Belmont-Paul Women's Equality National Monument, is a museum and the first national monument to women's history in the United States.

In 1926, Alva's daughter and the Duke of Marlborough, who had formally divorced in 1920, decided to pursue annulment as well. As Consuelo writes in her memoir *The Glitter and the Gold*, in order to grant the annulment, the church needed to believe Consuelo had undertaken the marriage completely against her will. Alva gladly testified that she had forced her daughter into the union, making her behavior sound far more severe than it was. The proceedings were supposed to be private, but news leaked and Alva was once more in the headlines, portrayed again as being selfish and cruel. Accounts of Alva's life almost always define her by these stories. None discuss the broader context, nor how close she and Consuelo were throughout Consuelo's adulthood—so close, in fact, that Consuelo often rented homes near wherever Alva was living at a given time, so close that when Consuelo built a home in Manalapan, Florida, she named it Casa Alva.

One of the reasons I was compelled to tell Alva's story (and Zelda Sayre Fitzgerald's in my previous novel, *Z*) is to combat the way notable women in history are too often reduced to little more than sensationalized sound bites. Strong women—especially if they elect to lead lives outside of the domestic sphere—are often depicted without appropriate context, are made to seem one-note (as if any of us could be defined by a single act in our personal history or a single aspect of personality), and are described with sexist labels. An intelligent, ambitious, outspoken woman is called "pushy," "domineering," "abrasive," "hysterical," "shrill," etc., most often by men but sometimes by other women as well.

Alva is regularly framed this way, said to be motivated solely by a desire for the trappings of wealth along with social prominence and power. Oliver's role in national politics is absent from almost every attempt to depict her (and him, for that matter). So it's no surprise that those who've written about her have found themselves unable to explain why she went to such lengths for the women's suffrage cause. Boredom is the theory most often advanced, if the matter is addressed at all. As for her support of African American women's rights, I've found no account that has attempted to address this.

It's worth noting that in Alva's point of view and dialogue I have used *girl* as interchangeable with *young lady* deliberately in keeping with the habits of nineteenth-century conventional usage. While I am a modern feminist, this book is an emulation of a nineteenth-century novel, with nineteenth-century characters and narrative style. I trust that when contrasted against our contemporary ways of thinking of feminist matters, this choice makes its argument without my forcing modern sensibilities on the work.

After passage of the Nineteenth Amendment, Alva (with the NWP) turned her attention to campaigning for equal rights, a far more complex matter than suffrage but one she was passionate about. She did not forsake her other great passion, however: she spent the remaining years of her life building and buying and renovating homes in Paris and the South of France, as well as a coastal mansion on Long Island called Beacon Towers, thought by many to have helped inspire F. Scott Fitzgerald's *The Great Gatsby*.

A stroke in the spring of 1932 debilitated her, and she died in early

1933 at her home in Paris, having just turned eighty years old. She was interred beside Oliver in the Woodlawn Cemetery mausoleum she had designed and built after his death. Her funeral was an impressive event, attended by more than fifteen hundred mourners. Her pallbearers, at her request, were all female. On her coffin was draped a picket banner that stated *Failure Is Impossible.*

Acknowledgments

A work of biographical fiction owes a lot to the historians and biographers whose primary research informs the materials the novelist makes use of. Key among the numerous publications I consulted are: *The Vanderbilt Women* by Clarice Stasz; *Alva Vanderbilt Belmont* by Sylvia D. Hoffert; *Fortune's Children* by Arthur T. Vanderbilt; *A Season of Splendor* by Greg King; *Victorian America* by Thomas J. Schlereth; *When the Astors Owned New York* by Justin Kaplan; *The Gilded Age in New York* by Esther Crain; and the Consuelo Vanderbilt Balsan memoir *The Glitter and the Gold*. In addition to these texts, however, I consulted many other books and articles that relate to the history, the places, and the people in this novel. The fiction of Edith Wharton and Henry James also helped to inform the story; they were there, after all.

The Vanderbilts as a family have not been the subject of as much scholarly research as I might have liked. This means that accounts of the individuals and their motivations vary widely from source to source, based, as most of them are, on anecdotes and apocryphal stories and newspaper articles that are often riddled with inaccuracies. I stuck to the facts inasmuch as fact could be determined.

It's my good fortune to have the support of the fine people of St. Martin's Press, and in particular, Sally Richardson, George Witte, and Hannah O'Grady; their hands-on participation in getting this book to press in this form is very much appreciated. I'm grateful to Jessica Lawrence, my publicist, and publicity head Dori Weintrab; Paul Hochman and Martin Quinn, marketing gurus; and the entire team of publicity, marketing, art, and sales folks who work behind the scenes. Also to Lisa Senz and Jennifer Enderlin, who have an important hand in things as well. Most especially I want to thank my editor, Hope Dellon, for patiently guiding this project from concept to completion, steadfastly supporting my vision for what the book would ultimately become, and for helping me see the ways it wasn't quite there—until finally it was.

Tremendous thanks go to Wendy Sherman, my literary agent, my friend, first reader, and the voice of clarity and reason in this murky, sometimes maddening business of writing and selling books. Also to Jenny Meyer, shepherdess of my foreign rights sales and second voice of clarity and reason. And while we're talking agents and business, my thanks to Lucy Stille for getting this book placed for television adaptation (may we see that tree bear fruit!).

I'm pleased and grateful to once again be partnering with Lisa Highton and Two Road Books for publication and distribution throughout the UK, New Zealand, Australia, South Africa, and all the other places outside of North America where folks buy books in English.

Shout-out to my sons, their wives, and my stepdaughter, as well as to my brothers and sisters-in-law: you might not all read my books, but you're all great cheerleaders and that counts for more than I can say.

Being an author full-time is a solitary occupation, but I am fortunate to have an array of fellow writers whose companionship, though often virtual, buoys me and reminds me there's fun to be had outside the walls of my home office. (You know who you are.) Queen among them is Sharon Kurtzman, who's been there for me since early in my journey to become a novelist, and whose friendship has been truly invaluable.

Earlier still in that journey was John Kessel, the first real-life, honest-to-god author I ever met, professor of literature and creative writing, first to tell me (in 2000) that I might, if I worked at it, have what it takes to write publishable fiction. He is my Oliver. The journey was long, the path twisted, but Reader, I married him.